# AN ALMOST PERFECT WORLD

Legend of East Series • Book 1

## CARRIE-ANN BARNES

Printed in Canada
First Printing: May 2014
Second Printing: April 2017

ISBN 978-0-9959013-2-2

Front cover images: iClipart & iStock/Thinkstock

PRO3 05 07 2017

Follow me on:
Twitter @C_A_Barnes
Facebook www.facebook.com/authorcabarnes

For George and Faye,
whose love and support
will stay with me always.

# Table of Contents

# One

★　★　★　★

"And that's why I did what I had to do," Miranda cried. Giving it her all, she let a few tears fall and covered her face with her hands. She sniffed loudly then whispered, "Surely, I thought you would understand."

Scott put a hand on her shoulder and read from his script, "I do understand Teresa. I just wish you had told me sooner. This Thanksgiving just wouldn't be the same without you."

"That's fine, you can stop there." The voice came from the almost empty auditorium and it continued, "That was lovely... from the both of you."

Sixteen year old Miranda Greenburg smiled to herself as she nervously straightened her navy blue shirt and retrieved her schoolbag from the front of the empty stage. "Thank you, Ms. Mahan," she smiled, looking down at her bag in her hands, which held the script. She had memorized it weeks ago.

The bright lights on the stage darkened the rest of the auditorium, so they heard Ms. Mahan's disembodied voice again, "I am going to need you to work harder on your lines, Scott. You can't have your script with you on Friday." Miranda and Scott both squinted out at them. Their fellow grade 12 student, to her left, nodded in agreement. "Hopefully you will have the last bit memorized before the dress rehearsal on Thursday.

Scott nodded and shifted uncomfortably, "I'm sorry Ms. Mahan, I will definitely have it all memorized by then."

"Hold on one minute," the grade 12 student, Jen, said as she walked briskly down the aisle and hopped up on the stage.

Miranda stood awkwardly as Jen pulled Scott back towards her. Jen stepped back to study the two of them while Miranda's cheeks flushed in embarrassment. She knew Jen must be comparing their height and she looked at the floor to hide her face. Miranda was very tall for a teenager, just over 6 feet 2 inches. Scott was approximately the same height but maybe her curly brown hair, which she wore in a high ponytail today, made her look taller.

"What are you thinking about Jen?" Ms. Mahan said, as she joined them on the stage. She pushed back a few graying hairs from her tired face.

Jen made a face. "Nothing really. I think Miranda should wear her hair down on Friday. It would fit with the theme better," she commented, and then added, "Scott has the perfect look." Jen gave him a winning smile and brushed his arm

Miranda scowled slightly, watching Jen make googly eyes at Scott. She let out an inaudible sigh. Perhaps she had been wrong assuming Jen was worried about their height but she had always been very good at guessing what people were thinking and could almost always tell when someone was lying to her. She had developed that talent when she was very young. A time she didn't like to remember.

Miranda shook her head to clear her thoughts and rearranged her face into a smile. "Helen is doing everyone's hair. I will let her know." Helen was Miranda's best friend. She was in the play as well but had been dismissed with the rest of the cast about an hour earlier. Ms. Mahan had asked her and Scott to stay later to work on the last scene.

Ms. Mahan smiled and nodded at Jen. She turned to Scott and Miranda, "Well, I will see you both Thursday for dress rehearsal! We will be wonderful!" She clapped her hands together in dismissal and she turned to head off the stage the way she had come. Jen followed, complaining to Ms. Mahan about the scenery. They were both stressed. The art class was working on the background and they weren't quite finished yet and the play was this Friday.

Scott sent Miranda a smile, motioned for her to follow and led the way out stage left. They heard Jen sigh in frustration as they left.

Miranda had a crush on Scott but she had never talked to him outside of rehearsals and the auditorium. Scott was a new student this year at their high school.

"Great job," Scott said, as they headed through the short corridor which would lead back out into the hallway of the high school. He walked slowly beside her, smiling at her, "You were amazing."

"Thanks," Miranda replied shyly, her eyes on the floor in front of her. "You weren't so bad yourself."

"Not as good as you," he complimented, watching her as they walked down the hallway, "I'm guessing you are the star of all the plays around here?"

Miranda shrugged her shoulders with a small smile, sneaking a quick look at him. She wasn't one to brag about herself but she had always been in the lead role. Miranda loved acting and it was her dream to be on television or in movies.

Their footsteps echoed down the drab, grey hallway. It was in the heart of the school and there were no windows. It was only lit by the overhead fluorescent lights and the only colour was from the blue and maroon lockers that lined both sides.

Scott smiled at her again, "I didn't think I would get the male lead. I wasn't really the best at my last school."

"You did really well," Miranda said, her cheeks colouring slightly. "I'm sure you will be great on Friday." Scott had to be one of the cutest boys in the school, at least that's how she felt, and he had become very popular, very quick. He had blond, curly hair, deep chocolate brown eyes and a gorgeous thin smile on a slim boyish face. He looked perfectly gorgeous right now in the school's uniform. She slouched a little bit so that she didn't feel as tall beside him.

"*We* will be great," he corrected her as he put a hand in his pocket, the other holding onto the strap of his backpack as he strolled casually down the hallway.

Miranda agreed. She wanted to add more, perhaps ask him about himself or if he liked this school so far, but she was tongue-tied. Her face flushed deeper and she scolded herself inwardly. She stopped walking as they had just reached her locker and she didn't want to pass it in case she got distracted by him and his smile. It was a great smile. "Um..." she started to say. She was going to ask him where he was from and then decided against asking him anything, "This is my locker," she said instead, motioning to it.

"Ok," he replied, as he continued his slow stroll down the hallway. "I'll see you tomorrow morning," he added, over his shoulder.

Miranda couldn't help but watch for a minute before he turned the corner. She let out a sigh as she opened the locker she shared with Helen, wishing she could be so casual and cool. Miranda had always been the shy type and kept a close group of friends. Her best friend, Helen, was the more outgoing of the two of them. They had been sharing a locker since they started high school.

Miranda gathered her homework and put on her zippered sweatshirt. The weather had just started to get cool outside. The leaves on the trees were just starting to change into dull browns, muted yellows and bright reds.

Miranda loved the fall. The air was always cool and crisp. She inhaled deeply as she exited the school and started towards home. Miranda walked to school almost every day since she was young. The high school was about twenty minutes away on foot.

Miranda looked at her watch which read 5:52 pm. She was almost home and her mother was probably waiting anxiously to hear about her day with dinner ready. They were the best adoptive parents anyone could ask for.

Miranda had been adopted when she was 2 and had lived in Woodstock, Ontario with her adoptive parents, the Greenburgs, since then. Before that, she had been with foster parents from just days after her birth. She had been left outside a maternity ward at a Toronto hospital with just a note, bearing her name *Miranda East*, asking them to place her with a good family and a large sum of money. The money was split in two ways. Half went to children's aid, as the note requested, and the other was set up in a savings account which would be available to her when she started university next year. Miranda didn't really want it, not wanting anything from her real mother or father, but it was more than enough to pay for her tuition and boarding for the next ten years, so her parents encouraged her to use it. She had been putting a lot of thought into taking a drama program and was considering the University of Toronto.

The Greenburgs never lied to her about her past. Her real parents had left no contact information, so Miranda had no chance of ever finding them, if they were even alive. She had tried to look through old records several years ago and searched for any clue about them, but found dead ends everywhere. No one could help her. There was no record of her birth at any hospitals in the area and no women had been admitted with the last name of East. Perhaps it wasn't even her real last name. The Greenburgs had encouraged her to keep the last name East but when Miranda was 13, she threw a fit and they took her to get her last name changed officially. She was no East and she never would be. She enrolled in high school as Miranda Greenburg. Mrs. Greenburg's eyes had sparkled with tears when Miranda's new birth certificate arrived bearing her new last name. She had hugged Miranda tight, so happy and proud to have her as her daughter. Miranda was happy too, feeling much more secure as a Greenburg. She didn't want to admit how hurt she was that her parents hadn't wanted her or even left any address to contact them later in life. She tried hard to convince herself that maybe they had a good reason for it, but sometimes the possibilities frightened her. Maybe her parents took drugs or were involved in some crime and now they were in jail. What if the money they had given her was drug money? She had no idea.

In the end, the Greenburgs, whom Miranda loved very much, were amazing people and they *were* her real family. They seemed to understand that she didn't search for her real family because she wanted to leave them. They knew she did it because she wanted to know why they had left her and who she was. Maybe even a medical history, though Miranda was hardly ever sick.

As Miranda walked home, all thoughts were on the play. She had always been able to memorize her lines with ease, leaving a lot of time to perfect her body movements and facial expressions. She had never been on the television yet but she was involved in the Stratford Theatre during the summer holidays.

Since her hometown was far from any major city, she was waiting until she was on her own and able to drive herself before she tried out for anything like a television show or movie. She never wanted to trouble her adoptive parents to drive her anywhere since they had already done so much just by raising her in a loving home.

Miranda walked down the residential street of old mismatched brick houses until she reached a short path. She smiled as she looked up at the beautiful colours of the maple trees that lined the path. It was still bright out, though the days had started to get shorter.

Through this path she emerged onto her own street and turned right. She could see her house across the street and five houses down, a cozy two-storey red brick house that she had grown up in. All the lights were on in the main floor and as Miranda approached, she could see the glow of the television in the living room. Her dad was probably getting ready to watch the news.

Helen lived two streets away. Normally, they walked to and from school together. Miranda didn't tell Helen about her crush on Scott yet. She knew Helen would probably do anything she could to help Miranda get together with him, but Miranda wasn't sure she was ready yet. The whole 'having a crush thing' was new to her. Some of the boys in her high school were cute but Miranda had no interest in any of them, until now. She knew exactly what she wanted and Scott fit into her ideal boyfriend perfectly.

Miranda climbed the porch stairs and smiled as she smelt something delicious coming from inside. Mrs. Greenburg emerged from the kitchen with a smile when Miranda walked in.

"How was rehearsal?" she asked as she tossed the tea towel over her shoulder, as Miranda put her school bag down and unzipped her sweatshirt.

She turned to her mother, her blue eyes sparkling, "It went great! I am so excited for you both to come and see it this Friday."

"Me too," Mrs. Greenburg agreed, "You are always such a hit!" She tried to put an arm around Miranda's shoulders, which were too high so her fingers slipped down across her shoulder blades, as she ushered her daughter towards the brightly lit kitchen. Miranda sighed at the height difference and wished she would stop getting taller. It was hard enough to find clothes as it was with her long legs and slender waist. Sometimes she worried that others were making fun of her height behind her back and she blamed it for her shyness.

. "We made your favourite," her father smiled, joining them in the kitchen. Miranda could hear the news coming from the living room. He took the plates down from the cabinet and started to set the table for the three of them. Miranda took three cups down from the higher shelf to help him.

It was bright in the clean kitchen with the soft glow from the potted lights on the ceiling bouncing off of the honey yellow walls. The white appliances and cabinets added to the brightness. The kitchen was also a shrine to cows since her mother loved them. They were on all of the dish towels, on magnets, on the cookie jar and on the wallpaper border. Even the salt and pepper shakers were small cows. Miranda picked them up and placed them in the centre of the table before she pulled out one of the light wooden chairs and sat, tucking one leg under her.

Miranda inhaled deeply again as Mrs. Greenburg placed a roast on top of the cow hot plate. Mr. Greenburg brought over the mashed potatoes and vegetables. Miranda was happy her mother enjoyed to cook so much. Miranda didn't share that passion, mostly because she just wasn't good at it. She had tried but it had always ended in disaster, like the time she almost started a fire by boiling water. Miranda never lived that one down. Jim, her dad, and the joker of the family, made sure to remind her of that incident every chance he could. It had only been one of the cow dishtowels she had accidentally left too close to the burner that had started the small fire but he still joked with her all the time.

But it wasn't just that one incident. She had tried so hard to cook things but never quite got it right. She always questioned if the chicken was undercooked and it would end up dry and overcooked. She over-spiced or she'd try different things that she thought would be good together and it ended up not quite right or absolutely disgusting. So she swore off cooking. Mr. Greenburg always told her that if she ever made it big, perhaps she could hire a maid to cook for her.

Miranda took the bowl of mashed potatoes her dad passed to her and started to create a small mountain on her plate. Her parents watched and then laughed at the same time.

"I love your potatoes," Miranda grinned as she passed the bowl to her mother.

"Well, we wouldn't want you to cook em," Jim chuckled, "I don't think the cows could handle another fire!"

Miranda rolled her eyes but smiled. It was never-ending.

Miranda adored her parents, though she looked like neither of them. She was taller than both now with curly brown hair, a diamond shaped face and bright blue eyes. Her perfectly straight nose was dotted with a few freckles, but no other distinguishing features. Her teeth were perfect, she had no moles or scars and her skin was sun-kissed all year round, no matter if there was a snowstorm in mid-winter. Both her parents had blond hair. Her stepfather was developing a bit of a beer belly, his shirts were starting to look a little tight around the mid-section, but both were still fairly slim. Jim Greenburg had a fairly large nose under his brown eyes, while her mother's was pointed slightly upwards. It gave her a snobbish look, but her light blue-gray eyes were soft and comforting. Sara Greenburg was very fair-skinned and Jim not far from that. Mr. Greenburg had a playful personality and Mrs. Greenburg was the serious one, but she still knew a good comeback or two when necessary. She needed to be quick-thinking with Jim, the joker, as her husband. Miranda smiled at the both of them and talked about rehearsal as they ate.

"So Scott, eh?" her dad said, wiggling his eyebrows, "Finally a lucky guy deserving of your attentions?"

Miranda paused with a forkful of mashed potatoes halfway to her mouth and blushed, while Sara giggled at Jim's antics. She lowered her face to her plate to try and hide her blush.

"Oh honey," Sara said, giving Miranda's arm a squeeze, "You are the most gorgeous girl I've ever seen. I don't know how we got so lucky. You are so smart and so beautiful! A total package! I'm sure Scott will notice."

Miranda looked down at her mother's hand on her arm and frowned. She bit her lip and wondered if her stepparents had ever noticed that she had no hair on her arms. No hair on her legs either for that matter. In fact, the only hair was on her head, her eyebrows and her mass of curls. Miranda never had to shave. Her mother *must* have noticed at some point that Miranda had never asked her how it was done. Perhaps she assumed Miranda had figured it out on her own. She had purchased Miranda a razor in a teen pack when Miranda entered grade nine and Miranda occasionally asked her for more when she remembered. She didn't want to be different and it was weird that she had no hair. Helen had noticed before, but Miranda had laughed it off and said she waxed.

After dinner, Miranda stood up and cleared their plates, bringing them to the sink. She turned the water on and added some soap to the left side sink.

Sara tried to help but Miranda shooed her away since she didn't mind doing the dishes after dinner. It was the least she could do since she couldn't cook.

Sara put a hand on her arm and gave a small squeeze, "I want to help and your dad and I wanted to ask you something anyways."

"Sure," Miranda said, filling the other side of the sink with rinse water, "Ask away."

"Well," Sara said, as she took the tea towel off the rack, "Jim and I have been talking a lot lately." She paused.

Miranda plunged her hands into the soapy water and started with the cups. She turned to Sara when she didn't go on with a questioning look. Sara looked like she was trying to figure out how to say what she was going to and Miranda looked to Jim who just smiled at Miranda, warmly.

"Well, honey," Sara continued, "We love you very much but..." She stopped again.

"We don't want you to take this the wrong way," Jim added.

"What?" Miranda asked, a hint of panic in her voice, as she pulled her hands out of the sink and dried them on the tea towel that Sara was fidgeting with. She looked back and forth between the two of them.

"It's nothing to worry about," Jim said quickly, "Sara, honey, spit it out! Like I said, she is going to take it just fine."

"We wanted to ask what you would think about us adopting again," Sara rushed out. Then she went on quickly explaining, "You see, we love children and next year you will be off to university and we're going to miss you like crazy! We will have no one to dote upon but each other." She sent Jim a smile that he returned.

Miranda looked almost shocked, but not because she thought she was being replaced. It was because they were asking her permission. She let out a little laugh, "Of course you should." She pulled her mother into an excited hug. "You two are the most wonderful parents!"

Sara smiled, her eyes glistened, "Plus if we get a small baby you will be here to help us for the year." Jim stood up and hugged Miranda too.

"Of course I would help! I would have a little brother or sister!" Miranda said excitedly.

"We actually have a meeting on Wednesday in Toronto and we were going to spend two nights in a hotel there," Jim said, "We'll be back on Thursday."

Miranda smiled and nodded, "I can't believe you asked me though. Of course I think you should."

Sara looked serious, "We just didn't want you to feel replaced since you are going to leave for university."

"No way! You both deserve to be happy and I think it's wonderful that some other unwanted child will be able to be brought up with such loving parents as you two." Miranda was most excited about having a sibling. She had never had a brother or sister, one that she knew of anyway. She smiled widely and hugged her mom again, "Why now? You should have done this years ago!"

"While you were growing up we were just so happy to have you, we never even thought about adopting again," Sara said, her eyes shining, "But now I am worried that the house will be so empty without you next year."

Even Jim's eyes glistened with excitement, "Miranda, I'm sure you have homework to do. Let us do the dishes," he said, taking her spot in front of the sink. Miranda protested, but she was overruled by the both of them and sent off to her room to start her homework.

"Oh, there is a comet tonight I wanted to check out," Jim stopped her just as she was about to leave the kitchen, "Maybe we can take a look when it gets darker?"

Miranda smiled and nodded, "Wouldn't miss it!" One of Jim's fascinations was of the sky. He had an expensive telescope he kept in the garage and took it out all the time.

Miranda headed up the stairs into the dark, automatically skipping the second step from the top, which was the creaky one. Her bedroom was to the right of the stairs. There was a spare bedroom directly ahead which Mrs. Greenburg used as an office. Beside that was her parent's bedroom and across the hall from them, and to the left of the stairs, was the bathroom. The door to her room was open about a couple inches, just enough for her cat to get through. Miranda flipped the light on.

Tinsel, Miranda's grey and white cat, was sprawled on her bed against the far wall. Tinsel yawned widely and blinked in the light.

"Hey kitty, kitty," Miranda said happily, taking a seat beside her on the bed. She stroked her back while Tinsel started to purr. "I was wondering where you were."

Miranda got up and stared at a movie poster that adorned her purple walls. She pulled her hair up into a pile on her head, like the girl in the poster and started mimicking the lines from the movie.

"Steve," she said urgently, in a country accent, "There ain't much time. Quick! Cut the blue wire..." She moved about her tidy bedroom, reciting the lines she had memorized from the movie.

She carried on until she caught her reflection in the full length mirror attached to her closet door. After realizing how silly she looked, she let her hair fall. Her brown curls fell down in front of her face and she blew them out of the way, sighing. Miranda stared at her reflection. She knew she was pretty, maybe not drop dead gorgeous, and also a little awkward, but she was alright. She looked herself up and down. Her grey slacks that were part of the school uniform looked like they were a bit short and Miranda tried to push them down a little more on her hips. *Ugh, I grew again*, she thought and she changed quickly into her plaid pyjama pants which had always been long on her anyways. They seemed to fit now and she sighed. How could she ask her parents to buy her new pants again, especially when a new baby may be coming? They had just bought her a new pair at the end of grade 11. She would just have to wear the school kilt while she worked up the nerve to ask them for another pair. She hated asking and it wasn't that they couldn't afford it but she always felt bad when they bought her anything. They already did so much.

Miranda wanted to get a part time job, but since she had all the money for her education supplied by her birth parents, her parents told her she should concentrate on school instead. She got top marks.

Miranda sighed, took out her homework, and sat down at her cream-coloured desk that matched the rest of her furniture. She decided to start with the biology assignment her teacher gave the class today. Miranda was taking drama, biology, calculus and English this semester. She liked science and had chosen biology as an elective along with drama. Drama was always her favourite class, followed closely by science even though they seemed on different ends of the spectrum.

Once her biology work was complete, she went to the window and looked up at the sky. The moon was almost full tonight. She couldn't wait to watch the comet with her dad. She loved the time she spent outdoors with him. They would sit for hours pointing out constellations and pretending there was life on other planets. Her dad had always been good at making up new civilizations and when Miranda was younger she would pretend she was an alien. Jim would laugh and tell her she was a great actress, playing out the parts he described perfectly. Her favourite had been the one legged planet, which her stepdad described as everything going to the right, leaning to the right, moving to the right. That was all they could do. Miranda had tied her legs together and hopped around all night, trying as hard as she could to only make right turns, ending every sentence with 'right?'

She was about to turn from the window when a strange sight caught her attention. A large motor home had pulled onto her street. It was mostly silver with an orange stripe. It slowly rolled by her house and parked a half block away. She watched but no one got out. A chill went through her body and she stepped away from the window. It had always been a little drafty since it was an older home and she laughed to herself.

She got out the novel they were reading in English class and lay in the centre of her bed, over her purple-flowered duvet cover. Tinsel moved closer to her and Miranda stroked her soft fur as she read.

Tinsel was now ten years old. Miranda had found her in a pet store and begged her parents to buy her. They had at first refused saying she wasn't ready for the responsibility of an animal. As the days went on, Miranda visited the store everyday trying to prove to them that she could do it. Then one day the kitten she wanted was gone. Heartbroken, Miranda had gone home only to find Tinsel sleeping in a basket of laundry on the living room floor. It had been an early Christmas present, so Miranda had named her Tinsel. Everyone called her 'Tinny' for short.

After Miranda finished the assigned chapters, she went to watch television with her parents who were curled up on the couch together. She picked up the blue-striped throw pillow and plopped herself down in the overstuffed brown leather chair, hugging the throw pillow to her chest.

Miranda watched her parents out of the corner of her eye. They were so happy together and she was happy for them to be adopting again. They had met twenty-four years ago when they were eighteen. Miranda had heard the story so many times. It was winter and Sara was driving in the early morning to meet her mother for Sunday breakfast. A car in front of her lost control and Sara swerved to miss but she ended up spinning into the opposite lane and a car hit her. Jim was following behind and saw the whole thing. He rushed to her aid while sending someone to phone for an ambulance. Sara remembered his face, *the face of an angel*, she describes to everyone. It was through this accident that she could never have children but she found the love of her life. Jim never left her side through the whole ordeal and they started dating shortly after she left the hospital.

Miranda smiled at them as Jim started tossing popcorn up in the air for Sara to catch in her mouth. One day Miranda hoped to be as happy as they were if she could ever get someone to date her. Her choices seemed slim because she was so tall and she never pictured herself dating someone shorter. At least Scott was the same height.

Her eyes roamed over the mantle above the electric fireplace across the room which was adorned with her school pictures. She had always been the tallest girl in the class and since Grade 7 she was taller than both of her parents. Her eyes fell on a family picture taken in Alberta at Lake Louise. It was taken during the summer before Grade 9 and she was inches taller than her dad. Now she was almost a full head taller.

Miranda sighed quietly and turned her thoughts back to Scott. She had sat behind him in class before and admired his broad shoulders. He had an amazing build. She wondered whether he played any sports. Perhaps she should ask him. If only she wouldn't get so nervous! All she had to do was talk to him like a friend.

She started to plan what she would say when she saw him next.

"So you still won't tell us what the play is about?" Sara asked, startling Miranda out of her daydream.

"It's a surprise," she smiled. She hadn't told them a thing about this play. Normally her mother would help her rehearse by reading the other parts but then they would always know what was coming. This one was special though. It was written by Jen, who was helping Ms. Mahan direct the play, especially for the Thanksgiving holiday charity fundraiser.

Sara smiled, "I can't wait to see it."

Miranda agreed, "It should be good."

A half hour later, the show ended and Jim got up and stretched, "Well, I'm ready to head outside! You are coming too, right?" He winked.

"Right!" Miranda laughed. It reminded her of the one-legged planet.

He rubbed his hands together, excited, "Get a jacket. It's a little chilly. I will meet you outside."

Miranda got up and grabbed her dark purple fleece jacket from the front hallway. Then she put the kettle on and fixed them both a hot chocolate.

By the time Miranda got outside, Mr. Greenburg had the telescope set-up in the driveway beside the house and pointed at the moon. Miranda shivered slightly and held the steaming mugs tighter in her hands. She waited until her dad looked back at her before she handed his over to him.

"Thanks sweetie," he said, holding the cup with both hands to warm them, "Take a look at the moon tonight"

Miranda looked up. The sky was clear and littered with stars and the moon was very bright. She stepped up to the telescope for a closer look.

"Did I ever tell you about the moon people?" her dad asked with a smile as he took a seat in one of the two lawn chairs he had brought out from the garage.

Miranda gazed at her father over her shoulder, a half-smile playing at her lips, "Really dad? I think I'm too old for make believe now."

It only made him smile wider, "You don't believe in life out there somewhere?"

Miranda shrugged. "It's a big sky. I am sure there is," she said as she stepped back from the telescope. She turned to her dad.

"Well the moon people are the guardians of Earth," Mr. Greenburg said, "They are always adorned in silver and they keep the other planets out there from reaching Earth. Most are hostile, of course, but we would never know it because the moon people fight valiantly to keep all Earthlings safe."

Miranda rolled her eyes at him and took a sip of her hot chocolate while he continued. Far-fetched as they were, she still loved his stories.

"There is a mighty queen who is the commander of the army and she has a beautiful daughter with long silky brown hair, who she is training to follow in her footsteps."

"Is her name Miranda?" Miranda asked with a smile.

Mr. Greenburg winked and nodded. He always worked her into his stories now that she refused to act out the parts.

Miranda turned to look up at the moon again, imagining a large silver city.

Mr. Greenburg took a sip of hot chocolate before continuing, "Miranda tries to be brave like her mother but she feels awkward with a sword in her hand. She doesn't want to fight and would rather read her books about peace and love. Then one day, a warrior catches her attention..."

"Dad!" Miranda said as she snapped her head around to look at him, a blush creeping up her face. Luckily it was dark outside. He never added a love interest before, "Please don't tell me this is your way of having a 'talk' about boys."

Mr. Greenburg shrugged, "You are growing up so fast, sweetie. You will be seventeen next month and next year you will be off to university and on your own. I just want to remember these little moments with you before you find a boy who takes up all your time."

"That won't happen," Miranda replied with a snort and raised her cup to her lips again. She almost choked as someone rounded the corner of the house. Mr. Greenburg gasped in surprise.

"I am so sorry to startle you both," the stranger said, "I was just out for a walk." He had a dark sweatshirt on with the hood pulled low over his face. He was very tall, much taller than Miranda.

Both Miranda and her dad gawked at him.

The boy stood awkwardly for a minute before he pulled his hood back. He no longer looked threatening at all. He was tall and lanky with short dark hair. His eyes looked bright grey in the moonlight. "Perhaps I should introduce myself. My name is Griffin and I just moved into the area. I was just out for a walk exploring the neighbourhood and I heard you both talking."

Mr. Greenburg stood and extended his hand, "Jim Greenburg. This is my daughter, Miranda." Her dad motioned to her over his shoulder. "We were just about to look for a comet I heard about."

Griffin shook his hand and then his eyes fell on Miranda. He smiled widely, "Nice to meet you both." Griffin tore his eyes away from Miranda to smile at Jim. "Do you mind if I join you? I have always had an interest in the sky."

"Certainly!" Jim replied excitedly, "Would you like a chair? I have more just in the garage."

"Thank you very much, sir," Griffin smiled and Jim went to retrieve one. Griffin turned to Miranda with a smile, "How are you tonight?"

Miranda had never seen someone so tall in person before. She couldn't tell how old he was either but she didn't think he was much older than her.

Griffin gave her a curious look, waiting for an answer.

Miranda shook her head slightly, "Sorry. I am fine. How are you?"

"I am well, thank you. That was an interesting story about the moon people."

Miranda snorted a laugh, "He makes them up all the time."

Griffin chuckled, "I do not believe other planets would be hostile though."

Miranda shrugged and nodded in agreement as her dad returned with a chair. "Miranda, would you mind getting another cup of hot chocolate?" he asked and then turned to Griffin, "Or would you like tea?"

Griffin bit his lip, "Uh, hot chocolate should be fine, thank you."

Miranda went inside for another cup. Her mother was just getting a glass of milk. She was in her rose pyjamas and her white terry cloth robe.

"How's the comet?" she asked as she put the milk back into the refrigerator.

"Haven't seen it yet," Miranda frowned, "Someone from the neighbourhood just dropped by. I came in to get another cup."

"Oh?" she asked, as she sat at the table with her milk, "Who?"

Miranda shrugged as she put the kettle on again, "He said he just moved in. He seems very nice and he is very polite."

Mrs. Greenburg reached over to pull the curtain aside and snuck a peek out the window, "Oh my! Is he ever tall!"

Miranda nodded.

"He looks young," she sent a smile to Miranda over her shoulder before turning her head back out the window, "What do you think?"

Miranda giggled and blushed, "I don't think he is my type."

Her mother laughed as she let the curtain fall back into place. "So, what is your type?"

Miranda thought about it for a second and shrugged, "I like muscles. He is too thin for me."

Her mother laughed, "Ah, yes. So does Scott have muscles?"

Miranda blushed deeper and nodded as the kettle switch flipped off to indicate it was finished.

"I can't wait to see what he looks like," her mother continued.

Miranda poured the hot water into the cup of chocolate powder and milk, and then stirred it all together.

Mrs. Greenburg finished off her milk and stood. She gave her daughter a squeeze on the arm, "Don't worry. We won't embarrass you."

Miranda shook her head, "I'm not worried about that. Sleep well, mom."

"Goodnight sweetie," Mrs. Greenburg replied and headed to bed while Miranda went back outside.

Mr. Greenburg and Griffin were talking animatedly about the sky. Griffin thanked Miranda for the hot chocolate before he turned back to her father.

"Yes, we are studying this constellation here," Griffin was explaining as Mr. Greenburg looked into the telescope. He hesitantly tried some of the hot chocolate. He looked delighted and tried another sip.

"I don't know this one," Mr. Greenburg said as he stepped back. He looked at Griffin expectantly.

"Well, we have determined its atmosphere is much like our own but well," Griffin paused and bit his lip, "We... assume... it could possibly... have life?" He started and stopped, like he was unsure of himself.

Mr. Greenburg laughed, "It is too bad we cannot just zip out there and check."

Griffin chuckled, "Yes." He took another, longer, sip of hot chocolate and smiled. He turned to Miranda, "This is very good."

Miranda smiled, "Thank you. The secret is to put the milk in and stir before the hot water."

Griffin gave her a half-smile and turned back to her father.

"So, are you studying astronomy at Western?" Jim asked.

Griffin nodded.

"I thought about doing that but I ended up in engineering. Astronomy is a hobby now."

"Oh? What do you do?"

"I'm an engineer at the car factory."

Griffin smiled.

"Where did you move from?" Miranda asked and took a look at the system they were looking at in the telescope. It was faint, even in the telescope, so it must be far away. She turned to look at him when he didn't answer right away.

He swallowed a sip of hot chocolate. "Down south," he replied, though he seemed unsure of his answer.

Miranda was about to ask him where down south he came from when Mr. Greenburg took over the telescope, "We should find that comet."

Griffin readily agreed and launched into a story about the first comet he saw when he was 3 years old.

Mr. Greenburg checked his notepad where he wrote the co-ordinates of the comet, "Three years old and you remember?" He turned to Griffin, surprised.

Griffin shrugged, "I suppose it is one of my earliest memories. My love of astronomy started from there."

Jim smiled, "We do tend to remember the most exciting moments, eh?"

Griffin chuckled and agreed.

Miranda stared at him. There was something weird about him. She tried to remember if there had been any houses that had been sold recently but she couldn't think of any.

"A-ha! Found it," Jim said, excitedly. He took a minute to watch it through the telescope. "Here Griffin, take a look."

Griffin thanked him and took a look. He watched for a minute and then offered the spot to Miranda.

Whcn Miranda peeked in, she wasn't as excited. It was nice but it didn't have a long tail like the last one she had seen. Those ones were beautiful.

Griffin chuckled, "It does have a short tail but the interesting fact about this one is that it only appears every 300 years."

Miranda looked at him strangely, "How did you know what I was thinking?"

Griffin looked down into his almost empty cup, "I saw you looked disappointed. I guessed." He shrugged slightly.

"Hmm," Miranda pursed her lips in thought. She was about to ask him again where he was from but another person stepped around the house. This time, no one was startled.

"There you are, Griffin," the new stranger said, "Mom and dad wanted me to come get you."

It was too dark to see his face, though Miranda stared. He was slightly shorter than Griffin but didn't appear as thin.

"That is my...uh... brother, Alex," Griffin said, biting his lip. He turned to Alex, "This is Mr. Greenburg and his daughter, Miranda."

"Please call me Jim," Mr. Greenburg said to Griffin with a smile.

Miranda stared at the new stranger. It was the first time that night she felt uncomfortable that she chose to wear her pyjamas outside. Even though her jacket covered her top, she was still in her plaid pants. She couldn't tear her eyes away. She wanted him to come closer so she could see him better but he stayed where he was.

"Nice to meet you both," Alex said. He smiled. Miranda could see his teeth in the darkness around his face. He wore a baseball hat which left his face in shadow. Was he staring at her too? She couldn't tell.

Jim nodded in his direction.

"I suppose I should be going," Griffin said, reluctantly.

"Please stop by anytime!" Jim replied with a smile and shook Griffin's hand.

Miranda had to tear her eyes away from Alex as Griffin stepped into her line of sight to shake her hand. His hand was very warm in hers and held on a second too long.

"Nice meeting you, Miranda," Griffin said, "I hope I see you again soon."

"Ya, sure," Miranda replied, distracted.

Griffin smiled and turned to follow Alex down the driveway.

"Well, he was nice," her dad commented.

"Yes," Miranda agreed and walked a little ways down the driveway. She peeked around the corner of the house and saw they were walking down the street.

"I thought I told you to wait," she heard Griffin say to his brother.

Alex looked back at the house and said something Miranda couldn't hear. They turned down the path and were out of sight. Miranda turned back to her dad, who was packing the telescope away.

"He seemed to like you," her dad said, smiling.

Miranda rolled her eyes.

"I hope I see you again soon," he mimicked.

Miranda giggled and shook her head.

"He asked a bit about you while you were inside," her dad smiled.

"Oh?" Miranda bit her lip, "What did you say?"

"He just asked how old you were and where you were studying. I can't remember why but I ended up telling him we had adopted you," Jim said, he paused and rubbed his chin, "But he was very nice."

Miranda wrinkled her nose, not liking that her father had told him that. She helped her dad put the chairs away and they went inside.

# Two

★　★　★　★

Miranda bolted upright in her bed, her breathing was heavy, after another bad dream so vivid she thought she was actually living it. She'd been having nightmares for almost a week and no matter what she did, ate or thought about before she went to bed the outcome was always the same. She would come so close to dying, always in a different way. The terror and the darkness that surrounded her stayed with her even after her waking moment. There was always someone or something sinister stalking her and trying to kill her. The ground would shake violently as her death neared, but then she would be rescued by someone she could never see, whether it was too dark or he kept his back to her. The rescuer in her dream was a male, she could tell by his stature.

She took a few deep breaths and looked at the time. It was just a few minutes before the alarm on her cell phone would go off so she turned it off and got up.

Miranda showered and got dressed in her uniform kilt. She pulled her hair into a high ponytail and added a touch of makeup. She didn't like to wear a lot, just a bit of blush and lip gloss.

Her mother was in the kitchen when she got downstairs already dressed in a long dark brown pencil skirt and matching suit jacket.

"Good morning, sweetie," she said as she spread jam on her toast.

"Morning, mom."

"Did you sleep ok?" she asked, concerned, "I thought I heard you moaning."

Miranda shrugged, "Bad dream."

"All week?" Her mother passed her the cereal as Miranda got a bowl out of the cupboard.

"Yes." She took the cereal, her bowl and a spoon over to the table.

"Aw," her mother said, sympathetically, "What about?" She took a small bite of toast and joined Miranda at the table.

Miranda shivered a little, "I'd rather not re-live it."

"Would you like a ride to school? It's raining."

Miranda looked out the window at the grey sky as she poured her cereal. She frowned, hating the rain. "I will just take an umbrella. I don't have rehearsal tonight but I have cheerleading so I will be a little later. Will you still be here when I get home?"

Sara shook her head. "Your dad and I are leaving after work. We'll make a quick stop at home and then we're going to hit the road."

"Ok," Miranda replied with a smile, "I'll be fine. Make sure you call! I want to hear about the interview tomorrow."

"Of course we'll call," Sara smiled assuredly, "I'll call you as soon as we get there tonight and tomorrow."

Miranda smiled and nodded.

"I'm just going to get ready," her mother said as she wiped the table clean of the few crumbs she had left, "We're going to leave you some money for dinner the next two nights. Let me know if you change your mind about that ride!"

Miranda stopped at Helen's house on her way to school. Helen was ready and waiting for her on the porch. Miranda had texted her to say she was on the way. Helen picked up her pink umbrella and her long blonde hair bounced as she skipped down the stairs. "Hey Mandy!" Helen had called her Mandy since first grade.

"Hi Hells Bells," Miranda laughed, as Helen joined her under her extra large red and white umbrella.

Helen smiled, "So, how was rehearsal with Scott?"

"It was alright. Scott still hasn't got that last scene," Miranda said as a blush crept up her face.

Helen looked at her out of the corner of her eye, "He'll get it. I'm not worried. He is *so* cute."

"Being cute won't help him remember his lines," Miranda said, avoiding Helen's eye. "And is he?" she lied, "I never noticed."

Helen giggled, "How could you not have?"

Miranda shrugged. She bit her lip. She wanted to tell Helen she had a crush on him but she worried Helen would make a big deal of it.

"I was thinking of asking him out," Helen said, dreamily.

Miranda's head snapped around, "Oh? Are you sure that's a good idea? I thought you were trying to work it out with Bryan?" Helen had dated Bryan since Grade 10. How could she just give up on him now? They had broken up over a silly fight! Miranda couldn't even remember what it had been about.

Helen waved her hand, "Bryan is fine but Scott is so hot! I know he doesn't hang out with our group of friends but..."

Miranda stopped walking. She was serious! This was the first she heard of this. Since when did Helen like Scott!

Helen, who had kept walking, stepped out into the rain. She laughed and opened her umbrella up, "Oh Miranda. I know you like him. I was just kidding!"

Miranda's face fell, "Oh? How did you know?"

Helen rolled her eyes, "Since you blush every time you see him or talk about him just like you are blushing right now." Helen giggled and bounced on her toes, "I am so excited you like someone! Want me to do anything? I can talk to him!"

Miranda shook her head vehemently, "Oh no you don't. Let's just let it play out. Like you said, he doesn't even hang out with our friends. Maybe he is dating someone else."

"Ok, ok," Helen rolled her eyes. They fell into step beside each other. Helen had to put her umbrella away again since Miranda's was so large they both fit under it without getting wet. "I know he isn't dating anyone else though."

Miranda smiled a little.

"So, when were you going to tell me?" Helen asked, pretending to be hurt.

Miranda shrugged, "I don't know. I just didn't want to make a big deal of it."

"This *is* a big deal! You have your first crush!" Helen squeezed her arm in excitement, "Aw!"

Miranda's face turned crimson.

"We should go to the school dance Saturday. I bet he will go! Want me to find out?"

"Uh," Miranda wasn't sure. She rarely went to the dances. She went a few times in Grades 9 and 10 but she hated standing in the middle of her friends, a whole head and shoulders taller. She felt like everyone was looking at her.

"Come on," Helen pressured, "It will be fun. You haven't gone with us in so long!"

"Oh, alright," Miranda sighed.

They walked in silence for a bit, until Helen asked how her night was.

"The usual. Homework, dad and I watched a comet. Some guy from the neighbourhood stopped in."

"Some guy?"

"Ya, some guy who said he just moved in. He's a university student."

Helen's eyes sparkled, "Oh?"

Miranda laughed, "You wouldn't like him. He was a science-y guy."

Helen's face fell.

"He had a brother but I didn't see him at all." She definitely wasn't going to tell Helen about how she couldn't take her eyes off of his brother despite his obscured features.

"You always get the guys," Helen complained.

Miranda laughed and gave her a little nudge. Helen squealed a little as the rain fell on her freshly straightened hair and she jumped in the next puddle which splashed Miranda's legs. They both erupted in giggles.

"Do you think your mom will let you stay over tonight? My parents are gone for two nights," Miranda asked when their laughter died down.

"I can ask," Helen said, calming herself, "I don't see why not. Where are they going?"

Miranda smiled, "To Toronto for a couple nights. They are looking into adopting again."

Helen squealed, "Really?"

Miranda nodded.

"That's so cool!" Helen smiled, "They are pretty awesome!"

"Definitely," Miranda agreed, excitedly, "I can't wait to have a little brother or sister."

Helen laughed. "They're not all they are cracked up to be," she said, referring to her two younger siblings, a brother, Trevor, who was two years younger and a half-sister, Gabriella, who was in Grade 3. Helen's parents had separated a long time ago and her mother remarried. Soon after, Gabriella was born. "I tried to train Gabby to be my slave. She never took to it."

Miranda laughed, remembering the times Helen had tried to boss her little sister around. Gabby would just run and tell their mother.

Tuesday seemed to creep by slowly and after her classes, Miranda headed towards the gym for cheerleading. She wasn't really into cheerleading like some of the girls were. Helen practically dragged her to the tryouts in Grade 9 and they had both made the team, but Miranda was sure that it was because she was tall enough to support the base of the pyramid. No matter what the reason, she was still happy to do it since it kept her athletic. The teacher in charge of the cheerleading squad kept them on a strict training schedule.

Miranda was also on the volleyball team, but that wouldn't start for another month, and she played street hockey in the church parking lot with her friends. Miranda liked hockey best but since equipment was so expensive, she never asked her parents to play. She was happy to just play a game with friends and once in awhile, she would go with Helen to London with Helen's dad to watch the Knights play. He had four season tickets.

After practice, Miranda and Helen walked back to Helen's house where Miranda was invited to stay for dinner. Helen's mother said it was fine that she stay at Miranda's that night, so Helen packed a bag and they walked to Miranda's.

As they were about to emerge from the path, Miranda noticed Griffin cross by with his brother. She still wasn't able to see the mysterious boy's face since he wore his baseball cap again. She stopped walking and Helen stopped as well. Helen gave her a funny look, wondering why she had stopped and then looked to the end of the path where Miranda was focused.

"What?" Helen whispered.

"Nothing," Miranda gave her a half smile, "That was Griffin." Miranda motioned with her head towards the end of the path.

Helen sped up a bit for a peek. Miranda rolled her eyes and lagged behind.

There were bushes on either side of the entrance to the path and Helen was hidden behind one looking around it when Miranda caught up.

"They're so tall!" Helen said, awed.

"I'm tall," Miranda reminded her.

Helen waved her hand, "Yes, but I know you."

Miranda laughed.

Helen stood up fully and pouted, "They are still walking. Should we follow to see where they live?"

Miranda thought about it for a minute. She wanted to know where they had moved in but she didn't want to be a stalker!

She was about to say yes when she noticed her parents' cars still in the driveway. She swore her mother said they were leaving right after work. "Hmm," she said instead, "My parents are still home."

"They said they would be gone by now?" Helen asked, still staring towards the corner the boys had just turned down.

Miranda nodded and headed towards her house. Helen reluctantly followed behind her and up the front steps.

"Hello!" she called out, cheerfully, as she entered the front door. She heard her parents' voices coming from the kitchen so she slipped off her shoes and headed straight through the short hallway into the kitchen. They stopped talking and their faces brightened immediately.

"How was your day?" Sara asked, a little catch in her voice. Sara glanced at Jim quickly. He wasn't looking at her but down at the coffee mug in his hand.

"Good! Helen is staying over tonight," Miranda said as Helen joined them in the kitchen. Helen smiled and greeted them as Miranda helped her father clear the kitchen table. Mrs. Greenburg washed the dishes slowly, her back to them. Miranda took a seat at the table. "I thought you were both leaving right after work."

"Yes, I just wanted to get these dishes finished first," her mother said, her back to them. She sniffed a little and her shoulders trembled.

"I could do them. You both go," Miranda urged. She went to her mother, knowing something was wrong.

Helen grabbed the drying cloth from where it was hanging on the stove, "I can dry."

Mrs. Greenburg turned and threw her arms around Miranda, "You are such a great daughter. I love you so much." She sounded emotional. Miranda patted her back and threw Helen a confused look.

"I love you too, mom," Miranda replied, "Is everything ok?"

Her mom pulled away and wiped her eyes, "Yes, I guess I'm a little nervous for tomorrow."

"I'm not sure we could get another child as great as you," her dad added, a little sadly.

Miranda laughed, "Oh dad. You guys go! Everything will go fine!"

Mrs. Greenburg nodded and Mr. Greenburg gave Miranda a hug before they both headed upstairs to get their overnight bags.

"Yeesh," Helen laughed, "They really like you, daughter of the year! Congrats!"

Miranda snorted a laugh, "Shut up! You know they're not like that all the time."

Helen shrugged, "They *must* be nervous."

Mr. and Mrs. Greenburg hugged her tightly one last time before they headed out the door. Miranda and Helen did their homework and spent the night watching a movie and gossiping about boys.

*Miranda walked slowly down the hallway of her school to the auditorium for dress rehearsal. There was no one there and Miranda looked down at her watch. She sighed and climbed the stairs to the stage to take a seat on the couch in the middle of the set. Suddenly every light went out. Miranda reached out into the darkness looking for something to grab a hold of to help her find her way in the dark.*

*Miranda froze with fear as she heard footsteps coming towards her.*

*"H-H-Hello?" she asked into the dark. She heard a weird noise, like right out of the movies when someone pulls a knife or a sword out of a sheath, and gasped. She felt the tip of it at her neck though it didn't strike. The blade traced its way down her neck and along her collarbone. A cold shiver went down her spine as she tried to speak, "Wh-What do you want?" The ground under her feet trembled and she felt the pressure as the blade moved to her heart.*

*"Die Miss East," a voice boomed from all around her.*

*Miranda screamed as she felt a rush of air but the sword never hit its mark. Someone was there with a sword of their own and knocked the other away from her heart. There was a little struggle and the sound of a sword fight, then a loud thud. Her rescuer turned to her, sheathed his sword at his hip and took her hand as his other touched her face lightly. He kissed her deeply and Miranda felt a tingle throughout her entire body.*

Miranda awoke then, placing a hand to her lips. It had felt so real. She looked at Helen, who was fast asleep on the air mattress on the floor and then at her cell phone which read 2:12 am.

Miranda rolled over and went back to sleep, where she fell into another dream about starting university. No one would talk to her. They thought she didn't belong with them. When Miranda awoke again, just a half hour after the first dream, she started to fret about university. Helen had decided she was going to go to the college in London and a few of their other friends had also chosen to go to college or university in London. She was likely going to be on her own and it reminded her of the very first time she started school and felt she didn't belong. Miranda allowed the memory she normally blocked to fill her mind. She had been different from the other students when she first started kindergarten. She was excited to be going to school to make friends but it turned out to be a bad experience. As the first few months passed, Miranda started to hear exactly what the other kids were thinking, though she didn't understand it much because she was so young. She could hear a person's voice in her head, even though their lips never moved. She thought it was normal and her parents never seemed to notice. This had scared many of the other children as she told them exactly what they were thinking or answered them even though they hadn't spoke aloud. They made fun of her, calling her a freak. It hadn't helped that she was also taller than all the girls and some of the boys so they had called her the giant freak. She had no friends at all. Miranda had cried almost every night, but never let her parents know about it. She knew she wasn't theirs and was worried they would get rid of her if she was different. She put on a brave face and asked them to transfer her to another school because they were not meeting her educational needs, which were big words for a 4 year old. Jim and Sara had laughed, but in a kind way. *You're so smart*, Sara had said, *how did we get so lucky?* Miranda realized quickly that mindreading wasn't normal and stopped it completely, blocking out all the voices she had ever heard. And that was how she knew what people were thinking sometimes and how she could tell if people were lying to her. She tried so hard to block it out, but she slipped up sometimes.

The next school Miranda attended was where she met Helen and she pushed all the bad memories of her first school away. What if she didn't fit in when she went to university?

Miranda rolled over again and tried to clear her mind. She really needed to sleep but she tossed and turned for a while before she fell asleep again.

Helen's alarm went off first and she went to get ready. Once she was ready she tried to wake Miranda, who refused to get up.

"Get up! We're going to be late!" Helen laughed and she jumped up on Miranda's bed.

Miranda rolled over and groaned.

Helen jumped a few times chanting 'Get up!' several times.

"No," Miranda moaned.

Helen sighed loudly and jumped down. She sat on the side of Miranda's bed close to her face. She pinched Miranda's nose and

Miranda swatted her away. Helen giggled and pulled Miranda's eyelid back.

Helen's light brown eyes were right by her face and she was making a silly face. Miranda giggled sleepily.

"I'm not asking you to stay over EVER again on a school night," Miranda joked, sleepily.

Helen laughed and stood, ignoring her comment. She motioned down to her clothes, "I'm ready!" And she was. She had the school uniform on and even had her blue polo shirt tucked into her grey slacks. It wasn't something she did often. The teachers were always telling her to tuck her shirt in.

"Ugh, fine," Miranda said, throwing the blankets off herself. Her plain blue t-shirt was wrinkled and twisted. She must have been thrashing around in her sleep.

Once Miranda was ready, they each took a piece of toast 'to go' and headed out to school. It was a grey, cloudy day but at least it wasn't raining.

"Hi Miranda," Griffin said, as he rounded the corner from the path and was headed towards them.

"Hi Griffin," Miranda smiled. Now that it was light out, she could see his face. His eyes were blue, not grey and his dark brown hair curled, though it was cut short. His black jacket and jeans made his tan stand out even more.

Helen cocked her head at him and then looked at Miranda.

"Oh, this is my friend Helen," Miranda introduced.

Helen smiled and shook his hand, "Hi Griffin. Out for a walk?" Griffin nodded.

"Do you have class today?" Miranda asked but Griffin looked confused. "At uh, Western?" Miranda added, giving him a wary look.

"Right!" Griffin said, "How silly of me. No, not today."

"What does your brother do?" Helen asked. She was curious about them and couldn't help herself.

"He is an actor," Griffin replied and rolled his eyes.

"Really?" Helen's eyes sparkled with delight, "So is Miranda. Or she wants to be." Helen clapped Miranda on the back.

"Oh?" Griffin asked with a smile and turned to Miranda.

Miranda shrugged and bit her lip.

"You know you do," Helen gave her a little nudge with her elbow, and then turned back to Griffin, "You should come see her. We're onstage this Friday for the Thanksgiving play."

"Helen," Miranda said through gritted teeth, "Why would he want to come see a high school play?"

Helen ignored her, "It starts at 7 pm at the high school. It costs five dollars which is going to be donated to the food bank to help feed families over Thanksgiving. You should come and bring your family." Miranda shot her a look.

Griffin smiled, "Thank you for the invitation! We would love to come." Miranda's head snapped towards him in shock.

"Great!" Helen said, excited, "Sorry, we would love to talk but we have class."

"Have a great day!" Griffin said with a smile.

"You too," Helen said, and took Miranda's arm, pulling her along.

Miranda cast another look at Griffin as he rounded the corner and headed to the right. She pressed her lips together, irritated.

Helen and Miranda rounded the corner, and then Miranda rounded on Helen. "What did you do that for?" she snapped.

Helen looked at her in confusion, "Why not? He is new to the neighbourhood. I was just being nice."

"There is something weird about him," Miranda shook her head, and looked back to make sure he was gone, "I don't know why but I have a weird feeling."

"Oh don't be silly," Helen said and she pulled Miranda along, "I think you two would make a cute couple."

Miranda made a gagging noise, "No thanks."

"He seems interested to get to know you," Helen smiled and nudged her.

"No way," Miranda said, doubtful, "Why do you think that?"

"Did you see his face when I said you wanted to be an actress?" Helen asked, grinning, "He's interested in you."

Miranda bit her lip. "What should I do?" She panicked. She didn't have any admirers before. How could she let him down gently?

"He's cute for a geek," Helen giggled and gave her a shrug.

Miranda paused, deep in thought.

"Well, just be friendly and if he shows he wants more you should just let him down gently," Helen said, "And don't worry so much! You look nauseous!"

Miranda forced out a laugh, "I'm fine."

Helen snorted, disbelieving. "I wonder what his brother looks like," she smiled, changing the subject in hopes of easing Miranda's mind.

"I didn't see his face at all," Miranda frowned, recalling his silhouette. "He isn't as tall and he looks stockier than his brother."

"He *must* be cute if he is an actor," Helen insinuated.

"I wonder if he's anyone famous," Miranda wondered aloud, "I don't even know Griffin's last name."

"Maybe we'll see him Friday!" Helen squealed when she realized.

Miranda was sitting at the edge of her friends at lunch and had just taken a big bite of her sandwich when someone took a seat beside her.

"Hi Miranda," Scott smiled.

Miranda swallowed roughly, "Hi Scott!" she said, a little overly excited. She tried to calm herself and noticed the conversation amongst her friends quieted. Miranda sent Helen a look and Helen pulled everyone into a conversation again. She turned back to Scott, "What's up?"

Scott put his lunch down on the table and pulled out a sandwich, "Not much. What's up with you?"

Miranda smiled, "Not too much." She tried to stop the blush she knew was creeping up her face.

"Oh, I'm sorry. I guess I should have asked if you mind that I sit with you," Scott said, pausing before he took a bite.

"It's no problem at all!" Miranda replied quickly, "I feel like I don't know you and we are both starring in the play!" She tried to remember what she was going to say to him the next time she saw him but her mind was drawing a blank.

Scott chuckled, "That's true. So tell me, have you lived here your whole life?"

Miranda bit her lip. The last thing she wanted to do was to tell someone right away that she was adopted. She wasn't sure where she lived as a foster child since she had been so young. So, she lied, "Yes, I have. Where are you from?"

"My family just moved from Goderich," he smiled and took another bite of his sandwich.

"Do you like it here?"

Scott shrugged a little as he chewed. "Everyone has been really nice. It was hard to move away from my friends especially in the last year of high school."

"Yes, that would be hard," Miranda sympathized. She cast a look at her friends. Next year she would be without them all and the thought frightened her.

"Don't get me wrong though, Woodstock is great! I'm glad my parents stuck to another small town. My dad commutes to London for work," Scott said.

"Helen and I go there once in awhile for the Knights games," Miranda smiled, happy Scott was carrying the conversation.

"You like hockey?" he asked, excited.

Miranda smiled and nodded, "We play sometimes too." She motioned over her shoulder with her head to her friends who had gone quiet again. "There's a church parking lot in my neighbourhood. Do you play?"

"Yes, I have played on the street back home. I mostly play baseball."

So he did play sports. Miranda smiled and turned to her friends who she knew were listening anyways. It wasn't every day that a new person joined them. "Do you all want to play Saturday?"

"Sure!" Helen agreed, happy to jump into the conversation, "Let's make it early so we have time to get ready for the dance. Are you going Scott?"

"I was thinking about it," Scott nodded.

"You should!" Helen smiled, "We are *all* going." Helen looked pointedly at Miranda.

"Ya ya," Miranda rolled her eyes, "I said I would go." Miranda's insides were jumping for joy. Scott was going and he was sitting here talking to her. She took a moment while he was looking away to eat some of her sandwich.

"So, I wanted to ask you if you would stay late to practice that last scene. I think I've got it but I just want to make sure before dress rehearsal tomorrow," Scott said after a minute.

"Sure!"

"Great! That's awesome!" Scott replied, "It's so much easier to memorize when someone else reads the other part."

"Definitely," Miranda agreed, "I'll meet up with you in the auditorium after the last bell."

"Thanks!" Scott smiled. He finished eating his sandwich and started cleaning up, "I'm going to go and get some research done for a project in the library but I will meet up with you later."

"For sure," she returned brightly, "See you later!"

When Scott walked away, Helen let out a squeal. Their other friend Laura Wong smiled and gave her thumbs up and Christina Venetti, who was sitting beside her, held up her hand for a high-five. The boys looked at them like they'd gone crazy.

"He is so adorable," Laura smiled.

Christina agreed.

"So, what time do we want to play on Saturday?" Bryan McCann, Helen's ex-boyfriend asked, mostly to Helen.

"Maybe noon?" Helen replied. She looked around the table for everyone's consent, to which they all nodded. Helen turned to Miranda, "Let Scott know."

The boys said they would let their other friends know and then Bryan stole Helen away for a chat.

Miranda cleaned up her garbage and played cards with those who were left for the rest of lunch, though she could hardly concentrate. She couldn't believe she had just had a normal conversation with Scott and that they'd be hanging out alone after school. It was just to practice and maybe it meant nothing so she tried not to get too excited.

Miranda was so anxious for her meet-up with Scott that the afternoon just dragged on. Finally the last school bell rang and Miranda bolted up out of her chair. Helen was waiting for her at their shared locker when she arrived.

"Good luck," Helen said, excited.

Miranda flushed and was quiet. She was too nervous.

"It'll be fine, silly," Helen reassured, "Just be your wonderful self." Helen looked like she was going to burst with excitement, "Oh, look at you! All grown up and meeting a boy!"

"Shut up," Miranda laughed.

"I never thought this day would come!" Helen continued, squeezing both of her arms.

Miranda rolled her eyes. "So?" she asked, changing the subject, "What did Bryan want at lunch?"

Helen rolled her eyes dramatically, "Oh just to get back together." She smiled.

"That's good," Miranda said, "And did you?"

"Yes, I guess the long distance thing *could* work," Helen replied.

That's what it had been about. Helen had broken it off with him because he wanted to go away to school and she said the long distance relationship wouldn't work for her. "I know it'll be hard," Miranda said, "But you have the rest of your lives to be together after school is finished," then added, "If it comes to that."

"Ya, I know," Helen shrugged, "I guess I should look at the big picture."

Miranda nodded.

"So, text me as soon as you get home tonight!" Helen said, "I can come over after if you don't want to be alone."

"Ok," Miranda smiled gratefully. She didn't mind staying in the house alone but she knew she would be excited to talk to Helen afterwards, "Maybe I can even swing by on the walk home?"

Helen winked, "Maybe you won't be walking home alone though."

Miranda's heart picked up but she tried to calm herself. Helen was getting carried away. This was just a rehearsal to help him memorize his lines. She voiced this to Helen.

"Yes but he chose you," Helen said, "He could have practiced at home with one of his family members or his friends he hangs out with."

Miranda made a face. A lot of girls did seem interested, why would he like her?

"He chose you," Helen said again, reassuring her.

Miranda was still doubtful as she packed her schoolbag with her homework and grabbed her sweatshirt before Helen closed the locker.

"So, text me!" Helen said in goodbye and disappeared to find Bryan.

Miranda took her time getting to the auditorium. She didn't want to seem too anxious but then she also didn't want to seem uninterested.

Scott just happened to arrive at the same time and held the door open for her. "After you," he said, bowing.

Miranda giggled, "Thanks."

"No, thank *you*," Scott said as he followed her down the aisle, "I fear the wrath of Ms. Mahan if I screw up my lines tomorrow."

Miranda smiled, "Ms. Mahan never gets angry," she said over her shoulder. She climbed the stairs of the stage and dropped her backpack near the couch. She shivered as she remembered her dream from the night before. It had been right here on this stage and she had been heading for the same couch.

Scott took the script from his bag and opened it to where he had it marked near the end. He moved closer to Miranda to show her, "Can we start from here?"

"Ok," Miranda said, "So I'll start." Miranda moved to where they should be and took a few breaths before launching into the act.

Scott did fine. Twice he looked at his script and when they ran through it for the third time, he nailed it.

"Thank you so much!" Scott smiled as he packed his script back into his bag. "I don't know how you memorized your lines so quickly but you never miss a beat!" He chuckled and gave her arm a squeeze.

"No problem! I'm happy to help," Miranda said, her blush creeping up her face at Scott's closeness. She turned away and went to retrieve her backpack before he saw her excitement.

"Oh wow, it's almost 6 pm.!" Scott said, checking his watch.

"No worries," Miranda said, "My parents are in Toronto anyways." Miranda realized that they had probably called her by now. They had their meeting today. She hoped it went well.

"I let my parents know I would be late. I should call my dad to pick me up," Scott said, "How are you getting home?"

"I walk," Miranda replied as she slipped her dark blue sweatshirt on.

"Oh? You don't live far?" Scott asked.

"Not really," Miranda smiled, "It's about twenty minutes to walk."

"Would you like a ride?"

Miranda bit her lip. She really liked her walks. "No, thank you. I like to walk."

Scott looked in thought and then asked, "Do you mind if I walk you home?"

"Sure!" Miranda said, excited, "Maybe we can stop and get dinner? My treat! My parents left me money to feed myself." Miranda laughed but didn't elaborate that it was because of her terrible cooking skills.

"I can't let you do that," Scott smiled, "What kind of guy lets a girl pay for dinner on their first date." He led the way down the stairs and up the aisle.

Miranda, who was following behind, let her mouth fall open in shock. *Date?* She took a few deep breaths. A friend date or a *date* date? She groaned inwardly wishing Helen was here to over-analyze.

Out of the auditorium, Scott fell into step beside her. Miranda let her eyes wander over to his face as they left the school. He caught her eye and smiled. Miranda could feel her cheeks heat up.

"So, uh... what would you like for dinner?" Miranda asked, "There are a sub or pizza place down the road and a burger place across the street from them." She bit her lip, hoping either of those would be ok. What if he didn't like any of them? She scolded herself inwardly. What teenage boy didn't like any of those?

"Do you have a preference?"

Miranda gave a half-shrug, "I'm starved. I'd eat all three right now!" She giggled a little but then stopped. What if he thought she was a pig for saying that? She bit her lip again.

Scott chuckled, "Me too. How about burgers?"

Miranda nodded in relief as her stomach grumbled, "Sounds good!"

"This burger place is one of the best in town," Miranda said as she smiled her thanks to Scott for holding the door to the restaurant open for her.

"Great!"

They were seated at a table and given menus. Miranda ordered a strawberry milkshake and Scott got a chocolate one.

"Hope you don't mind if I just call my dad and let him know where to get me?" Scott asked and put his menu down.

"No worries. I'm going to text my mother as well," Miranda said. She gave Scott her address and some quick directions to pass along and then pulled out her own phone. She had two voicemails, both from her mother's cell phone. She quickly messaged that she was out for dinner and would call her back when she got home. Then she texted Helen to let her know that she was out to dinner and would call her when she got home as well. She tucked her phone away as Scott disconnected.

Scott was hilarious, to top it all off. He made her laugh throughout the entire dinner and then he snatched the bill before she could even blink. Miranda hoped he found her funny as well. She got her sense of humour from her father, which could be quite quirky at times. He had laughed too, so she hoped he was enjoying himself.

"At least let me pay my half," Miranda insisted.

"No way," Scott replied as he put some money down on the table and got up. He held his hand out and Miranda took it. He pulled her up.

"Do you work?" Miranda asked, flushed that he was still holding her hand as they headed out the door.

"Yes," Scott replied, "Just on weekends. Do you?"

"No," Miranda bit her lip, "I wanted to but my parents wanted me to concentrate on school."

"Are you doing any post-secondary school?" he asked as Miranda led the way back to her house.

"Yes, I am trying to get into a drama program either at U of T or York. I haven't decided," Miranda replied, "How about you?"

"I want to get into a trade, I think," Scott said, deep in thought, "My dad is an electrician and praises the trades all the time. It's what I want too, though. I like to fix things."

Miranda smiled and they walked in silence for a bit.

"It's a nice night," Scott commented as they exited the park onto a residential street.

"Mm-hmm," Miranda agreed, "Smells like autumn. My house is not much farther. Just through that path up ahead." Miranda motioned to it with her free arm.

"And you walk every day?"

"Yep. Helen lives just that way a couple streets," Miranda explained, nodded he head in the direction, "I pick her up and we walk together."

"That's nice," Scott said, "Better than the bus. I outgrew those seats in Grade 8!"

Miranda laughed, "Ya, me too." She stopped laughing abruptly and wanted to pinch herself. Why did she always have to point out that she was so tall?

"Why the face?"

Miranda made another face. Should she just lie and say something else? But that wasn't a good way to start a relationship, "Just my height. I hate that I'm so tall."

Scott chuckled, "Well, I like your height. Don't be ashamed."

Miranda blushed again, "Thanks."

They had reached the path and were headed down it when Miranda noticed Griffin was leaning against a tree up ahead. He looked at the two of them when he heard voices and made a face.

"Hi Miranda," Griffin said, once they were close enough.

"Hi Griffin," Miranda replied, she cast a look at Scott before turning back to Griffin, "Out for a walk again?"

"Yes," Griffin smiled, "How was school?" He looked down at their adjoined hands as they stopped in front of him.

"Great!" Miranda replied and motioned with her head to Scott, "This is Scott. He's starring in the play with me. Scott, this is Griffin. He just moved into the neighbourhood."

Scott and Griffin shook hands, though neither said anything.

"I'm excited to see the play," Griffin continued, talking only to Miranda.

"It should be good!" Miranda said, "Sorry, we should get going. Perhaps I'll run into you again soon."

Griffin chuckled, "Seems that way."

Miranda sighed quietly as they reached the end of the path. It almost seemed like Griffin had been waiting for her. What should she say to him? What if he did like her? She pushed that thought away and smiled at Scott. "I just live right there." Miranda pointed out her house.

"Nice," Scott said.

"Would you like to come in for a bit?"

"I really would," Scott smiled and looked at his watch, "But only for a bit. My dad has to get up for work early and he said he would be here at 8."

Miranda looked at her watch. It was 7:23 pm.

Miranda showed him around the main floor and he paused at the pictures of Miranda on the mantle. Miranda wished he wouldn't look at them and started to chew on her lip again.

Scott smiled, "My parents have pictures of me all over as well. Are you an only child?"

Miranda nodded. He must notice that she didn't look like her parents. She wondered if she should just tell him that she was adopted.

"Me too," Scott said.

Miranda smiled and motioned for Scott to sit on the couch, "Would you like something to drink? I make a pretty mean hot chocolate."

"Sure!" he replied.

Miranda flipped on the television and passed Scott the remote, "Here, you can find anything you like."

Scott smiled and took the remote. Miranda went to make hot chocolate and when she returned, Scott had a hockey game on the television.

"I hope you don't mind," he said, "I assume you like hockey."

"Definitely," Miranda said and took a seat beside him. She normally watched with her dad but she sat back beside Scott and sipped her hot chocolate. They watched in silence for a minute until a goal was scored. Scott cheered but Miranda booed and then they both laughed.

"Not a fan, eh?" Scott chuckled.

"I'm afraid we can't be friends if this is the team you like," Miranda smiled and gave him a playful nudge.

Scott gave her an overdramatic sigh, "I may just have to overlook it."

Miranda shrugged, "I suppose I could as well." She smiled at him and he returned it.

"Did you ever play ice hockey?" Scott asked.

"No," Miranda said, "Just on the streets with friends. Sometimes we play pond hockey in winter if the weather allows but we don't put any equipment on."

"That's pretty cool," Scott smiled, "I would love to join you all."

"We're aiming for noon on Saturday. St. Patrick's Church is just around the corner on Station Street. You can come here first if you like and we can walk over."

"Sounds great! I'm really excited," Scott said.

"Where about do you live?"

"Not too far. On the outskirts, more the London way."

"The new neighbourhood?" Miranda asked.

"Yes, the house was a new build. We moved in the summer."

"I really hope you like it here," Miranda said, genuinely, "Let me know if you need anything, ok? I can tell you all the good spots."

Scott smiled and leaned in to kiss Miranda on the cheek. His lips lingered a little and Miranda held her breath but before anything happened they heard a knock on the door.

"Oh," Scott frowned and they both looked towards the sound, "That is probably my dad." He let out a breath and stood.

Miranda smiled and got up, following Scott to the door.

"I'll see you tomorrow," she said a little breathlessly, her stomach doing backflips.

"Yep," Scott said, "Thanks again for helping me with the lines today."

Miranda smiled, "No worries."

Miranda answered the door while Scott got his shoes on.

"Hi," Scott's father said, "You must be Miranda. I've heard a lot about you."

Miranda flushed, "Hello, Mr. Thomas. Please come in."

"I'm excited to see the play Friday," he replied, as he stepped in the door, "Scott tells us you are a great actress."

Miranda sent Scott a smile, "Thanks." She turned back to his father, "Scott is pretty good too."

Mr. Thomas chuckled, "Yes. He's too modest."

"Thanks for picking me up, dad," Scott said, as he rose from tying his shoes. His face looked a little pink as well, whether it was because of his father or the fact that he was just bent over to tie his shoes.

"No worries kiddo," he replied.

Scott flushed a little bit more, "On Saturday can you drive me back here? Our friends are playing hockey."

Mr. Thomas turned to Miranda, "You play hockey?"

Miranda nodded and smiled.

"Nice," he smiled and turned back to his son, "Sure. All set?"

Scott nodded, smiled at Miranda and followed his dad out the door.

Miranda shut the door behind them and did a little dance on the spot. Then she ran for the phone and messaged Helen to come over. She couldn't wait to tell Helen about her night. She thought Scott may have been about to kiss her! Miranda had never been kissed before. She had the opportunity during a friend's boy-girl party in Grade 8 and again at several co-ed parties in high school where they played 'Spin the Bottle' or 'Seven Minutes in Heaven'. Miranda always refused to play. Helen always laughed at her pickiness but Miranda didn't want to kiss someone who didn't mean that much to her and on top of that, she'd never liked a guy before.

Miranda checked her mother's voice messages before she called her. They were just hang-ups so she gave her a call while she waited.

"Hello?" Mrs. Greenburg answered. She sounded upset.

"Hi mom," Miranda replied, "What's wrong?"

"Nothing sweetheart," she said, "I was just worried about you when you didn't answer."

"I'm so sorry mom," Miranda frowned into the phone, "I didn't think you would worry."

"It's ok," she sniffed, "I just... thought you were gone..."

"Gone?" Miranda asked, confused. "Gone where?"

"Gone out, I guess," she replied.

"Well, how was your interview?"

"It went great," she replied miserably.

"Doesn't sound very great," Miranda said. She giggled a bit hoping to cheer her mother up.

Sara sighed and changed her tone, "I'm sorry Miranda. It did go wonderfully. They think we're excellent candidates and will be checking through some references. They may even call you as well."

"Of course I will give you an excellent reference," Miranda assured her.

"You are the best," Sara said, her voice sad again, "I have some bad news though."

"I knew it," Miranda frowned into the phone, "What's wrong?"

"We're not going to be able to make it back for your play."

"Oh? Why not?" Miranda asked, concerned and a little disheartened.

Sara sniffed again, "I'm sorry. I know you are so disappointed but we have to go see your dad's mother. She's not well."

"Do you want me to come too? Can you come get me?"

"No sweetheart," Sara said, "You stay home. We will take care of her."

"Ok mom. Don't worry about missing the play. They always record them. I will get a copy. Just take care of grandma and send her my love."

"Oh, that's great," she replied, "I'm so glad I will be able to watch it after."

"Me too," Miranda said, "Is grandma in bad shape? What happened?"

"She's just sick. Your dad is worried because she is alone."

"Oh, ok," Miranda said, a little sad.

"Are you going to be ok for a few more days? I have some emergency money upstairs in my first drawer if you need more money for food," Sara said, "Make sure you go get it."

"I will if I need it. I still have the money you gave me. I was at Helen's the first night and Scott bought me dinner tonight."

"Oh?" Sara asked, as she drew in a sharp breath, "You were out with Scott?"

"Yes, he needed help with his lines so we stayed after school. Then he bought me dinner. I think I really like him, mom," Miranda admitted, excitedly.

Sara sighed, "I... I... That's good Miranda. Just take it slow and be his friend."

Miranda bit her lip, "Ok mom." She didn't want to take it slow. She wanted a boyfriend especially since she felt so inexperienced. Her friends had all at least dated someone else.

"Well, I will call you in the morning."

"Have a good sleep," Miranda replied.

"I love you Miranda."

"Love you too mom."

# Three

★　★　★　★

Helen let herself in the door and found Miranda sitting on the couch, her cell phone still in her hand. "What's up?" Helen put her overnight bag down beside the stairs and went into the living room.

Miranda shook her head slowly, "Just a weird conversation with my mom. They are going to my grandmother's for a few days. She's not feeling well and my dad is worried because she is alone." Normally only one of her parents went when her grandmother was sick but Miranda assumed that since they were both already halfway there and they had the time off anyways, that they both decided to go.

"She's going to miss the play?"

Miranda nodded.

"Hmm," Helen sat on the couch beside her.

"I wonder if it is worse with my grandmother than they are letting on and that is why she sounded so upset. Maybe just to spare my feelings?" Miranda sighed, and looked at Helen, "What do you think?"

"Makes sense. They don't want you to worry with the play coming up or feel obligated to be there with them?"

"I'm not sure," Miranda said. Her parents had always been honest with her. It didn't seem like them to make anything up.

"She sounded upset?"

Miranda nodded.

Helen looked deep in thought and then saw the game on the television, "What made you put this game on?" She wrinkled her nose.

"Scott picked it," Miranda replied, smiling.

Helen giggled and threw her arms up triumphantly, "Finally something wrong with him. He has absolutely *no* taste in hockey teams."

Miranda laughed.

"So?" Helen asked, a smile lit her face.

"I think I just went out on a date!" Miranda replied and went into every detail of her night, right down to where he almost kissed her and what his dad said. "He must have mentioned me before at home."

Helen squealed, "I'm so happy for you!" She squeezed Miranda's arm with both hands in excitement.

They talked about Scott and Helen helped her analyze the date for the rest of the night. Miranda completely forgot about the conversation with her mother.

*It was just after sunset and Miranda was being chased through the streets of Woodstock. The man behind her was going to kill her. She ran past her house and into the park, hiding in one of the playhouses. She held her breath, her heart beating wildly, as a shadow passed. She could feel his confusion in thinking that he had lost her.*

*She heard footsteps walk away and decided it might be safe to take a peek out the window. Her hands were shaking and she took deep calming breaths. She poked her head out again and didn't see a soul around so she crept out of the small shelter but was grabbed from behind. He took her down and knelt overtop of her. Miranda looked up at him but his face was covered with a black ski mask. Miranda pleaded with him and he just laughed at her. She kicked him in the groin and he doubled over, giving her a few seconds to escape but she didn't get far before the lights in the dimly lit park went out. Even the stars in the sky disappeared.*

*Miranda fumbled in the darkness as she heard the man in the ski mask get closer.*

*"Prepare to die Miss East," he said in a cold, deep voice and then she heard the sound of a gun being cocked. Miranda could feel his hot breath on the back of her neck and screamed, reaching out in the darkness.*

*Finally a hand took hers and pulled her away. He hugged her to him tightly as the Earthquake hit. A dark scream rose up from behind her but Miranda couldn't bear to look to see what was happening.*

Miranda awoke with a small gasp, darkness all around her. She could almost still feel his arms around her. She rolled over and concentrated on that rather than her nightmares to calm herself. She wished she wouldn't have these dreams anymore. They were starting to frighten her. Like something drastic was going to happen soon. Was she afraid to have a boyfriend and that was causing them?

Helen was the first to get up again but this time Miranda's alarm woke her up while Helen was in the bathroom.

When Miranda opened her closet door she noticed half of her wardrobe was missing! Panicked, she opened up all her drawers and noticed they were half empty as well. She looked again around her room and started to notice little things missing. All the pictures of her and her friends were gone, even the ones that were in frames on her desk and dresser. The frames stood there empty.

Miranda's laptop was still there and she knew nothing was missing from downstairs. Then she remembered she hadn't seen Tinsel since her parents left.

"Tinny!" Miranda called out. She went into her parent's room even though the door had been closed. She called her name a few times as she checked all her normal hiding spots.

"What's going on?" Helen asked, coming out of the bathroom.

"My clothes are missing! And my pictures!" Miranda said, a little hysterical. Her eyes filled with tears, "I just realized I haven't seen Tinsel!"

"Calm down," Helen said, trying to stay calm herself, "We'll find her."

They searched the house up and down, calling her name but they didn't find her.

"Your clothes were here yesterday, right?" Helen asked when they had reconvened in the living room.

Miranda nodded, tears streaming down her face. Her clothes were all there when she got dressed yesterday morning but she had laid her pyjamas under her pillow so she had no need to open her drawer last night. She couldn't believe she didn't even think of Tinsel! She left food for her yesterday morning but when she looked today, it hadn't been touched. Did someone take her clothes, pictures and cat sometime yesterday? Miranda tried to remember if she had to unlock the door when she got home last night. There were no windows broken. Did she leave the door unlocked and if she did, why wouldn't a burglar steal the computers or televisions they had? "What should I do? Call the police?"

Helen frowned and gave Miranda a hug, "Yes. I would. I'll stay here with you."

Before Miranda could call, the phone rang.

"Hello?" Miranda croaked.

"Hi honey," her father said. At least he didn't sound sad. "I didn't get to talk to you last night so I wanted to say hello this morning. How are you doing?"

"Not very well dad," Miranda replied.

"What happened?" he asked, worried.

"Someone stole my cat!" Miranda broke down. Her clothes and pictures could be replaced but what about Tinsel?

"What?" Mr. Greenburg said, shocked, "How?"

"I don't know," Miranda cried, "My clothes are missing too and my pictures but nothing else."

"That's certainly strange," Mr. Greenburg said, "Do you want us to come home?"

"No dad," Miranda shook her head. As much as she wanted them home, she knew her grandmother needed them more, "I will call the police."

"Hmm," he said, "I don't think you should call the police. We can buy you more clothes and I don't think Tinsel was taken. Maybe she got outside?"

"Do you think? Should I search the neighbourhood?"

"She will come home Miranda," Mr. Greenburg assured her, "If she is not home by the time we are back on Sunday, we will help you find her."

"Um," Miranda was torn. She wanted to do all she could to find her now! And why was her dad so nonchalant about a burglar in the house? Miranda started to pace the kitchen with the cordless home phone tucked between her ear and shoulder, "Are you sure I shouldn't call the police?"

"Most of your clothes were too small anyways," he replied, "We can buy more."

Miranda was almost too shocked to be upset anymore, "But they stole clothes that still fit," she said stubbornly.

"It's ok," he said, "We will sort it all out when we get home."

Miranda made a face at Helen and Helen mouthed the word 'what?' Miranda shrugged.

"Ok dad," Miranda finally said, "If you are sure, I will wait."

"Yes," he said, more firmly, "That is best. I love you Miranda."

"Love you too dad." They disconnected.


"He didn't want you to call?" Helen asked, folding her arms across her chest over the bright white shirt of her school uniform.

Miranda shook her head, "I guess he doesn't think it's worthwhile. I don't know! There was someone in our house!"

"Your parents have been really weird lately."

Miranda agreed and her blue eyes filled with tears again. She missed Tinsel.

"We can stay home and look for her," Helen suggested, "We'll make some flyers and paper the whole town!"

Miranda gave her a grateful smile.

"I'll call my mom and tell her to call the school to excuse us for the morning? Or the whole day?"

"We have dress rehearsal tonight. We can't let them down," Miranda frowned again, "Maybe just the morning."

Helen nodded and called her mom. She explained to her that the cat was missing but didn't mention the stolen clothes. Her mother agreed to call the school and wished them luck at finding the cat.

"Wanna split up?" Helen asked once the flyers were made up.

Miranda shook her head as she took a look at the stack of flyers in her hand. There was a picture of Tinsel in the middle and a description including her light purple collar and vet tags, plus Miranda Greenburg's contact information. "I don't think I can go around alone."

Helen put a comforting arm around her, "We'll find her."

Miranda nodded and they both put on their sweatshirts over their school uniforms. It was the only sweatshirt Miranda had left and she had to put her school kilt on since her pants didn't fit. The burglar had at least left her school uniform behind.

Helen and Miranda walked up and down the streets putting up the flyers on the hydro poles and calling out Tinsel's name. Miranda got more and more upset as they went, shuffling from pole to pole in a daze. Tinsel was going to be her only companion when she went to school. That was, if she was allowed to bring her. She was hoping to be able to.

"Miranda, don't be upset," Helen said, putting an arm around her again, "We'll find her. I'm sure of it."

Miranda fought a fresh wave of tears and tried to nod in agreement.

They were taping up another flyer when someone came up to them from behind.

"What have you got there?" Griffin asked.

Helen and Miranda both looked back with a gasp.

"Geez," Helen said, "You scared us. Where did you come from?"

"Just out for a walk before class," Griffin said with a shrug. He turned to Miranda and saw her face, "What is wrong? Why are you upset?" He looked like he wanted to console her, but held back.

"My cat is missing," Miranda managed to say. Another tear slipped down her face as she handed Griffin a flyer.

He took it and bit his lip as he read.

"Have you seen a cat around?" Helen asked, "Since you are out walking all the time?"

Griffin shook his head and pocketed the flyer, "I will be sure to look around."

Miranda thanked him.

"I am sorry you are upset," Griffin said, stopping her with a hand on her arm as she passed.

"Thanks," Miranda mumbled and continued on.

"You are right," Helen whispered, taking a peek back to make sure Griffin was far enough away, "There is something weird about him."

Miranda sped up and Helen followed. They rounded the corner and she stopped.

"He's been around me a lot lately. You don't think he's the one who broke into my house?" Miranda asked, quietly.

"No," Helen said, equally as quiet, "He's weird but I don't think he's some sort of pervert."

Miranda took a second to think and then nodded, "It just seems weird that he keeps showing up while I'm out and he seems so unsure of some of his answers. Like when I asked him about his classes yesterday and he also said he was from down south but never said where."

"He said he was going to class today," Helen said with a shrug.

"I guess," Miranda replied. She sighed and looked at the time on her cell phone, "Well, let's keep going. We only have another hour before we should head to the school."

After an hour, with no luck, they picked up their schoolbags from Miranda's house and headed to the school. Miranda made a point of making sure she locked the door and checked it before they left.

The afternoon went by in a blur. Miranda couldn't concentrate. She was so worried about her cat. She almost didn't want to go to dress rehearsal. She needed to be out there looking.

Helen met up with her at their locker at the end of the day.

"I know it sucks, Miranda," Helen said, comfortingly, "But we can head out again after this. Bryan and Christina said they would come too. And maybe Scott will help."

"I don't want to bother Scott," Miranda said, quickly. She hated pity. She got it a lot when people found out she was adopted and she hadn't even told him that yet. Everyone always looked at her with that pitying look, like she was broken. But they shouldn't pity her. She had the best parents ever!

"He'll want to help too," Helen assured her as she put an arm around her and ushered her off to the girl's dressing room where their costumes awaited. The play was set back in the early 1900s and they had elaborate dresses as costumes which Miranda had on lend from Stratford.

"Hi Miranda!" Scott said when she reached the stage. He was smiling and dressed in his costume. The set was all complete. Ms. Mahan had replaced the contemporary couch with another that looked antique. There was an antique table and chairs and the backdrop had finally been completed by the art students.

Miranda sent him a small smile. He had the perfect face for a man of the early twentieth century. That's probably why Ms. Mahan picked him for the role. He filled out the brown suit pants nicely.

"You look good," Scott said, looking her up and down, "I wasn't sure if you were here. You missed class this morning and I couldn't find you at lunch. I didn't have your number so I was worried."

Miranda blushed the same colour as her full bodied pink lace gown, "Sorry Scott. I should have given you my number yesterday. I was out of school this morning."

"I'll get it afterwards," he said as he took her hand and kissed it.

Miranda's smile widened, "You look pretty good too."

"Thanks," Scott replied.

"Ok everyone!" Ms. Mahan said, calling for attention. Everyone turned to her. "You all look amazing! Thank you so much to Miranda for getting us the costumes!" Everyone applauded in appreciation. "Ok, so we're going to run through this like it's the actual night! Places everyone and show me what you got!" Ms. Mahan spread her arms wide like she wanted to hug everyone and then she turned and headed off the stage. She took a seat a few rows back, where Jen was seated, while everyone made their way off stage. The house lights were lowered and the curtain pulled.

The dress rehearsal went smoothly. Scott needed a small coaxing near the end for his line, which Miranda helped him by improvising a little. Scott easily caught on and they were able to finish the last scene without a problem.

Ms. Mahan and Jen both applauded as the curtain closed and stood as the curtain opened again and the whole cast was on the stage for the final bow.

"Woohoo!" Jen catcalled.

The music cut away and the house lights went back on.

"Excellent work everyone!" Ms. Mahan called out. Jen was grinning from ear to ear beside her. For once, she had no criticisms.

Scott turned and pulled Miranda into a hug, "Thank you so much for the line," he said.

"No worries!" Miranda smiled, pulling back a bit, "You did great!"

Helen was beside Miranda next, she was smiling as well. Everyone crowded around them, all excited for the play tomorrow and congratulating them on a rehearsal well done.

"Everyone get a good sleep tonight!" Ms. Mahan shouted out above the crowd.

The cast agreed and slowly started to head back to the dressing rooms until it was just Helen, Christina, Bryan, Miranda and Scott left on stage.

"We should celebrate!" Scott said.

Miranda's smile faded and Helen put a hand on her arm.

Scott's face fell, "What's up?"

Miranda's eyes filled with tears and she bit her lip. She was grateful that Helen stepped in. She didn't want to cry in front of Scott.

"Her cat is missing," Helen explained, "We were all going to look for her. That's why we weren't in school this morning."

"Oh man!" Scott said, sending Miranda a pitying look, "I would love to help!"

"Great!" Helen smiled, "We are all going right now and then heading to Miranda's for pizza. You are welcome to join!"

Scott agreed and they all headed back to the dressing rooms to change.

They decided to split up once they got into Miranda's neighbourhood to cover more ground. As Miranda walked along, she could hear her friends calling for Tinsel around the neighbourhood. She called out her name a few times, her eyes darting around for any sign of her. She strained to listen for any kind of meowing.

As Miranda turned onto the path that led to her street, she noticed another boy walking towards her.  She slowed her pace and stopped walking altogether when he pulled back his hood. He was the cutest boy she had ever seen in her life. They stared at each other for almost a whole minute as the world around her seemed to vanish and it was only them.

"Did your mother ever tell you it is not polite to stare?" he grinned at her. The smile lit his whole face. Miranda had never seen such a gorgeous smile.

She shook her head to clear it and flushed a deep red, "Did yours?" She would have continued on, embarrassed for staring, but he stepped in front of her. He was so tall she had to look up to him.

"I guess not," he said, continuing to stare at her. His blue-green eyes seemed to be looking deep inside of her.

"Excuse me, I-I" Miranda stammered but she couldn't remember what she was doing. She took a step closer to him.

"You are looking for your cat?" he finished for her, also moving closer.

"Yes, Tinsel is missing. Who are you?"

He just smiled at her, "You are Miranda East?"

Miranda nodded, lost in his gaze again. She stared dazed, like she should know him from somewhere, "Well yes and no. I'm... wait, how did you know that?"

"Your posters say Miranda Greenburg," he continued, avoiding her question again.

"I changed it," Miranda said, shaking her head again. She tried so hard to think clearly but failed, "I'm Miranda Greenburg now." She answered his questions easily enough, like she was in a trance. An uneasy feeling finally settled in and she took a step back from him. She was getting annoyed that he was avoiding her questions and it broke the spell he put on her.

"Why?"

"I was adopted. I'm not a part of any East family." She took another step back. "I have to go. I have to find my cat."

"Wait," he pleaded, stepping in closer again, "I have something to ask you."

"No," Miranda said stubbornly, "You haven't answered any of my questions."

"I will soon," he said with a mysterious smile.

Miranda stared again. She couldn't help it. She felt drawn to him.

"Would you like to go out with me tomorrow? We could get a coffee or something of that sort?" he asked, though he wrinkled his nose slightly as he finished the sentence.

"I really would like that," Miranda said, without thinking. She shook her head before she dropped her gaze and it took her a second to realize that she had something to do already. "Can I take a raincheck? I have school."

"Raincheck?" he asked, confused.

"It means some other time," Miranda explained.

He shook his head and smiled, "I knew that. How about after the play?"

Miranda blinked a few times, "I don't even know you."

"You will," he said, confidently. He was about to reach out to touch her but pulled his hand back. "Please Miranda?"

"What's your name?"

"Alex."

The name echoed through her thoughts. Alex, Griffin's brother? Aside from the tanned skin and the height, he didn't look a thing like him. He had a square jaw and his hair was lighter, plus he looked much more toned. Despite his sweatshirt, Miranda focused on his broad shoulders. She needed to concentrate and focus on not being swayed by this really cute guy. After the play they normally went out as a cast to celebrate and plus, she had Scott now, sort of, and she didn't want to ruin things by going out with someone else.

"Sorry Alex, I can't. I'm busy this weekend."

He made a face.

Miranda's face fell too. Despite her feelings for Scott, she wanted this guy in front of her even more and she didn't even know him.

"You think about that," Alex said, smiling secretively. He pulled his hood back up. "I will see you soon." And he turned and headed back the way he came from.

"Miranda!" Helen called from behind her.

Miranda spun towards her as the world seemed to rise back up around her and all her senses returned. She remembered that she was supposed to be looking for her cat.

"Who was that?" Helen asked, stopping in front of her.

"Alex," Miranda replied.

Helen went wide-eyed, "Griffin's brother?" She peeked around Miranda and rose on her toes, trying to get a better look at his retreating frame.

"Yep," Miranda said. She turned to watch as he rounded the corner and headed to the left.

Helen gave her a sideways glance, "You looked like you were having an intense conversation."

Miranda coloured slightly, "He was asking me out."

Helen's head snapped back to her, "Seriously?"

Miranda bit her lip and nodded.

"So what did you say?" Helen asked, excited.

"I said no!" Miranda replied, as if it were obvious, "What do you think I'd say?"

Helen rolled her eyes, "Oh Miranda. You are not even dating Scott. If another guy comes along, you can give him a shot too."

"How would you know I'm even interested in him?"

"You should have seen you both," Helen snorted, "A bomb could have dropped five feet away and it wouldn't have mattered."

Miranda gave her a doubtful look. They didn't know each other at all. This was the first time she had seen or spoken to him. Why would she be so drawn to him?

"Come with me," Helen said, pulling her along, "I'm going to find out where they live."

Miranda protested but Helen wouldn't let her go. They reached the end of the path and Helen headed to the left to follow but he was nowhere to be seen.

Helen swore, "We lost him." Despite that, she continued to pull Miranda along. "He must have turned down the side street." They quickly crossed the street and reached the corner and turned right down the next side street but he had vanished. Still Helen pulled her, calling out Tinsel's name so it looked like they were just looking for the cat. They reached the next corner and Helen stood on her toes and looked both ways down the street. Miranda refused to look but when Helen took her arm to pull her along again, she glanced to the left and saw the same motor home that she had seen pull onto her street on Monday night. She stopped abruptly and Helen gave her a questioning look.

"I saw that motor home a few nights ago on my street," Miranda commented, pointing towards it.

Helen looked at the massive silver vehicle and laughed, "Well, they certainly don't live in a motor home."

Miranda shrugged, "Just pointing it out. It's strange. I've never seen it before."

"Someone probably just brought it back from up north. It's getting colder and time to shut down the summer parks," Helen deducted and pulled Miranda along again.

Miranda watched the motor home while allowing Helen to pull her along until it was out of sight. All the curtains were closed. She couldn't see inside at all though she did think she saw the curtains flutter a bit like someone had looked outside.

Helen pulled her to every intersection, looking left and right but they couldn't find where Alex had gone. She let out a big sigh. "Next time, we won't let him get away."

Miranda's stomach grumbled and she looked at her watch. It was almost 7 pm. They should really get back and have dinner. "Well, we should really go back. The pizza is going to be delivered at 7 pm. It looks like Tinsel really is lost." She looked down in defeat.

"I bet someone picked her up," Helen suggested, "Once they see the flyers, they will call you."

Miranda nodded half-heartedly and they both headed back to Miranda's house just on time to meet the pizza delivery. Miranda paid him and they went inside.

Helen messaged for everyone to come back.

"No luck?" Scott asked when he and Bryan entered the kitchen.

Miranda shook her head sadly, "We hope that maybe someone picked her up and they will see the flyers. She also has her vet tags on so they could call the vet to find out who she is."

Scott sat at the kitchen table with Helen. Bryan joined them.

"Help yourselves," Helen said, pushing the pizza box around so the opening faced the boys. Bryan was the first to dive in and Helen rolled her eyes. He was always hungry!

Christina joined them a few minutes later with no luck as well.

Miranda poured out drinks for everyone and then grabbed her desk chair from upstairs to join them.

The conversation was a little subdued. Miranda didn't join in at all. Between worrying about her cat and her encounter with Alex, she couldn't concentrate on the conversation.

Scott looked at his watch as it neared 8pm, "My dad will be here shortly," he announced, "Does anyone need a ride?"

Bryan nodded.

Christina shook her head, "I live the other direction. I can have my dad pick me up."

"Thanks everyone for your help," Miranda said sadly, snapping out of her thoughts, "I really appreciate it."

Scott gave her a sad smile, "I have a cat too. I would do the same."

"Let's go wait outside," Helen suggested, "It's a nice night." Everyone agreed and they all headed towards the front door to put their shoes back on. Miranda lagged behind to clean up. When Scott noticed, he stayed behind too.

"You don't have to help," Miranda smiled at him as she cleared the table of the plates and cups.

"I'm happy to help," Scott replied and collected the garbage and recycling.

"Thanks!"

"So, are you going to the dance?" Scott asked as he broke down the pizza box to fit into the recycling, "It sounded like you weren't sure the other day."

Miranda laughed a little, "Yes, Helen would have my head if I didn't go."

"Ok," Scott smiled, "I was only going to go if you did."

Miranda blushed a little, "And I probably would only go if you did."

"So," Scott laughed, "Let's go!"

Miranda agreed as she quickly wiped down the table. Then the two joined the others outside.

Helen was seated on the step below Bryan and was leaning up against him. He fiddled with her hair. Christina sat on the steps across from them so Miranda took the ledge around the front porch and Scott sat beside her. They talked about the hockey game coming up on Saturday but it wasn't long before Scott's dad pulled in the driveway.

Miranda waved to Scott's dad, who smiled and waved back. She joined the others on the steps to say goodbye. "See you tomorrow," she said to Scott, "Thanks again for the help."

"Anytime," Scott smiled.

Bryan, on the other hand, said goodbye to Helen with a kiss. Miranda and Scott shifted uncomfortably but luckily it was Christina who made the gagging noises, causing them to laugh.

"Uh, bye," Scott said awkwardly to the others and headed down the steps to his father's car.

Bryan said goodbye to Miranda and Christina and followed Scott.

Miranda took a seat between the two girls and watched them drive away.

"He really is a sweetheart," Christina commented when they were out of sight, "I'm glad you got him than one of those other girls he was hanging around."

"He is super nice," Helen agreed, "I hope he will hang out with our group now."

"Hope so too!" Miranda agreed as well.

"Are you both dating officially?" Christina asked, "I'll happily help spread the word so the others will back off!" She smiled wickedly.

"Not officially," Miranda said, "So not yet. I'll let you know if and when you can."

"Ok," Christina agreed as another car pulled in the driveway. It was her dad. Miranda thanked her as well and said goodbye.

"You wanna stay at my house tonight?" Helen asked once she had gone.

Miranda smiled with relief and nodded, "Definitely." She needed to get out of this house. It was frightening to her that someone else had been inside. She packed a few things, one of the few pairs of pyjamas she had left that actually fit and some toiletries. She also had to make an outfit of what she had left in her closet for after school and after the play.

"Just wear this shirt and I'll let you borrow a skirt," Helen suggested, rummaging through her drawers, "You've got killer legs so it won't matter if it's too short."

Miranda made a face, "It matters to me!"

Helen rolled her eyes, "You got it. You should flaunt it."

Miranda sighed. She really didn't have much choice. She packed the shirt Helen had passed her and they headed out the door. Miranda made sure it was locked.

<h1 style="text-align:center">Four</h1>

★  ★  ★  ★

It didn't take long for Miranda to fall asleep that night. She was exhausted after the long day but she awoke in the middle of the night after another nightmare. This time she had been attacked at the school dance by the man in the black ski mask.

"You ok?" Helen asked sleepily.

"Yes," Miranda replied, "Sorry to wake you."

Helen yawned and rolled over. Miranda could tell Helen fell back to sleep immediately by her breathing. Miranda tossed and turned a bit, thinking about Alex and how much she wanted to be with him instead of Scott. Why was it she was so attracted to him? He could have a horrible personality even though he seemed nice enough. And why did he want to date her? He didn't know her either? She was confused because she thought maybe Griffin was interested. Was Griffin trying to befriend her for the sake of his brother? But that was silly. They didn't know her at all!

Miranda was finally able to fall asleep after probably an hour of her mind racing.

"Happy Friday superstar!" Helen called out and jumped on the bed.

Miranda groaned, "Remind me again why I slept here."

"Because you loooooove me!" Helen sang out and continued to jump until Miranda grabbed her ankle and pulled.

Helen erupted into a fit of giggles as she landed on her backside on the bed, "Up and at em! We have a play to do today!"

Miranda smiled and sat up. Helen was already dressed in her school uniform and ready. "I don't know how you do it."

"What?"

"Have so much energy in the morning."

Helen laughed and shrugged. She was always the morning person. Miranda on the other hand needed a couple hours before she could function.

The day went by quickly which made Miranda happy. Scott even joined their group for lunch which made her even happier. Scott and Bryan got along really well and they planned a double date for dinner that night before the play. By the last bell, Miranda's excitement was at its peak. She had decided throughout the day that she was going to think positively. It was what her dad always taught her. They would find Tinsel soon, she shouldn't mope around. She also had two guys who were trying to date her, which was sort of overwhelming, but it sure made her feel good about herself.

Back at Helen's house, Helen opened up her large closet. She had a ton of clothes for someone who had to wear a uniform every day.

Helen pulled out a multiple hangar that had about six or seven skirts hanging from it and smiled. She looked at them in thought and then pulled off three of them. She tossed all three at Miranda, "One of these should be good. Try em all on!"

All three were a jean material, two blue and one black. The black was really short. When Miranda held it up to herself, she sent Helen a look of disgust and tossed it back at her, "Oh heck no!"

Helen threw it back at her, aiming for her face but Miranda caught it. "Just try it. It will look best with that top rather than the blue."

Miranda groaned, "Fine," and went to the washroom to try them on.

"I wanna see!" Helen called after her.

Miranda put the longest blue one on first and looked at herself in the mirror. She sighed. Helen was right. The black probably would look best with her dark purple shirt. She loved this top and was glad it wasn't stolen. She had gotten it from her parents at Christmas and would have never bought it for herself because it was expensive. She thought Helen may have had a hand in helping her parents choose it. It wasn't normally a shirt they would buy her. It had a low v-neck and cap sleeves. The kind of shirt she should probably save for the dance tomorrow night but since she had very slim picking in her wardrobe, she would have to wear it tonight.

Miranda took off the blue without showing Helen and put on the black. It was about mid-thigh on her and she tried to pull it down more. She turned to the mirror. It looked really good with the top but Miranda didn't think she would be comfortable showing so much leg. Reluctantly, she went to show Helen, who squealed with delight.

"I don't know," Miranda shifted uncomfortably and tried to pull it down again.

Helen swatted her hand, "It looks amazing on you. I really wish I had your legs!"

Miranda pursed her lips and looked into Helen's full length mirror.

"Do you wax your legs too?" Helen asked, "They look so smooth!"

Miranda nodded.

Helen shook her head in disbelief, "For someone like yourself, I can't believe you wax!"

Miranda looked at her, "Why?"

"Well, it's expensive to do it, isn't it? I haven't known you to spend a quarter without overanalyzing!"

Miranda forced out a laugh, "I do it myself. I learned."

"Maybe you could do mine someday," Helen said, looking down at her legs. She had changed into a short khaki skirt and a light blue halter. She put her white sweater on overtop and went to stand beside Miranda at the mirror.

"I'd be afraid to hurt you," Miranda said, trying to think of something quickly, "It kinda sucks but I like the outcome."

"Your legs always look so great. I'm so jealous!" Helen exclaimed. "So, I think you should definitely wear that." She smiled encouragingly.

"I'll be so uncomfortable!" Miranda sighed.

"You look amazing," Helen shook her head, "Whenever you feel uncomfortable you just look at me and I can reassure you."

"Alright fine," Miranda finally caved. She took another long look at herself. It wasn't too short, she tried to convince herself.

Helen looked at her watch, "Bryan will be here soon. His dad is letting him use his car for the night and his parents are taking his mom's car to the play."

"Ok," Miranda replied, finally turning away from the mirror.

Helen smiled at her and then led the way downstairs, "Bye mom!" Helen shouted, "See you tonight!"

"Break a leg, ladies!" Helen's mother called, poking her head around from the kitchen, "Oh Miranda, you look nice!"

"Thanks Mrs. Beauchamps!" Miranda giggled. She felt the urge to pull the skirt down again and looked at Helen.

Helen rolled her eyes, "You look good! Stop fidgeting."

Miranda made a face and followed Helen onto the porch. "I don't know what I'll wear tomorrow. All my good clothes are gone."

"I can ask my mom if we can run to the mall tomorrow after hockey." Helen suggested.

Miranda shook her head, "I don't have money."

Helen waved her hand, "We'll figure out something. Don't worry!" She gave Miranda a wide grin.

Miranda looked down at herself and groaned, "It's gonna be short and tight, isn't it?"

Helen laughed, "Possibly."


Scott was in the car with Bryan when he pulled in the driveway. He got out of the front to let Helen have shotgun and held the door to the backseat open for Miranda. Miranda caught him giving her a once over before he smiled at her.

"You look stunning," Scott said.

Miranda blushed, something she was doing a lot of lately. "Thanks." She glanced down at his jeans, which fit him nicely and his striped rugby shirt that hugged his biceps and bit her lip. He looked pretty good himself.

"So should we just grab something quickly?" Bryan asked from the front seat, "Ms. Mahan wants us there an hour before curtain?"

"Ya," Miranda replied, "I'm fine with that."

"How about Chinese?" Helen suggested, "The buffet. That way it'll be fast."

Everyone agreed and Bryan made a left out of the street towards the restaurant.

By the time they reached the school, Miranda had decided to choose Scott over Alex. There was no way she was going to jeopardize the blooming relationship with Scott by going on one date with Alex. Scott was super sweet, really cute, though not as cute as Alex, and he got along with Helen and Bryan very well.

"Oh I am so glad you are here," Ms. Mahan said when she saw them, "I was hoping you boys could go get a table from the cafeteria, please?"

"Sure, Ms. Mahan," Bryan said. Scott followed him down the hallway towards the cafeteria.

Ms. Mahan was holding a brown cash box and a stack of tickets which she placed on the steps to the auditorium. She turned to look at Helen and Miranda, deep in thought. "If you ladies would like to get ready and come back out here, you can help greet the audience. The boys are going to be ushers. I think it will be a nice touch to show off your costumes since it's a play no one has seen."

They both agreed and headed to the dressing room.

Before getting dressed, Helen pulled out her makeup case and did both of their makeup. She put a few pins in Miranda's hair but left it down.

Miranda got dressed while Helen did the makeup of some of the other ladies in the cast.

"I'll meet you out there," Helen said, as she was applying blush to Sabrina's face, "Let Ms. Mahan know I'm almost finished with everyone."

Miranda checked herself in the mirror and headed out.

"Oh, good!" Ms. Mahan said, sounding a little stressed, when she saw Miranda, "We need help!"

There was a long line of people waiting to get in and just Jen and Ms. Mahan were there. Miranda took a seat and started collecting money and giving tickets. She peeked over and saw that some of the boys were taking the tickets at the door. Others were inside acting as ushers. Almost everyone was in character. She heard Bryan trying to use his horrible English accent. It added a bit of humour to the play and Ms. Mahan had told him to keep doing it.

With the three of them there, the line started to move quicker. Miranda greeted some of her classmates and some of her friend's parents as they arrived. She got nervous thinking Griffin and Alex might show up.

"I'll take over for a bit," one of the other girls said to Miranda, "You should get backstage and relax before you go on. Rest your voice."

"Thanks Tiffany," Ms. Mahan replied before Miranda could.

Miranda stood and sent Tiffany a smile. She took a look at the line and of course spotted Griffin and his brother and her stomach lurched. They were the tallest in the line but they hadn't seen her looking so she averted her eyes quickly. Miranda passed Helen, who was heading to the front.

"I'm going backstage," Miranda told her, "There's still a bit of a line if you wanted to help."

"Yes, I might as well. I'm not in till the fifth scene anyways!" Helen smiled, excitedly, "Break a leg Mandy!"

Miranda smiled, "You too. I saw your family. They are in already."

"Is Griffin and his brother here?" Helen asked, wide-eyed, as she just remembered they were coming.

Miranda coloured slightly, "I saw them in line. They didn't see me."

"Gotta go!" Helen said and took off in a hurry.

Miranda laughed to herself as she watched her friend go.

Two minutes till the show, Helen found Miranda warming her voice in the wings.

"You didn't tell me he was so hot!" Helen squealed. She squeezed Miranda's arm with both hands. "You have to go on a date with him!"

"What?" Miranda laughed, "No!"

"Come on!" Helen giggled.

"You think he's hot, you date him!" Miranda could see in her face she was actually considering it. "Helen!" she said, pretending to be scandalized. She put her hands over her ears, "I can't be hearing this. Whatever will Mr. McCann think?" She sighed dramatically.

Helen gave her a playful nudge, giggling, "You are such a dork."

Miranda stuck her tongue out at her.

Ms. Mahan came up behind them. She had a huge smile on her face, "We're sold out! Are you all set?"

Miranda nodded enthusiastically, ignoring the butterflies in her stomach. She was always more excited than nervous. She took a few deep breaths and sent Helen a wide smile.

"Knock em dead!" Helen whispered and squeezed her hand.

"Ok!" Ms. Mahan said and turned to everyone, "Places everyone!" And she took the stage to do the introductions. She tapped the microphone to see if it was on before beginning. "Ladies and gentleman, thank you so much for joining us today. With your help we have raised five thousand dollars for charity tonight." She paused while everyone applauded. "This play we are about to put on is one of a kind! Written by our grade 12 student, Jennifer MacMillen. So sit back and enjoy!" Ms. Mahan left the stage and went into the pit. The house lights dimmed and the curtain opened.

*   *   *

The crowd roared as the lights dimmed on the final scene. In the dark, Scott found Miranda's hand and they took their position in the centre of the line. The lights came up again and the whole cast was on the stage. The audience was standing and cheering. They all bowed together. Then Jen came out onto the stage and took a bow and Ms. Mahan. The curtain closed.

Jen was so happy, she let out a squeal, "You all did just amazing. I couldn't have asked for a better cast to perform my play." She turned to Ms. Mahan, "Thank you so much for believing in me." She gave her a hug.

"You all did wonderfully," Ms. Mahan said, turning to the cast. Everyone was in a happy buzz.

Miranda turned to Scott, "Great job! You nailed it!"

"Thanks to you," Scott smiled. He gave her a hug, "You were awesome!"

"Thanks."

"Mandy you were amazing!" Helen exclaimed, interrupting the two of them, "We have to celebrate!" Helen glanced around to everyone, "Where shall we go?"

"Sorry," Scott frowned, "I actually can't go out tonight."

"Oh no," Helen said, her face fell, "We always celebrate after!"

"My aunt and uncle came to see the play and my parents wanted me to spend some time with the family."

"That's ok, Scott," Miranda smiled, and put a reassuring hand on his arm, "We'll see you tomorrow!"

"I'm bailing too," Bryan said with a shrug.

"What!" Helen turned to him with shock.

82

"That's fine," Miranda cut in, trying to diffuse Helen before she got angry with Bryan for something so silly, "We've still got everyone else."

"I'm in!" Christina said.

Tiffany, Sabrina, Brad, Jacob, Jen and Michelle also agreed so they headed to the dressing rooms to change.

Miranda changed back into her skirt and pushed it down on her hips so it wasn't as short. She sighed.

"You look fine," Helen laughed at her from across the dressing room.

"Ready girls?" Brad called from outside their dressing room door.

"Keep your pants on!" Helen yelled out, "Perfection takes time!" She smiled at her reflection as she dabbed on some lip gloss.

Brad snorted so loud, they heard it through the door.

"Ok, done," Helen said and turned to everyone else, who were all ready to go.

Miranda shook her head as she exited the dressing room right behind her best friend, "I also don't know how you manage to make it to school on time."

Helen threw her a smile over her shoulder, "I get up early."

In the school entrance, they split themselves into two groups. Helen, Miranda, Christina were in Tiffany's car and the rest went with Jen, who had a bigger vehicle.

"Oh I left my keys," Tiffany said, as she checked her pockets, "I'll just run and get them, you all go ahead."

Jen and the others left so only three of them were startled when someone stepped around the corner from the gym.

Christina's mouth dropped open when she saw the really cute stranger. Miranda stopped what she was about to say. She couldn't remember what she was about to say when she looked at him.

"Hi Alex!" Helen recovered first.

"Hello," he said and sent her a smile, "I just need to speak with Miranda. Will you please excuse us?"

Christina and Helen nodded.

He stepped in close to Miranda and put a hand on her shoulder. The world fell away from Miranda again as she stared into his eyes. She could feel the warmth of his hand through her shirt. "Can we talk? Please?"

Miranda nodded numbly.

He spun to her just before the doors to the outside, "Do you have everything you need?"

"Yes, why?" Miranda replied, looking down at the backpack in her hand, "What do you need to talk about?"

"Remember that raincheck?" he asked, as he held the door open for her, "Can I take you up on that now?"

Miranda stopped abruptly. Once in the cool October air, her daze lifted and she shivered, "You mean a date? Are you crazy? I said no! I'm going out with my friends."

"I really need to talk to you and I am running out of time. Just please, come with me for five minutes."

"Out of time for what?" Miranda asked but he had already spun around. He glanced back in hopes she would follow. Sighing she stomped after him but planned all her exits. She knew the high school very well and the surrounding area. She was slightly worried that there was no one in the parking lot. Almost everyone had cleared out but there were houses across from the school.

He led her around the corner of the school heading towards the back.

"Where are we going?" Miranda asked, cautiously.

Alex rounded the corner to the back of the school without answering, so Miranda rolled her eyes and followed. She stopped dead in her tracks when she saw the large silver motor home was parked in the back parking lot. Miranda recognized it immediately. It was the one that had been parked in her neighbourhood all week. She was about to bolt for it when he turned around quickly and grabbed her, spinning her against the wall. She tried to hit him but it was as if he anticipated it and caught her fist. His other hand moved so quickly, she couldn't even see it but she felt a sharp pain in the side of her neck, like a pinprick. She put a hand to her neck as she felt her legs get heavy.

"What did you do to me?" she gasped, frightened. She couldn't move her legs and she felt a numbness flow through her. She fell forward into his awaiting arms.

"I am so sorry it had to come to this," Alex sighed, brushing a stray hair from her face with one hand while the other held her.

Miranda looked up at him accusingly, her eyes full of fright. She tried to move her arms but they only twitched and now she also wasn't able to speak. Her voice just wouldn't work.

"Do not look at me that way," Alex said, sadly, "I promise you will be safe."

Miranda's eyes filled with tears. She wanted to believe him but he had drugged her. She broke his gaze and searched for anyone walking by before she realized anyone walking by would probably mistake them for a couple making out in the shaded area of the school.

"Miranda, do not fight it. Just go to sleep. You will be awake shortly," Alex said.

Finally she closed her eyes and everything around her disappeared.

"Alex! What did you do that for?" someone said behind him.

"She was about to run," Alex snapped, holding Miranda up, "And I told you we went about this all wrong."

"Now I feel like we are kidnapping! Here let me help," Griffin said, taking Miranda's other side.

"Just leave her, I have her," Alex said, irritably, and he bent down to pick up her legs.

"Are you sure?" Griffin asked.

"Yes," Alex said with no hint of strain in his voice, "And we *are* kidnapping. If you had just let me see her earlier this week, I could have talked to her."

"She was always with someone. I couldn't get her alone so what makes you think that you could?" Griffin replied, matching his irritable tone. He took a quick look to make sure no one was watching them and opened the door to the motor home so Alex could carry her inside, "We have wasted enough time already waiting for this play as her parents asked. This is for the best, I guess."

"It was ok for a senior school play," Alex said with a smirk.

"Ok?" Griffin smiled as Alex laid her down in one of the beds, "It was great! She was wonderful!"

"I cannot believe you thought she was not the right one," Alex replied, rolling his eyes as he adjusted Miranda's body so that it looked comfortable.

"I had to check! The paper she showed me said Greenburg was her last name."

"And the part where we met her parents who told you she was adopted and that her last name was likely East. That did not convince you?" Alex replied irritably, casting Griffin an annoyed look, "And the picture you have from your mother that looks exactly like her. That did not convince you?"

"Ok. I *am* glad we called the Greenburgs last night to let them know that we would be taking her home tonight instead of tomorrow. It makes me feel less like a kidnapper," Griffin rolled his eyes and then addressed the driver, "We should go."

"We should have told her right away," Alex continued, taking a seat on the end of the bed. He looked up at Miranda's face. The tears that had filled her eyes slipped down her cheeks, "It was not necessary to frighten her. She could have been included in the conversation with her adoptive parents."

Griffin grimaced, almost regretting how they went about this. He was just so nervous. He had wanted to have the time to talk to her, not just tell her the truth, he wanted to show her. "Take her cell phone and send a message to that girl, Helen. Tell her that she is coming with us so they do not worry."

Alex rolled his eyes and searched Miranda's backpack for her phone. He lifted it out with two fingers, as if it had germs all over it. "Look at this thing," he said, disgusted, "It is ancient."

Griffin rolled his eyes, "Yes, well, what do you expect." The motor home started moving.

Alex managed to work the phone and sent Helen a message, pretending to be Miranda. 'Sorry to leave. I am going on that date with Alex,' he typed.

'Seriously?' he got back seconds later.

'Yes,' he messaged back.

'OMG! Be safe! LOL :)' was the message he got back. He had no idea what she meant so he tossed her phone back in her backpack and turned to Griffin, "Are you sure about this? We could be in big trouble you know."

"My mom wanted this," Griffin mumbled as he stared down at her motionless form.

Alex sighed and took Miranda's shoes off, feeling horrible about what he did. She would be a little lightheaded when she awoke, a small side effect, but it was probably for the best.

# Five

★ ★ ★ ★

Miranda's head ached so she lay still with her eyes closed on the soft pillow. She wriggled a little. Everything around her felt soft and silky and she nuzzled into the pillow a little more, turning onto her side. If this was dream and she was floating on a cloud, she didn't want to wake up. It was much nicer than being almost killed in her other dreams. She could feel the weight of someone sitting beside her.

"Mom?" she asked, leaving her eyes closed.

"No, sorry," a male voice said to her.

Miranda's eyes snapped open when she didn't recognize the voice. The bright lights made her blink a few times and she put her hand to her aching head, trying to remember exactly what had happened. When her eyes came into focus and she saw Griffin sitting beside her, everything came back to her. He had been stalking her for days. He was probably the sick pervert who stole her clothes and now he was going to kill her. She put a hand to her neck where she had felt the sharp pain and pulled her hand back to check for blood.

"Wait just a moment. Do not be scared," he said to her, placing a hand on her arm, "I am very sorry it had to come to what we did to get your attention."

Miranda screamed, throwing the blankets off her and tried to get away but the boy caught her wrist.

"I promise you that we are not going to hurt you," he told her comfortingly, trying to reassure her. He held tight to her wrist.

Miranda turned to him, stopped struggling and asked in a forced calm voice, "Well, what do you want?"

"We are taking you home."

"My home or your home?"

"Our home."

"Oh, ok then," Miranda said sarcastically and screamed again, trying to pull from his grasp. She didn't notice the other boy sneak up from behind her until he had covered her mouth with his hand.

Frantic, Miranda bit down hard and he yelped, letting her go.

"Griffin, she bit me!" Alex exclaimed, shaking the pain away from his hand.

Miranda kicked at the shin of the one that held her wrist and he let go as well with a cry of pain.

Free, she ran for the door not caring that she was now barefoot and it was cold outside. Alex recovered quickly and grabbed her from behind. "Trust me you do *not* want go out there," he said threateningly.

"Like hell I don't!" Miranda screamed at him, struggling to break free but he was too strong for her. Instead of pulling her away from the door, he pushed her against it, pinning her there with his body. He let go with one arm and pulled the curtain up.

"Relax," Alex said calmly in her ear and Miranda stopped struggling, letting out a small gasp. His voice was like silk, rushing over her. She was very aware of his proximity and felt the strong curve of his arms around her, the firmness of his chest and stomach along her back. She inhaled and could smell him. His smell was intoxicating, like the smell of everything she liked rolled into one. He released her slowly, but kept his hands on her hips, pushing her skirt back down which had hiked up a couple inches. She had a strong urge to turn around into his arms, but when Miranda looked out the window she forgot all about him. She couldn't believe her eyes at the most magnificent sight she had ever seen. It seemed like something out of the movies. Streaks of light enclosed whatever vehicle they were in like a vortex. Miranda couldn't even fathom just how fast they were moving. Faster than anything she'd seen on television. She had been kidnapped by aliens! She didn't know why, but so much anger and rage filled her.

"Let me go," Miranda seethed and Alex did as he was told and took a step back.

After a moment she turned to stare at her captor. Miranda slapped him and scolded herself inwardly because she had been so attracted to him and he probably wasn't even a real human. He could probably just take on a human form like in that movie she saw last year. What did they want with her? Why were they stalking her all week?

"You..." he started to say, raising a hand to her. Miranda cringed away, bracing herself for the blow.

"Alex! What do you think you are doing?" Griffin said, limping over to the pair.

"I would not do it," he insisted, "Unlike her, I will not resort to violence! Are you sure you want her because I would love to bring her back now."

"Good!" Miranda agreed shouting, "Bring me home!" Angry tears filled her eyes. How could she have been stupid enough to follow Alex around the back of the school?

Griffin wasn't listening, he turned to Miranda, "Come sit down Miranda, we have a lot to talk about."

Miranda stared at the second giant above her. Compared to them, she actually felt small. Now that she saw them without a sweatshirt or a jacket on, she could see Griffin was definitely much more lanky. He looked a lot nicer than the first one though. At least he was smiling while the other only scowled at her.

She thought of fighting them but knew it would be impossible and pointless since she was being whisked away to some unknown place. Fury was replaced by terror as she thought of all the alien abductions she'd read about. *What if they cut her open to study her or implant her with some weird mind-altering device? Maybe they had already!* Alex let out a chuckle and Miranda shot him a glare. The tears spilled down her cheeks and she wiped them away hastily.

Griffin took her hand and led her to the kitchen table. Miranda took that time to look at her surroundings. It looked like the interior of a motor home but it must have been some kind of spaceship. Everything was stainless steel or some kind of silver metal and was decorated with blue accents. There was a blue comforter on the bed she awoke in which was towards the back end of the space ship. It didn't look as though there was anything beyond it. All the curtains on the windows that lined the spaceship were blue and were all closed. There was a doorway to that first bed that was open and two others, which were closed, to the left and right which she assumed could have been a bathroom and another bedroom. The doors slid inside the wall to reduce space. The small booth-style table was silver with blue cushions which were amazingly comfortable when she sat down and across the walkway was a small counter surrounded by cupboards and one larger one on the right side, possibly a fridge? Near the front, there was another closed door which, Miranda assumed, led to someone driving. Her fears became denial. There was no way this was real. *I have been drugged so this must be a dream*, she thought breathing a sigh of relief. *This can't be real.*

"I assure you, this is no dream," Alex told her, then chuckled again, "We are not going to cut you open or do any crazy things to you." He paused for a second, then shuddered, "And I am *never* going to Earth again," he brushed off his arms, "Absolutely disgusting. I cannot wait to get home and bathe."

Miranda frowned. *Shit, now what?*

"Well, you could remain quiet and listen," Alex suggested.

*I didn't say anything*, she retorted in her mind, then felt silly. *Is he reading my mind?* She glared at Alex, who she was starting to dislike now that she had gotten over the initial shock of his good looks.

"I do not care if you like me or not," Alex scoffed, "I only came in support of my friend here." He motioned to Griffin.

*Stop it!* Miranda shouted in her head.

"You stop it."

"Both of you stop please," Griffin said, mildly annoyed.

Miranda sat back in her seat and folded her arms across her chest as Alex made the same motion across the table, neither looking at each other.

Griffin sighed loudly and threw his hands up in the air in exasperation, "This is not going as I planned. I was hoping you would not awake till we got there to show you. It is hard to explain."

"What did you expect? She has been with the small minded for far too long," Alex said, still looking in the other direction.

"What do you mean small minded?" Miranda glared angrily at Alex.

Alex turned back to her calmly. "Well where we come from, we have evolved into a higher form of human beings," Alex taunted very slowly as if Miranda was stupid, "Where your people only use a percentage of your brain, we use the whole thing."

"And where do you come from? Smart Ass City?" Miranda retorted sarcastically.

"Better than Dumb City!" Alex said, his teeth clenched, glaring again at Miranda.

Griffin sighed heavily, "We come from a planet called Utopia," he said, shooting Alex a look that said 'be quiet'.

"I've heard about that in books," Miranda said, thinking back to school. She was sure it was in a book she read in high school, "Isn't it supposed to be some sort of perfect place?" she asked, sarcastically.

Alex rolled his eyes, "Yes, right out of your book and we are here to grant you three wishes," he replied, matching her sarcasm.

"Alex..." Griffin chastised.

"I would assume Mr. Perfect here would come from a perfect planet," Miranda said to Griffin, nodding towards Alex.

"Miranda..." Griffin started to say but was interrupted again.

Alex's face grew red, "I would assume that someone as stupid…"

Griffin slammed a fist down on the table to get their attention, "Ok, enough Alex! Go away and let me talk to my sister alone!" He elbowed Alex out of the booth.

Alex stomped away to the bed area, reached over to touch the wall beside the door which slid closed.

Miranda's mouth dropped as she ignored Alex's exit. She couldn't believe her ears, *Sister? Are you kidding me?*

Griffin's face flushed slightly. "No, not kidding," Griffin finally said and Miranda closed her mouth. He took her hand from across the table, "I am your brother, Griffin East. I was sent to find you, Miranda."

There was a long pause, each staring at the other. *He looks so much like me*, Miranda thought, *how did I not see that before?* Her shocked turned to anger in seconds, anger at her family who left her alone for so long. She wrenched her hand out of his grip. "No," she said, "I'm not an East. I'm a Greenburg." She said stubbornly.

"Please let me explain before you get angry," Griffin pleaded.

As curious as she was, Miranda didn't want to hear it. She was mad at how they approached it. Did he think kidnapping her would make any of this ok?

"I tried not to have it come to that," Griffin explained, "It is just that you would not cooperate and we really needed to leave."

"I don't care," Miranda snapped, "You should have said something right away! You didn't have to kidnap me."

Griffin looked down at the table, "I am sorry. I know now that I did it wrong. I just did not think you would understand and every time I saw you, you were with someone. I could not risk exposing us or you as an 'alien' as you call it."

Miranda paused and tried to calm herself, taking in slow deep breaths. She should probably let him explain before she got angry. "I could do that too," she said finally, "Read minds, I mean. I've forgotten how though"

"I can try to teach you again," he assured her with a small smile, "Now where shall I start?"

"Let's start at the beginning, I guess," Miranda suggested, a little snippish.

"Ok, well, we are taking you back to your home planet, Utopia," Griffin started, "Not the one you read about, in fact, completely different from any one you have read about I am sure. There are so many things that our race of humans has passed on to your race," he chuckled, "English being one thing but we will not get into that yet.

You have another brother. I am the oldest and then our other brother and then you. I think? How old are you?"

"Almost seventeen," Miranda replied numbly.

"Yes, then you would be the youngest," he replied carefully.

"I have two brothers," Miranda repeated to herself in shock, she looked at Griffin, "I'm the youngest? Why?" *Why was I sent away?*

"In Utopia, each family is only allowed two children to help keep population growth down. We would not want to end up like Earth. We assume our mother must have been overlooked for child bearing deterrents so when she got pregnant with you, she must have hid on your planet throughout her pregnancy pretending she was doing some research. She had you and returned, leaving you where you would be safe. Thankfully you were still in Canada. We would have had a lot more trouble if you had moved anywhere else. We have an alliance with the Canadians. Whenever we land, it has to be in Canada or else someone may track us."

Miranda let his words sink in. This was far too much for her to handle now. What about her family? Friends? She had just started dating a guy for the first time. It was no wonder why she had never had any clues regarding her mother or her family. They weren't even from Earth. *She* wasn't even from Earth. "Why are you taking me home?" she asked finally.

"Our mom wanted you with us."

"Wanted?" she asked, not missing the past tense.

"She just died," Griffin said quietly, clearing his throat and looking at his hands on the table, "Just last week. We found out about you after she died. She had it all recorded in a message," he paused again and gave her hand a squeeze. He looked at her, his eyes glistening, and said softly "Her cremation is tomorrow which is why we needed to leave today. I understand if you would rather not go. We just wanted you to have the option"

Miranda let go of his hand as the tears started to fall. She covered her face with her hands. Her mother was dead and she didn't even get to meet her. Griffin moved to her side of the table and put his arm around her shoulders.

Miranda buried her face in her hands, her mind racing. *I'm expected to go to a funeral for a mother I never knew and I'm leaving everyone behind I know. I will never see them again and I'll never even meet my mother.* She pushed her brother out of the way and went towards the back of the motor home. Her brother didn't follow, knowing she might need time to process.

Miranda managed to open the sliding door to find a startled Alex lying on the bed that she had first awoken in. He held a small electronic device in his hands that it looked like he had been reading from.

"Get out!" she barked at him.

Alex made a sour face at her but got up. He looked at her before he left, like he was going to say something but thought better of it and went to join Griffin at the table. Miranda closed the door and threw herself on the bed. She cried into her pillow until she fell asleep.

"It never went well, did it?" Alex asked Griffin, taking a seat across from him.

"I guess we cannot blame her," Griffin sighed, rubbing his face with both hands in frustration.

"She will be fine. She still has a dad and her brothers."

"Yes but maybe we *should* have left her. We pulled her away from everyone she knows. Did you hear her say that in her mind? I guess I was being selfish to want to meet her. I have a sister! A little sister that I know nothing about and it appears she wants nothing to do with us." He frowned and rested his head on his hand.

"She just needs a little time to adjust. You did the right thing," Alex reassured, giving him a comforting pat on the shoulder.

"I do not know anymore. She is so angry *and* she changed her last name."

"I know if I had another sister, I would look for her as well."

Griffin gave Alex a pitiful look and tried to smile, "I guess you are right. I just hope she will be safe."

Alex's face hardened, "That will never happen again, not to us."

"Yes but..." Griffin started to say, his face lined with worry again.

"I do not believe it and I am surely not going to live my life according to it," Alex cut in, stubbornly. He changed the subject quickly as he saw an image of him and Miranda in Griffin's mind. Griffin had not missed that short exchange by the door, though it was short-lived when she slapped him. "Are you sure we picked up the right one. I thought your sister would be a little nicer!"

Griffin laughed, "She got you good, right? Look at her though. She looks just like my mom."

"And she has the typical blue eyes, curly brown hair like the rest of your family. I cannot believe you thought for a second that she was not your sister." Alex smiled and Griffin laughed. "*But it says Greenburg*" Alex mocked making Griffin chuckle again. It was all they could do to not think of the upcoming funeral.

"I know and I do know now that we did go about this all wrong. We should have tried harder to get her to sit and talk with us. To explain," Griffin paused, frowning.

Alex sighed, "I did tell you that."

"Do you think she will want to be an East again?"

"You are her real family. Of course she will."

* * *

*Miranda was talking to someone but couldn't see his or her face. Just a normal conversation about the weather and how beautiful her new home was.*

*She noticed construction signs nearby. The building they were standing beside was being renovated. The conversation was halted as a jackhammer started up, and Miranda looked up at the building annoyed.*

*She turned back to her friend, "So much for that," she yelled over the jackhammer, and bid him or her farewell. The other walked away while she stood there rummaging through her bag.*

*She didn't see one of the workers as he sent a demolition ball into the wall behind her and it started to fall on top of her. Everyone around her was screaming and fleeing.*

*Miranda turned and saw the building coming closer to her. It was falling and going to crush her!*

*Like a deer caught in the headlights, she stood there, horrified at the falling building. As she glanced around her, she saw someone in all black and he seemed to be laughing, "You will die this time Miss East," he cackled.*

*Everything happened in slow motion. When the building was five feet away, Miranda finally turned to run before she was flattened. She reached out as she ran and the milliseconds ticked by.*

*A hand reached out and took hers, pulling her down to the ground. The ground rumbled like an Earthquake hit. The person held her protectively and after a minute, Miranda pulled her head away from the person's chest and looked up. The building had stopped, just inches above her head, but seemed as if whatever was holding it up was about to give way. She screamed.*

Miranda sat up in the strange bed. She was still in some sort of spaceship being shipped off to a faraway planet to which she supposedly belonged. Her mother had died and she was leaving the only family she ever knew behind and her nightmares *still* plagued her. *Ignorance IS bliss*, she thought sarcastically as she got up and straightened her clothes. She pulled at the hem of the skirt, wishing she had something else to wear.

Miranda paused just before she opened the door. She almost didn't want to go back out there with the million questions she had. She wanted to go home where she could pretend her biological mother was alive and well somewhere. It almost felt better than the truth.

When the sliding door silently opened, her brother was nowhere to be seen. Only Alex sat at the table eating and she made a face at him behind his back. Her face turned to shock and she watched in awe as he somehow caused a knife to slide across the table into his hand.

"It is very easy" Alex said, turning to face her.

Miranda rolled her eyes and went to sit down across from him. She couldn't stand the fact that he could hear what she was thinking and she couldn't read his mind.

"If you were not such an open book I would never be able to do it. It is controllable though," he explained, smiling smugly.

"How?"

"It takes practice but you can block other people from hearing your thoughts by putting your hands up on your head," Alex explained. He demonstrated, running his hands through his hair, his fingers spread apart.

"Really?" Miranda asked and put her hands on her head like Alex had showed her. She kept them on her head while she sat down. A thought dawned on her then. Griffin said she had another brother. It couldn't be the boy sitting across from her, could it? She eyed him suspiciously. He didn't look like her or Griffin but he *could* have gotten traits from another part of the family. She hesitated a moment before asking, "You aren't my other brother, are you?"

Alex laughed and shook his head. "No, as I said, I am here to support my friend. Your brother, *Evan*, and your father had to work."

"There isn't some crazy thing going on that we're betrothed and I'm a Utopian princess?"

Alex snorted a laugh.

Miranda let out a relieved sigh, glad she wasn't related or being sent to marry this tool. And also glad he couldn't hear her thoughts anymore. A little part of her was happy her body hadn't reacted the way it did to a family member. He was incredibly gorgeous.

"Nice outfit by the way," Alex chuckled.

Miranda looked down at her skirt with a frown. It may have been short but it didn't look that bad on her. Or did it? She regretted putting it on now but she wasn't going to let Alex know he was getting to her, "What is wrong with it?"

Alex laughed, "Earth, ha!"

"Seriously? Are there skirts in Utopia?"

"Of course there are but I meant the material. How you can wear that?"

Miranda took her hand off her head and ran it across the material at her neckline. It felt fine to her. Hesitantly she reached across to touch the sleeve of Alex's shirt. She was shocked at how silky it felt, even though it didn't look it. A warm rush went down her spine as she accidentally brushed the skin of his arm. The warmth pooled inside her, filling her completely. She held his gaze, staring deeply into the blue-green colour of the ocean in his eyes. She couldn't describe the feeling she felt. She pulled her hand back quickly and placed it back on her head. *Thank you for not being my brother!* And then she scolded herself. No, she would not fall for this guy.

"S-so," Alex faltered. He took a breath before continuing, "You see? Earth is so full of disgusting and dirty things. You all ruined everything, even your own clothes. I do not understand why Griffin thought you should bring your own clothes. You can buy more."

"What do you mean bring my own clothes?" Miranda asked. Then it dawned on her. They *were* the ones who broke into her house and took her stuff. She gasped aloud and stood up, her hands still on her head. "Where are they?" she snapped.

"In the closet by the door there," Alex said calmly, motioning to the doorway beside the door with the window that he had pressed her up against.

Miranda took her hands away from her head and stomped over to the closet. There were two suitcases inside. She pulled one out and knelt in front of it. Inside were all her missing clothes. She stood up quickly.

"HOW COULD YOU?" she screamed and put her hands back on her head. They had gone through all her things, her underwear! She blushed a deep red.

"It was not my idea, obviously," Alex replied. He got up and put his empty plate into what looked like a dishwasher.

"WHERE'S MY CAT?" Miranda continued to scream.

"With the Greenburgs," Alex said, calmly, as he sat back down and put his hands behind his head, reclining.

Miranda's face dropped, "They knew?" Her stomach felt like it dropped to her knees.

"Yes, it was only right of us. We met with them on Tuesday and told them everything. They took your cat with them."

"Tinsel is alright?" Miranda asked. Her eyes filled with tears. *Why didn't her parents tell her?*

"We asked them not to tell you," Alex said, "We asked them to stay away while we planned on gently explaining it to you but you would not come with us. And then I think Griffin got nervous we had the wrong girl. But that was just silly." Alex shook his head, smiling at the thought.

"It's not like you ever asked me at an appropriate time! Should I have dropped everything to go off with a stranger?" Miranda demanded, staring at him, bewildered. How dare he sit there so calmly! He just ruined her life and tore her away from two amazing and loving people.

"If you were smart, you would have noticed that Griffin looks just like you. Your friend Scott noticed when he met Griffin."

Griffin entered through the door towards the front as Miranda sent Alex a dirty look, "What are you doing?" he asked her, motioning to the arms on her head.

Miranda instantly knew Alex had been lying and turned to glare at him again.

"Jerk," she said huffily and folded her arms across her chest.

"What is a tool anyways?" Alex laughed.

"You!" Miranda snapped and Alex rolled his eyes.

"You can control it though, we will have to teach you," Griffin said, and then paused, "I am sorry about your parents. We just..."

"It's fine," Miranda interrupted, "I just wish I could have said goodbye properly."

"I-We are sorry," Griffin said, motioning to Alex.

"Speak for yourself," Alex mumbled.

Miranda bent down and closed up her suitcase, ignoring Alex's comment, "Griffin... My clothes?"

Griffin's ears went a little pink, and he shifted his feet, "Sorry. I just thought you would want some things from your planet. Your pictures are in the front pocket."

"You missed some of my good clothes," Miranda grumbled. She hated to think that they went through her undergarments. She could picture Alex making fun of them as he packed them away and wondered if she was reading his mind. She shuddered.

"We could not bring anything with labels on it. It would be too noticeable on our planet," Griffin explained, "You will have to change your shirt."

Miranda looked down at the label that was on her shirt and frowned, "Oh." She got out a different purple shirt she had and closed the suitcase again.

"Not like any of it is good," Alex laughed.

Miranda rolled her eyes and ignored him again. She put the suitcase back in the closet. She stepped into the bedroom and shut the door to change.

"Can I move things too with my head?" Miranda asked as she returned back to the table and took a seat beside Griffin. She didn't want to get close to Alex.

"Our brain is only capable to move small things."

"I thought Alex said we have full use of our brain?"

"The brain is very complex and we do use much more than your race of humans do."

"We are more evolved," Alex piped in, "Our planet is older than yours and we have had more time. Your planet is 4 billion years old correct?"

"Yes."

"Well ours is almost 8 billion years old. We are no longer classified as *Homo sapiens*, but *Recto superiorus*."

"Superiorus?" Miranda questioned, "So, you think you are superior?"

"No," Griffin said, quickly before Alex opened his mouth to agree, "but we have not evolved anymore in billions of years so we think we have reached a peak."

"I guess that makes sense," Miranda told them, "I was taking biology but I was more into drama, as you both probably know." She rolled her eyes. No wonder Griffin had wanted to come to her play.

"You did really well," Griffin smiled.

Miranda returned it, uncertain, "Thanks."

"You seem a lot like Evan, our brother. He would be the creative one in the family," Griffin said, sounding slightly disappointed, "Dad and Evan. I was always more studious, like our mother."

Miranda smiled, "What does Evan do?"

"Evan is a producer and director at the television station. Dad and I work at the space centre," Griffin explained.

They sat in silence for a while. Miranda was thinking about what sort of technology she would run into on this new planet. There was probably so much she would have to learn, it all seemed a little overwhelming. At least she understood now how she could read minds when she was younger. She wished she had never stopped. Now she would have to learn it all over again.

"Are you hungry?" Griffin asked.

"A little," Miranda replied. She was actually very hungry. She had been ignoring her rumbling stomach since she had woken up and seen Alex was eating but he never offered to get her anything and she didn't want to ask him, "How long has it been since we left Earth?"

"About eight hours in your time," Griffin said. Miranda moved and he slid out of the booth, "I will get you something to eat." He fumbled around in the small kitchenette for a minute, put something in what looked like a microwave and pushed the button. It only took a second before the microwave beeped and he pulled out a plate full of food.

Miranda sighed inwardly wondering if her friends knew she was missing or if they were worried about her. She was startled out of that thought quickly as Griffin placed the food in front of her. She stared at it in shock. It looked like chicken, mashed potatoes and carrots but it hadn't looked like that before it was put in. In fact, it hadn't looked like anything.

"What did you do to it?" she asked, not wanting to put it in her mouth, even though she eyed the mashed potatoes hungrily.

"New technology," Griffin said, "Well, old for us. It is how we eat. We get all the nutrients we need from these meals. There are plenty of different flavours and they take the shape of what it tastes like but without having to grow or slaughter anything."

"Oh," Miranda said and hesitantly tried a small bite. It tasted just like it should and she ate hungrily while the boys just conversed amongst themselves. She listened intently, noting that they had no funny accents. They sounded a lot like aristocrats, speaking very articulately and it sounded kind vain. Miranda knew she used a lot of slang, it was how everyone talked. Perhaps she could try to speak better.

She studied Griffin's face. They even looked like normal human beings, no antennae or green skin like the aliens in movies. In fact, they both were very nicely tanned, especially Alex. *Just like me*, Miranda thought looking down at her own arm. She looked at her brother's arm beside her. He had no hair on his arms either.

"That is what aliens are portrayed as?" Alex asked.

"Ya," Miranda replied with a shrug.

"Stupid Earthlings," he said and Miranda glared at him, getting annoyed at his total disregard for the race of humans who raised her.

Griffin cleared his throat and fidgeted, "You may want to know that we messaged Helen pretending to be you so that she would not worry."

Miranda sent him a glare too but didn't say a word. When her parents got home, they would be the ones who would have to explain to Helen where she was.

When she had finished, Griffin took her plate and put it in the dishwasher-looking device. It was cleaned within seconds.

"Small things amuse small minds," Alex commented and Miranda shot him a dirty look, again.

"That's a big deal where I live," Miranda said.

"Yes, well, you might as well get accustomed. Our planets are very different. Ours is cleaner, smarter and better in every way possible," Alex replied, smiling.

"How long till we get there?" Miranda asked Griffin, deliberately turning away from Alex. She knew from her dad that her own solar system would take two light years to cross and the next closest was 4.3 light years away, "Please tell me it's not going to take years to get there. I don't think I can stand him much longer," she added, motioning with her head at Alex.

"Actually, we should be there in fifteen minutes," Griffin said, checking his watch, "We are only a few systems from yours, approximately 165 light years."

Miranda laughed. A few systems seemed ages apart to her.

Alex laughed, "Too bad we are neighbours there, short one. Relatively speaking, we are close to yours. I know that our galaxy is made up of billions of systems and we are not the closest, but relatively close to yours than ones on the other side of the Milky Way."

"Trust me, we are moving a lot faster than light speed," Griffin added.

Miranda groaned. Of course she would be neighbours with the planet's biggest jerk! She was sick of him and his attitude already. Nobody had ever called her short before.

Alex laughed, listening to her thoughts, "Oh yes, you are short. The average height on our planet is 215 cm or approximately seven feet if you need the conversion."

"I guess that makes you short then," Miranda commented, smirking.

Alex's mouth dropped, "I am *exactly* 214.5 cm. *You* are nowhere near it." He huffed and looked away again.

Miranda's smile widened, knowing she was just as much of an annoyance to him as he was to her. She turned to her brother, "What else should I know? So we're more evolved, what else?"

"Yes, compared to most people on Earth you should have been taller and super smart. You also should only have hair on top of your head. Well, we should be bald, but a long, long time ago, a geneticist added the gene of hair on the top of your head. I guess everyone missed having hair," Griffin explained, and grinned, "You should see the historical pictures of when everyone was bald. Now you will notice no one has facial hair."

"I am so glad they did. I love my hair," Alex agreed, not staying out of the conversation for long, running a hand through his gorgeous light brown locks.

"Oh, so you're shallow too?" Miranda cut in, glaring at him.

"Shallow?" Alex frowned.

"Let's see, you don't know shallow? Try conceited? Vain? Arrogant? Any of those work for you?" Miranda suggested, her voice becoming more irritated with every name she called him.

Alex opened his mouth to say something, but Griffin cut in, "Anyways," he shot, glaring between the two of them, "Ever have to shave your legs, Miranda?"

Miranda nodded, thinking about the times she had lied to her mother for more razors and telling Helen that she waxed. She remembered the one time she actually tried to shave, even though there was nothing there, hoping to encourage it to grow.

Alex cracked up with laughter, "You are hilarious." He laughed so much he put his head down on the table and pounded with fist.

Miranda flushed, angrily. It wasn't her fault she'd been dumped on Earth so different from them. She was made fun of her whole life for being tall but at least now she knew why she was so different. Griffin glared at Alex again and he stopped laughing immediately. Tears were stinging Miranda's eyes. She wanted to go home where she had worked so hard to fit in. She didn't want to have to go through that again. She liked someone for the first time and someone liked her!

"Will you stop upsetting her?" Griffin said to Alex, annoyed.

Alex took a few deep breaths and rolled his eyes, "Please, he was an Earthling."

"He did have good intentions though," Griffin said, "He really liked you, Miranda. I could read his mind when I met him." Griffin laughed, "He was actually a little jealous you were talking to me but then he thought I was your brother because we looked alike."

"Like he had a chance against anyone from *our* planet," Alex added.

"Well he was much nicer than you are! Please tell me that not all people from your planet are like him!" Miranda snapped.

Griffin shook his head at Alex, "Well, I have never seen him like this."

Alex snorted, "I have never been in the company of Neanderthals."

"Shut up," Miranda said, frowning.

"Come on Alex, leave her alone," Griffin chastised.

"I can take care of myself," Miranda huffed at Griffin.

"Sorry," Griffin said quickly.

Miranda paused for a second. She didn't want to be angry with Griffin so she smiled apologetically, and shook her head, "No, I'm sorry I snapped. I guess I've never had a brother to stand up for me before."

Griffin smiled at her and squeezed her hand, "You do not have to worry. Evan, dad and I will help you adjust in no time."

## Six

★ ★ ★ ★

It wasn't long before the door to the front opened and a really tall bald man walked in.

"We're preparing for landing," he announced.

Griffin got up and followed him into the front but not before the man shot a smile at Miranda.

"Who was that?" she asked Alex, who was the only one left. If it was up to her, she wouldn't speak to him ever again but she was curious about this place and the people in it.

"He is a friend of your family who works with them at the space centre. He was one of the few your family confided in about bringing you home. We *are* only supposed to have two children."

Miranda looked away. *Why did they bring me here if I'm not wanted?* she thought then added aloud, "So why are you here? Obviously you could care less about me."

"So for the third time because obviously it has not quite sunk in to that little brain of yours, I am just here for Griffin. Your dad and Evan had to be back at work and I did not want him to go alone. You are wanted," Alex assured her, "By them at least. Do not worry so much."

Miranda noted he had as much compassion in his voice as a wet noodle.

This time it was Alex who shot her a dirty look, "I can see we are going to be good friends," he said sarcastically.

"You started it," Miranda retorted.

"You bit me," Alex replied, "And then you slapped me. I would say you started it."

"Well you didn't have to be so mean!" Miranda said, her voice rising. She stood on her side of the table trying to stare him down.

"How was *I* mean?" he said, rising as well. They both glared at each other, neither backing down.

"You two scared me to death kidnapping me and then you knocked me out with some, probably carcinogenic, substance! So what did you expect? Then you pushed me up against the door and it hurt!" she screamed at him. She tried not to remember how attracted she had been to him as he held her against the door but it all came rushing back to her when she thought about it. He was so close to her right now. It would be so easy to just move in a foot and take in his amazing scent.

"For one, nothing from our planet is carcinogenic and two, I was trying to stop you from opening the door. WE ARE IN SPACE IF YOU DID NOT NOTICE!!!" he screamed back.

"WELL YOU HURT ME!"

"I do not believe you," he said and moved in closer, whispering in her ear, "I think you actually enjoyed it." He smirked.

Miranda felt his breath on her ear and neck and shuddered but she wouldn't let him get to her like that again, "SHUT UP DAMMIT!" She swore at him and jumped so far away from him she almost fell over the back of the booth. Her face was bright pink. She would definitely mind what she thought from now on.

Griffin poked his head out from the front, "Can you two please just get along for two seconds and sit down. We are landing you know."

Miranda composed herself and sat back down, waiting and refusing to look at Alex. She tried to think of nothing so that he couldn't read any of her thoughts.

Alex got up quickly when Griffin came back through the door. He grabbed his bag from the back and opened the door. Miranda didn't even feel the spaceship descend or touch the ground.

"Finally, fresh air," Alex said as he disappeared through the door without a look back.

"Come on. I will help you with your things," Griffin said, sending an annoyed look at the empty doorway, "I do not understand. He is not usually like this." He pulled her suitcases out and his own bag and placed the shoes Miranda had been wearing on the floor for her to step in to.

Miranda rolled her eyes and frowned as she stood up, "I can see I made a friend." She took a suitcase and one of the bags from Griffin and grimaced as she stepped into her black ballet flats. Now she had all flats and she was so short.

Griffin smiled, "Do not worry about him. I am sure he will come around. You may have just hurt his pride when you slapped him." He opened the door again that Alex had so rudely closed behind him, "Are you ok to carry that?"

"I'm fine." When Miranda stepped out, she was shocked at the sight. She expected only buildings, foreign chatter, tall white skyscrapers and flying cars like she'd seen in movies but this was so different. For one, it was so vivid, so colourful. There were trees, tall trees with shrubs and flowers she'd never seen before. She spotted some rooftops, but none rose above the tree-line. They appeared to be in a large valley surrounded by rust coloured mountains which were covered in vegetation. They had landed nearby the ring of mountains and were higher in elevation so it overlooked much of the city. The city was very large and she could see rooftops extending all the way towards the one opening in the valley. There were flying cars high above her head, but it wasn't the crazy bustle that she expected. Miranda took in a deep breath, completely entranced at the beauty around her. The air even smelt so fresh with a hint of a floral scent. She thought she could breath in all day. It was wonderful and exotic. It was so intoxicating she felt her head cloud as she realized she hadn't moved away from the spaceship. Alex had stopped and he was waiting just ahead.

"Like I said, there are laws against too much population growth. We limit it so that our planet can stay green and beautiful," Griffin said coming down the steps of the spaceship and motioning her towards what looked like a bus without wheels. It was parked on some sort of platform which kept it directly off the ground. It had an orange stripe running lengthwise across it which declared it to be 'City 217 Bus Services' and had a flower emblem which looked like a sunflower. Miranda looked back at the spaceship, which was exactly the same on the outside as the bus without the writing and with fewer windows. The flower symbol was there though and there were tires while the bus in front of her had none.

Miranda started to feel a little dizzy and stopped walking. The boys stopped just ahead.

"Come on," Alex urged, "It is just about ready to leave."

"I don't feel well," Miranda replied, putting a hand to her head.

"That would be the lack of pollution in the air," Alex retorted, hitching his bag higher up on his shoulder, "We have a clean planet, so you might want to remember that the next time you wish to go back to Earth."

Griffin gave Alex a weary look, silently begging him to be quiet and went to his sister's side, "We have a small amount more oxygen in our air than on your planet," he explained, "Your lungs are built for it. They just have to become adjusted." He took the bag from her and slung it on his shoulder with the other bag.

Miranda took her brothers arm that he offered and went towards the bus. She glanced back at the spaceship towards the driver who had just stepped out with what looked like a tablet in his arms. He was walking around the vehicle like he was doing a final inspection. They reached the bus, put their things in the storage outside the bus, and then she climbed aboard and took a window seat. She was so nervous, her eyes scanned the crowd several times. She felt like everyone could tell she was from Earth and were watching her. She did a quick smell check of her hair but it just smelled like her ginger shampoo and her clothes like laundry detergent. She didn't think she smelled bad, but she had lived on Earth for a long time. What if she was just used to the smell?

The bus started to move when all the passengers were seated, rising steadily into the air before moving forward.

She stared out the window as they flew over the trees. There were many small apartment buildings, but no houses. No two buildings were exactly alike but were made mostly of windows. They were all shapes and sizes and most had parking on their rooftops. Miranda counted some of the floors of the apartments they passed. None of them had over ten floors. There were no power lines either she noticed and wondered how they generated electricity. Probably some well advanced technology that Earth could only ever dream of, she thought and sighed.

She saw a few rivers with sparkling blue water and the trees and bushes were spotted with vivid colour that could only come from flowers. It was all so exotic.

She watched the many flying cars pass her. The people inside were well dressed and she looked at her companions. She didn't realize before, but they were wearing clothes much like they wore on Earth not some silver jumpsuit aliens wore on television. Her brother had on a blue button-up shirt and black slacks, and Alex had blue jeans and the striped polo shirt she had felt before. She blushed as she admired his body again. There was a strong look to him, obviously from working out or some kind of physical activity. His arms were muscular, which sent a chill down her spine when she remembered them around her. His face was thin, but not too thin, he had a rectangular jaw and his eyes were a gorgeous colour, so much like the Caribbean Ocean, a bright blue-green. Miranda had to force herself to look away. She was convinced he was much cuter than any boy she had seen on Earth, even Scott, but he had such a bad attitude. Miranda thought she saw Alex's eyes glance at her quickly but he was conversing with Griffin and she prayed he couldn't listen to her thoughts and talk at the same time.

Miranda scolded herself and looked back out the window. He was such a jerk! Why was she so attracted to him? She looked down at her own outfit again and felt out of place. *And why does he have to look so good while I look like I've been dragged through the dirt?* She tried to smooth down her skirt which was wrinkled from the trip. She longed to look in a mirror to see if her face looked as bad as she felt. She rubbed her face and wiped at her eyes, then ran her hands a few times through her hair, which got tangled in her curls. She sighed again and gave up, turning her attentions back out the window. She'd never seen anything so beautiful. Everywhere she looked was so sharp and colourful. The suns shone more brightly then she had ever seen in the cloudless bright blue sky. *Suns? That's funny, there are two suns*, she thought as she did a double take.

"Yes, there are two suns," Griffin leaned towards her, interrupting her thoughts.

"Huh?" Miranda asked, distracted. She hadn't been listening to the boys' conversation.

"There are two suns. The second one trails a little farther behind the other. The one in the lead is much closer to us," he explained and pointed out the window at them.

"Oh," she replied.

"It is your system that is strange," Alex added, "Most systems have two."

"I knew that," Miranda snapped, remembering her father had said it before, "It's not like I leave Earth on a daily basis. I've never seen it before."

"Prepare yourself for a lot more that you have not seen and only dreamed of," Alex said.

Miranda ignored him. "Can you hear my thoughts while you are talking? How does it work?" she asked Griffin, curiously. He must have been listening for them to answer her about the suns.

"All I heard was you commenting on the suns," Griffin said, "I had just stopped talking. It is like a normal conversation. If you are talking then you normally do not hear what another person is 'saying' in their mind."

Miranda looked at Alex, who was not looking at them. He stared out the window with half a smile on his face. Miranda knew that he had heard everything and she groaned quietly, her cheeks colouring slightly.

They reached their destination and were left atop of a small apartment building about seven floors high. Miranda asked Griffin about the lack of houses.

"It is all about balance on this planet," Griffin told her, "Houses are unnecessary and occupy too much space in the city for only one family to live. We all live in apartments that are decorated in any way we want."

Miranda followed them inside thinking again about how much she would have to learn. On the elevator, Griffin pushed the sixth floor. Instead of going six floors up, the elevator went six floors down.

The doors opened on six to reveal a small hallway with ivory walls and a solid light brown floor. There was a door with the last name East on it to the left and West on the right.

"This is us here," Griffin said directing her towards the left.

"I don't think I could have figured that one out," Miranda smiled, sarcastically.

"I will be there in a minute," Alex said, heading for the door on the right, "I just want to have a shower and get the disgusting Earth smell off me."

"Wow, East and West," Miranda joked, "Where is North and South?"

"Actually, it was just coincidence," Alex rolled his eyes as he opened his door, "Last names are passed to children just as they are on Earth."

Miranda turned away from Alex with a sigh. He had absolutely no sense of humour at all. She watched as the door slid open like on a track and disappeared into the wall, and took a deep breath before stepping into the apartment, her new home. The small foyer was decorated with light coloured floors and taupe walls. It led two ways. Straight ahead was a big open room, with black leather couches and the same solid floor continued into what must be the living room, she supposed. The walls were a stone grey, with many interesting looking paintings of various landscapes that appeared so real and the large window took up most of the far wall. The living room had black end tables and coffee table with glass tops. She peeked in and saw a large screen on the wall across from the couch. There were pictures scattered throughout the room and on the shelves that embedded into the wall.

To the left was a hallway. It had two doors on the left, two doors on the right and one at the very end. They were all closed.

"Well, I guess I will give you a tour," Griffin said, taking off his shoes. He turned, touched the wall beside the door and the front door closed. "We never lock our doors. There are no criminals here to break in so you do not have to worry."

"Oh?" Miranda asked as she copied him by removing her shoes and he led her down three steps and into the living room, "No criminals at all?"

"No. This is the living room," he said, motioning around. He pointed up three small steps, which opened to the kitchen, "Kitchen."

They walked up to the kitchen, which was painted a cranberry colour, with white countertops, cupboards and drawers. There was another room to the right of the kitchen, a large dining room painted a golden yellow with a long black table and eight chairs around it. There was a big marble fake fireplace and mantle, which was lined with family pictures that appeared digitally in the frame, like a holograph image. Miranda wanted to touch them to see if she could put her hand through but she didn't want to see the pictures up close. They were of her mother, who left her abandoned on Earth and was not here to explain herself, and of her family to which she didn't belong.

"Dining room." If Griffin heard her thoughts, he didn't show it.

They went through a set of double sliding doors in the dining room which also opened with a touch and they led back to the foyer and her brother showed her down the long hallway. The first door on the left was the bathroom, which was fairly large itself. It was painted burgundy and had white floors. There was a stand up shower with about three shower heads, each on different walls of the shower. The next door was the first on the right, Evan's room.

"I will let Evan show you his room when he gets home."

"Everyone is still at work?" Miranda asked as she was led through the door beside Evan's room, which was Griffin's. The room was a navy blue and there was a large picture of a constellation on the far wall where the window should be. Griffin pressed a spot by the window and the constellation disappeared, replaced by the window. Miranda smiled in appreciation. *That* was cool.

"Not today. They must be out. I guess we got here sooner than expected," Griffin told her, "This is my room."

"Nice," Miranda said, taking a look out the window. They weren't that far off the ground. She looked around the room. It looked so much like they did on Earth but everything looked tidier. She couldn't figure out why. Miranda quickly scanned the pictures along his desk, which appeared like the ones in the dining room. Smiling faces of his friends and family stared back at her and she turned away quickly. She didn't know who anyone was.

Griffin led his sister to the room at the end of the hall before the last door on the left.

"This is mom and," Griffin caught himself and cleared his throat, "I mean, just dad's room."

Miranda stepped in and was met with the same lilac colour that her room was at home.

"My room was this colour," she told her brother.

"It was mom's favourite, purple."

"It's my favourite too." Miranda said, sadly. She stared at a picture on the wall of her family, ignoring the rest of the room. One she didn't belong to. Four smiling faces stared at her, all with curly brown hair, whether short or long. All had bright blue eyes. She moved closer to the portrait, ran her hand over the front and she realized she couldn't put her hand through it. Her eyes welled with tears.

"You look just like mom, you know," Griffin said quietly.

Miranda didn't answer, just stared through blurry eyes at her mother. She only picked out the differences. Her mother was beautiful and her nose was smaller. Her hair fell in silky waves, unlike Miranda's tangled mess. She shook her head and looked at the rest of her family. Her dad was tall and handsome, and her two older brothers looked so much alike they could have been twins, except Evan didn't seem to be as lanky as Griffin.

She felt a twinge of jealousy that she had never been able to be a part of this family. *How could she have left me on Earth to grow up alone?* she thought as the tears spilled down her cheeks.

Miranda turned away from the picture and wiped her eyes. Griffin wasn't looking at her, his sad face staring at the floor. She went over to him and he looked at her, helplessly. "Thank you for bringing me here." Miranda hugged her brother tightly. He was startled by her action at first but put his arms around her while she let a few tears fall for her missed life with her family. He rubbed her back while she cried. "I've never had a brother," she sniffed, her voice muffled by his shirt.

"Now you have two," he said, hoping to cheer her up. He felt bad for taking her away from her life. He just assumed she would want to live on her home planet with her real family, but she had a family there and they probably loved her as much as they would.

Miranda couldn't hear what he was thinking, even though she strained to listen.

"Would you have preferred us to leave you there?" he asked quietly, "Evan and I have never had a sister and we really wanted to bring you here."

"I would have come with you either way. I am not very happy with how you took me away. I could have said goodbye."

"I am so sorry Miranda," Griffin said, filled with regret, "I was afraid and worried. I guess I assumed you would be miserable and I was rescuing you from your terrible Earth life."

Miranda frowned and stared up at Griffin, "I was happy. I had people who loved me."

Griffin looked away from her accusing eyes, "I am sorry," he repeated, "There is a letter from your parents. It is in your suitcase with your pictures."

Miranda's face softened. There was no sense in accusing Griffin. He did what he did and now it was over. She would have to get over it. "Ok. Let's go see this last room."

Griffin nodded and went down the hallway to retrieve Miranda's suitcases. Miranda waited outside the last door on the left. Griffin opened the door and Miranda followed him in. The walls were painted the same lilac as her dad's room. It had a large white bookcase embedded into the far wall beside the window that took up the rest of the wall and a large purple chair. There was a double bed that had a pile of linens on it, ready to be made. The comforter was the same purple, just like hers had been on Earth.

"I think mom was thinking of you when she painted this one. Mom always came in here to read, as you can see. Those books were hers. And I guess dad and Evan have been busy while I was gone. They must have bought you a bed and linens."

Miranda ran her hand over the soft, silky comforter.

Griffin pulled out his phone as it beeped, "I have a message from dad. He says to rearrange your room how you like and he will see you soon."

Miranda liked it the way it was so they made the bed. He showed her a desk which came out of the wall, which even though it looked like a wooden desk, it clanged like a metal when Miranda tapped on it. Miranda was about to suggest they unpack when they heard someone calling from the foyer. She had noticed the doors did not make much noise as they opened.

"I am home," she heard the voice say. It sounded like it was getting closer.

"We are in here, dad!" Griffin called excitedly, a huge grin on his face.

Miranda stomach dropped. She was about to meet her real dad for the first time. Her palms immediately started to sweat and she sank slowly down on her bed.

The man that entered looked exactly like the portrait on the wall, except seven feet high, about the same height as Griffin. He looked tired and drawn, but that was expected since he had just lost his wife. His face lit up when he saw her. Miranda froze.

"Hi Miranda," he said, not coming any closer.

"Hello," she managed to squeak out. She didn't know what to say, all kinds of crazy thoughts rushed through her head. *What if he doesn't like me? What if I get them in trouble? What do I do?*

She stood up and he stepped in closer. She threw her arms around him without thinking twice. He squeezed her tightly and smiled.

"I am so happy they found you," he said, still hugging her.

"Me too."

"Look at you though," he said, pulling away slightly and held her by the shoulders, "You are beautiful."

Miranda looked away shyly, "Thank you."

He hugged her again.

Miranda didn't know if he knew how Griffin had decided to take her from Earth.

Mr. East let go and looked to his son, "What did you do?"

Griffin bit his lip.

"Oh, he was fine," Miranda lied, "He just scared me a little."

"I am so sorry Miranda," Griffin said again.

"You can tell me all about it over dinner. I will go make it and call you when it is ready," he said to the both of them. He smiled and kissed Miranda on the cheek, "Welcome home." Reluctantly he left to make dinner.

Miranda let out the breath she didn't realize she was holding.

Griffin laughed and the tension in the air broke. "That was tense!"

"Do you all think Earth is a terrible place and you have just rescued me?"

Griffin shook his head, "Mom told us a lot about Earth. She went often and now we know why. It was to see you. But we were not sure how the system worked. We do not have adoption here so we did not understand it."

Miranda frowned again, "What happens to a child when his parents die or don't want him or her."

"The closest relative will watch the child if the parents die and there are no unwanted children here," he replied as their father called to signify dinner was ready.

Miranda followed her brother out into the hallway. She had a lot to learn about this place. As they neared the front door it opened and both Alex and Evan walked in.

"…then she slapped me," Alex was saying to him and Evan laughed. Alex noticed Miranda first and glared at her.

"Jerk," Miranda huffed.

Evan turned around and smiled. He was the tallest of the group. He took two steps and Miranda felt herself being plucked up off the ground in a big bear hug. Evan spun her around once and planted a kiss on her cheek.

"You are absolutely beautiful, little sister," he said. Miranda smiled into his twinkling blue eyes. She immediately liked him. Why was everyone but Alex super nice?

Evan laughed, "Do not worry about that. He is going to *love* you."

Alex snorted and Miranda rolled her eyes at him.

"Ya, when pigs fly," Miranda said.

"Actually, what you would call pigs on Earth *can* fly on Utopia," Alex said.

"Oh," Miranda said, making a face.

"She is also very gullible did I mention?" Alex said snidely.

Miranda laughed, "Alright, that's not fair. I don't know anything about this place."

"You should have seen her with her hands on her head," Alex said chuckling, putting his hands on his head. He made a funny face at her and she rolled her eyes. Griffin looked like he was trying not to laugh and Evan looked confused.

"Never mind that," Miranda said, turning away from Alex.

"Dinner is ready, are you staying?" Griffin managed to ask while holding his sides, trying to keep the laughter in.

"Sure, anything for a laugh," he said motioning with his head to Miranda.

Miranda made a look like she was in pain, wishing her brother hadn't invited the jerk for dinner but followed the three boys to the dining room where her father had prepared a huge dinner within seconds.

Miranda sat as far as she could from Alex but it wasn't far enough to her liking, just diagonally across the table. She shot him looks all throughout dinner while politely answering questions her father asked her about her childhood. It made her a little uncomfortable to tell them she stayed in foster care till she was two years old, but then was adopted by the most wonderful people. Her father was glad that they took good care of her but she could tell he was sad that he couldn't have been there. He apologized many times repeating over and over again that he never even knew about her. Her mother went to Earth often to study the history, sometimes for months at a time.

"How did she die?" Miranda asked quietly. Not that she wanted to bring it up but it seemed that there was nothing bad on this planet. How could she have died?

Silence followed and Miranda strained to hear the thoughts around her again but heard nothing. She glanced around at everyone who looked deep in thought, except Alex who shook his head at her with a glare. She bit her lip.

Griffin cleared his throat, "Last week she was teaching a class at the school and there was an attack. She must have known they were coming because she wrote a quick note about you on her phone before she died. Like I said, she went to Earth often and now we know it was to watch over you."

Miranda stared at her plate. If her mom had been watching her, why hadn't she shown herself? Miranda felt the tears coming again.

Griffin, who was sitting beside her, put his arm around her. "Do not cry Miranda, please."

Miranda nodded slowly trying to force her tears back. She didn't want to cry again especially in front of Mr. Perfect Alex.

Evan and her father laughed to break the tension. "She really does not like you, does she?" her father asked Alex.

"Yes, I do not know what I did!" Alex exclaimed, innocently.

"The mere fact that you exist on this perfect planet just doesn't seem right," Miranda said, smiling smugly. Everyone laughed except Alex. He just rolled his eyes.

With dinner over, they all strayed into the living room after putting the dishes through the washer. Miranda's dad took a seat beside her on the couch, overjoyed that he had his little girl home.

Miranda was in the middle of telling them a story about her high school when she was interrupted by the television that Alex had turned on. It was television but Miranda was shocked. It looked so life-like, like 3-Dimensional. It felt like you were right there in the picture. She watched as he flicked through the channels and saw many people, all normal looking. She still felt like she was going to run into some weird looking fish-faced alien but they all looked human.

Everyone noticed her pause and turned to where she was looking. Even Alex looked back wondering why she just stopped talking.

"I thought they had television on Earth?" Alex laughed.

Miranda glared at him for what seemed like the millionth time that day, "I'm sorry, I didn't know I was boring you," she snapped.

Alex flicked the television off, "Sorry," he mumbled but Miranda just laughed.

"I'm kidding! You can turn it back on. It just looks different. Very real, like I'm there," Miranda explained.

"Much better than Earth television," Alex said smugly, as he turned the television back on.

Miranda ignored the last comment and finished telling her family about some of her classes.

"So tell me what happened here. What was it like here growing up?" she asked, finally noticing she was really outnumbered male to female.

"Well, your mother and I moved into this place when we were married," Mr. East started, "That was 22 years ago. We met at the Space Centre, where I work as well, but as a designer. I use computer graphics to make model constellations. We had Griffin, he is 21 and he works there as well, and then Evan, who is 18. He works at the television station producing Northern Shores, a very popular show that airs every day on television. I am sorry honey. I do not even know how old you are."

"I am almost 17," Miranda smiled. She grew up thinking she would never find her family, especially after all these years with no clues, but here they were. Her smile faltered a little as her thoughts turned to the family and friends she left behind.

"The West family moved in here about a year after us so I have watched Alex like a son as well. He is 20. His parents moved out last year but at least he is still here," Mr. East continued, glancing at Alex.

Miranda also looked at Alex, who was watching the television. He didn't seem interested in talking, which upset her. Why was he here then? She convinced herself that she didn't care what he did. "Yes! He's still here!" Miranda cheered with sarcastic enthusiasm.

Alex turned away from the television and frowned at her, "Sarcasm is very unbecoming."

Miranda stuck her tongue out at him, "Whatever."

"Your English skills could also use some work," Alex said and then repeated her "Whatever."

She let out a loud breath and turned away from him.

"I used to beat Griffin up," Evan said, puffing out his chest. Miranda had noticed the difference in the muscle tone. Griffin was more on the scrawny side.

Griffin just rolled his eyes at Evan, and then added, "I am smarter."

Each told her a few stories about when they were kids, and then Evan went into the long-winded story of how he'd come up with the idea for his television show when he was just 15 and finished school. He knew he wanted to get into film production and was hired to shadow a director. From there, the ideas started to flow and he spoke to the producers and they loved his ideas. He explained how it was a show about Earth, "They are all so full of problems those Earthlings, according to our mother anyways. It was her interest and stories about Earth that gave me ideas" he concluded. The show had been running successfully for the past two years.

When they were finished their stories Miranda thought it should be getting late, but when she looked outside, it was still light out.

"Why isn't it dark yet?" she asked, a little worried that it may be like the North Pole in summer where it was constantly light.

"No, we have 36 hour days. Not like the Earth. You will get used to the change. Our rotation around the suns is different. Right now we are closer to the Alpha sun, but for the last half of the year we're closer to the Beta sun. We have only 312 days per year and each month has 26 days. It gets dark around the 35th hour and stays dark till about 10," Griffin said.

"Thirty-six hours!" Miranda said, shocked.

"Well, we have 50 minutes to an hour and 50 seconds to a minute," Griffin explained, "So if you really think about it, our days are not much longer than on Earth."

"Oh boy, that's a lot to get used to. What time is it now?" Miranda asked.

"Thirty-four twenty," her father said looking down at his watch, then he reached into his back pocket, "Before I forget, I got these for everyone," he said, handing four small metal framed flat glass objects to Evan.

"This is great!" Evan said, after taking a quick look at them.

"What?" Griffin said, snatching them away. Then a huge grin flashed on his face, "Feel up to a concert the day after tomorrow Miranda?"

Miranda's eyes sparkled, "Really? What are those?"

"They are tickets," Evan said and handed one to Miranda.

It was only the size of the palm of her hand. When the glass caught the light, Miranda could read what it said in the hologram. It listed the concert details.

"They are reusable, just by changing the hologram," her dad explained.

"They don't break?" Miranda asked.

"No, it is a strong clear substance used in the middle," Griffin said, "Not like what you would call glass on Earth. Just like our windows." He motioned to the window, and then turned back to Miranda, "Go ahead, throw it."

"The Trees," Miranda read aloud before she raised the ticket above her head to throw it, "Are you sure?"

Griffin laughed, "Go ahead."

Miranda squeezed her eyes shut and threw the ticket as hard as she could against the wall where it hit with a thud and then dropped to the floor still intact.

Everyone laughed but Miranda went to pick it up. "Cool," she said examining it and then the wall, which she knocked on lightly. It sounded almost metallic but it was painted and flat and looked just like a normal wall. Alex chuckled.

"They are great! What kind of music do you listen to?" Evan asked excitedly.

"Uhh…" Miranda thought about it for a second, she really didn't have a favourite type of music. She liked so many different songs from different types. She returned to the seat between Evan and her dad.

"This band is in the classic genre meaning they play with no sound generating panels, only classic instruments. They have four men in the band, two play guitars, one bass guitar and a drummer," Evan explained, and then turned to Alex, "There are four, you know."

Alex smiled, "Thanks Mr. East."

"You are very welcome," Mr. East said, "I would never leave you out."

"But you do not want to go?" Alex asked.

"You know I prefer different music," Mr. East laughed, "It is all yours."

The boys talked excitedly about the concert, while Mr. East continued to ask Miranda questions. She was only mildly annoyed that Alex was coming too. Apparently, it seemed she would have to get used to him if her father treated him as part of the family but she wasn't going to let him ruin her night or any night.

"So, what else is there about you? Any nicknames?" he asked.

"My friends called my Mandy," Miranda replied and then made a face, "Unless you count giant freak."

Alex snorted a laugh, "No one here will call you that, short one."

Mr. East looked annoyed that his daughter was made fun of but ignored Miranda's last comment, "Mandy? I guess you cannot shorten Miranda any other way. I chose Miranda you know. If any of the boys had been girls that would have been their name. I guess your mom liked it."

"Speaking of which," Griffin interrupted, "We have the funeral in the morning."

Everyone grew quiet. As much as they wanted to keep the atmosphere light for Miranda, they couldn't help but be overcome with devastation at the loss. Miranda put her head down. She didn't want to think about it.

"Well, we could call her Maddix," Alex said after a minute, trying to lighten the mood.

Evan chuckled.

"Do I even want to know what that means?" Miranda asked, turning to her dad.

He just smiled at her and shook his head. Miranda rolled her eyes at Alex.

Miranda enjoyed the company of her family as they tried to talk about other things but dozed off just as the sun's rays extinguished.

"Miranda?" Mr. East said softly.

"Hmmm…" Miranda said sleepily.

"Someone want to carry her?" Mr. East asked.

Miranda felt herself being lifted off the couch. Too sleepy to notice, she wrapped her arms around Alex's neck and laid her head on his shoulder, falling back to sleep instantly.

Evan smiled at Alex.

He just rolled his eyes, "Not like any of you could pick her up."

"I could so have," Evan smiled, "So what do you think?"

Alex rolled his eyes, "Just because you have a sister, does not mean anything."

Evan's face fell, "Yes, it does."

"She is beautiful," Griffin cut in, looking pointedly at Mr. East, "It is scary how much she looks like mom."

Mr. East smiled, "I am so glad she is here. Thank you so much for bringing her home you two." He put a hand on Griffin's shoulder.

Griffin smiled, "I think we may have scared her a little but she took it well."

"Yes," Alex agreed, annoyed, "Well enough for an Earthling. I suppose I deserved that slap." He carried her into her room, pulling her soft comforter over her.

"Goodnight," he said as he left.

Miranda mumbled an incoherent goodnight.

## Seven

★　★　★　★

*Miranda was riding around in one of the flying cars she'd seen out the bus window. It was a pretty smooth ride and she fell asleep in the backseat being so tired.*

*When she awoke, her driver had been replaced by a large person in a black hooded robe. He cranked the wheel and the car was veering left and right, out of control. He laughed wickedly then pushed a button and was ejected from the car. Miranda screamed and tried to grab the wheel, but there was a glass partition stopping her from entering the front part of the car. Frantically, she banged on the partition, trying to break through it as the car started its nosedive to the ground. Miranda's stomach was in her chest and she couldn't scream anymore. Horrible laughter rang in her ears as it felt like she was plunging down from the top of a really high rollercoaster.*

*As she neared the ground, Miranda held her breath and closed her eyes. That was when she felt someone in the seat beside her. The person wrapped his arms around Miranda and the car shook. A bright white light erupted between the two of them. Miranda could see it even with her eyes closed. The car never did hit the ground. When Miranda opened her eyes, she found the car had landed safely.*

*"What's going on?" she asked her companion. She couldn't see him though since he was wearing a hooded sweatshirt with it pulled low over his face.*

*He reached out and touched her cheek.*

Miranda awoke with a start. The sunlight filled her room and she tried to calm her fast beating heart. She was a little shocked at her surroundings when she opened her eyes, not used to her new room and the memories of the day before came flooding back to her. She got out of bed still wearing the skirt she had worn yesterday and opened one of the suitcases for something else. She dug around and pulled on a pair of dark blue sweatpants and a grey plain t-shirt and went to see if she could find someone.

Griffin was in the kitchen getting breakfast ready. He was dressed in an all black suit, a black collared shirt with a navy blue tie. Miranda could feel the sobering atmosphere surrounding him.

"Morning," Miranda said quietly as she entered.

"Good morning. I was just about to come wake you. Did you sleep well?" he asked, just as quietly.

Their whispered conversation continued. "Yes. Are we leaving soon?" Miranda asked.

"You have about an hour," Griffin said and gave her a quick hug, "Let me get you some breakfast."

"There's really only 50 minutes in an hour?" Miranda questioned.

Griffin gave her a small smile and nodded in reassurance.

Miranda could tell he was really upset about the upcoming funeral. He barely looked at her as he moved around the kitchen and she could tell he was fighting back the tears.

Miranda ate quickly and went back to her room. She was a little annoyed that they hadn't woken her sooner. It would take her a lot longer than the forty minutes she had left if she had wanted to wash and style her hair, so she decided just to get dressed and do what she could with her face and her hair. Luckily she had a short sleeve black dress to wear and a pair of nice black sandals.

*I really need to go shopping*, she thought as she dressed. Even though it was half her wardrobe, it still wasn't much.

She went to the washroom and brushed her hair. She had no idea what she wanted to do with it so she just left it down. She had no styling products and only one hair elastic. She fussed with it, trying to make it look nice but was struggling.

Evan knocked on the bathroom door a half hour later.

"Come in," Miranda said, annoyed at her hair. She was done with it. She had put it into a ponytail.

The door slid open, "Are you ready?"

"I guess."

"You look great," Evan complimented. He knew this would be very hard for his sister, maybe as hard as it was on the family even though she never met her mother. He felt sorry that she had never met her. He gave her hand a squeeze then led her out to the door to meet with the rest of the family.

Miranda had only been to one funeral a few years back when Helen's grandfather had died. Her parents had left her behind when her father's aunt died years before that. They thought she had been too young. She seemed to understand why everyone wore dark colours to a funeral. She could feel the blackness in the mood around her and her eyes filled with tears. She felt bad for them. Should she feel badly for herself too? It was her mother but she didn't know her at all. If anything, she cried for what could have been.

They met Alex in the hallway, who looked really good wearing a navy blue shirt and black tie under his suit jacket, and took the elevator up to the first floor where they all got into the family car. It was just like the others she had seen but was dark blue in colour. The doors even lifted up, just like the futuristic cars on Earth. They drove in silence for about ten minutes. Miranda sat between Griffin and her least favourite person, Alex, in the backseat which was stretched out a lot further than cars on Earth. They all sat comfortably with plenty of leg room. She had become so used to sitting all cramped up in the back of her parents' sedan. She recalled how comfortable she had been in the bus and through the doorways in their apartment as well. Everything was made for taller people, of course.

The sign on the top of the building read 'Sunsent Funeral Home' in large black lettering. Everyone piled out as the silence continued and Mr. East put his arm around his daughter and ushered her inside.

It was quiet. Miranda thought there would be more people, "Isn't anyone else coming?" Miranda whispered to her father, breaking the silence.

"No, we have already had a public service. We waited for you for the cremation," Mr. East explained quietly.

Miranda's eyes welled with tears and she slowed her pace. She almost wished they hadn't waited and had just gone ahead with it and she was really glad that she hadn't been there for the public service. Having to explain who she was and meeting more of her family would be too overwhelming right now.

They met up with the funeral director who led them down a large staircase and into a large room where there was a table and a lavish sheet covering a body. The walls were a light grey and there were large bouquets of sweet-smelling flowers, whose scent filled the room. Beside the body was a door, which led to a large incinerator where she would be cremated. Miranda looked away, trying not to think about what was happening. She wondered about the beautiful sheet and how there was no casket. She supposed the Utopians would think it a waste of a tree. She looked to the flowers, the beautiful exotic flowers that looked like orchids and birds of paradise.

"Would you like to see her one last time?" the director asked, interrupting Miranda's thoughts. She flinched, not wanting this to continue. She couldn't believe she was about to see her mother burned. Is this how they did it here in Utopia?

Everyone turned to Miranda who shied away. She didn't want to be the one to decide.

"It is up to you," Mr. East said, "We have seen her."

Miranda couldn't decide. She wished to remember her mother as in the picture where she smiled brightly, not dead lying on a table. She bit her lip and tried to process her thoughts, uncomfortable that everyone around her knew what she was thinking. Finally, she gave the director a quick nod. She wanted to see her in real life so that she knew where she came from and it would feel real.

The director quickly turned and pulled the sheet back to just under the shoulders, then walked to the door pausing, "I will leave you for just a moment."

All Miranda could see was a side profile. Her father nudged her forward and her mother's full face came into view. She moved closer, drawn to it. Tears streamed down her face as she rested her hands lightly on the side of the table. *Why did she have to die?*

Her mother was so beautiful, even this way. Her crimson lips were full and her long eyelashes could be seen even from a distance. Miranda could only guess that her eyes were as bright blue as the sky. It was true, her mother looked exactly like her and it scared

Miranda. Her dreams came rushing back and she shook a little at the thought of death. Miranda drew in a shaky breath.

She felt a hand placed on her shoulder and turned, burying her face into him. He wrapped his arms around her tightly, resting his chin on her head, running a warm hand down her back. Mr. East stepped up to the table next and rested his hand lightly on the top of the sheet where her hand would be.

The funeral director returned a few minutes later, "Are you ready?"

Mr. East nodded, "Thank you for keeping her so long," he said in a choked whisper.

Miranda turned her head to watch the sheet flow over the woman who gave birth to her for the last time. She didn't know her at all. What had she been like? What were her hobbies? Why didn't she ever speak to her while on Earth?

Miranda turned back and realized she had been hugging Alex. She pulled away from him quickly and turned away, wiping her eyes. What the hell was he doing? Did he think he could make up for being such a jerk to her? She took a step towards her father and took his hand. He gave it a squeeze.

The funeral director turned to speak to them, "What happened was terrible and I hope that you will find comfort in each other. She was a wonderful, intelligent wife and a loving mother. May your years to come be filled with fond memories," he paused, "You are welcome to stay but it is not necessary."

Mr. East didn't move, "I will stay. Miranda, boys, you do not have to."

Griffin and Evan stood rooted to the spot but Miranda wanted to go. She couldn't bear to see her mother put into a fire. She excused herself and went up the stairs, as quickly as she could without running, into the large reception area wanting to be as far away as possible. The reception area had dark brown panelled walls and large burgundy sofas and Miranda sunk into one of the couches.

Back in the cremation room, Alex agreed to follow Miranda to give the family some privacy.

"Thank you Alex," Mr. East said, "but you are always a part of my family, you know that."

Alex gave a half smile, touched the sheet as a sign of farewell and left the family as the director opened the small door to where the body would go. He found Miranda sitting on one of the sofas hugging herself and staring at the wall. He listened closely to her thoughts as he approached quietly.

*Why did she have to die? Why couldn't I meet her?* Miranda rested her elbows on her knees and leaned forward to bury her face in her hands, *but if she never had died, where would I be now?* She let out a small sob. If her mom was still alive, she wouldn't be here right now. She would be on Earth with her friends and family, everyone she knew and loved dearly. Miranda felt so confused, which should she prefer? Life on Earth with her parents and friends while her mother lived and breathed on this beautiful planet or her real family and being here at the funeral of her mother.

Alex sat beside her, "I think being here would be best."

"What would you know?" Miranda snapped, keeping her face in her hands, "I don't care how much you hate Earth. My parents are wonderful people and they took good care of me!"

"This is your real family. You belong with them," Alex snapped.

"My mother is dead!" She sent him a glare.

He frowned, "I know that. Of course you should be upset about it but your brothers and your father are so happy you are here. Do not ruin their happiness by wishing to go home."

"Are you kidding me?" Miranda whispered harshly, "I'm not going to pretend to be happy because I have feelings too! I loved my home and my parents."

"Obviously your brain is not as fully functional," Alex snapped, "but you could not hear your father think as you told him about your *wonderful* parents. How did you think that would make him feel? And your brothers?"

Miranda's mouth dropped open, "I know how he felt. I could see it clearly but what am I supposed to do, lie? I love my parents. You have no idea how I'm feeling right now, Alex. I will never see them again!"

Alex sat quietly for a moment and then cleared his throat, "I saw how torn up your family was when they found out what happened to your mother but when they found out about you, it brought them hope. They could think and plan how to get you while worrying about the funeral details."

"I'm not leaving but I will miss my parents so much, Alex! They were all I had for almost 15 years of my life!"

"But they were not your real parents."

More tears streamed down her face, "They sure felt like it! It's not like my mother talked to me or explained anything. I thought I was abandoned!" she cried, and stood "Just stop making my life more miserable." Miranda stomped away towards the elevator and took it up to the roof where they had parked and walked around taking in the sights. There were a few clouds in the bright blue sky today and the air carried that floral smell to her. She inhaled deeply, trying to focus on the beauty around her but her mind kept wandering to the face of her mother lying there and how much it looked like her. She shook her head to clear her thoughts. It was just those horrible dreams she was having.

She tried to think about something else but her mind wandered to the tingling on her spine from where Alex's hand had been. She was surprised that it had been him comforting her down in the cremation room. Perhaps he was trying to be nicer to her after yesterday? Miranda shook her head again, a few stray hairs that had come loose from her ponytail whipped at her face from the gentle breeze. If he was trying to be nicer, he wouldn't have been so mean in the reception area. How could he expect her to be happy, to just fall into her place here and forget everyone? He was arrogant and inconsiderate and she didn't know why she was so attracted to him.

"I will never fall in love with you," she grumbled to herself, determinedly clenching her fists over the railing. It's not like she had much of a choice so far. He was the only one she knew aside from her brothers. There were probably tons of males in Utopia, but first, she wanted to find her place here before she even thought about dating.

She stared out to the rust-coloured mountains and sighed. She would never forget her family and friends on Earth but she was more than willing to try to be a part of her family here.

When the East's came up the stairs, they found Alex sitting alone.

"Where is Miranda?" Griffin asked first.

"Upstairs," Alex said, standing, "She needed air."

"Is she alright?" Mr. East asked.

"I am sure she is," Alex said, forcing himself not to roll his eyes.

Griffin hung back to talk to Alex as Evan and Mr. East went to push the button for the elevator.

"Did you say something to her?" Griffin asked, annoyed at him.

"We argued again," Alex replied, sullenly, "If that is what you mean."

Griffin sighed, "I thought we talked about this last night. At least try to be nice to her. I do not understand you Alex. I have never known you dislike anyone."

"You know that is not how it is. She just..." Alex stopped as they reached Mr. East and Evan. He ran a hand through his hair, "I do not know."

They all joined Miranda on the top of the building and drove home. They ate an early lunch and then Miranda closed herself in her room for hours, trying to keep herself preoccupied. She didn't know what to say to her family, didn't know them at all.

Miranda lay on her bed thinking about everything again. Her Earth mother's voice as she said goodbye to her for the last time. How she had been upset all week since the day she had met up with Griffin. It was no wonder she had been acting so strangely. She didn't blame either of her parents for keeping it from her, it must have been hard to find out your daughter wasn't even from the planet. She wondered what they would tell Helen and what they would do with the things she left behind. Probably collect it all and bring it to goodwill. She hadn't been able to give her recommendations to the child services agency. What if they weren't able to adopt again?

Thinking about her parents, she remembered that Griffin told her they wrote her a letter. She opened the suitcase and checked all the zippered compartments till she found it.

She opened it slowly and read.

*Dear Miranda,*

*I know we didn't get to say goodbye properly, so we included this note. I'm sorry we couldn't tell you that we met your family and are just allowing them to take you away from us. He believes to be your brother and gave the last name*

*East. He looks so much like you. He said he was going to make sure they had the right girl and call us if they were going to take you home with them. He told us everything. About being from another planet, about your mother and we're really sorry to hear. If she was anything like you, she must have been wonderful.*

*I hope you are all right with your new family (your brother was very nice) and maybe someday you will be able to see us again. We'll miss you very much sweetie and we'll never forget you. Take care of yourself, and remember, you are a wonderful, talented young woman. Don't ever forget it. Jim says he was right about life on other planets by the way and when he looks at the stars, he will think of you.*

*We will tell everyone here that your birth parents found you and you left immediately and we will take care of all your things. If you ever need to come back, we'll be here for you, always.*

*Love you lots,*

*Sarah and Jim.*

*P.S. We'll take good care of Tinsel. She says goodbye for now too. I'm sorry we must have frightened you when you saw she was gone, but your brother thought it was for the best. I didn't agree but we decided finally to trust his judgment.*

Miranda cried as she held her mother's stationery in her hand. She could picture her parents sitting at their kitchen table writing this and crying. She wished Griffin had allowed her to say goodbye in person. She would never see them again. Miranda sank to her bed and put her face in her hands, still clutching the page.

There was a soft knock on the door.

Miranda hastily wiped her face and cleared her throat, "Come in?"

Alex stepped through the door and shut it behind him quickly. Miranda frowned and wiped her eyes again. She didn't need any advice from him right now.

"What are you doing in here?" he asked, his arms folded across his chest.

"I don't know," Miranda replied sullenly, tucking the letter back into its envelope. She stood, turning her back to him, and placed it on the bottom shelf in front of a row of books.

"I was just in the hall and I heard you were upset."

"You can hear my thoughts from another room?" Miranda spun to face him in shock.

"No," Alex said, "I heard you sniffling."

Miranda frowned again, "So? What do you care?"

"I am here to make you even more *miserable*, according to you, so that you will stop moping about your old family and start interacting with your new one," Alex explained, with a hint of sarcasm.

Miranda was instantly fuming, "Get out!"

"No. Not till you tell me why you are in here and not out there," Alex said, motioning with his arms, "Your family is worried that you have been in here all day. They think that you do not want to be here."

"I don't have to explain myself to you, Alex."

Alex stood there with his arms crossed and didn't reply. Miranda ignored him and turned to her suitcases.

"I'm done talking to you," she said, not looking at him. She stood with her back to him, trying to calm herself so she wouldn't shout at him.

He still didn't reply and she took a deep steadying breath. She didn't want her family to hear her shouting. "Alex, please," Miranda pleaded, "I don't know what to say to them. I can't replace her."

"They do not expect you to replace her," he finally said, "but you should not just hide in here. They want to get to know you. We all do."

Miranda gave him a doubtful look, "You do?"

Alex didn't answer, "Are you going to leave your bedroom?"

"I don't expect you to understand, Alex," Miranda said, turning away from him again, "Obviously you are beyond all *human* emotions."

Alex took a step towards her, "The only things I can tell about you are that you are selfish and inconsiderate..."

Miranda cut him off. "I'm inconsiderate?" she snapped, "I am? Ha! You are the most inconsiderate ass I have ever met!"

Alex took her arm, "Do not be so foolish. Get out there and be nice to them." He pointed to the door.

Miranda shook her arm free, "You can't make me!"

There was another knock on the door and Alex sent Miranda a look before he said, calmly, "Come in."

Griffin entered and took in the scene. Alex and Miranda both had a forced smile on their faces, he could tell. "What is going on in here?" he asked.

"Nothing," Miranda replied, "Alex and I were having a *lovely* conversation."

Alex rolled his eyes as Griffin sent him a glare, "Leave Alex." He motioned him towards the door.

Alex left grumbling about how it was not his fault and something about stubborn-ness.

"You ok?" Griffin asked.

Miranda tried to force a smile again but she knew her face was red from crying, "Of course Griffin. I'm just unpacking." She motioned to her opened suitcases.

"Unpacking? You really want to stay?" Griffin asked, hopefully.

"Of course," Miranda replied, nodding, "I'm sorry I'm being a little antisocial. I'm just a little shy."

"You should not be shy. We are your family," Griffin smiled, leaning against the desk.

"I know," Miranda looked down at her feet. She really did want to get to know them but what about her parents? She was going to miss them a lot.

"I know this must be so hard for you and Alex does not seem to be making it any better," Griffin sighed, "Would you like me to talk to him?"

"No," Miranda sighed. She really didn't want Alex to have the benefit of knowing he was really getting to her. "Thanks though."

Griffin sighed, "I really do not understand. He is such a good person and then…" He broke off from what he was about to say. "I am sure once he gets to know you."

"Sure" Miranda snorted.

"Yes," Griffin agreed with himself, not seeming to hear Miranda and she wished she could hear his thoughts. "He just needs time. Are you sure you want to stay?"

"Of course Griffin," Miranda said, giving him a small smile.

"Here, let me help you unpack," Griffin said, "You will have to enter your clothes into the system."

Miranda gave him a confused look and he smiled and went to her closet. He opened the doors by placing his hand to the right of it. Inside there was a small screen of glass that lit up like a computer. It was hanging from the ceiling by a metal arm. Griffin fiddled with it and then turned to Miranda, "Come here."

Miranda went to stand beside him.

"Alpha, this is Miranda," Griffin said.

"Hello Miranda," a female voice spoke which made Miranda jump a little, it continued, "Please hold still while I enter your profile into the system." It sounded so human, not robotic at all.

Miranda stood still, but nothing happened. She shot Griffin a questioning look but the computer indicated it was complete, she had been added as a new member of the family.

"So now you can just scan each garment by pushing this button," Griffin showed her which, "And Alpha will put it away for you."

"Oh?"

"Yes and each day you can choose from the computer what you would like to wear and she will get it for you. You can do this from your own room or the bathroom."

"Cool!" Miranda exclaimed.

Griffin smiled, "I can help you with the first few."

"Can you show me how you put a picture on your window?"

"Alpha will do that for you. Just tell her what you would like to see."

"Anything?"

Griffin nodded, "Space, meadows, underwater, mountains. There are several sceneries to choose from."

"Alpha, can you change my window to an underwater scene?" Miranda asked. She smiled with delight when the window changed to spectacular blue-green water with tropical fish and the whitest sand bottom. She went to the window and put her hand on it but could only feel the hard surface of the window. It looked so real. She turned back to Griffin with a smile. The picture reflection danced on his face like waves.

"Alpha controls the entire house. She will turn your lights on and off or dim them. All you have to do is ask," Griffin explained, "Alpha, please turn the lights on." The light in Miranda's bedroom went on making the reflection off Griffin disappear.

He helped her with most of her wardrobe and each time a small clamp would reach out and take whatever she was holding and put it away.

"I can do the rest if you had something you needed to do," Miranda smiled. This was already so cool.

"I will go tell everyone that you are staying!" He left in a hurry and Miranda could feel the excitement in his voice as he left. She smiled to herself and tried closing her bedroom door again. She had to touch several places alongside it before she got the right spot and it closed.

After he left, she finished with her wardrobe and then took out all of her pictures, taking in every detail of every one of them. She would miss everyone so much, but this *was* her family and she wanted to know them. She put some of the pictures on the shelves beside the letter from her parents.

As it neared dinner, Mr. East knocked softly on her door.

"Come in," Miranda called. She was lying on her bed, staring at the ceiling. A position she had been in for the past hour. She held her Earth cell phone in her hand. It had a half battery left. Miranda had shut of the network since it couldn't find one and she didn't want the battery to die while it searched for service. She was going through her last messages with her friends, her parents and saw the messages that Griffin had sent Helen so that she wouldn't worry or raise an alarm.

"Hi," he began. He hesitated for a second then went to sit on the edge of Miranda's bed.

She sat up beside him, putting her phone on the bedside table.

"Did you want to talk about anything?" he asked, finally.

"No, I'm alright," Miranda said, looking down at her hands.

"I know we pulled you away from everyone you know and love and I am sorry. I hope you will come to love us someday as much as I know I love you, even though I do not know you," he said and put a hand on top of hers, "You are my daughter. I so wish you had not been apart from me for so long."

Miranda gave him a small smile and hugged him around his neck, "Of course I love you, dad... uh... father?" she said. It didn't feel strange at all that she called this man her father. It wasn't his fault she didn't know him, "I guess I'm just frightened that I won't fit in here and I'm afraid to say the wrong thing. I just don't know anything about this place. I don't know the customs or even the time!"

"Dad is fine, sweetheart," he said, "That is a word here." He looked at his watch and told her it was 28:19, "I will get you a clock to put in here so you will know the time and I know that you could never say the wrong thing. I believe you will be just fine here. You are so beautiful and I can tell you are very intelligent, patient and caring. You are everything I hoped to have in a daughter."

Miranda smiled shyly, "Thank you."

He gave her a kiss on the cheek, "Evan is making dinner now if you are hungry." Miranda nodded as her father continued, "If there is anything you need, just let me know."

"I will."

He smiled at her once more then stood and left. Miranda sighed. Her dad and her brothers had been nice so far. She couldn't ask for more. She left the sanctuary of her bedroom and joined her family for dinner where she heard more about their jobs and answered more questions about herself. After dinner they moved into the living room again and Miranda talked with them for an hour until Alex showed up. She excused herself saying she was tired, not wanting to be in the same room as him. They both glared at each other as she left the room. As she walked down the hallway, she wondered why he had changed into this jerk. What did she do? Was it because she had hit him because what else would he expect? She thought they had kidnapped her. He was nice to her on Earth but that had only been to try and get her to talk to him. If only she had skipped school and gone out with him. Everything would have been different.

*Miranda was at a funeral home. She walked down a set of stairs and into a crematorium. When she got there, she spotted an open casket in the centre of the room. She looked inside, but it was empty.*

*Nervously, she looked around feeling like she was being watched. Suddenly, the incinerator roared to life. She jumped away from the heat, bumping into something hard. She turned to see what it was and screamed when she saw this large man dressed in all black and a black mask standing in front of her. He picked her up like she was weightless as she screamed, trying desperately to break free. He put her into the casket and closed it tight. She felt it move and grow very hot. Miranda pounded on the lid but it wouldn't open. It was dark and she was frightened. The oxygen began to dwindle and Miranda started gasping for breath.*

*Then she felt someone close to her. "It is ok. I am here," he whispered, touching her face lightly.*

*She clung to him tightly, "Get me out of here," she cried.*

*The casket started to shake and the lid swung open, but they were no longer engulfed in the flames.*

Miranda awoke with a start. She looked around frantically and sighed with relief. She was in her room.

She went to look for someone and found a note for her on a small device on the kitchen counter which said they all had to be at work today but that they would check in on her at lunch. There were also instructions on how to use the phone and the oven. The clock in the living room said it was just past 11.

Feeling a little apprehensive about being alone in this apartment on an unknown planet and a little shaken at her dreams, she went into the bathroom and decided to shower. How hard could that be?

She opened the shower door just fine and started up the shower with a push of a button. There were no temperature adjustments so she shut the door, hoping it would warm up and undressed.

She stuck her hand in to test the water and it was alright, a little on the cool side but she hopped in anyways.

"Brr… that's cold!" she said aloud. Just then the water got colder and she had to press herself against the side of the wall to avoid the jets. She let out a squeal. "No, hot!" she said, hoping it would warm. She stuck her hand to test it but the water had already turned a scalding hot. She pulled her hand back quickly and laughed at herself. "Uhh… warm?" she tried.

She put her hand in and it had settled at a nice temperature. She put her whole body in. She looked around for shampoo or soap, scolding herself for not checking firsthand to see if there was anything in the shower.

"Where's the soap?" she muttered, but as soon as she said soap, she was covered from the neck down in bubbles which had come pouring out of the shower head. She was amazed at how precise it landed but assumed it must have been because her profile had been programmed in. The water ran clear and she was rinsed clean.

"Shampoo?" she tried next but nothing happened. She tried to think of what it could be called here. She tried 'conditioner' and 'hair cream' before saying 'hair wash' which worked. Another soapy substance came out of the shower head that landed on her head. She massaged that in, absolutely loving the floral scent of it and the magic it did to her hair. It felt so amazing after she had washed it out. Then the water automatically shut off.

Miranda pouted. She liked longer showers but guessed that it would be considered a waste here. Her hair felt so silky, she knew they must not have conditioner.

She stepped out onto the rug in front of the shower and before she had time to even think about where a towel might be, large blow dryers dropped down from the ceiling and she was dry in seconds.

"Woah, that was weird!" Miranda said, checking herself in the mirror. She was completely dry.

"What would you like to wear today Miranda?" Alpha said, startling her.

"Uhh…"

"Would you like a suggestion?" Alpha continued and a screen dropped down in front of her. Several of her outfits matched together perfectly were on the image in front of her, "I would suggest this one as it is a lovely day outside and it matches your body type perfectly," Alpha said, highlighting one on the screen. It was her jean skirt and white peasant top with purple and green flowers.

"Ok," Miranda replied, a little shocked at how much the computer knew. Her clothes were handed to her and she dressed quickly. It was so weird talking to a computer and she didn't want to stand naked for too long, feeling a little shy about her body, even if it was a computer.

"Would you like your hair and makeup done or will you complete that yourself?" Alpha asked as soon as she finished dressing.

"Wow, hair and makeup too? That's amazing! Yes!" she smiled.

A dome like object came out of the ceiling and encircled her head. It was sort of scary but she tried to stay calm.

"Please choose a hair style," Alpha said and several hairstyles appeared. Miranda wanted to scroll through them all, but there were so many images all of her own face and hair. She chose a simple ponytail. Her hair was dried and styled before she knew it, then she was given a list of makeup that could be worn. She chose something simple, just foundation, some natural blush and eyeshadow, and a hint of pink lip gloss. She closed her eyes as instructed and seconds later the dome had left her head and wished her a good day.

"Awkward!" she laughed looking in the mirror in front of her. She looked so well put together and it was so fast. No wonder her brothers hadn't woken her up earlier. She could have been ready in minutes yesterday.

"You are telling me!" a voice said from the doorway.

Miranda jumped at the noise and turned to see Alex in the doorway.

"How long have you been there?" she snapped and blushed. It had only taken her minutes from when she got out of the shower to now. What if he had seen her naked!

"Do not worry. I would never look at you naked," Alex laughed, "I heard you in the shower and just stayed around the corner until you were finished.

"You scared me," Miranda sighed.

"I was sent to check in on you," he said leaning on the doorway.

"Don't you knock?" Miranda asked, "Someone should seriously rethink locking the front door!"

"No. *We* do not need them and it is your own fault for leaving the bathroom door open."

"Ok, well, do *you* mind?" She hit the spot on the wall hard for emphasis and the door slid shut. After she did that, she felt silly though. She was completely ready and didn't need to be in the bathroom anymore. She opened the door again to Alex's smug face.

"Done in there?" he laughed.

She was irritated so she stomped to her room.

"I will make some food and you can come to the kitchen whenever you are done pouting," he called to her and went to the kitchen.

Again she felt silly as she stood in her room, her stomach rumbling. Why did they have to send him to check on her? He was so annoying and it was so obvious he didn't even want to be friends.

"Do you always eat here?" Miranda asked him when she found him in the dining room eating pancakes.

"No," he said between mouthfuls.

"Where's the pancakes?"

"Where *are* the pancakes," Alex emphasized, in a mocking tone.

"That's what I asked," Miranda huffed.

"No, you said '*where's* the pancakes' and it was not proper. Perhaps we should send you back to class for three year olds."

Miranda's cheeks went a little pink, "Where *are* the pancakes?" she said through gritted teeth.

"In the cupboard beside the washer," he replied, smiling smugly.

Miranda rolled her eyes and searched the cupboard for a bottle marked pancakes. Of course he was setting her up for failure. Well that didn't matter, how hard could it be to pour some liquid on the plate and push a button. She did just that and put it in the 'oven'. She checked the note and it told her to push seven. The oven beeped after just seconds and she opened it. Inside were about thirty pancakes all toppled over one another. Miranda shut the door quickly.

"When are you leaving?" she asked Alex, praying he wouldn't see her mistake. It would just be more ammunition for him to make fun of her for. It was worse than her Earth dad! At least he did it lovingly. Alex just wanted to see her fail.

Alex glanced over, a smirk on his face, "Well, I am supposed to watch you all day," he said painfully, as if it was a horrible chore.

"Are you kidding me? I'm not a baby. You don't have to watch me!"

"I *am* not a baby and you *do not* have to watch me," Alex retorted, "Apparently I have to teach you too, my little Maddix."

Miranda growled at him.

"It is not polite to growl at someone, little Maddix. Although it does suit your name," Alex laughed and got up from the table, "Where is your breakfast?"

"Um…I *am* not that hungry," she said, mockingly, standing guard at the oven.

"Oh really?" he asked, unconvinced as he strode back into the kitchen with his empty plate.

Miranda pressed her back against the oven, guarding it. She wasn't going to let him make fun of her for this.

"For what?" he asked, smiling as he sent his dish through the washer.

Miranda cursed under her breath, *Damn mindreading.*

He easily pulled her away from the oven and opened it. He doubled over laughing when he saw the piles of pancakes inside.

"Oh Maddie, when I said I was hungry I did not mean *that* hungry," he guffawed, laughing so hard he almost choked.

"Shut up," she snapped at him, pulling out another plate from the cupboard. She took out two pancakes from the oven, went to the table and started eating, knowing she would have to do something about the piles of pancakes in the oven and wondering what a Maddix was. She should have demanded to know the other night. Alex would never tell her.

Alex was laughing so hard he was clutching his sides and Miranda tried to ignore him while she ate. Just when she thought he was going to stop, he would open the oven and start right up again. When she finished the two, she got up to clean off her dishes, nudging Alex roughly out of the way as she opened the washer and put her plate through.

Miranda was starting to get angry, *It's not my fault, nobody told me how much to use!*

Finally Alex stopped laughing. "It is reversible," he said, and pushed 'U' on the oven.

It beeped and he opened it to show her. The pancakes had disappeared and there was the liquid on the plate again.

"Oh," she said taking the plate, "Do I just put it back?"

"Yes."

She got the bottle out and poured it back in.

"We do not waste things like Earth does."

She ignored him and sent the dirty plate through the wash, "Well, they sure wasted time making you," she snapped at him when she was done.

"Sure," he retorted, "I have to go, I was just making sure you did not ruin the place yet."

"I thought you were staying?" Miranda asked, desperately, following him to the door. It was bad company but it was better than no one at all, especially in a strange place.

"Sorry, I have to work too," he said pushing the elevator button, "Goodbye pancake!"

"Bye," she groaned, wishing she could slam the door.

She sighed with relief as she turned to go to her room but she was instantly filled with loneliness. *What am I going to do all day?*

She went to her room and decided to read. She told Alpha to remove the underwater scene and open the window, to which she complied. *I'm never closing this window*, she thought breathing in deeply, and took a seat by the window with the first book she pulled off the shelf.

The book she chose was about the animals on the planet. She devoured it for a couple hours learning a lot about the evolution that took place and perhaps will take place in the future of some of the animals on Earth. Some of the animals were similar and others she had never seen before.

She went into the living room to watch television when she was tired of reading, praying that this wasn't what her life would be resorted to. She wondered if she would ever get a job or go to school here. *If they accept me, that is*, she thought. What if she wasn't accepted here and had to be hidden in an apartment her whole life? Would they let her go back to Earth? Did she want to go back to Earth now that she found her real family?

Flicking through the channels she noticed *Northern Shores* and pressed enter, remembering that it was her brother's show. It had already started so she watched a few minutes of it and realised that it was definitely a soap opera like the ones on Earth. Not being a big fan of soaps but a little curious, she watched the whole thing instantly becoming hooked. Of course it was interesting to her because it was about Earth. Perhaps this could be her one thing she had left of her old home.

After it had finished she raced to the phone to call Evan.

When Miranda picked up the receiver, it asked her who she would like to call. "Evan East?" she asked it, a little unsure if she needed to say his full name. The screen in front of her read dialling and after three short beeps, her brother answered. She could see his face on the screen in front of her.

"Hi little sister, what can I do for you?" he said, not looking at the screen. Miranda noticed he was fumbling with some device on his desk and knew she had probably caught him at a bad time. Something seemed to click and he turned his full attention to Miranda, "Is something wrong?"

"No," she said, shaking her head at the same time, "I just watched your show. Do you have a few minutes?"

"Did you like it?" he asked excitedly.

"Ya I did! I'm usually not one for soaps, but that was interesting! I was wondering if you could tell me a bit more about the characters."

"Soaps?"

"Oh, umm…It mustn't be called that here. What type of show was that?"

"Daytime Drama," Evan said, smiling, "Really, soaps? What do they do, watch people shower?"

Miranda laughed, "No, just an Earth expression I guess."

Evan laughed, "You say a lot of Earth expressions that we do not understand. Alex has no idea what a jerk is. He could only assume it was something bad."

"Oh," Miranda laughed, "You know, I don't even know what it means. It's just something you call someone when they are making you mad or jerking you around, I guess. So, do you have time to talk?"

"Sure, I have time," he said happily and reclined back in his desk chair, "Well, where shall I start? There is Bethany and Steven Gould. They are like the parents or grandparents of everyone. They just got together a while ago. They have each had marriages beforehand but just so you know, no one gets divorced on this planet. This show is all about Earth. Bethany used to be married to Jack Williams, which is the father of Dean and Jake. Dean's wife died and he has only one son, Jeff…"

"Wait, who's Jeff? He wasn't on today," Miranda asked, cutting in.

"Jeff has been away for a week doing some business. Jeff is engaged to Janet, but that is going to change soon. Jake is the older brother to Dean.  He is married to Lisa, but Lisa is starting to hang out with her first love and she might leave him for the other guy, Matt Marshall, whom she shares her first child with, Alana. Lisa and Jake have kids too and they are 16 and 14, Christy and Katy. They are starting to get in with a bad crowd and Christy's ex-boyfriend, Ben, is trying to get them away. Ok, now, Steven was once married to Alison Waters. They have two children Crystal and Ocean. I am sure by watching today you know their stories," Evan paused and Miranda nodded, "Crystal's daughter Janet is engaged to Jeff and her son David is more of an outcast. Ocean is married to Trevor, but is actually sleeping with her sister's husband, Eric. I have not decided yet if Ocean's daughter is actually her husband's or her sister's husband. That should be coming up soon. I am focused on Jeff and Janet now. Well, I could go on but I am sure you will get to know it if you watch it more."

Miranda smiled, "Thanks! Is it on everyday at 23 hour?"

"Yes but you can search up any episode you want. Just the new ones are released everyday at that time. We usually tape the episode four days earlier. Maybe you would like to come see the studio sometime?" Evan laughed, "Being an Earth expert too, you could always give me some new ideas!"

"Sure," Miranda smiled, excited, "You could really bring me there sometime?"

"Sure can! I am the creator AND director of the show."

"Oh wow! Maybe you could hook me up someday then," she said winking at him.

Light dawned on Evan's face, "That is right! You are into the drama thing! We have an opening! Like I said, Jeff is leaving his fiancée. We are writing in another character but do not tell anyone," he whispered the last part with a smile.

"You're kidding right? Who am I going to tell?"

He smiled, "We have already had an open video audition and narrowed it down to eight women but I will have a word with a few people. I am sure I can get you an audition."

"Oh wow, that would be awesome!" Miranda was ecstatic. She took a second to daydream about being a big star.

"Did you need something to wear tonight?" Evan interrupted.

"I don't know. What should I wear?" Worry lined her face. What if she looked stupid in her Earth clothes?

"Do not worry about it. I will get you something nice from wardrobe," Evan said, seeing the concern all on her face.

"Thank you so much!" She was instantly relieved, knowing that she will at least look like a Utopian.

"Anything for you," he smiled, "But I do have to go now. I will see you in a few hours."

"Ok. Bye!"

Miranda hung up, probably happier than she had been her whole life. She skipped around the house for the rest of the afternoon, wishing she had someone to share her good news with.

# Eight

★ ★ ★ ★

When Griffin came home at 27 hour, Miranda practically jumped on him as soon as he walked in the door, talking excitedly. Griffin was stunned, hardly deciphering a word she had said.

"Evanisgoingtogetmeanaudition!I'msoexcited!Ican'twait!"

He paused as he was taking off his shoes and stared at her, his mouth hanging open. "Slow down, what?" he asked.

"I talked to Evan today," she said breathlessly, "He said they're looking for someone for his show and he'd get me an audition! Isn't that awesome?" She bounced up and down a few times.

"That is great!" he said smiling, "So how did it go here?" He put his shoes away, and then stepped into the living room and looked around.

Miranda finally frowned, "Fine. I guess." She didn't really want to tell her brother how bored she was. They didn't really give her anything else to do but watch television and the day felt so long.

"Well, I may have some good news." He turned to her with a smile after surveying the room.

"Oh?"

"Well, dad and I went to the councilman of our city before work to ask for permission for you to stay. That is why we did not wake you up. We left very early." He took a seat on the couch.

"And?" A twinge of nervousness ran down her spine. She watched him apprehensively. His face showed no emotion so she had no idea whether it was good or bad news.

"It is absolutely fine. He said that since our mother died so young, it would not affect the population too much if you were added to it. But he would like to meet you and he wants some tests run to make sure you are not harmful to the planet."

"Me? Harmful?" Miranda asked incredulously. She had been about to sit as well, but stopped, shocked.

"Only to test and see if you have any diseases that you are bringing back. Not to worry."

"Oh, ok. When is that?" Miranda sat on the chair and tucked one leg under herself.

"Tomorrow. Dad took the day off so that he could go with you. He will be home in an hour to talk more about it."

She nodded.

"So everything seems to be ok," he chuckled, looking around again, "What did you do all day?"

"You didn't expect it to be?"

"I was only joking. So really, what did you do?"

Miranda told him about her day, how she had read and watched television mostly.

"You ate? I am so sorry again that we had to leave you behind but we have missed a lot of work recently."

"It's ok, stop apologizing. I had breakfast," she said looking away, her face flushing slightly. Truthfully, she hadn't wanted to touch the food since her little mishap this morning. She couldn't cook on Earth and no matter how easy it was here, she still managed to mess it up. She was afraid to put too much and clog the oven or something awful like that.

Her brother was talking so he must have missed her thoughts of the mishap earlier with the pancakes, "That is all? Just breakfast? You must be starving! Come on, we will get something to eat now," he said, pulling her off the chair and leading her to the kitchen.

"I wasn't hungry but I am now," she said as her stomach rumbled slightly.

"I thought Evan and Alex were going to check in on you to make sure you ate."

"Alex did at breakfast or lunch. I am not sure what times those are normally at."

"Oh, I thought one of them would take a break later as well. They must have been too busy."

Miranda rolled her eyes, relieved Alex hadn't come back. He would only have put a downer on her good mood, "I'm glad *he* didn't come back," she said aloud, knowing Griffin would know exactly who she meant, "And I called Evan and we talked for awhile. He probably assumed I was fine."

"*He* really is not that bad," Griffin smiled at her as he took out a few bottles from the cupboard. He put only a dot of each on the plates and put them in the oven. It beeped and he pulled out dinner. It was chicken and a salad.

*So that's how much I'm supposed to use*, Miranda thought.

"Did you use more?" Griffin asked, hearing her thought.

"Umm...no, of course not... just a drop." She smiled as innocently as she could muster.

He looked at her quizzically, not really sure if he should believe it and then took the plates into the dining room. Miranda took special care to clear her mind so that he wouldn't know what she did.

"You look nice," Griffin commented as they ate, "I guess you figured out how everything works in the bathroom?"

Miranda laughed and told her brother all about it. "It was so cool but very weird!" she concluded, "I can't believe how fast you can get ready here. I wish someone had told me yesterday!"

Griffin smiled, "Sorry. I think we forget how different things can be here."

About an hour later, both Mr. East and Evan walked in the door. Evan carried a bag and a small electronic device.

"Hi," Evan said excitedly, coming into the living room where Griffin and Miranda watched television.

"How was work?" Miranda asked, looking at him with a smile.

"Great," Evan said, tossing the silver thing in his hand to Miranda.

"What's this?" she said, picking up the silver object that landed beside her on the couch. It was a flat glass object framed with silver and almost looked like the concert tickets her dad had given them the other night, but it was bigger. Without waiting for an answer she pushed the silver button on the top and the screen came to life. She used her finger and scrolled through the open document. It looked like a small computer.

Evan could hardly contain his excitement and smiled, "You have an audition in three days!"

Miranda squealed, "Are you serious?!" she said excitedly jumping up off the couch and throwing her arms around her brother.

"I bought it for you. It is a computer and it is also a phone. I will teach you how to use it tomorrow. The document that is open is what we need you to rehearse for the audition. If you make it, we beam all the scripts directly to your device."

"What's it called?"

"A pocket notebook," Evan told her, then lifted the bag in his hand, "And I got you something nice from the wardrobe at work to wear tonight." He passed it to her.

"It is much like some of the more advanced cell phones you have on Earth," Griffin added, and took it out of her hands. He pulled at the frame and it got bigger like it was elastic but it held the shape. He gave it back to her and she stared at it in awe. All the letters had gotten bigger. "You can make phone calls, pass messages, load books, music. Anything you can think of." He paused as he watched Miranda push on the frame so it went back to its original size. "We do not ever use paper. It is a waste. Even assignments for school are handed in through personal or the school devices."

"Just do not ever lose it especially with the scripts loaded onto it. I really hate it when everyone ruins what is going to happen on the show," Evan sighed.

"That is wonderful Evan. That is one less thing I will have to get you, Miranda. We should go shopping tomorrow to get you some more clothes after our appointments," Mr. East suggested, "Sound good?"

Miranda nodded enthusiastically and then went to her room to change. Her brother had brought her a short black skirt and a shiny red halter-top that was long enough so that her skirt just peeked out at the bottom. She had the perfect pair of red ballet flats to wear with it. The skirt wasn't as short as Helen's so she was a little more comfortable but the red halter dipped lower on her chest then she was used to. Although they didn't look it, they were so soft and Miranda spent a good five minutes just rubbing her skirt before she rejoined her family in the living room. Alex was already there, wearing a baseball cap on his head which was pulled low, shadowing much of his face. She was reminded of the first time they met especially when she knew she could feel his eyes on her.

Evan whistled low when he saw Miranda re-enter the living room and she immediately crossed her arms over her chest to cover the bit of cleavage that was showing. She ignored Alex's gaze, if he was even looking at her. She couldn't tell.

"Does it fit?" Evan asked, concerned that he hadn't gotten the proper size.

"Yep," Miranda said, smiling nervously and fidgeting.

"Ok, time to go!" Griffin said, checking his watch and getting up from the couch.

Miranda sent Alex a glare. She wondered why he was wearing that stupid baseball cap again. It didn't even match his dark blue shirt that had 'The Trees' written above a tree symbol that must have been the band logo.

Miranda followed her brothers and Alex to the top of the building where the bus picked them up five minutes later. Alex and Evan talked excitedly about the band. Miranda watched Griffin closely as they sat together on the bus bench. She could tell he was the typical older brother type, always looking out for the younger ones. She wished he had been there for her growing up. Maybe then she wouldn't have been made fun of. Griffin smiled at her and gave her a one arm hug.

"I wish I was too," he whispered and gave her a quick kiss on her temple.

When they reached the concert hall, Miranda looked excitedly around at the people. She really was short! There were thousands of people around her, most of them taller than her. She followed Evan and Alex to the entrance, darting between people and praying she wouldn't get stepped on. A huge change from how she felt on Earth. Griffin stayed close to her like the overprotective brother even though they had told her there was nothing harmful on the planet.

"I think Earth stunted your growth," Alex laughed, turning back to them.

"Shut up," Miranda snapped. She absolutely hated mindreading, especially when Alex could do it and she couldn't.

He laughed and she stuck her tongue out at him.

The inside of the auditorium looked like the ones on Earth. It had high ceilings and long concrete floors with hundreds of people milling around. There were vendors all over selling various foods and beverages, as well as the band's paraphernalia. Miranda scanned the crowd. She took in as much as possible as they headed down towards their entrance to the hall. Everyone seemed to have the same tan skin of different tones. Most people seemed to be either blond or brunette in varying shades, however there must be hair dyes because there were unnatural colours and highlights, like blue. Facial characteristics were all different just like on Earth. There were some larger noses, some small and some almond shape eyes and some round. No one appeared to be too overweight and she wondered if it was the food they ate or high metabolism. She assumed it must have been metabolism since she was raised on Earth food and was still slim. Another difference she noticed compared to Earth was the smiles and the happy chatter from all around her. She didn't see anyone that looked like they were going to get into mischief or cause trouble. In fact, a girl waved to her that just happened to catch her eye and Miranda smiled and nodded back.

Miranda's dad had gotten them level one tickets so they walked all the way to the end, where Evan showed the usher the tickets again and he motioned them through the curtains.

She got excited again as they entered the large auditorium. There were about four levels and the high ceiling glittered with designs of instruments and music notes. It was beautiful. There were so many people there. Miranda had only been to one concert before and that was when she was much younger. Her parents had brought her and Helen to see a boy band. Miranda had liked the music but Helen was always gushing about how cute the one guy was. Miranda didn't listen much to the boy bands anymore, finding them to be irritating with all their publicity. She wasn't like a lot of girls, never really caring about celebrity drama. When she had made it famous she wanted to be different, a good role model for girls all over the world. Now she wasn't sure what she could be.

She followed her brothers to the front of the stage. There were a number of seats if anyone wanted to sit but everyone was standing in groups. The background music played really loud so they had to yell to hear each other.

"Have you ever been to a concert before?" Evan asked Miranda.

Miranda smiled, "Only when I was little. This is so exciting!" They were right by the stage!

"We go all the time!" Griffin added, "Dad has a friend at work whose brother runs the auditorium."

"Cool! How many people fit in here?" She looked around again.

"The capacity is 10,000. I think he made sure to get level one to make it special for you," Evan said, throwing an arm around her shoulder.

Miranda smiled shyly. She'd never been spoiled before. Her adoptive parents did what they could but never excessive. Miranda never really asked for much anyways, always grateful just for them being there.

The band started several minutes later and everyone crowded the stage. Miranda listened to everyone around her singing along with the band. She should have asked her brothers for a CD or whatever they had here and listened to the music earlier that day to better prepare herself.

"You think too much," Alex said. He had been forced closer to her when Evan moved to talk to Griffin.

"Don't listen then," Miranda said, annoyed. If he would just keep to himself he probably wouldn't hear her. Couldn't he shut it off? It's obvious that she had.

He rolled his eyes at her and turned his attention back to the band.

In the middle of a slower song 'I Fall Apart', the lead singer moved closer to the audience and shook some hands. When he got to Miranda, he smiled down at her and handed her the guitar pick he had been playing with two of the glass tickets he had in his pocket. Others around her looked on jealously while Miranda blushed and smiled at the singer.

Miranda sighed as the singer moved on, clutching the pick close to her. *Wow, he's so cute*, she thought, biting her bottom lip. Finally she looked down at the tickets and her mouth dropped open. He had given her two passes backstage.

"Evan!" Miranda yelled so that he could hear her.

He looked down at her and saw the passes, his eyes lighting up. He leaned in closer, "Well, there are some benefits to having a beautiful sister."

"There are only two," Miranda said sadly.

"That is ok. You can take whoever you want."

"That's the hardest decision I've ever had to make!"

Evan shrugged, "Well, do not think about it now. Enjoy yourself and wait till the end."

Miranda sighed. She tried not to think about it but how could she choose between her brothers? They both had been absolutely amazing to her. Which liked the band more than the other? She wished she knew them better.

Miranda forgot what she was thinking about as the singer strode by again and winked at her. She sent him a huge smile and became fully engrossed with the singer for the rest of the night. She was having so much fun. The whole crowd was energized. Throwing their hands in the air and moving their hips to the music. It was incredible. The instruments looked similar but not exactly the same. The guitar had more strings and the drums were just flat discs. She couldn't see any wires or microphones but the singer's voice and the music radiated throughout the hall.

Miranda had never been very musical. She couldn't play any instruments but she did like to sing. Once she had performed in a musical but she didn't think she was very good. Her parents and friends had told her otherwise.

When it was over, Miranda followed her brothers out of the auditorium and out into the hallways.

"That was so much fun!" Miranda squealed, "They were awesome!"

"I am glad you liked it," Griffin said, throwing an arm around her shoulders.

Miranda pulled out the passes, "So, who wants to go backstage?"

"What?" Alex said, snatching the passes.

"When did that happen?" Griffin asked, looking over Alex's shoulder at them.

"When the singer gave me this," Miranda smiled, pulling the guitar pick from her pocket. It was plain blue with the band logo on it.

"Wow, that is great!" Griffin said, "I saw him give you that but I did not know the passes were with it."

Miranda took the tickets from Alex, "Why don't you and Evan go? I mean, I loved the band but they're your favourite." That would leave her alone with Alex, but at least her brothers could enjoy themselves.

"No way," Evan said, "You got them from the singer. You have to go."

Miranda sighed, "But I can't choose between the two of you."

"How about you go with Alex?" Evan suggested.

Alex looked away. He knew that he was Miranda's last choice.

Miranda hesitated. Did she really want to go with him? She had never even considered it. "Do you want to go Alex?" she asked, finally.

Alex shook his head, but Evan jumped in, "Of course he does. The Trees are his favourite band on the planet."

"Yes, let Alex go with you," Griffin agreed, "He loves that band more than the both of us combined."

"It will take hours to clear the place anyways," Evan added, nodding around to the filled hallways "We will go get something to eat and meet you in two hours. Is that ok?"

Miranda shrugged and turned to Alex, "Well, let's go." She would rather not be going with him but it seems as if she would be stuck with him anyways. She didn't have a problem being nice to him as long as he was nice to her.

Alex nodded and they headed off towards the backstage area.

"You did not have to bring me," Alex said, staring down at her. He had obviously heard her thoughts.

"My brother's suggested it, not me," Miranda replied.

"Thanks anyways," Alex said coolly.

Miranda rubbed her forehead. *So much for being nice*, she thought. They walked to the back in silence to where an eight foot man stood checking passes. Miranda showed him the passes and he motioned them through.

"There is my girl," the singer stood as Miranda entered. The room was large with about twenty people chatting happily about the concert. The band sat on the mismatched couches in the centre.

Miranda smiled as the singer approached and kissed her cheek. She blushed.

"Sorry if I embarrassed you before. I always choose someone in the front to come on back. It is usually a girl," he gave an embarrassed smile and a shrug, "I am Aaron, as I hope you know." He took her hand and squeezed it gently.

Miranda smiled, "I am Miranda and this is my friend, Alex." Miranda tried hard to make it seem like she fit in. She pronounced every word fully.

"Nice to meet you both," he said, taking Alex's hand as well, "Are you dating?"

"No," Miranda said, quickly.

"Definitely not," Alex added.

"I guess that is better for me," he winked at Miranda, who blushed deeper in return. "We have drinks and food over on that table. Help yourselves. Feel free to ask us whatever you would like," he continued and smiled before returning to the couch.

Alex left her and went over to the couch to talk to the band. He finally pulled the baseball cap off his head and tucked it into his back pocket. It was an old thing, and Miranda wondered why he was wearing it anyways.

It figures Alex would ditch her right away. Miranda only brought him backstage. *Ungrateful jerk,* Miranda thought. She was going to follow but she was very thirsty. She went over to the side table instead and took a look at the kinds of drinks they had in the bottles. There were all sorts of colours but no labels. She didn't know what any of them were so she grabbed the purple one, hoping it was grape. She looked on the bottom of a bottle which was blank. She took a sip slowly and it tasted like grape juice. She smiled, happy to find something similar to Earth. When she turned back around she saw the singer and Alex getting along quite well. She thought she heard the singer say 'I thought I recognized you' so she headed over to see what they were talking about.

"Everyone, this is Alex West," Aaron said excitedly to his other band mates. They all smiled and nodded enthusiastically. Miranda paused on her way over. Alex looked like he was happy so Miranda changed her mind, sighed to herself and decided to leave him alone. She walked around the room looking at the large pictures on the wall of different singers and bands that had performed in that auditorium. They were the same hologram images as the pictures at home. A girl about her age came over to talk to her as she stared at an old band picture of the Trees.

The girl was gorgeous. She wore a black leather tube top and tight leather pants which hugged her curves. Her long blond hair was tied in a high ponytail and her green eyes sparkled under her long eyelashes. Despite the get-up she was very sweet and her voice was quiet as she spoke.

"Hi there," the girl said, "Did you have a good time?"

"I did. They're great eh?" Miranda motioned to the picture she was standing in front of.

"They sure are. I am dating the drummer," she blushed and motioned to him on the end of the couch. He happened to catch her eye and gave her a little wave and a smile. She blew him a kiss.

"Oh, that's cool. Do you tour with them?"

"Only once in awhile. I miss him when he is gone."

"It must be hard," Miranda said sympathetically.

"Yes, I am just starting out in promotions so I hope to one day be the band promoter. I am Senika, by the way," she said, extending her hand.

"Miranda." She took her hand.

They found a couch away from the band along the back wall and talked for a long time about the concert, the band and the singer. Senika tucked both her legs under her and she was such a positive and happy person. Miranda liked her right away. She was drawn to her good mood. It reminded her of Helen. They glanced toward the band often as they talked and Miranda was able to admire the singer.

Aaron had light blond hair styled into a faux-hawk and his deeply tanned skin complimented his warm chocolate brown eyes. He had the muscle tone of a rock star. Senika talked about her boyfriend, Mike, the drummer, who wore his hair a bit longer, down to his shoulders, but it suited him.

Miranda had to tell Senika she was from Earth because she couldn't lie. Senika would be able to read her thoughts.

"I thought so," Senika said, smiling, "The way you speak, you have a slight accent."

Miranda laughed, "It's funny. Everyone here has an accent to me."

"So, what happened? How did you end up on Earth?" Senika asked curiously.

"I'm not sure I'm supposed to tell anyone but I'm a third child because there was some mix up with my mom," Miranda whispered.

"Oh, that is ok. I think I have heard of a family with three children. It is not their fault," Senika said in a normal voice, as if it was no big deal.

"That's a relief! I was afraid they would send me back," Miranda smiled.

"I would hope not," Senika agreed, "So, what is your number? Maybe you would like to hang out some time. I live along the ocean coastline to the west."

Miranda gave her a puzzled look, "There's an ocean? Cool! How far is it?"

"About an hour drive," Senika replied, laughing.

"So, 50 minutes?" Miranda asked, still not believing the hour was 10 minutes shorter.

Senika laughed, "Yes, 50. Is it different on Earth?"

"Yes, there are 60! It is going to take me some time to get used to it," Miranda laughed with her.

Senika helped her sort out her pocket notebook and they exchanged numbers.

"Your boyfriend is motioning to you," Senika said, pointing to the couches once they were done playing with Miranda's notebook.

"Who?" Miranda said, looking over to the couch, "Oh, no. He's definitely not my boyfriend."

"Oh, sorry. He is adorable and he looks so familiar."

Miranda nodded slowly, "I suppose. Well, hopefully I will see you soon. It was great to meet you."

"Yes, you too. I have got your number in case I am ever in town and if you are heading west, give me a call."

Miranda smiled, happy to have made a friend so easily. She sat beside Alex on the couch.

"You having fun?" Miranda asked.

"Yes," Alex replied beaming.

"Here Miranda," the singer said, aiming his pocket notebook at her, "I heard this is the first time you have ever heard us so hopefully this helps."

Miranda gave him a confused look as her notebook beeped in her pocket, "Sorry. I've only been on this planet for two full days," she smiled sheepishly. Obviously Alex had told them about her.

"I just sent all of our songs to your notebook. That way you can listen anytime you like," Aaron smiled.

"Oh wow!" Miranda exclaimed, pulling it out, "That is so amazing, thank you!"

"Alex was telling us about how you lived on Earth," the guitarist said, taking a sip of his drink, "What was that like?"

"It's hard to explain," Miranda said, completely unsure of herself, "I mean, my life seemed normal enough. It was just normal!" She laughed not knowing how to describe Earth especially when she wasn't on Utopia long enough to be able to compare it.

Aaron smiled, "Well, I hope you like it here."

"I do," Miranda said, returning his smile, "It is so beautiful, the colours and the air are just absolutely amazing. I like Earth and I will miss everyone a lot but everyone here has been very nice and welcoming. The only one I met here who has been rude to me is this guy." She put her arm around Alex and gave him a smile.

Alex glared at her.

"And yet you are here with him?" Aaron asked, laughing. He picked up his drink off the table in front of him and took a long sip.

"Him and my brothers but they're meeting us outside," Miranda said as Alex shrugged her arm off.

"He seems alright" the singer said, shrugging as he set his drink back down again.

"She is just cranky because her brains have been muddled by that disgusting planet she is from," Alex said, still glaring at Miranda.

Miranda rolled her eyes, "Whatever."

"Whatever," Alex repeated, rolling his eyes as well, and then turned back to the band, "Well, we should meet up with our friends. It has been two hours already." Alex stood. "Thank you for the shirts. Keep up the good music."

"Sure will, Alex," the singer said, standing to shake his hand, "You keep doing what you are doing."

"Thank you so much for everything," Miranda said and kissed the singer's cheek. She blushed after she did, wondering if she should have done that. She'd never done that before but he had greeted her that way.

"I have got Alex's address so next time we are in town. We will send you all passes again," the guitarist added, taking Alex's hand and then placing a kiss on Miranda's cheek.

"Yes, I met Senika and we exchanged numbers," Miranda smiled, motioning over to her. Senika was talking to a group of girls in the corner of the room.

"My beautiful girlfriend," the drummer smiled in Senika's direction. Senika just happened to look over and she motioned for him so he waved goodbye to Miranda and Alex and went to join her.

As they left, Alex put the hat back on and Miranda made a face at him. She hated how it shaded his face.

They didn't speak at all as they made their way through the building and met up with Evan and Griffin who were almost at the front of a bus line.

Alex passed around the shirts the singer had given him. He handed one to Miranda. Hers was the blue baby tee with the band logo on it.

"Oh man. Why did I let Alex go?" Evan said, laughing as he held up the shirt.

"I hope you two had a terrible time," Griffin added with a smile.

"Sorry but it was great!" Alex said, excitedly "I sat with the band the whole time. They have seen me before, you know."

"Oh really?" Evan smiled proudly and then whispered something that Miranda couldn't hear. She thought something was up but didn't care if it involved Alex. They boarded the bus and she sat by the window thinking about the singer and humming his song. He *was* gorgeous but not as cute as Alex, of course.

Miranda sighed and pressed a fist into her forehead, *why do I keep thinking about Alex like that? He can probably hear me! Stupid arrogant, conceited...*

Alex turned to look at her and she stopped her internal rant. He was seated in the bench in front of her so of course he heard her. He always did. The guy was always around, he never went away. She refused to meet his eyes.

"Thank you for taking me backstage," he said and she almost sighed with relief. Either he finally wasn't listening to Miranda's thoughts or he was just ignoring them. "I know you did not choose me to go but I still appreciate you letting me."

Miranda cocked her head, trying to catch any sort of sarcasm. "You're welcome," she said finally when she detected none.

Then he smirked at her, whispering, "You are right though. I am cuter than the singer."

"Ugh! You arrogant bastard!" she swore at him, loudly.

Both Griffin and Evan, who had been talking to each other, turned to her with disapproving looks. Miranda folded her arms across her chest and turned to look out the window, pouting. She wasn't even embarrassed anymore. He just made her angry now.

When they got back to the apartment, the boys said good night to Alex but Miranda ignored him, completely.

"Do either of you have like headphones or something so I can listen to the songs?" Miranda asked.

"I do," Evan said, and went into his room.

While he was gone, Griffin took the opportunity to chastise his sister for her bad language.

"We do not normally call people names unless it is jokingly," he explained.

"Well, if he would just be nice to me," Miranda grumbled, and then added, "And just stay out of my thoughts!"

"That is not possible, Miranda," Griffin said, "We cannot simply just stay out of your thoughts. We hear them like in conversation if you do not know how to properly close your mind. You cannot blame Alex. It was like you told him he was cute to his face."

Miranda blushed, "But it was just a random thought. I don't think he is cute, he..." she stopped herself since it was no use lying about it, "Ok, so apparently I do, but still! How do you block just a random thought?"

Griffin thought about that for a second, "I do not know," he said after just a moment, "I suppose it is just something you concentrate on."

Evan returned with the headphones which were just small wireless earpieces. He showed her how to work them with her notebook and she went to bed, falling asleep as she listened.

*Miranda was back in the auditorium watching the band play again. Thousands of people crowded her, pushing her closer to the stage. When the band went for a break, a man in a black cloak came onto the stage. He put his hands up and suddenly the ground started shaking. Everyone around started screaming in panic as pieces of the beautiful ceiling started to fall all around them and everyone bolted for the exit.*

*Miranda tried to keep up with her brothers but lost sight of them. She tripped over something and hit the floor. She turned her head to look up and saw a large chunk of the building coming straight at her. She would either be trampled or crushed.*

*Miranda screamed as the chunk got closer but then someone took her hand and pulled her to safety. A white light shone around them and everything went dark.*

Her dad startled her from her dream just as the first sun's rays started to peak through the window. She pulled the earphones out, which were still playing The Trees music.

"Are you ok? Bad dream?" he asked, looking at her worriedly.

"Yes," Miranda said, "I've been having bad dreams since before I came here."

"I am sorry, sweetheart," he said, "They are just dreams, no need to worry."

"I know, dad."

"Did you want to get up now to get ready?" he asked her quietly, "We have to leave in 75 minutes."

"Ya, I'll get in the shower now," she replied, yawning.

"Did you have a good time last night?"

"It was great, dad. Thank you so much."

"You are welcome."

He was just about to leave when she stopped him, "Hey dad?"

He stopped and turned in the doorframe, "Yes?"

"Do I ever have to charge this notebook? How does the electricity work here?"

He smiled, "No, you will never have to charge it. Every apartment is lined with an electric field which everything runs off of. That is why there are no power cords. And we get our energy from the suns."

Miranda smiled, "Cool!" Then it dawned on her why everything looked so neat. It was because there were no power cords lying about on the floor.

Mr. East laughed and shut the door so Miranda could get ready. She looked at her notebook. It was already after ten. Somehow she had picked up on their times very quickly. She got out of bed and headed for the bathroom.

Today's shower was much less awkward than the day before, now that she knew what to expect. She chose the outfit Alpha suggested since her dad had been casually dressed in khaki shorts and a blue button-down shirt. She dressed in her jean shorts and yellow polo then she went out to the kitchen where her family sat, along with Alex, to her great disappointment.

"Good morning, pancake," Alex said, smiling at her as she entered the dining room.

Miranda huffed at him and went to sit down at her plate of bacon and eggs, blushing furiously, "You really know how to make my morning, don't you?"

"I do what I can," Alex replied nonchalantly.

"Last time I take you backstage," Miranda grumbled.

Everyone laughed.

"You can make pancakes for all of us someday," Evan said, grinning at her.

Miranda smiled back, happy they weren't mad at her.

"How could we be mad? It is our fault we never told you how much to use." Griffin said to her.

Mr. East looked like he was trying not to laugh and cleared his throat, taking on a more serious tone, "We will leave in about a half hour, ok?"

"Yep," Miranda agreed before shovelling a fork full of eggs in her mouth.

"Yes," Alex said, shaking his head at her.

Miranda narrowed her eyes at Alex. Did he really have to point that out in front of her father? "Whatever," she snapped at him.

"What does that even mean?" he asked, glaring back.

Miranda took a second to think about a good retort, and then smirked, "A polite way of saying 'I don't give a shit what you have to say'".

Alex's and her father's mouth dropped open. Evan chuckled but Griffin, who had been glaring at Alex, turned it on Miranda. "Remember what we talked about?"

"Of course Griffin," she turned her sweetest, most innocent smile, at him. "I *was* only joking." She cleared her mind, hoping no one would catch that lie.

Her father forced out a small laugh. "I still cannot believe you got backstage," Mr. East said, changing the conversation.

"Well, it was lucky we were in the first level!" Miranda said, grateful for the subject change.

"Lucky you are beautiful or else he would have passed us by," Evan said.

Mr. East choked a little, "What?"

"Yes, the singer said they usually choose girls," Alex explained, as Miranda shifted uncomfortably. Didn't he know that would bother her father or was he trying to start something? To her horror, he continued, "I think he liked you Miranda. He kept asking about you." Miranda glared daggers at him.

Mr. East shifted, "Miranda, I know you are 16 and you probably talked to your other parents about… well, your mother was better at this…"

Miranda turned crimson as the three boys burst out laughing.

"Now is not the time to embarrass your daughter of three days," Evan said, through laughs.

Mr. East flushed a little bit, "Oh, sorry. Should we talk later?"

"Not ever," Griffin added.

The table went silent as everyone continued to eat until Miranda started to giggle, terribly embarrassed, but it was a *little* funny and everyone joined in.

Miranda hugged both her brothers goodbye and they wished her luck at the appointments today and then she followed her dad to the parking garage on the top floor of their building. Miranda could finally take it all in. Last time she was up here, all she could think about was the funeral. The parking garage was plain, just like the ones from Earth, with grey walls and pillars. The family car was dark blue and almost looked like an actual car but with no tires. It was parked on what looked like a rubber post platform. Where the two front tires should be it was wider. The interior was a little different with many more buttons on the dark grey dashboard than an Earth car. Also the steering wheel was just two handles at three o'clock and nine o'clock, on an Earth clock.

The trip there, Miranda gazed out the window as they hovered about a hundred feet off the ground, just above the highest of buildings. There were no roads beneath them but long plains of grass which were indicators of the road that wound through the city.

Reaching their destination, her father parked on the top floor of a ten-story building. They got into the elevator and he pushed one.

Miranda guessed that 'P' on the elevator meant parking and 'R' meant roof. They were at the top of the list followed by the numbers 1 through 8. She confirmed it with her father.

They went one floor down, which was the topmost floor below the parking garage and the door opened to a reception room. It had panelled walls of a dark red colour and one desk directly in the centre towards the back. It was a beautiful room with many plants and a small waterfall cascading down a glass pane. The floor was flat and grey.

She followed her father as he approached the desk.

"We have and appointment with Councilman Hope," he said to the older lady behind the desk who was reading what looked like a magazine. It had a metal-looking frame and appeared digitally in the centre just like the photographs.

"Your name?" she asked, setting it aside with a small clink on the desk.

"Edward East."

The woman smiled at him, and then turned to look at Miranda, "I think it is wonderful you are here. Have a seat. I will let him know you have arrived."

Miranda smiled back at her as she got up and headed into the door on the right.

They sat down on the beige chairs that lined the left side of the wall beside the waterfall but didn't have to sit long before she came back out and told them they could go in.

Miranda's palms started to sweat, her typical nervous reaction, as she followed her father into the next office wiping her hands on her shorts. It was bigger than the first one they had walked into with many bookshelves filled with books lining the right side wall.

Miranda and her father sat down in the two black leather-looking seats in front of the desk of a tall, of course, grey haired man in a dark grey suit that seemed to match his eyes.

He smiled at her and rose off his seat to shake her hand.

She took it nervously, "It's nice to meet you."

"And you as well," he said excitedly, smiling at her. Then seemed to calm himself, "Never met an Earthling before but I guess in reality you really are not one, are you?"

"No, I guess not," she agreed. She liked him. He seemed genuinely happy that her brother had found her and she relaxed.

"Well now, I have read over your family's case and I find no grounds as to not allow you to live here. Your family did not know about you except your mother. Seems it is our fault considering she was overlooked for birth deterrents after your second brother was born. It has happened before but not very often and we have let a few families keep the accidental third child. However because you were on Earth, I would like a few tests run to check for viruses and that sort before I grant full citizenship and you can get your identification."

Miranda let out a sigh of relief and smiled. Her father stood and shook the councilman's hand excitedly.

"I just wish we had found out sooner," the councilman said and turned slowly to Miranda, "But I guess your mother was nervous that you would be in trouble. We allow a third child in special circumstances but not too many people know about it." He cleared his throat before continuing, "We do not want the wrong ears to hear about this."

Miranda frowned. It was sad to hear that she could have lived here this whole time but she pushed that feeling to the back of her mind. Maybe Alex was right for once. At least she was here now.

"I have also been thinking about training. Of course you are too old for school but I have set up a special trainer at the school who will gladly catch you up in your education."

"Too old? I am only 16," Miranda told him.

"Here we only go to school until the age of 15," Mr. Hope explained, "You should have picked you career by now and be shadowing a professional."

Miranda's cheeks went pink. She was already too old for school? She wasn't sure how to feel about that.

"That is wonderful!" Mr. East exclaimed, "I was so worried she would not be able to receive an education."

The councilman smiled, "This is definitely an odd circumstance. Very rarely have we had to begin an education so late in life."

Miranda frowned, "I am a very fast learner and I did very well in Earth school," she argued.

"Oh I did not mean it that way," he said, alarmed "I am very sorry to have offended you."

"It's fine," Miranda replied quietly.

"I just meant a Utopian education with Utopian history, science, philosophies. You will not take anything very basic and definitely no English or mathematics courses. I am sure you have been sufficiently trained. We keep a very close watch on the training of youth on other planets."

"Excellent," Mr. East said, "When shall she start?"

"I should think Monday would be fine. That will give you plenty of time to be settled into your home."

Miranda looked quizzically at her father, who knew immediately that she had no idea which day it was, "It is now Wednesday. We have the same seven days of the week, all the same, Sunday to Saturday," he explained and turned back to the councilman, "Is she to dress for school?"

"Yes."

"Thank you very much," Mr. East said smiling still.

Councilman Hope rose from his desk to walk them to the elevator, chatting happily about the planet and how much Miranda was sure to enjoy it but just before they got to the elevator he put a hand on her shoulder and whispered, "You be careful and watch yourself. Tell only who you must that you are a third child. I fully trust your trainer."

Miranda nodded and followed her father back to the car thinking about what he said last. She didn't know anyone to tell anyways.

They arrived at the hospital quickly and her father escorted her to the third floor. They didn't have to wait long before it was Miranda's turn.

The tests were awkward because the machines they had were a hundred times faster than those on Earth. They took a blood sample and generated a long list of results, immediately. Then she was scanned by a hovering piece of equipment. She was in and out within fifteen minutes with a signature that declared her in perfect health.

After the hospital, they went back to city hall and received her identification and documents. She accidentally called herself Miranda Greenburg when they asked for her full name and she sent an apologetic look to her father.

"You can use that name if you like," he encouraged, "I do not want to take anything away from you anymore."

"No, dad," Miranda insisted and turned to the receptionist, "Miranda East."

"Do you have a second name?" the receptionist asked.

"No," Miranda said, turning to her dad, "Mom never left one on the paper with my name."

"Would you like to pick one?" her father asked.

"Yes, Sara," Miranda replied, looking at her hands, "My Earth mother's name was Sara."

Mr. East put an arm around his daughter's shoulders. An easy thing for him since he was taller, "That is a great idea."

After she received her identification, her father took her to get a school uniform at the school. It was one of the larger buildings she had seen and her father told her that all the senior school aged children in the city went here. There was only one senior school per city as well as one middle school and one junior school. At least she was used to wearing a uniform. As she stood in front of the mirror with it on at the shop, she thought this one looked pretty cool. It was a plain burgundy fitted smock type dress with the embroidered city flower logo in yellow on the left breast pocket. It read 'C217 S.S.' above the flower in gold stitching. It had thick tank top sleeves, a thick black belt and fell to just above her knees. Above all else, Miranda loved the silky feel.

With her uniform purchased, they headed to the shopping centre where she was dragged around going store to store for hours where countless designers all helped feverishly to find outfits that suited her. They were all wonderful help and all very cheerful. Miranda seemed to fit right in since she had always been such a positive person. She smiled and laughed with the sales clerks and her dad all day. Her dad explained that each storeowner made their own clothes. It was the career they chose and all loved doing what they did. Her father tried to explain that all the clothes were synthetically made, but could not explain what it was that made them so soft. 'Just years of trying to get it perfect!' he had said.

Miranda learned a lot more about her new home that day. She found out that children went to school from the age of two until they were 15 taking all general courses and then they chose which career path they would follow. Junior school was for ages 2 to 6, middle for 7 to 11 and senior for ages 12 to 15. After senior school, for the next one to five years depending on which job a student wanted, they would work closely with a professional in their field of choice. Some chose doctor or scientist or even a chef, who manipulated the liquids to make extravagant dishes that were served at restaurants. It all depended on what you wanted but everyone on the planet worked. There weren't any poor families, everyone was paid well. Every city was fairly self-reliant. What was made in the city normally stayed in the city boundaries. It was completely balanced, set out by ancient laws that no one ever broke. The only things shared between the cities were television shows and aviation, for the most part.

"If everything is good, how was mom attacked? I don't understand," Miranda asked quietly as they drove home, the car loaded with shopping bags for which Miranda had thanked her father several times. It was all too much. She wasn't used to having so many clothes to pick from.

Her father nervously cleared his throat but didn't say anything. Miranda looked at him, hopefully. It was hard to believe that there was an attack since this place and the people in it seemed so wonderful.

"There is a group of individuals," he started quietly, "Who are not like everyone else. They only attack every so often and it is not understood why but it can be guessed that it stems back from some ancient legend of good and evil. The majority of Utopians love the peace and quiet and we respect the laws which are there to protect the balance of life."

"Oh," Miranda said quietly. Figures even the most perfect place could have some crazy people.

"Do not be afraid. It is the only harm on this planet."

Miranda wasn't afraid. She would have had more to fear on Earth than one thing here, "So there are no murderers? What about diseases?"

"We do not even produce any kind of weapon on this planet and most diseases are eradicated as soon as they arise. We have the most intelligent people in the universe on this planet."

"Are there other planets?"

"Of course but we have yet to find one as evolved as ours. We have space explorers who live most of their life researching."

"If there are no guns, how do they attack?"

"We do not understand how. Everyone who has encountered them has not survived so we have no way of knowing what happens."

"But mom was attacked at the school?"

"She must have been just getting into her car," Mr. East said sadly.

"How did you find me?" Miranda asked, her eyes downcast.

"All the note said on her notebook was 'Find Miranda, Read My Will'. She explained it all in her video Will which was tucked inside the pages of a book on her bookshelf."

Miranda frowned.

"She also had a few pictures with her Will," Mr. East continued, "Obviously you were oblivious to the camera but I knew what you looked like even before you came here. I remember finding one of the pictures in your mother's drawer. She told me it was her when she was younger. I believed her because you two look alike."

Miranda blushed and her eyes welled with tears. Her mother carried a picture of her. So she did care.

"I have an idea," Mr. East said excited, "Do you mind if I introduce you to some of my co-workers? You can see the inside of the space centre!"

Miranda nodded, "I'd love to see it."

As they drove, Mr. East pointed out some really great restaurants and some of the other things in the city. They even passed the studio where Evan worked. The car dipped slowly and pulled onto the large open area of grass that was set aside for parking. He easily set the car down on a pair of the rubber posts that were on the ground and got out. She followed her dad into the centre. It was a large two story beige building with a decorated sign that had the building's name on it.

"Do all cities have these?" Miranda asked.

"All cities have a small airspace but not every city has one as large as this. Only one city every two thousand kilometres squared. We collaborate all the time," he explained, "And this is where you have to go for tickets to other planets. You should have arrived here when you first landed."

"Oh, right!" Miranda said, "I was a little dizzy when we got here but it does look familiar." She looked out over the city.

Mr. East smiled, "Yes, your mother said there was a big difference in the air quality."

"Seems so," Miranda said glumly, following her father up the stairs. She worried about the health of her family and friends on Earth and wished they could be here just to smell the air.

They stepped into the middle set of the five double doors and Miranda was met with a large room that encompassed the whole building. The whole solar system seemed to be projected on the ceiling. The room was full of large desks and what must have been Utopian computers. There were a few separate rooms at the back enclosed in glass. Several people were bent over a long holograph image in one of the rooms.

"Griffin works at the back right. I work just to the left here," he said pointing. He led the way to his desk.

"Oh Ed!" a lady said, as she looked up when they approached, "My goodness, I thought I saw a ghost!"

Mr. East laughed, "This is my daughter, Miranda. Miranda, this is Susan."

Susan jumped up and shook her hand, "They were not kidding when they said you looked like your mom!"

Miranda smiled. She met so many people that day that she'd never remember all their names. Everyone had the same thing to say. She looked so much like her mother. Many had questions about Earth. She promised she would come in soon to try to explain some things they didn't understand about her old home and her solar system.

When they reached home after a long day, her father helped her carry her things to the chute that deposited things into the apartment.

Back at the apartment, her brothers were already carrying her bags to the room.

"I guess it went well," Evan said excitedly, when they walked in lifting up the bags in his hands as evidence.

"Yes, I have full citizenship now," Miranda squealed, showing her brothers her identification.

"Good picture. Most do not come out so well," Evan said with a sly smile, motioning to Griffin.

"Be quiet," Griffin said, frowning.

Miranda laughed, "I'll have to see that later," she said as she picked up a few of her bags and followed the boys down to her room.

"I will have these sent back to the stores," Griffin said, picking up the bags after Miranda had dumped out the contents onto her bed.

Miranda looked at him curiously.

"They go down into the mail and are sent back to the stores so they can reuse them," Griffin told her.

"Right," Miranda smiled, "Everything is reused."

Evan picked up the school uniform that he saw lying on the top and laughed, "Someone has to go to school?"

Miranda snatched the uniform from him, blushing, "Yes but with a private trainer."

"Well, at least you will learn all about the planet," Griffin said, smiling.

Evan sighed, "If you make it into my show we should have no problem accommodating your time in school."

"Really?" Miranda asked, hopefully.

"It should be fine," Evan said and smiled, "A little inconvenienced but it really does not matter. Besides, I am not writing in the new character for a least a month. I need some other things wrapped up before then."

"Your education should be your first priority," Mr. East added.

Miranda smiled, "Of course dad!"

"We will get supper ready," her dad said, smiling and the three men left. Miranda could hear her father scolding Evan down the hallway about not interfering in Miranda's education if she makes it on the show.

Miranda started to put away the clothes she bought, excitedly holding up to her the latest fashions on the planet in front of her full-length mirror before programming them in with Alpha. Her family seemed to have quite a lot of money and Miranda wondered if everyone on the planet were *that* well off.


After dinner she tackled her brother into showing her his I.D. It wasn't as bad as he thought but he wore a goofy grin.

Evan had promised her he'd work on some lines with her for her audition so she spent the rest of the night going over the script with her brother in her room.

He gave her a few pointers but was amazed at how good she was. She knew exactly was kind of body expression to give at the right time.

"You know, compared to many girls here you are very cute," he said playfully, receiving a small punch in the arm, "You should not be so self-conscious. Confidence is a good thing during these auditions."

"Whatever. You have to say that! I'm your sister."

"No, I am serious. I may have to watch out for you! Look at last night! That singer thought you were too! That is why he picked you."

Miranda smiled at him, "He picked me 'cause I'm a girl, that's all." She never got much attention from the boys on Earth but then again they could have been intimidated at her size considering she was taller than most.

"That must have been it," Evan said, nodding in assurance, "So did you have a boyfriend on Earth?"

"Not really. I had a couple dates though," Miranda told him returning his smile. Her thoughts trailed off to Scott. She wondered if he missed her.

"See?" Evan laughed, "Well, I am exhausted. I had a long day on the set and we had a meeting afterwards." He gave her a quick hug, "Good night!"

"Night Ev," she said.

As Miranda lay on her bed, she wondered about what would have happened with Scott if she had stayed on Earth. Would they have started dating exclusively? Would they have had fun at the dance? Would he have kissed her goodnight? Miranda was sure that if his dad had not shown up the first night, he may have kissed her then.

She *was* very self conscious when it came to boys. When she was younger and not as tall, she had a couple little 'boyfriends' but as soon as she grew past them, no one seemed interested. She had been afraid she was destined to wander the globe alone until Scott had asked her out. Miranda had been a little jealous that Helen had a boyfriend but she changed her mind quickly when she never became interested in any of the boys at her high school. They also never seemed to become interested in her though either. She thought Helen was so much prettier than her and she wished to be more like her so she would get a boyfriend as well. Not too long ago, Helen had told Miranda that she had gone all the way with Bryan and here Miranda hadn't even kissed a boy. Miranda didn't even want to think about sex yet. She hadn't even had her first real kiss.

Briefly, her thoughts turned to Alex. She hadn't seen him since that morning and she actually was a little disappointed. Miranda groaned as tried to fall asleep, *what am I thinking!* He was so mean to her and he obviously wasn't interested, just as most boys weren't, so why couldn't she stop thinking about him.

# Nine

★　★　★　★

The next day, Miranda spent the day alone in the apartment, though she was in much better spirits than she was the day before. She couldn't believe she had an audition for Evan's show tomorrow and spent a lot of the time nervously pacing the living room with her pocket notebook in her hands, practicing the script. It distracted her from her nightmare the night before. Miranda had awoken in a cold sweat that morning. It would have been a very gruesome way to die if her rescuer had not been there.

Miranda was going to be a new character entering the plot. Some guy, Jeff, has a fiancée but would immediately fall in love with her. She wasn't sure yet of how that would turn out and her stomach fluttered to think that maybe she may have to kiss someone on television or possibly more. She let herself fall onto the couch and laid back. What if she did have to kiss someone onscreen, would she be terrible? *Of course I will. I've never even been kissed*, she thought sadly to herself.

The part she would be reciting in her audition complemented her well. She would be having an argument and that was her specialty.

That and crying since she could easily start crying her eyes out right on cue.

When she was bored with the script, knowing it practically be heart, she went to her room and flopped down on the bed.

She felt so lonely. There was no one for her to talk to and no way of communicating with her friends from Earth. She stared at her favourite picture of her and Helen on her shelf and her eyes welled with tears. *What is Helen going to think of me when I never call her again?* she thought. A small wave of homesickness washed over her and she tried hard to brush it away. She picked up her Earth cell phone and turned it on. She only had a quarter left of battery power. She read through all her text messages she had sent the past week. She had nothing of Scott, no pictures or messages. All she had were a few memories.

She tried to be positive. Once she met some people and got out of the apartment, she would feel better about this place, hopefully. She turned on her Earth cell off, hoping to conserve the battery a little bit longer. They were the only words she had from home aside from the letter from her Earth parents.

Miranda decided to go for a walk around the building, desperately needing to get away from the confinement of the apartment. She changed from her sweatpants she had gotten used to wearing around the house to a new outfit her father had bought.

Miranda twirled in front of the mirror, admiring her new black shorts and short-sleeved top. The store owner said it was cotton but it sure didn't feel the same as Earth's did. Every material was much silkier against her skin and much lighter. She thought of the time she had touched Alex and the same jolt went down her spine. *Oh, please don't tell me it's love at first sight*, she thought but shook her head at her reflection, her curls bouncing and she laughed to herself. There was no way she was going to let herself fall for that guy. He was so mean, drove her crazy and there were a ton more people she could meet. She just hadn't had any other options yet. Perhaps when she started school? But she was older than everyone there. Miranda sighed and ran her hands through her hair. The few days in Utopia had softened her curls and her hair was glossy and shiny. She loved the feel of it now. What was she going to tell everyone at school where she came from and why she was behind in her studies? The councilman had told her to keep it quiet that she was a third child.

She left the apartment and took the elevator to the very top. It was only ¾ parking garage she noticed the day before. There was another door to the left after getting off the elevator. Through the door she found a small lobby.

"Hello," a man said from a desk. It looked much like a security desk but she was puzzled because they shouldn't need it.

"Well, I am a member of the law enforcement but you do not need it. They station us around the city," he said smiling, reading her mind, "I take care of the surrounding buildings."

Miranda was really going to have to learn to control her thoughts now. Everyone could hear anything she thought of. How could she make up any stories about where she came from or why she was behind in her studies?

"You must be Miranda," he said coming around the desk extending his hand, which she took shyly, "I am Bill Manchester. It is really great that your family found you and I am so sorry about your mother. She was a wonderful person."

"Did you know my mom?"

"Yes. I have lived here about as long as your parents have. You must be bored! Would you like a tour of the building?"

Miranda brightened, "I'd love one if you have the time!"

Bill smiled and nodded. He motioned around the room, "This is the lobby, of course. There is not much to do here except talk to boring old me or have your laundry done," he motioned to a door across the room that read Laundromat, "All the fun is on the bottom floor."

He led her to the elevator and pushed seven. "You are on six, correct?"

Miranda nodded.

"Well, it is all apartments from one to six and seven is the entertainment floor. I am on the first floor, if you ever need anything after hours," he explained.

The doors opened on seven and Miranda was shocked that her family hadn't told her about this. It was a small square room with white walls and beige carpeting with three clear glass doors. The one on the right was marked 'Exercise Room', in the centre directly across from her was 'Game Room', and the third on the left was 'Movie room'.

Bill moved towards the exercise room and Miranda followed. It led to a large room with a pool in the centre, surrounded by lounge chairs. There were windows instead of a wall and several were open to allow the warm breeze to flow through. It was a beautiful sunny day outside and there were even lounge chairs just outside to enjoy it. Miranda knew exactly what she wanted to do. She loved to lie in the sun.

There was nobody at the pool this afternoon. A large hot tub was tucked away into the back beside another door which led to a room full of exercise equipment.

"Wow, this is wonderful!" Miranda gasped.

"Yes, it is. This entertainment caters to some of the surrounding buildings so not everyone who uses this is from this building," Bill said, "Come with me. You will like the game room!"

He led her back to the small hallway and stepped into the game room. It was a little smaller than the last one but was filled with a bunch of games Miranda recognized, such as pinball and air hockey and some that she didn't.

Bill placed a card on the reader and then opened the final door which lead down a small ramp and opened up to a fair sized room with a large screen and seats for about thirty people. There was a movie playing on the large screen and a group of four older women sat watching it quietly.

Miranda was quiet so that she wouldn't disturb them and they had not noticed the pair walk in.

Miranda finally spoke when they reached the small room again. "I didn't know all this was down here!"

"Yes, they usually show the latest movie in the movie room about five times a day. I forgot that one had started. You just swipe your bank card and it deducts 20 from your account to watch the movie."

"Thank you for the tour!" Miranda said, shaking his hand again.

"No problem Miranda. I am glad to help. I will just leave you to it and head back to the desk. You let me know if you need anything."

They both got in the elevator and Miranda got off at her floor, waving to Bill.

She went into her room and changed into her new bathing suit her dad had bought her. He seemed a little embarrassed about her choice in bikini, obviously never raising a daughter before, but it was plain purple and Miranda loved it.

Miranda decided to grab the same book off her mother's shelf about Utopian animals. She had only gotten a part way through the last time.

She made her way to the chairs outside. It had been getting cooler on Earth, so her skin was starting to get slightly paler than normal. Everyone else in her family was so tanned and she wondered if they even had winter on this planet. Her family had talked about the two suns but never said anything about snow or winter when they were near the second smaller sun.

Miranda sat outside for hours with her straps pulled down so she wouldn't get tan lines. It was so relaxing with the sun on her skin, not once did she feel too warm.

She really enjoyed the animal book. The planet was split in half with people living on one half of the planet and animals on the other so that they wouldn't disturb each other. Utopians wanted to make sure that they didn't interfere with the natural evolution of animals. The book didn't talk about any domestic animals and Miranda thought about Tinsel back at home. It would be sad not to have a pet.

Miranda was reading through the small jungle cats section when she came across a Maddix, or *Leopardus maddixon* as it said in the book. It was a tiny cat-like creature with spots like a leopard. It was the cutest animal she had seen in the book so far and she let out a laugh. She read about it and despite its adorable appearance, it had a terrible little mean streak and was known for attacking prey much larger than itself and devouring it in just a few sittings. It also had an uncharacteristic loud growl which made it sound like a much larger animal than it was. Miranda rolled her eyes. Of course Alex would think she represented the latter description of it and definitely did not call her a Maddix because he thought she was cute. She sighed.

She was so enwrapped in the book and her thoughts that she didn't hear the sliding doors open behind her.

"Hi there," someone said to her and Miranda turned startled.

When she saw it was just a girl in a pink bikini with a blanket slug over her shoulder, she replied, "Hi, sorry, I didn't hear the door open."

"That is ok," the tall blond said to her, laying her blanket on the lounge chair beside her. She had her pocket notebook in hand, "What are you reading?" She took a seat and stretched her long legs out.

"A book on Utopian animals," Miranda replied, "I found it in my mom's collection."

"Oh, are you studying to work with animals?" she said, gazing at the cover, "Books are very rare! That must be very old!"

Miranda blushed, wondering if she should tell the girl she was from Earth, but the girl's eyes widened and Miranda knew she heard her thoughts.

"You are from Earth?" she asked skeptically.

"Ya, I'm not sure if I'm supposed to tell many people. My mom left me on Earth because I was a third child. She just died though and told my brothers where to find me."

"Wow, you must Evan and Griffin's sister! I know your brothers. I am so sorry about your mom," she said downcast, then straightened up, "How rude of me, I am Alicia Manchester."

"Miranda."

"Nice to meet you."

"You too. Are you Bill's daughter?" Miranda asked.

"Yes," she giggled, "Have you met him?"

"He gave me a tour not too long ago. He seems very nice."

"Well, dad is great!" Alicia laughed.

"So books are rare?" Miranda asked, closing her book and looking at the cover. It didn't seem to be that old.

"For some time now we just buy books over our notebooks," she said, holding hers up for a second, "Although they stopped using trees like Earth does billions of years ago and started making books from another material. I would say that one probably is not billions of years old because it has not yellowed and fallen apart like it would if it was made from a tree, so it is probably a few hundred million."

Miranda gasped, "Really? Wow!"

"Check the print date on the first page," Alicia laughed.

Miranda opened the book, "It just says 7.8B."

"That is 7.8 billion years and we are just over 8.16 now, so yes, it is over 300 million years old."

"Gosh! I don't think I should be even touching it!"

Alicia laughed again, "I am sure it does not mind. It is not worth anything but they are fun to see."

The two girls sat and chatted for a long time, Miranda's book forgotten. Miranda told her about Earth which Alicia was very excited to hear about and Alicia told her that they lived in the mid latitudes of the planet and they didn't see snow, only near the polar region. Miranda found out she was 15, almost through her last year of school. Miranda talked about how she would be starting school on Monday with a private trainer to catch her up and Alicia was excited that she would be going to the same school. Miranda was happy she didn't think her stupid for being in school at the age of 16.

"Of course not," Alicia laughed, reading her mind, "No one can blame you for what happened and I am sure you will be very welcome. You may sit with me at lunch, of course, and I will introduce you to everyone."

"Thank you so much," Miranda smiled, but sighed, "I'm not sure I am supposed to tell many people that I am a third child. But I do not know what else to say. The councilman said to me that I should tell only who I must."

Alicia looked in thought, "Well, your mother was an Earth expert. I would just say you travelled with her. A friend of mine started school when she was 10 because her mother was a space traveler and she spent the first 10 years of her life travelling."

"Will that work? Do most people know about my brothers?" Miranda asked, hopefully.

"Well, everyone knows Evan because of the show," Alicia laughed, "but I think we can pull it off."

"Speaking of the show," Miranda smiled, excited she finally had another girl to share the news with, "I have an audition tomorrow!"

Alicia squealed, "Really?"

"Yes, I was acting on Earth so my brother got me an audition."

"Oh, you must be so happy!" Alicia said excitedly, "Were you in many shows on Earth?"

"Oh no," Miranda frowned, "I was still studying."

"You must be so nervous then for your first big audition!" Alicia said, sympathetically.

"So nervous!" Miranda chewed her lip.

"I am sure you will be just fine!" Alicia encouraged, "Northern Shores is awesome! I watch it every day! Your brother is a genius and..."

"Genius is a little overdramatic," a boy's voice interrupted from the doors behind them, "There you are Miranda! Your family is worried about you. We were searching all over the building."

Miranda turned and saw Alex at the door and rolled her eyes, "What I can't understand is why YOU really care?" Miranda noticed Alicia had gone quiet and was ogling Alex.

Alex smiled at the attention and Miranda rolled her eyes again. He looked away from Alicia and made a face at Miranda, "Well, your brothers were worried when they found the apartment empty and asked for my help. I am always here to help my friends."

"That is very sweet," Alicia said, flashing a bright smile to Alex.

"Well, tell them I'll be up in a few minutes and go away," Miranda snapped, irritated at Alex for interrupting.

"Nice to see you too Maddix!" he said sarcastically and closed the door behind him.

Miranda watched his retreating frame through the sliding glass door. It probably wasn't made of glass. It was probably something like the tickets and windows were made of. She sighed heavily and Alicia looked at her strangely.

"He is so gorgeous," Alicia said.

"I can't stand him. He's been so mean to me ever since I met him."

"Really? I wonder why?" Alicia asked to no one in particular.

Miranda shrugged.

"Still, he is really cute," Alicia smiled dreamily.

"He's all yours." Miranda rolled her eyes at her new friend and got a flash of Alicia making out with Alex on a beach while the waves crashed around them. She wondered if she had finally read into someone's thoughts. That's not something she would think about. If anything, it would have been herself and Alex. Alicia continued to stare at the door that Alex had just walked through.

"What are you thinking about?" Miranda asked, "I'm not too good at the reading minds thing and I just wanted to know if it worked."

Alicia blushed, "Oh... just kissing Alex."

"On a beach?" Miranda asked. She felt bad invading Alicia's privacy but was hoping she was finally getting her mindreading back.

Alicia flushed more and nodded.

"Sorry," Miranda added quickly, a little excited she read into someone's mind, "I really am not good at the mindreading and I didn't mean to embarrass you. If you like, I can find out if he likes you."

"Do not worry," Alicia smiled, "Would you do that for me?"

"Sure," Miranda smiled back. Alicia dazed off again but Miranda couldn't see any more of her thoughts. "Well, I should go tell them I'm alright," she continued, snapping Alicia back to reality.

"Oh, yes. Before you go, I am in school tomorrow, but do you want to meet for the late movie tomorrow night?"

"Sure, that'd be great!" Miranda smiled.

"It starts at 27 hour," Alicia told her, "and you can tell me how your audition went. Good luck!"

"Thanks! I'll see you tomorrow."

Miranda put her pink sundress back on and went upstairs. Her family was in the living room. Mr. East was pacing behind the couch.

"There you are," he cried when she walked in.

Miranda looked at her brothers and they wore worried faces too.

"I'm sorry. I didn't realize how long I was down there for," she said looking down at her arms. She didn't look sunburned.

"It is ok," he father said, letting out a sigh, "Just send a message next time, please."

"We do not sunburn," Griffin explained, reading her thoughts, "I suppose it is just one of the mutations we have developed to withstand the ultraviolet rays of the sun."

Miranda smiled at all of them and they all seemed to let out a collected sigh of relief, "Why didn't you tell me about all the stuff downstairs? I had to get Bill to give me a tour."

Her dad smiled and gave her a quick hug, "Sorry, we never really thought of it, but I guess it would have been smart considering we left you here alone all day."

"Yes, we should have assumed you needed to get out of here," Griffin said, turning his attention to the television.

"Well, look at you though," Evan said, "Got some colour back for your audition tomorrow."

"And I met a girl downstairs named Alicia," Miranda told them.

"Oh, I know her," Evan said, "She is on the first floor and is really nice. I should introduce you to more people around the building. There are some that are our age. Would you like to go down to the game room tonight?"

"Sure!"

Alex came in the front door with a large stack of books in his hands, which he placed in Miranda's arms.

"I noticed you liked to read," he laughed, "Perhaps these will help you learn a little about the planet."

Miranda placed the books at her feet and picked up the top book. *Learning the days with Ellie the Ellasaur.*

"I think you will need this one too," Alex mocked, picking up the second book, *Counting with Ellie the Ellasaur.* There were other books that explained the solar system, the utopian clock, etc.

Miranda thought they would definitely help her learn a little about the planet, even though they were recommended for children age two to five. They seemed a little advanced for a two year old, "Oh, you've brought me down to your reading level! How nice!"

Alex stopped laughing as Miranda opened the book.

"We mature faster than the babies on Earth," he said through gritted teeth, "I did not expect you to have to read the counting book," he added, snatching the book away.

She shot him a dirty look, "I just wanted to see what an Ellasaur was." It was something that looked like an elephant, but smaller and its skin was green and scaly, like a reptile. "Is it a real animal here?"

"Yes," Alex said.

She looked to her dad for confirmation and he nodded. She didn't trust Alex to tell her anything.

"Just be careful with them. Books are rare."

"I *know*," Miranda retorted, happy that Alicia had told her about books earlier. Finally she didn't have to get schooled by Alex. Miranda, who didn't know whether to be offended or not, mumbled, "Thanks," and went quickly to change and put the books away. At least if she looked through some of them before school on Monday, she wouldn't feel as dumb. She rejoined her family and, to her dismay, Alex in the dining room for dinner.

"Guess what Maddie? I am coming to the game room too," Alex said mockingly as she sat down across from him.

Miranda was going to protest but decided it wasn't worth her breath, "Fine," she muttered before stuffing a few carrots in her mouth. She certainly wouldn't let Alex ruin her night. She'd ditch him as soon as they got down there. "Just so you know," she snapped as she remembered why he called her Maddie, "I know what a Maddix is now and if you don't leave me alone I just might attack and devour you in a few sittings."

Everyone laughed, including Alex.

"Well it suits you, so that is what I will call you from now on," Alex smiled and Miranda rolled her eyes at him, "Such a big growl for such a tiny person."

"You know, maybe you should have Alex run through those lines with you," Evan said, changing the subject, "You know, to get a good feel for the character with someone else?"

Both of them stopped smiling and glared at Evan.

"Why would I want to do that?" Miranda snapped.

Evan shrugged, "Just a suggestion." He made an encouraging face at Alex but Alex just looked away.

After dinner, they settled in the living room to digest for a half hour before going downstairs. Miranda asked her family about their day and what they were working on at work though she almost regretted it when Griffin excitedly told her about the findings of some research they were doing on an empty planet. It sounded incredibly boring but he was so excited about it.

There were a lot more people downstairs than there was earlier. A group of ten people that looked about Miranda's age littered the game room that night when Miranda, Evan and Alex walked in.

"East! West! How are you?" one of the boys said, coming up to them.

"Good, Nathan. This is my little sister, Miranda," Evan said, motioning to Miranda.

"Since when did you get a sister? And a fine one at that!" Nathan said moving closer to Miranda.

Miranda inched away and smiled.

"Do not even think about it," Evan threatened and Nathan raised his hands.

"Just kidding, it's nice to meet you Miranda," he said, taking her hand and kissing it. Miranda was a little shocked. She picked up on the slang right away after being around her family for so long. He sounded like he was from Earth.

"You too," Miranda blushed. She could get used to the suave attitude Scott and now Nathan showed her.

Alex took that moment to go over to a group of girls that were beckoning him and batting their lashes, giggling.

Evan steered Miranda to follow Nathan over to the group of five people who stood away from the group of girls, all looking slightly annoyed.

"Everyone invites their friends over just to see Alex," Evan said.

"And what would possess them to do that," Miranda asked as they reached the group.

"He is *famous* around here," Evan laughed.

"Can't understand why," Miranda said rolling her eyes and looking over at the group. One girl had taken Alex's arm and was staring at him with googly eyes. The others appeared to hang off his every word. It made her jealous and want to vomit at the same time. It was a shame he was so cute.

"Miranda, this is Rebecca, Jane, Pete, Dave and Greg. Everyone, this is my sister. She is from Earth and we just picked her up," Evan said, putting his arm around Miranda's shoulders.

A round of 'hello' went through the group and they all started bombarding her with questions about Earth and if she was happy here. Miranda was excited they had accepted her so quickly and answered everything they asked, forgetting completely about Alex and his admirers. She noticed that she was shorter than anyone from the group. How does it happen that she goes from being the tallest to the shortest?

"We should play something now!" Jane whined after a few minutes, her eyes gazing at the pinball machine.

"Jane holds the highest score right now," Dave explained to Miranda.

"Well, I'm good at hockey being from Canada and all," Miranda said, which was true, she loved playing back on Earth and always seemed to beat her friends. She noticed the other day it looked like there was an air hockey table.

"I will take that challenge," Alex said as he rejoined the group, he turned to Evan and whispered, "*That* was annoying." It seemed only Miranda overheard. Everyone else was moving towards either pinball or hockey.

"Why do you go then?" Evan asked, raising an eyebrow.

Alex pretended to be offended, "Now why would I ignore them?" He laughed then turned to Miranda and saw she was listening. He smirked, "Are we playing Maddie?"

Miranda almost refused but he put a hand on her back and pushed her to the big hockey table. It was a little different upon further inspection. In fact there was no air involved at all. There were no actual paddles or puck. The puck moved digitally across the top and the player was to use their hand as the paddle. It worked by touchscreen. Everyone but Jane and Dave had gathered around, even the group of giggling females. If they bothered Alex, he sure didn't show it. Another fit of giggles erupted as Alex flashed them another gorgeous smile.

"You're on," Miranda challenged and Evan started up the machine.

Miranda was really nervous with everyone's eyes on them and Alex scored on her right away.

"Are you kidding?" he complained, "Put a little effort in."

"Did I mention Alex is on a winning streak?" Greg said as the puck appeared by Miranda's hand indicating it was her turn to shoot.

"Ya, well that ends now," Miranda said, as she executed a perfect bank off the side and into Alex's goal, "Did I mention that I never lose?"

"Ouch, watch yourself Alex," Nathan said, "She's a hot one."

Evan sent him a glare but Nathan smiled innocently.

The game went back and forth, a really close score and everyone cheered for Miranda when she would score, except the giggling females who cheered for Alex. Miranda finally got the last goal before the timer sounded.

She jumped up and down excitedly, throwing her arms in the air and doing a little dance on the spot, "Oh ya! I rock!"

Alex looked thoroughly disappointed and Pete clapped him on the back.

"Alex, I thought you were a professional!" he said mockingly to which he received a small punch in the arm.

The group of giggling girls were glaring at Miranda, who didn't seem to notice or care and they went over to console the loser.

"I do not know how to play that game but I would have let you win," Miranda swore she heard one of the girls coo to Alex.

"So, who's next?" Miranda challenged, ignoring the pathetic attempts to cheer Alex up. They all stepped up, aside from the group of girls, one by one and Miranda defeated them all.

After they were done, Evan suggested they go back upstairs so she could get some rest before her audition tomorrow. Miranda was so happy she had made friends so easily. She told them that she was going to the movies with Alicia tomorrow and everyone agreed to meet them and wished her luck for the audition tomorrow.

In the elevator, Miranda finally noticed that Alex wasn't with him.

"I think he was a little embarrassed about losing to you," Evan said laughing.

"Are you serious?" Miranda hoped.

"I am not sure but he also needed to get away from those girls," Evan said.

"Or go home with one," Miranda snorted, "They disappeared when he left."

Evan gave her a confused look and thought about that for a second before he shook his head, "No, Alex is not like that. He told me they were annoying him."

"Why does he bother talking with them then?"

"Well, he likes the popularity. He...well, you would not understand. I will explain another time. So, you like hockey then?"

"Oh, for sure," Miranda said laughing, "It *is* Canada's game."

Evan laughed, "Yes, you are correct. It is an Earth game."

When they reached the apartment, Miranda was far too excited to go to bed but Evan suggested it might be a good idea that she be well rested for the audition tomorrow and she finally conceded, going to her room. It took her ages to fall asleep. Her mind full of excitement at her audition and her new friends and when she finally did, she fell into her nightmares again.

*Miranda awoke in her bed. When she went out to the kitchen she noticed a note from her brother telling her to meet him at the studio.*

*Miranda was angry he was making her go by herself, considering she didn't know the way.*

*When Miranda finished getting ready she took the bus to the studio.*

*'That was easy' she thought to herself as she reached her destination.*

*Venturing through the building, she found a large empty newsroom with video cameras and equipment all around. Curious, she stepped inside and the door shut behind her.*

*She stepped onto the set and sat behind the desk, looking around. She was so glad her brother got her into the television industry. This was so cool.*

*Suddenly, all the remaining lights shut off and Miranda was in darkness.*

*She started to get nervous and got up.*

*As she did, the door opened and a group of people walked into the room. They all carried large brown books and wore what looked like make-up, painted in a weird character over their eyebrows and on their hands.*

*Miranda tried to run but she was frozen to the ground. She screamed as they neared her but then she felt strong arms wrap around her waist. The whole building shook and a brilliant white light appeared with no source. The people who were coming after her screamed this time.*

Miranda awoke. *That was a weird dream*, she thought. It was still early, but she decided to get up to get ready, butterflies dancing in her belly. She showered and then spent an hour trying to decide on an outfit, ignoring Alpha's suggestions. Finally she chose black pants with white pinstripe stitching down the length and a black short-sleeved sweater that was off the shoulder.

She put on a touch of makeup by herself to calm her nerves and the perfume her dad had bought for her before joining her brothers at breakfast.

"Dad had to leave for work early so he said 'good luck'" Evan told her as she sat down.

"Ok," Miranda said staring at her breakfast. She was really nervous now.

"Do not worry Miranda, you will be great," Evan said, rising from his seat to clean his plate, "I have confidence in you and when you walk in there, you have to be confident too." He winked and added, "We like that."

Miranda smiled weakly at him.

"You look beautiful," Griffin added.

"Thanks."

Miranda picked at her food, thinking. Everyone else was more advanced and she just got here. How would her acting skills compare to people who have been here their whole life?

"I would know, Miranda," Evan smiled, coming back into the dining room, "I have dealt with plenty of actors. From what I saw, you were great! Trust me."

Miranda half smiled, "Stop reading my mind."

"It is as easy as if you were talking to us," Griffin reminded her.

"I really should start concentrating on shutting it off," Miranda said, glumly. She didn't want to inflate Alex's head anymore with thoughts of thinking he is cute.

Evan chuckled and Miranda laughed. Griffin smiled and shook his head at her.

After breakfast she followed Evan out to the roof where a bus showed up a few minutes later and they were on their way.

Miranda stared at her notebook, reading the same line over and over again as the bus made its way in the morning traffic to a large oval building made mostly of windows where the pair got off along with about five others who greeted Evan.

Miranda followed Evan to the elevator and they went eight floors down. She kept telling herself that she was good enough in hopes it would boost her confidence till Evan took her hand and gave it a squeeze.

"Miranda, you *are* great!" he said when she looked up at him.

She sent him a small smile.

"Good morning Mr. East," the receptionist smiled brightly at them as they got off the elevator.

"Morning," Evan smiled back, "Everyone ready in there?"

"All the casting crew is ready," she replied, "Jeff is not here yet, though."

"He will be here. I had him doing a few scenes this morning so that he could take the time to come down here," Evan said and turned to Miranda, "You stay here and we will call you in when we are ready."

"Sure," Miranda replied numbly. Her stomach was really fluttering now and her palms got sweaty. She stood there feeling a little silly and a lot nervous. What if she let her brother down? Would people not want to hire her because she was related to the director/creator? Would they think she was favoured because of that? Her stomach sank.

"I assume they are trying out too," Evan said, pointing to a row of nervous looking girls, who appeared to be approximately Miranda's age. He gave Miranda a small push towards them, whispering, "Have confidence in yourself," then turned to the receptionist, "Miranda will be first followed by the order we talked about." She nodded.

Miranda went to sit by the girls who watched her carefully, scoping out the competition. It wasn't long before the secretary, who just got off the phone, told her she could go down the hallway to the last room on the left.

Just as she was getting up, the elevator doors opened and Alex walked out.

Miranda made a face at him, "What're you doing here?" she said as she opened the door and started down the hallway. He followed and she was puzzled.

"Umm…well, there is something you should know Maddie," he said as they walked into the last room together.

"Good Alex, you are here," a woman said from behind the long desk.

There were three people behind the table, Miranda's brother and two women.

"And I see you have met one of our tryouts," the other woman said.

Alex just stared glumly, not looking at Miranda and it finally sunk in. Griffin had told her on Earth that Alex was an actor.

"Alex is our Jeff on the show," Evan told his sister though her face said it all.

She was going to kill her brother for not telling her. *Why hadn't she seen him when she watched it?*

Alex rolled his eyes, "I have been on a work trip on the show. But in real life I had to have some time off to make a pointless trip to Earth," he added, "If you continued to watch, I came back yesterday but obviously you did not." He seemed to send Evan, an 'are you kidding me?' look. Evan shook his head at Alex, sending him an angry glare.

Miranda composed herself, not wanting to let them ruin her audition. If Alex was going to be her co-star, she'd just have to put up with him, somehow. That's why the band knew him and that's why he was always eyed by giggling girls. Miranda knew that they were up to something but never expected they were keeping this from her. Why did they keep it from her? Did Evan think it would have stopped her from trying out?

"Ok," the first woman said, confused and looking to the second woman, "We have obviously missed something."

The other woman nodded at her smiling, "Shall we start?"

"I'm ready," Miranda said, glaring from her brother to Alex. This would be perfect anyways. The scene called for anger and she was feeling a lot of anger right now.

She walked straight up to Alex, pointing a finger at him.

"How could you Jeff?" she screamed at him.

Alex was taken aback, "What?"

"How could you not tell me you had a girlfriend?" she glared at him.

"I know," he said calmly, running a stressed hand through his hair, "I just…"

"This is ridiculous. You are a horrible person," Miranda said a little more calmly, jamming a finger at him, "I want you to leave and I do not want to see you again." She turned to walk away but Alex grabbed her by the arm.

"Please…Please do not say that," he pleaded.

"Do not touch me," she said, yanking her arm from his grip.

Alex pulled his arm back like he'd been stung. He looked so hurt, "Please Cara. I know you like me."

This infuriated Miranda even more, "And I thought you liked me," she said angrily, her eyes filling with tears. *Yes!* she thought in her mind. She'd nailed the crying part right on.

"I do like you," he said, reaching to touch her face. Her and Alex had fought from the moment he kidnapped her. It was so strange to have him looking at her so lovingly.

Miranda leaned into his caress, seeming to enjoying it but inside she was so mad at him. "You should have told me from the start," she sobbed, "How could you? I thought you were such a nice person."

"Please Cara, do not cry. I want to be with you," Alex said sweetly, reaching out for her with his other hand, "Last night was so great. I have not had that much fun in a long time."

Miranda melted into his embrace, into his smile and into his eyes. He was so good, and she hoped she at least looked the part even though she would love to hit him right now. Maybe a good slap like she did in the space shuttle when she thought they were kidnapping her, "What about the girl I saw you with? She was your girlfriend and you were talking about getting married."

"I do not want to anymore. I honestly never did want to marry her. I met you and I realised I should not just settle on someone I feel comfortable with. Someone I have known for so long that everyone just assumed we should marry. You are wild and spontaneous," he said, his hand sliding to her neck, "Not to mention beautiful."

Miranda smiled at him, all of Cara's anger evaporating immediately, "So, you will break it off with her," she asked hopefully, gazing deeply into his eyes. Miranda wondered how he felt about this. He looked so into the scene, it almost seemed real.

"Y-Yes," he stammered, breaking eye contact and releasing her.

Miranda's eyes fired up again, "You are not going to, are you? What kind of person do you think I am?"

"I just said yes. Is that not good enough?"

"Get out of my house!" she screamed, brushing past him towards the left, opening an imaginary door.

"I really do want to be with you, Cara. Just one chance…one more date and we will see what happens," Alex said, not moving.

"Yes, one more date so you can break my heart by staying with your fiancée. I do not wish to put myself through that," Miranda said, motioning with her head for him to leave.

"But…"

Just GO!" Miranda shouted and Alex went through the imaginary door.

Once he was far enough, she closed the invisible door on him and moved back to the centre where she began her soliloquy. She sat on the chair, which would be a couch if it were the real scene and ran her hands through her hair.

Miranda understood this next scene perfectly. Knew exactly how Cara felt, "How could I fall for the first person I met? There are so many males in this city and I fall for the first one I lay my eyes on. Why does everyone do this to me?"

She paused and stood up, wiping at her eyes, "Oh, who am I kidding? I have no luck when it comes to love. I always get caught up with men who are in relationships already. I just have to be strong... and stay away from him." She turned, pulled out her pocket notebook and started fiddling with it, but didn't read it. She looked as if she was trying to concentrate on something, sighed and then quietly added, "How can I stay away? In one night he swept me off my feet and I am so in love... Why am I so pathetic?" Miranda sighed.

Evan started clapping, followed by the two women on either side of him. They all stood up, giving her a standing ovation. She smiled at them, pleased with the way she performed.

Alex was looking at the ground and Miranda wondered whether or not he liked her performance as well. If he did, he certainly wasn't showing it.

"That was excellent Miranda," the second woman said, "And the two of you looked great together!"

"Wow, I actually thought you were torn up and upset! Wonderful job! I know we have others to see today but I would not be worried," the first woman agreed as the three sat down.

"Thankfully you cannot hear what is going on in someone's mind through the television," the second woman laughed, "With you wanting to hit Alex and him singing, our audience would be so confused."

Evan agreed, laughing himself.

Miranda looked at Alex and giggled, "Singing?"

"Better than the violence you seem to enjoy," he snapped, finally looking at her.

Miranda stopped giggling and stuck her tongue out at him.

When the second woman stopped laughing, she pushed a button on the device in front of her and Miranda's device beeped in her pocket, "If you could please open that document," she paused as Miranda withdrew her notebook and opened the document, "As you know, this show is a daytime drama. There may be things we need you to do that you may not have done before. I know you are 16 so, well, maybe you have done some things," she smiled and winked, "Also there may be some heavy kissing scenes and that sort but obviously no sex scenes. We fake those with camera angles and blankets."

Miranda blushed wishing her brother and Alex weren't here.

"You are an adult Miranda. At 16 we are classified as adults on this planet. You can make your own decision," Evan said, showing a bit of embarrassment himself. He wasn't listening to Miranda's thoughts because he was a little worried that maybe she had done things like that before. He had not been there on Earth to protect his little sister from her boyfriends and be a role model for her.

"Yes, I can do it. Not a problem," Miranda said with a hesitant smile.

"Ok, we just need your signature on the bottom of that and you can send it to our receptionist's device in the front. Then just relax in the waiting room while we interview the others just in case we need to bring you in again," the first woman said, and then turned to Evan, "She would be good too since she knows so much about Earth. We may be able to get some ideas." She turned to Miranda smiling, "Which we would pay for."

Miranda thanked them and went back out into the waiting room where she read the document quickly and signed the bottom with the little pen on her device and the receptionist showed her how to send it.

"Congratulations," the secretary smiled at her, "Have a seat and I will let you know if they need you back in there."

Miranda sat down in the burgundy wing-back chairs which were more comfortable than any waiting room chairs on Earth. The receptionist area was small and white on three walls but the fourth was all glass. There was a low coffee table in the centre of the ring of chairs with what looked like metal frames. Hesitantly Miranda picked one up. It was the same kind of material as the picture frames and when it was off, she could stick her hand through it. Once it was on she realized it was a newspaper, she had a choice of articles which she could scroll through and once she decided on one, she tapped it with her finger, which would no longer go through the screen, and it opened. She read about the happy lives of the movie stars on this planet and watched out of the corner of her eyes as the other girls poured over their own notebooks probably reciting their lines. Girl after girl were called into the back room and each came out close to tears.

When the last girl had gone into the back hallway, Miranda let out a little sigh of relief. Only one person left who could compete against her.

But 15 minutes later, that girl came out close to tears as well. As she went to pick up her jacket, she smiled at Miranda, "Congratulations I guess," she smiled through her tears.

"Thank you," Miranda returned with a smile, but then frowned and added, "I am sorry you did not get picked."

"Oh, that is alright," she said, drying her tears, "I am just glad I made it this far. Perhaps next time I will get the part. I am still studying in school anyways."

"Definitely," Miranda encouraged.

"I wish you all the best. See you on television soon." She went to the elevator and was gone.

Miranda stood up, too excited to sit anymore, "Were there a lot of auditions before this?" she asked the receptionist.

"There was one mass audition where everyone was to send in a video of them reciting lines from a scene. Just a preliminary screening," she replied. The phone beeped and the secretary picked it up. "You can go back in now," the secretary said, smiling at Miranda as she hung up the phone.

Miranda thanked the receptionist and then headed towards the back room.

They were all standing and stretching when she walked in. Evan came over to her and picked her up, spinning her around as he did when they first met.

"You did wonderfully," he smiled, "We will be talking about it this afternoon and will make the official decision on Monday."

"Evan, seriously?" Miranda looked shocked. She thought for sure by the other girl's reaction that she had got the part.

He gave her a mischievous smile, "Official announcement on Monday. You should receive a call from my secretary tomorrow to invite you into the office." He winked.

Miranda groaned, "You can't just tell me at home?"

"Miranda, we have to make it official. Just because you are my sister," he looked to the other woman, winked and looked back to Miranda, "No special treatment."

The woman laughed, "Oh Evan, do not tease her. Of course you…"

Evan cut her off with a loud clearing of his throat, "Official announcement Monday. That was the agreement."

The other woman laughed, "Ok Evan." She turned to Miranda, "I am Sandy Markham and this is Patricia Donolley. We help Evan with the writing of the show. The co-director, Melissa Steer, wanted to be here as well but she is handling the scenes upstairs right now. You will meet her Monday." She winked.

Evan laughed.

Miranda looked at him quizzically, still waiting for him to cave and say she got the part but it appeared he couldn't be swayed.

"Alex will take you home," Evan said instead, "He is finished filming and I have to get upstairs. I will see you at home."

"Evan, come on," Miranda laughed nervously as she followed him out and down the hallway.

"No official announcement till Monday," he repeated.

Miranda looked back and saw that Alex had followed but the ladies were still in the room. She knew Alex would never tell her.

She tracked her brother to the elevator as the doors opened and they all got on.

She watched Evan the whole way up to the parking garage but he refused to look at her. She knew she must have the part by the way Sandy and Patricia had acted but she still wanted her brother to say it. He *could* still change his mind.

"So, I will have my secretary call you in the morning," Evan smiled and motioned them to get off the elevator. They had reached the top of the building where the bus would pick her and Alex up.

"Fine. Be that way," Miranda laughed and stepped out. She turned, "I look forward to her call."

Alex trudged along behind her and Miranda wished she knew what he was thinking. He didn't seem too happy the way he was moping behind her.

They sat in silence the whole bus ride home while Miranda gazed out the window daydreaming. She must have the part but what if she didn't. Maybe they did things differently on this planet? What if she was reading too much into it? What if she actually didn't have the part?

Alex tsked loudly and rolled his eyes at her.

"What?" she snapped.

"Unfortunately, you did really well," he said, though it didn't sound like much of a compliment, "Your brother just has to make it official. He might receive some poor comments because you are his sister. Some may say it is favouritism."

Miranda's eyes sparkled with tears. The last thing she wanted was for people to think she only got on the show because of her brother.

Alex groaned, "Do not cry! Once people see you on television, they will know he made the right choice."

Miranda drew in a breath and forced the tears away. He sounded sincere. Could she have really gotten the part? She didn't want to get excited until she heard the words on Monday.

"You really are impossible," Alex sighed and rolled his eyes. He turned his attention back out the window.

When the bus stopped at the apartment as Alex had directed, they got off together however Alex pushed 'P' and 'six' on the elevator.

"Where are you going?" Miranda asked, as the doors opened to the parking garage and lobby.

"I have things to do," Alex said and left it at that, "You are a big girl, Maddie. Surely you do not want me around."

She almost stuck her hand out to stop the doors before they closed, but they did and she was alone again. Back in her bedroom, she took a few books from the stack Alex had given her and went to the lounge chairs outside to educate herself.

The books really were a big help. She spent the afternoon learning the Utopian clock, the Utopian holidays and calendar, food, populations, culture and currency. She quickly flipped through basic mathematics, counting and the alphabet since she was sure she knew everything anyways but wanted to check to see if there were any differences.

When she was tired of reading she dove into the pool, did a few laps and headed upstairs where she found her brothers in the living room watching television and proceeded to annoy Evan to the brink of his sanity to tell her if she had gotten the part. He was good. He never caved and went stomping to his room to listen to music so she wouldn't bother him anymore.

# Ten

★ ★ ★ ★

The group Miranda met yesterday were waiting outside the theatre, along with Alicia, who practically jumped on her when the doors opened that night.

"Did you get it?" she exclaimed.

Miranda couldn't contain her smile, "I find out Monday but it looks good!"

Alicia squealed and she pulled Miranda away to ask her about the audition. Miranda asked her what she thought about her getting the part. Only another girl would understand her fears.

"Oh it sure sounds like you got the part!" Alicia encouraged.

"Already a celebrity being whisked off by fans," Evan commented quietly to Alex, who laughed.

They all moved into the theatre, Alicia sat on Miranda's right and to her surprise, Nathan moved in quickly to sit on her left. She sat back as the movie started, taking quick glances at Nathan. He was quite cute and seemed really friendly. He was very tall, taller than most of the group and his eyes were so dark they were almost black.

As Miranda turned her attention to the movie, she fantasized about being on the big screen in one of the movies. She was halfway there practically, if she got the part. Television may even be better. In movies, it's a one-time deal but the show would be aired daily.

* * *

Miranda was exhausted when the movie was finished and politely declined Nathan's invite to the bar with Jane and Dave.

"I'm sorry," Miranda yawned, "It would be fun to see since I've never been to a club but I am so tired."

"Next time then?" Nathan asked hopefully.

Miranda smiled and nodded, wondering if he was asking her as a date as she got into the elevator with Alicia, Alex and Evan, who had also refused the night out.

"See you early Monday for school!" Alicia said excitedly to Miranda as her, Alex and Evan got off the elevator.

"Oh I'm so nervous," Miranda admitted, holding the elevator as the boys went ahead.

"Do not worry at all. I will be there to show you around!" Alicia said, smiling, "You will have a great time and meet lots of people."

"Thanks," Miranda tried to smile, "What time does the bus come at?"

"Nine," Alicia said, "I will see you then."

Miranda allowed the door to close and went to bed.

She bolted upright the next morning after another horrible dream and almost completely gruesome death. She was tired of the dreams. They felt so real and were so terrifying. She took several deep breaths reminding herself it was only a dream. She climbed out of bed and went to the window. It was another beautiful day outside but big, puffy clouds moved quickly across the sky, blocking out both suns as they went. Miranda assumed everyone would be at work and sighed, bored already. She had breakfast and read through Alex's stack of books again so that she could commit some of the finer details to memory, and then she went down to the exercise room, watching the clock so she would get upstairs on time to watch her brothers show. She was worried it wasn't on because it was Saturday but found it on the same channel as before. She watched the opening credits and frowned when Alex came onto the screen. *Well, this proves it now*, Miranda thought and scolded herself for not watching the show any other day. Her frown deepened every time she saw Alex on the television. He was so good. Could she even possibly compare? She didn't want him to get angry with her anymore and this would put a strain on their already mediocre friendship if she didn't do well. Would she also embarrass her brother? Maybe she wasn't good enough.

When the episode ended, she went to her bedroom and picked up her Earth phone. It gave a warning sound when it turned on indicating the battery was low and her eyes filled with tears. She needed Helen or her parents to reassure her that everything would be ok.

When Griffin came home, she asked him why Saturday wasn't a day off. Were there no weekends on Utopia?

"Everyone has Sundays off and that is all," Griffin explained, "Do you really need more?" He smiled.

"I suppose not," Miranda said, thoughtfully.

"Work is much more relaxed than I have seen on Earth though," Griffin went on, "Whenever you need a day off, you just take one."

"Oh?"

"We do not need to ask permission," Griffin went on, "We are our own bosses and work as a group. It is polite to inform the others that you will not be there if it is important but we do not usually have deadlines." Griffin chuckled, "Well, except for Evan. He has to produce a show in just a few days to go on the air. Actors are paid pretty well for the added stress of deadlines."

Miranda forced a smile, "Sounds great."

Miranda was in her room when Evan knocked.

"You ready?" he asked after she called for him to 'come in'. Miranda was sitting on her bed, her legs stretched out in front of her, with a book in her lap. She hadn't been reading from it but daydreaming about Earth.

"For?"

"We are going to the race track tonight," Evan gave her a quizzical look, "Griffin did not tell you?"

"Oh, I forgot!" Griffin called from his bedroom.

"Race track?" Miranda asked as she sat up straighter. That sounded exciting.

Evan smiled, "Almost every Saturday night we go to see the cars race."

Miranda's eyes lit up, "Cool! They race?"

"Yes, there is a track through the mountains," Evan explained, "There are about 25 cars and they go around the track about 500 laps. It starts in one hour so we better head out soon."

"What should I wear?" Miranda asked, looking down at her clothes and then at Evan's. He was wearing a shirt with the number 8 on it. It was dark blue with two black and white racing stripes down the side. The name, in script, across the top of the '8' was Allan Westin.

"Just put anything on and we will get you a shirt like this when we get there," Evan smiled, pointing to his shirt. Griffin came into the room, wearing a similar shirt with the same driver on it.

"Ready?" he asked.

"Shall we go?" their dad called from the hallway.

Miranda followed her brothers out and saw that her dad also supported the same driver.

"So, is this guy any good?" Miranda laughed, motioning to the driver name on their shirts.

"He is ok," Griffin laughed, leading the way out the door and pushing the button to the elevator.

"What, you mean *Alex* isn't coming with us," Miranda inquired as they waited. He always seemed to go wherever they were.

They all laughed.

"He will meet us there," Evan said.

Miranda groaned. For a minute she hoped she would spend the night with just her family.

Her dad put his arm around her, "It *is* family night."

Miranda was happy to be getting out of the house after her depressing day. They drove towards the mountains. As they got closer, Miranda could see it all lit up. A large track twisted and turned through the mountain passes, with flying lights that marked the route. They parked on the grass where everyone else had parked their cars and then started towards the entrance with a number of people. Mr. East paid for them all by sliding his card through one of the many terminals lined up in a row. Miranda noticed most everyone was headed towards the centre of the track where a large group was already gathered. It seemed a little dangerous to Miranda, as she watched her dad and brothers follow and once they found an open space they scattered the blankets they had brought on the ground. What if there was an accident? What about flying car parts? There was no protection at all.

"Have a seat," her dad patted the spot beside him.

She gave him a confused look and sat.

All of them laughed. "Nothing could harm us," Griffin explained, "Just watch. There are accidents but the cars just do not fall apart. They are built to keep the driver safe and those on the ground. Our vehicles are very intelligent."

Evan smiled, "I almost forgot. Would you like a shirt?"

"Perhaps after," Miranda laughed, "Maybe I won't like this Allan Westin guy."

Evan and Griffin both cracked up again. Her father chuckled.

"It's Alex isn't it?" Miranda said, rolling her eyes, "You should tell him next time he wants a disguise name, he should try something that doesn't even remotely look like his."

"Yes, we tried to tell him," Evan said laughing, "But he would like a tiny bit of privacy which is why he does not use his real name. He thinks if everyone knew he was racing, the fields would be flooded with fans of the show."

"Wow," Miranda shook her head, "He really does have an abnormally big head."

"But unfortunately he is correct," Griffin explained, "Alex is really popular, especially amongst the women. He never announces where he is going, he goes in and out of places quickly before he is noticed and almost never gives his real name."

Miranda frowned, "You do not think that will happen to me, do you? Why don't you have that problem?" She turned to Evan.

"I am rarely seen on television," Evan said, "And if you are a star like I think you are going to be on the show, then yes, you may have that problem."

"So I guess that means I did get the part?" Miranda smiled a huge grin.

Evan gasped, "You tricked me," he laughed and sighed, "Of course you did."

Miranda threw her arms around her brother's neck and squealed, "Yay!"

"Remember now," Mr. East said, "School comes first."

Miranda smiled and nodded, "So who is the second best driver?"

They all thought about it for a second and all answered differently. Her dad said Arnie Winter, number 26, Evan said George Dives, number 2, and Griffin said Mike Power, number 9 and then they all started arguing for their driver.

"Oh nevermind," Miranda sighed, "Can I borrow someone's card?"

Griffin handed his over, "Would you like me to come with you?"

"No, I can find it," Miranda said, "Just point the way." She was used to being an only child and didn't mind going alone.

Miranda followed Griffin's directions to the place where they sold the shirts and stood there for a long time reading each one and trying to decide if she liked it. Perhaps she should have waited until after the race.

An announcer said the race would begin in ten minutes and Miranda could hear the crowd roar.

"Can I help you?" a man asked from behind her.

Miranda laughed and turned. He looked to be her age and was only a couple inches taller. He had a handsome face with bright green eyes and black hair and Miranda blushed slightly.

"I am just trying to decide on a driver," she smiled, returning her eyes to the displays of shirts, "This is my first time here."

He looked thoughtful for a minute and didn't question why she had never been there before. His face turned into a smile, "I am sorry. I have a favourite driver so I cannot really give you an unbiased answer."

Miranda laughed, "Well, who is yours? I am open to biased opinions."

"My older sister," he blushed and pulled out a shirt from the rack, "Danielle Fletcher. I am Ben, by the way." He held out his hand and Miranda took it, and then he passed her the shirt for her to look at.

"Miranda," she replied and looked at the shirt. It was pretty and it was dark purple, her favourite colour, with black sleeves. It had a number '11' on it and the 'i' was dotted with a flower, "Are there a lot of female racers? How does she do?"

"Well, she has not won since last year," Ben laughed, "And there are eight females in the pack of twenty-five I believe?"

"Well, I think you have convinced me," she smiled, "I will get this one."

She followed him to the machine to pay with Griffin's card.

"You have a very pretty smile," Ben said as he swiped the card.

Miranda smiled again and blushed, "Thank you."

"So what brings you to the races tonight?" he asked and handed her back her card.

"I am here with my family. They are here all the time," Miranda explained as she tucked the card back into her pocket.

"And you never wanted to come with them?"

"Well," Miranda thought quickly. Perhaps now was the time to try out what her and Alicia had said could be her explanation. "I travelled with our mother. She is an Earth expert."

"That sounds like fun," Ben smiled, "Are you going to follow in her footsteps?"

Miranda laughed and continued, not thinking of anything else so that he wouldn't catch her lie, "No, I suppose that was only my mother's dream. I am acting now."

"Anything I know?" Ben asked.

"I am not supposed to tell anyone yet," Miranda held a finger to her lips, "I start in about a month's time on a very good show."

"Congratulations," Ben said, sincerely, "You must be very excited."

She nodded in reply.

"I will look for you on television then," he winked.

"What do you do?" Miranda asked, leaning on the counter and flashing her biggest smile, "Besides sell shirts on race night."

"I teach 8 year old students."

"That is exciting! What is your favourite part of it?"

"Well, I like gym class, of course. The ability to combine physical and mental capacities has always been my favourite subject. And, of course, I love my students. I have a great class this year." Miranda admired his physique. It was obvious from the curves of his forearms that he spent a lot of time with sports.

"What is your favourite sport?" she asked.

"Amanuins," he said, as if it should be an obvious choice.

She was spared her confusion by the announcement that the race was to begin.

"I am sorry," she said, "I should go back. My family must be wondering where I am."

"Will you be back soon?" he asked.

"Yes. I think so," she smiled and waved goodbye.


She met Griffin halfway back to her seat. He smiled when he saw her, "There you are. We were wondering what took you so long."

"Sorry, I could not decide which to pick," she said as she pulled the shirt on overtop the one she had on.

"Danielle Fletcher?" Griffin laughed.

"What?"

"She is not one of the better drivers. Why did you pick that one?"

Miranda thought about Ben.

"Oh. Now I understand," Griffin winked and then started back towards their seats, then turned and called over his shoulder, "We should not let you out of our sight. You attract too many men."

Miranda laughed, "'Cause it is purple!" She said quickly and followed a few steps behind.

"Sure," Griffin laughed. Before they reached the rest of the family they stopped to buy some drinks for everyone but he was still laughing when they reached Evan and their dad and told them how a boy had made her decision.

Evan laughed too but Mr. East looked stunned.

"We are going to have to watch out for you," Evan said to Miranda as she sat.

"It's *purple*," Miranda stressed, pointing to her shirt, "You know I like this colour."

"No dad, she does not need to talk about that," Griffin said to their dad.

He looked concerned.

Miranda blushed and rolled her eyes, "Not that conversation again."

"He has never had a daughter before," Griffin smiled and patted their dad on the back, "Give him time."

Mr. East looked resigned but his attentions were shifted as there was a rumble of engines and the cars began to move out onto the track.

Everyone around seemed to lie back at the same time. Miranda looked around stunned and then laid back so fast she banged her head on the ground. "Ouch," she massaged it gently as Evan chuckled beside her.

A pace car led the pack around the circuit. Evan explained, pointing up in the air, that the first car led them around the track once and then it would dip off and the race would begin. The underside of the cars were coloured the same as the rest of the car and was moulded to its contents though it looked fairly flat. Each had their numbers emblazoned on the underside with the name of the driver. Miranda found number 8 and then number 11. Alex was two rows back from Danielle.

Once the first car dropped off, the race was on. Miranda thought it was exhilarating. The cars moved so fast around the track that they had already completed 25 laps in 10 minutes!

There were two larger accidents which slowed the race. Alex was involved in the second of them which happened near where they were seated. Miranda bolted up to a sitting position, worried about him, but like Griffin said, there were no flying car parts and the car slowly descended vertically to the ground.

Miranda watched to make sure he got out safely. He seemed fine and even looked over to her. He was wearing his usual baseball cap, so Miranda wasn't sure if he was actually looking at her but then he waved. She smiled in relief and waved back before she lay back down and Griffin passed her a drink.

"What are these anyways?" she asked, opening the bottle.

"Since we get all the nutrients we need from our meals, it is basically flavoured water," he explained, and then mumbled, "Mixed in with a little alcohol."

Miranda almost spit out the sip she had just taken. She swallowed hard, and coughed a bit, "I'm sorry, did you say alcohol?"

Griffin smiled at Evan and turned back to Miranda, "Yes."

"Seriously?" she asked, looking between the two of them.

"Yes," Griffin said again.

"You guys have alcohol?"

"It is not the same as Earth's alcohol," Mr. East said, "Earth's alcohol is harmful to your body. This is not. It will give you more energy and make you forget your worries like Earth's does but it does no harm at all; However, like Earth, you drink too many and you may make silly decisions and you definitely should not drive."

"Is there any non-alcoholic drinks? I have just been drinking the water from the tap when I am thirsty," Miranda asked.

"Yes," Evan said, "It is the same flavoured water with no alcohol but there are different bottles for the non-alcoholic beverages. The non-alcohol bottles are straight. You see how yours is curved?"

"Why are they so similar?" she asked looking at the curve of her bottle.

"It just makes it easier to recycle," Griffin said.

"So what is the legal drinking age here? In Canada, I wasn't allowed to drink yet. I had to be 19."

"It is 16 here," Mr. East said, "As soon as school is finished when you are classified as an adult."

"Have you ever had a drink before?" Evan asked.

"Yes, a couple times but never excessively. I had a glass of wine with Christmas dinner before," Miranda explained. She thought back to a Helen's birthday party this past year. She knew some of her friends got pretty drunk that night but she had only one drink, just to try. Helen actually threw up in the bushes behind her house.

Mr. East smiled proudly, "I am so glad to hear you are so responsible."

It was an exciting race to the finish. Griffin's second favourite, Max Power won the race. Danielle came third and Miranda was happy that she had chosen a good driver.

"Come on, let's go see Alex," Evan said after the award for first was handed out.

They walked towards the driver's area which was separated with a temporary fence. Evan gave their name to the woman who was standing there who checked their names on her device and let them pass. They found Alex, who was talking to the winner of the race, Max.

"Hi everyone," Max said, smiling.

Miranda looked to her family who returned the driver's greeting like they had known him forever.

"Great race Max," Griffin said.

"Thanks," he replied and noticed Miranda, "So this is your sister?"

"Yes, this is Miranda," Mr. East said, putting and arm around his daughter, smiling. "Max has worked with me and Griffin at the space centre for years," he explained to Miranda, "He was not at work the day we brought you to visit."

Max shook her hand, "Yes, I was pretty sad to have missed meeting you."

"Good race," Miranda smiled.

"Thank you. I hope you enjoyed it," Max replied.

"I cannot *believe* you picked that shirt! Danielle Fletcher? Really?" Alex exclaimed, when he finally noticed her shirt, "She cut me off in that accident. I could have pulled away from it."

"I guess she is just the better driver," Miranda smirked.

Someone laughed behind her, "I like her Alex," she said.

Miranda turned and a pretty woman with long straight black hair and big brown eyes stood behind her. She was tall and slim and wore a dark purple racing suit with number '11' on the front. She looked a lot like a female version of her brother, Ben.

"I am so sorry Alex," she continued, "It was the only spot open to me."

"I forgive you," Alex rolled his eyes playfully and smiled. Danielle went to his side and kissed his cheek before he continued, "Congratulations on the third place finish."

Danielle smiled at him longingly, "Thank you."

"You have met the rest of the family but this is Miranda, Evan and Griffin's sister," Alex said, motioning with his hand. Danielle turned and smiled.

"Nice shirt," she said, shaking Miranda's hand.

Miranda laughed, "Your brother sold me on it."

Danielle laughed too, "He is my biggest fan." She turned to Alex, "We are going out for a post-race celebration at Ernie's. Are you coming?"

"Sure," Alex smiled at her.

Miranda could definitely sense there was something going on between the two of them. She looked away, uncomfortable.

"Everyone is welcome, of course," she turned to everyone else, including the Easts.

Griffin looked like he was about to say no but Miranda gave him a pleading look. She really wanted to see Ernie's, whatever that was. She had declined going to the bar last night because she was tired but she was really curious to see everything on Utopia, even a bar.

"For a bit perhaps," Mr. East said, "We have an early morning."

"Excellent. We will meet you there," Danielle smiled and took Alex's hand, addressing only him, "Will you ride with me?"

Alex nodded and he headed off with Danielle hand in hand.

Miranda watched them walk away, shaking her head. She had no idea what everyone saw in him. "So, what is Ernie's?" she asked her father.

"It is called Ernie's Final Lap. It is just a bar that Ernie Landshaw opened after he stopped racing. Everyone who races will usually go there after the race," he explained. He motioned to Evan and Griffin, who were still discussing the race with Max, "Shall we go? Will we see you there Max?"

"I will be there," Max smiled, "I have to celebrate my victory." He looked over to his award which was on top of his car. It was made out of the same clear 'glass' substance and was shaped like a car. On the way to the bar, her family explained to her that one was given out after each race.

Miranda was excited to see her first Utopian bar, in fact her first bar ever, which turned out to be not far from the race track. Ernie's racing car was on display on the wall of the building and it was lit up with a neon red sign and lights.

Inside, they joined Alex, who was sitting at a table with Danielle, and ordered a round of drinks. Miranda looked around, curiously. The bar looked like the ones she had seen on Earth television. It was dimly lit by lights that seemed to float in mid-air and was decorated with a racing theme with pictures of racers and cars adorning the walls in the Utopian digital image. Some of the images were even moving, showing race wins. Apparently the frames were capable of video as well. The floor was a checkered flag and Miranda wondered if Utopia had provided that idea to Earth or if Utopia had taken the idea by studying Earth.

"So, you have three children?" Danielle asked Mr. East and then turned to Miranda, "I have never seen you around the track before."

"Well, Evan and I are twins," Miranda blurted out, "And I spent a lot of time with our mother travelling. She studied Earth."

Mr. East almost choked on the sip of his drink he took but Evan caught on quickly, "Yes, she would be gone for months at a time."

Danielle smiled excitedly, "Oh that sounds like a lot of fun. Did you enjoy it?"

Miranda nodded, "Yes, we had a lot of great times together but I will not miss the smell of Earth, ugh!" Miranda wrinkled her nose and looked pointedly at Alex, "You get used to the smell but when you first step out, it is kind of disgusting." She laughed and Evan and Griffin joined in. Mr. East was still in stunned silence.

Danielle asked Miranda a lot about Earth but never once did she question if Miranda had grown up there so Miranda thought she may have pulled it off. Danielle admitted she had wanted to be a space traveller but chose to be a teacher instead. Her brother had followed in her footsteps.

"Where is the washroom?" Miranda whispered to Griffin as she stood.

"Just towards the back on the right," he replied, pointing.

Miranda started to walk away and Alex rose as well.

"This I have to see," he said when Miranda was out of earshot, smirking.

Griffin started to protest but Evan laughed.

Alex caught up to Miranda just as she had reached the door with plaque that declared it the 'Washroom'. Miranda peeked inside and gave him a puzzled look.

"Where is the girl's bathroom?" she asked.

"What do you mean?" Alex replied, as innocently as he could muster.

Miranda went inside and Alex followed. She spun to face him, "Are you serious?"

Alex smirked, "What is wrong?"

Miranda sighed and went into a stall. Luckily, the walls and door went all the way to the ground. She stepped into the bathroom and put her hand where she thought the door closing button would be but it didn't closed.

"There is no need to separate males and females. It is unnecessary," Alex smiled, watching her struggle.

Miranda felt around, growing more frustrated until finally she got the right spot and it slid shut.

"So I am fine," Alex said.

"What is that supposed to mean?" Miranda snapped as she stood there. She didn't want to use the washroom with him there.

"You looked worried about me after I crashed," Alex replied with a smile.

Miranda blushed, even though he couldn't see it. "Please do not talk to me right now," Miranda said from behind the door, "You are distracting me."

There were a few moments of silence.

"Don't you have to use the bathroom?" Miranda snapped.

"No," Alex chuckled, "I just came to wash my hands."

Miranda sighed, "So wash them."

Alex laughed again and put his hands under the faucet which was on a motion sensor. He kept it on long enough and pulled his hands away when he thought she was done.

"So thanks for making my first public bathroom experience completely awkward," Miranda laughed awkwardly from the stall.

Alex chuckled but stopped short as someone else entered the bathroom.

"There you are Alex," Miranda heard Danielle say. She paused with her hand just inches from the door opener.

"Oh," Alex replied, "Did you need something?"

Danielle crossed the bathroom and threw her arms around Alex's neck, kissing him deeply.

He pulled away but she kept him close with her arms around his neck, "I told you Danielle, I am sorry."

"It is not fair, Alex. A few dates and you will not even give it a try."

"I just do not feel the same way."

"I know Alex but I thought we could just enjoy the *pleasure* of each other's company," she stressed, pressing her lips to his neck.

He gently pushed her away, "No thank you."

She pushed out her bottom lip, pouting.

"I think you are a beautiful woman," Alex said gently, "So do not think like that. I just do not feel that way about you."

"It was worth a try," Danielle said sadly and turned to leave, "I will see you next time at the track."

Miranda exited the stall when Danielle had left. She sent Alex a puzzled look as she passed him to wash her hands.

"Go ahead and say it. I know what you are thinking," Alex snapped, glaring at her reflection in the mirror.

"Obviously you do not," Miranda snapped back, "In fact, I was wondering if casual sex is something that happens a lot on this planet. Is it a normal thing?"

Alex opened his mouth to retort but stopped, stunned. He was not expecting that question. He cleared his throat, "Yes. It is normal but everyone has their own opinions. We have learned long ago that sex is for pleasure as well as to procreate. It is natural and we are educated at a young age. Some wait and some do not. It is respectful to honour someone's choice."

Miranda's bit her lip as she dried her hands under the warm air. It wasn't a conversation she wanted to have with Alex but she was glad to learn this now, "What about waiting for love? Wouldn't it hurt feelings? That just doesn't seem to be an ideal that Utopia would support."

"There is nothing wrong with waiting for love or just using it for pleasure," Alex replied, "You will learn more about philosophy in school."

"What about sexually transmitted diseases or teen pregnancy?" she asked, in shock. So many questions and fears filled her mind. She turned to look at him, a thousand questions in her eyes.

"You know we do not have diseases like Earth," Alex said, "And if you did not notice, your cycles did not start until you were around sixteen, right?"

"I think I was fourteen or fifteen," Miranda said with a blush.

"It might have been Earth that changed your cycle," Alex assumed, with a shrug. He didn't seem as embarrassed to be talking about this as Miranda was. "Your cycle is very easy to track. It is on a perfect 35 day schedule and you will ovulate on day 17. Obviously you will avoid having sex on that day. If you do have a child then it is your own fault for not keeping track."

"And if you don't love that person?"

"Love everyone Miranda," Alex said, "And respect everyone. *That* is what Utopia supports."

Miranda looked down. She didn't understand. She felt so inexperienced. What would men expect from her? She wasn't ready for anything like that.

"I do not know Miranda," Alex shrugged, "I have not heard of any unwanted children since everyone is mindful of their cycles. And if you want to wait, no one will pressure you." He reached out to try and comfort her but felt awkward so he just patted her shoulder lightly.

"Oh," Miranda said, feeling the heat of his hand as it came to rest on her shoulder, "Are you waiting?"

Alex made a face and pulled his hand back, "That is none of your business but yes. I have not met anyone I would like to share that with."

Miranda gave him a questioning look. It was hard to believe considering how cute he was and her dad did say he was what, twenty? That and there were all those women who were throwing themselves at him.

Alex's mouth formed a hard line and he was about to retort to her last thought when Evan walked in.

"What are you two doing?" he asked, stopping abruptly when he saw them, "Everyone is wondering what is taking so long."

They both stuttered and went red.

Evan laughed, "Well, I suppose someone should have that discussion with her."

Miranda made a look like she was in pain. She really wanted to learn how to shut her mind down so no one could read her thoughts. How embarrassing that she had to be caught talking about sex with Alex.

"I think we are ready to head home," Evan continued, "We have to wake early tomorrow."

Miranda followed him out the door, casting an embarrassed smile at Alex following behind her, before asking her brother, "What are you doing tomorrow?"

"*We* are going hiking," Evan said, "With dad."

"Oh! Excellent," she smiled and turned to Alex, "Are you coming?"

"Normally I would but I have things to do," Alex grumbled in reply.

"Griffin isn't coming?" Miranda asked, turning back to Evan. She was surprised Alex wasn't going with them. He seemed to go everywhere with the family.

"Griffin is staying home with Greta. She is coming home tomorrow," Evan replied.

"Who's Greta?" Miranda asked, as they reached the table.

"My girlfriend," Griffin answered first.

"Really? Why didn't you tell me you had a girlfriend?" Miranda asked, excited, as Griffin and her father stood to leave, "Where have you been hiding her?"

"She was visiting her relatives these past few days. They live about two hours away in City 1428."

"City 1428?"

"Yes, something else you will learn in school. We are all divided into different sections on this planet. Kind of like cities on your planet but all our cities are numbered and are about the same size with approximately the same people per square kilometre. It helps keep the balance," her father explained as he led the way out, waving goodbye to some of the others he knew there.

Miranda recalled her identification. She was in City 217, "I did read about populations in those books Alex gave me. I did not know our cities were numbered." She turned to Griffin, "What's Greta like? Where did you two meet?"

"She is amazing," Griffin smiled, "We met at work."

"How long have you been together?" she continued, turning to walk backwards so she was facing her brother, "Where does she live?"

"Three years," Griffin replied, "She actually lives with us in my room." He smiled sheepishly, "You will meet her tomorrow after your hike. I would like one day alone with her. I have not seen her in over a week."

"And here I thought you guys were alone here, all boys with no girls to take care of you," Miranda sulked as she climbed in the backseat.

They all laughed.

"If it helps," Evan said, putting his arm around her, "I do not have a girlfriend anymore. We just broke up last month."

Miranda glared at him too. *Come on guys, I'm your sister! You have to let me in on these things!*

"Sorry Miranda," Griffin said, "We just wanted you to get used to your family before we started introducing in more people."

"I forgive you, I suppose."

# Eleven

★　★　★　★

*Miranda woke up to a strange woman in the kitchen whom she thought must be Greta. The woman's back was to her and when Miranda was close enough, she turned. Miranda froze. The woman had a knife in her hand and she took a wild slash at Miranda. Miranda jumped back, but wasn't fast enough. The knife cut into her forearm and she ran.*

*The woman chased Miranda around the apartment until she was cornered in her father's room. The woman advanced on her brandishing the knife, a wild look in her eyes. Miranda was stuck. She thought of fighting her but the long, sharp blade frightened her. The woman got close enough that Miranda felt the tip of the blade press lightly on her chest, over her heart. Miranda's eyes streamed with tears and she caught the picture of her family in the corner of her eye. How could they leave her alone with this psychopath? She would be joining her mother soon. The ground shook violently and she clung to the wall for support.*

*But the door banged open and her rescuer was there. He took the woman down and drove the knife into her.*

Miranda awoke with a start and shivered a little at the gory end of her dream. Even though he had come to her rescue, it was still scary to see him stab someone like that. There was more light than usual in her dream. Usually it was plunged in darkness but she still couldn't see his face. It was strange. She saw the woman's face clearly. Why couldn't she see her rescuer?

Miranda looked down at her arm where the knife had pierced her skin. It tingled slightly and looked red. She rubbed at it, thinking she must be imagining it, but the pain didn't subside for several minutes.

Miranda was the first one awake that day. She decided to wait till after the hike to shower and changed into a comfortable pair of shorts and a tank top. She looked down at her arm again. The redness had gone down and she couldn't feel any pain. Her brain must have produced the pain.

Miranda managed to put enough liquid on the plate to make two eggs, toast and three strips of bacon, the first perfect meal she made on Utopia. She smiled as she sat down to eat.

Her dad joined her in the dining room when she was halfway finished her breakfast with a plate of his own.

"Well, look at that. You did it," he smiled at her half empty plate.

"Yes!" Miranda smiled, proudly. So the eggs had been a little big and the bacon somewhat on the small side, at least she had done it, "So where are we going today?"

"I was just thinking through the mountain path," Mr. East smiled, taking a bite of his egg sandwich, "We will start with something close by. It has a very nice view of the outer land."

"What is out there?" Miranda asked.

Mr. East chuckled, "Not a whole lot, mostly vegetation. There are animals but it is nothing like the other side of the planet. Though there are some predators that lurk out there, most are afraid of humans."

"Are they in the city as well? I don't remember seeing any birds or anything like that around," she asked.

"They are not allowed in the city. There are invisible fences that they cannot cross. I am sorry to say the birds went extinct long ago. Without the insects, it started a horrible chain reaction of extinctions."

"No insects? That's incredible!" Miranda's mouth dropped in shock. She didn't remember reading about that but then again, she hadn't come across any birds in that book she had been reading.

"Unfortunately, earlier humans a billion years ago wiped out the entire insect kingdom. Our biologists have been hoping they would arise again on the other side of the planet but so far only insects that do not fly have recovered."

"I know bugs are important to the whole food chain but wow!" Miranda said, thinking of how annoying mosquitos and blackflies could be when she had gone camping with her Earth parents.

"Bugs?" her dad chuckled.

Miranda smiled and shrugged, "Yes. They bug you, so we call them bugs I guess." She laughed.

An hour later, she headed out with Evan and her father to hike in the mountains. She asked them about everything she saw, the trees and the flowers, as they took a path along the opposite slope of the mountain than the one facing the city. Miranda saw trees as far as her eyes could see. Her father told her that the next city was about half hour away by car. They even showed her the invisible fence surrounding the city. It was only ten feet high and was lined with trees that were tightly packed together. It would probably be easy to accidentally walk into it but the trees did help. She put her hand on it just to prove to herself it was there. At first, she hesitated, thinking it might be electric but Evan had laughed at her.

"Don't you feel confined?" Miranda asked as she glanced up and down. She couldn't see how high the fence went.

Evan shrugged.

"No, our cars fly so we can leave when we need to," her dad said, "And it keeps the animals out so it is safer for them to live."

They walked for hours heading back upslope before taking a more direct path back to the car. Miranda was sweating buckets but her father and Evan seemed to still be managing fine.

"Why aren't you two all sweaty?" Miranda laughed as she lagged behind the two of them, dragging her sore feet.

"You should have worn a pair of shoes from here," Evan said, looking at the bulky running shoes on her feet. His were sleek and fitted and probably so comfortable.

Miranda made a face and thought about just getting rid of all her clothes and shoes from Earth. If only she thought she could bear to part with anything. Maybe her shoes could go but she couldn't bring herself to throw away her Earth clothes.

"We do this every Sunday," Mr. East said, "Your body will get used to it. Did you ever hike on Earth?"

"Sometimes. I mostly played street hockey for exercise. Sometimes basketball, volleyball and I was a cheerleader in high school so we had a gym training schedule."

Mr. East and Evan shared a confused look. Evan turned to her, "Cheerleader?" he asked.

"Don't you guys have people who cheer on sports teams on the sidelines?" Miranda asked, "You know. People who do cartwheels and flips? I couldn't do anything too spectacular. I was mostly the base of the pyramid because of my height."

Evan shook his head, "We have announcers who start cheers and lead the applause and there *are* gymnasts. But there is no mixing of the two."

"Oh," Miranda said and shrugged, "Well, I only did it because my best friend Helen wanted to. It was alright."

Evan laughed, "You will have to show me that some day."

Miranda shrugged, "Watch this then." She bent her back into a bridge and managed to flip herself over, even though she was tired. Then she just did a quick cheer, "T-I-G-E-R-S, Tigers really are the best!" she shouted, doing the choreographed moves, "Go-o-o-o-o Tigers!" She stood and gave her family a shrug. "That was our sports team in high school. We were the Tigers."

Evan, who was staring with his mouth open, burst out laughing. Mr. East chuckled.

"You *have* to show that to Alex," Evan said, laughing. He bent double, his shoulders going up and down.

Miranda made a face, "If that is the reaction I'm going to get then not in this lifetime." That's all she needed was for Alex to make fun of her even more.

"That was really cute," Mr. East said with a smile.

Miranda smiled, "Uh, thanks?" She giggled.

Miranda liked the thought of spending every Sunday with her family but as they continued, she thought of all the time she missed with her mother. She fell farther back from her dad and brother, hoping she wouldn't upset them with her thoughts.

When Miranda had fallen far enough back to be comfortable that her thoughts wouldn't be heard, she got sad about the good times she had missed here, especially with her mother and how much she was going to miss her parents and friends on Earth. She was just thinking about the last time she had gone hiking with Helen when she heard a branch snap just beyond the tree line. It startled her since it sounded like someone had stepped on it. She looked ahead and saw her family had just rounded a bend on the well worn path.

Without warning, the ground beneath her feet started to tremble and Miranda's heart jumped in her throat. Was this an Earthquake? She stayed rooted to the spot afraid to move. Her mind raced. She couldn't remember what you were supposed to do in an Earthquake, especially being outside? Her head turned to the forest to where she thought she had seen someone but there was nothing there.

The rumbling stopped about thirty seconds later and Evan and her father were racing back to her. Mr. East pulled out his phone when they had reached Miranda.

"Hi Griffin," he said, looking at the screen, "Are you and Greta ok?"

"Yes, we are fine," came Griffin's voice.

Evan looked strained and Miranda glanced between his and her father's apprehensive faces. "What just happened?" she asked, frightened.

"Our planet does not have Earthquakes. Whenever the ground shakes, it means there is an attack," Evan said, a little shaky as he pulled out his phone. It looked like he was scrolling through and then he tapped the screen.

Miranda's eyes grew wide, "You mean the bad people?"

"Alex," Evan said before nodding to Miranda.

"Everyone ok?" came Alex's stressed voice through the phone.

"Yes," Evan answered, "You?"

"Good. I will see you at home," and he was gone.

"We should go home," Mr. East said as he typed furiously on his phone, "I just let the rest of the family know we are ok."

Evan nodded grimly and turned to Miranda, "Want a ride?" He bent down and Miranda hopped on piggy-back.

"Never too old for a piggy-back ride from my big brother I guess," Miranda let out a small giggle, hoping to ease the strain around her.

She could feel Evan smile, "Piggy-back?"

"That is what we call this type of carrying on Earth," Miranda explained.

"Oh, I did not know pigs carried their young like this," Evan said, chuckling, "We call it a monkey-ride."

"Um, no. Pigs don't carry like this. I have no idea where the name comes from. So you guys have monkeys?" Miranda asked and saw Evan nod. "Do they talk?" she asked.

Evan snorted a laugh and shook his head.

Miranda shrugged, though he couldn't see it. You never know if the movies are true, she thought with a smile.


They reached the car in only fifteen minutes and Miranda hopped down and climbed in. Mr. East checked his phone once he slid into the driver's seat, "Looks like everyone is accounted for."

"Is that like text messaging?" Miranda asked curiously.

"Yes. You can send a message to any of your contacts and we have a group message with all of the family to keep in touch," her father replied, "I guess we have not set you up yet?"

Miranda shook her head and pulled out her own notebook. She looked at her short contact list. Everyone had a picture beside their name, her dad, Evan, Griffin and Senika. Just then Alex showed up on her contact list, followed by Alice and Ray Sampson, Fred and

Sally Freight, a Grandfather East, a Grandmother and Grandfather Teller. Miranda looked up to see Evan had his phone pointed at hers. A 'Family' group showed up which Miranda pressed it with her fingertip. There were a few messages addressed specifically to her. Her family welcoming her and hoping they would get to meet her soon. Miranda quickly typed her thanks and expressed that she would love to meet them soon as well. When her message popped up, it was the same picture as her identification.

Evan explained that Alice was their dad's sister, married to Ray, and Sally was their mom's sister, married to Fred, so they were her aunts and uncles. Teller was her mother's maiden name.

When they got home there was a somber feel to the house. Alex, Griffin and a woman were in the living room talking.

The woman smiled wide when she saw Miranda and bounced up off the couch. Miranda took her in. She was almost as tall as Griffin with short pin-straight blond hair and dark eyes. Like all the people of Utopia, her face was flawless though her nose was slightly on the larger side. She looked nothing like the woman in her dreams and Miranda smiled back. *This* must be Greta.

Greta hugged her tight, "Nice to meet you finally Miranda. I am Greta."

"You too," Miranda replied with a smile.

"Oh I heard so much about you today. Your brother was so excited he had a sister. Look at you, though, you are so beautiful. I heard you got a part in the show, Congratulations!" Greta rambled as she pulled Miranda away from the boys and into the kitchen. Greta loved to talk.

"Not official yet Greta," Evan laughed from the living room as they walked away and Greta rolled her eyes dramatically and continued on.

"Thank you," Miranda replied as Greta opened up the cupboard and fixed them ice cream within a few seconds. She handed Miranda a bowl and then motioned for her to follow her into the dining room away from the boys.

"I just brought you in her because I wanted you to know if you need anything at all, any womanly advice, you can always come to me," Greta gave her hand a squeeze, "I just know we are going to get along great!"

Miranda stared at her. That was possibly the nicest thing she could hear right now.

Greta smiled, had a spoonful of ice cream and then frowned, "I know you did not get to meet your mom and now you are stuck living here with three, well with Alex, four boys. It must be tough."

"Thank you so much!" Miranda exclaimed. It was so nice to be in the company of another woman, "So, are you and my brother serious?" Miranda looked down at the ice cream and wondered how it was cold if it was made in the oven. She tasted a tiny bit and it was definitely cold!

"Well, I hope so!" Greta said smiling again.

"Good, 'cause I think you're the perfect one for him. I heard you were on a trip, how was it?"

"Oh my grandparents are very well," Greta laughed and told her all about her trip.

Miranda and Greta chatted on for a good half hour before the rest of the family joined them for dinner.

"Did you spoil your dinner?" Griffin asked them when they walked in, eyeing the empty bowls on the table. He kissed Greta on the top of her head.

Greta laughed, "Of course I did! What are you boys doing to this poor girl?"

Griffin frowned a little offended but then Miranda laughed.

"You have a wonderful sister," Greta commented and Miranda blushed as she rose and cleared her and Greta's bowls.

"I guess," Evan teased and Miranda stuck her tongue out at him.

"Where did Alex go?" Greta asked.

"He said he had to meet a girl for a date," Griffin said pulling up a chair beside her.

Miranda dropped the bowl to the ground, which luckily, even though it looked like ceramic or porcelain, did not break. *A date?*

"Not with Sidney though, right?" Greta moaned then turned to Miranda, "This girl is madly in love with him and they have only been out a few times."

"Yes, I think it was her," Griffin said, rolling his eyes.

"What about Danielle?" Miranda asked, irritably, picking up the bowl.

Griffin gave her a quizzical look, "Who?"

"I got her racing shirt," Miranda explained, "They were pretty comfortable with each other in the bathroom. It sounded like they were dating."

"Oh, right," Griffin rolled his eyes, "I can never keep track of who Alex dates."

Miranda tried to smile and remembered what she was doing. She went to send the bowls through the washer and returned to the dining room.

"What happens to the dish water?" She focused hard on controlling her thoughts. She didn't need anyone to know what she was thinking right now.

"It's only food that's on them and a mild detergent that breaks down immediately in the environment," Evan answered first.

"Doesn't it hurt the environment with the extra nutrients? Wouldn't it cause eutrophication?" At least to her it sounded smart but Griffin went into a discussion about the chemical breakdown of what they ate and in the end, no, it didn't hurt the environment. Evan made silly faces at him behind his back as he explained and Miranda and Greta had to suppress their giggles.

They all smiled and laughed that night, Greta bringing a whole new light over the place despite what had happened that day. At least Miranda had someone on her side.

*   *   *

Miranda shivered slightly when she woke up the next day from another graphic dream which took place at her new school. Greta had spent the night telling her a lot about the senior school she would be attending which probably contributed to the setting of her latest nightmare. Greta told her not to be nervous, but of course, Miranda was. She worried incessantly that she wouldn't fit in.

She went to shower and then chose her school uniform and dressed quickly. She let Alpha do her hair and makeup and emerged from the bathroom, hoping she looked polished and gorgeous.

Her dad was the only one in the apartment, waiting to see his daughter off on her first day of school.

"Smile," he said holding up his phone.

Miranda giggled and she heard a click, "Really dad?"

Mr. East just smiled. He pointed his phone at an empty frame on the wall and Miranda's picture showed up in the frame. Miranda went to look at it up close. At least she thought she looked alright.

"I am so happy you are going to school," Mr. East said, "Do not be nervous, you will be just fine."

"I still feel like I'm missing something," Miranda said, looking at her large purse that her father had bought her. Of course she did not need a school bag, Griffin had explained once Miranda had told them what exactly a school bag was. There were no books. She had her pocket notebook in her purse which was all she would need for school.

There was a knock on the door and Mr. East went to answer.

"Miranda!" Alicia said, smiling as she stepped into the living room wearing her school uniform, "I figured you might be a little nervous so I thought I would come get you."

Miranda smiled appreciatively and went to the front foyer. She chose her black ballet flats from a list and they were deposited in front of her. She slipped them on and she turned to her dad, "Thank you for waiting." Miranda smiled nervously.

"You are very welcome. Good luck today and do not be nervous," he said and gave her a quick hug, "Alex will pick you up when you are finished to bring you to Evan's studio."

Miranda's stomach dropped and she frowned, "Alex is picking me up?"

Mr. East nodded and Alicia smiled, "Lucky girl."

Miranda groaned inwardly and followed Alicia out the door and up to the bus, thanking her for stopping by the apartment.

"I have to admit, I am very nervous," Miranda admitted.

"Do not be nervous," Alicia assured her, "Everyone is going to love you. Plus getting picked up by Alex? That will definitely make an impression."

They were picked up by a bus like the one she had ridden in before except it had 'C217 S.S.' on the side. The bus was mostly full and everyone seemed to turn and look at her when she climbed on. She was a new student, so of course there would be stares. Alicia let her have the window seat and introduced her to a few people that were sitting nearby. Everyone was very welcoming but that didn't stop Miranda's stomach from fluttering.

They only made a couple more stops and were at the school in about fifteen minutes. Miranda's stomach dropped as she saw all the people. Like at the space centre, the bus dropped them off in front of the school on the grass rather than on top of the building.

"Are you coming?" Alicia smiled kindly.

Miranda forced a smile, "Oh alright. If I must." She let out a nervous giggle.

"I will show you the office and they will be able to direct you," Alicia smiled. Miranda stopped just before she walked into the school to take it in. It looked like a typical Earth-type school building. It was just a large rectangular gray building with several large double doors and evenly spaced windows, very institutional looking. She was sure the interior would probably be much more advanced and she was right. Each room was enclosed in what looked to be glass, but probably wasn't glass. There were long desks with chairs in a line but there were no chalkboards. Of course, that would be a waste of chalk. She giggled inwardly. It certainly didn't smell like a school should. Everything smelled like flowers in Utopia, where in a school, especially a senior school, it should smell like chalk, gym shorts and fear.

Alicia introduced her to a few of her friends as they made their way to the office. Miranda answered politely and stuck to the story that she had been away studying Earth with her mother.

Alicia left her in front of the office and headed off to her first class. Miranda took a deep breath as the glass door to the office slid open automatically.

She approached the first woman she saw, who smiled at her, "Can I help you?"

"Yes," Miranda answered nervously, "My name is Miranda Gre-East. I am supposed to be having private lessons." Miranda had to correct herself. She almost said Greenburg.

The woman's smile widened and she nodded, "Of course. I will show you where you will meet your trainer."

She came around the desk and Miranda followed her out the door and through the school. She pointed out a few areas of the school as they walked.

They reached a set of elevators in the centre of the school. There was an atrium in the centre enclosed in glass and the elevators were glass as well. Miranda looked at the atrium as they rose to the sixth and highest floor. The atrium was grassed with trees and shrubs. There were a few benches with students milling about, waiting for classes to start.

It was quieter on the top floor.

"I am Miss Mackily, the head secretary here," she smiled at Miranda.

"Nice to meet you," Miranda smiled nervously.

"Do not be nervous. Your trainer is wonderful. He just finished one year as a shadow-teacher of ages 14 and 15 students and is more than willing to do his second year of shadowing as a private trainer."

Miranda nodded.

"I told him that he could use this room or move to the atrium whenever you wish," she continued, "Please do not feel confined to one space. You may use the gym room and he can teach you Utopian sports as well."

Miranda smiled, glad that her education will be so thorough.

Miss Mackily showed her into the room. Her trainer had not arrived yet.

"He should be here shortly," Miss Mackily smiled, "Have a seat. I am sorry but I should be getting back to the office."

Miranda sat and waited in the large classroom, looking around. The cream coloured walls were fairly plain, only decorated with a digital map of Utopia which took up a large part of the wall. Miranda sat at the first chair in the row. It was very comfortable. Not like the high school chairs she was used to. She noticed there was a screen on the desk in front of her which turned on when she touched it. It was a computer.

A minute later the door opened and Miranda turned. Her breath hitched and she could have sworn it was Alex walking in the room, but when he faced her fully, she could see plainly that it wasn't. He had the same light brown hair and blue-green eyes but he was taller, his eyebrows were thicker and his mouth not as full. He had the same square jaw and one huge difference was that he smiled when he saw her.

"Hi Miranda," he said as he approached, taking her hand, "I am Jackson West, your private trainer."

Miranda's mouth dropped open. *What do they feed these West boys?* she thought to herself.

He chuckled and Miranda blushed.

"If you are referring to Alex West, he is my cousin. And yes, I am mistaken for him sometimes," he smiled.

Miranda found her voice, "I am so sorry Jackson… uh…Mr. West? It is just that Alex is my neighbour."

"Jackson is fine," he said, taking his notebook out of his front pocket and leaning casually on the front table, "So you know Alex personally and not just as a celebrity?"

Miranda nodded and coloured, "We actually do not get along at all. I have no idea why so many women are interested."

Jackson laughed, "Well he does seem to have a big ego. We do not talk much. Not since his parents moved away."

"Oh," Miranda shrugged.

"So, I do have a lesson plan I have prepared," he stood again, "I am not sure how much you know about Utopia."

"Just the basics actually," Miranda smiled sheepishly and described Alex's books he had let her borrow.

Jackson smiled, "I know those books. So anytime I am explaining something and you know already, just let me know. Is there anything you would like to start with though?"

Miranda thought about it for a minute before she answered, "Do you think you can teach me how to close my mind and read other people's minds? I am afraid I must have stopped listening for so long that I cannot hear anymore." Miranda frowned.

Jackson ran a hand through his hair, "Hm. Ok. I honestly do not know how but let us say we work on it, one on one."

He took a seat beside Miranda and turned her to face him. He took her hand which warmed at his touch. He was incredibly cute. Miranda put her head down blushing as Jackson chuckled.

Miranda spent one embarrassing morning trying to suppress her thoughts. Once in a while she would think about how cute he was or how near he was to her and they would both flush.

"Close your eyes," Jackson instructed, "And picture yourself putting up a brick wall, one brick at a time so no one can get into that mind of yours."

It seemed to help but it wasn't until near lunch that Jackson had finally not been able to read into them. She didn't even know what she changed in herself so that he didn't hear them but she seemed to have mastered it. The brick wall was completed.

"Let's go down to the atrium after lunch to work on *you* listening to *my* thoughts," Jackson suggested.

Miranda nodded.

"Are you going to the lunch area?"

"Yes. My friend Alicia from my building invited me to meet her friends," Miranda replied.

Jackson looked downcast.

"You can join if you would like," Miranda said, confused. Surely he must be sick of her by now.

"No, that is fine. I am going out for lunch," he checked his watch, "We can meet in the atrium in one hour."

Miranda smiled, "I will see you there."

Lunch seemed to fly by. Miranda met a lot of Alicia's close friends who were all really nice. They were all excited about her potential part in the show. She knew she had the part but like Evan had said, it wasn't official so she didn't tell them.

When Miranda walked with Alicia out of the lunch room, she asked her if she knew Jackson.

Alicia giggled, "You have Jackson West as your private trainer?"

Miranda smiled and nodded.

Alicia's eyes sparkled, "Wow, you *are* lucky. He is two years older than me so I did know of him in school but we have never spoke personally. He shadowed one of my teachers last year and what a transformation! He used to be very skinny and studious. Then it looked like he started working out and now he looks gorgeous! It must run in the family." She winked.

Miranda blushed a little bit, "Well he is a lot nicer than the *famous* Alex." She rolled her eyes.

"Have you had a chance to talk to him about me?"

Miranda frowned, "No. He does not talk to me much and he had a date Sunday so he was not around." She noticed Alicia's shoulders fall so she continued quickly, "My brothers do not think it is serious though. They said she is very in love with him but he does not reciprocate."

She shrugged, "I do not expect anything anyways. Not after we dated last year."

Miranda stopped walking, "You dated him last year?"

Alicia shrugged, "Just once. He is too busy to notice me."

"Don't be sad," Miranda tried to reassure her, "I think you are gorgeous! You have as much a chance as anyone."

Alicia smiled, "Thanks."

When Miranda got to the atrium, Jackson was already there. He smiled as she approached.

"Ok," he said, slipping his notebook in his pocket. He took her hand which sent a tiny shiver down her arm and she sat next to him.

It smelled really good in the atrium, almost intoxicating.

"So, I think I have an idea as to why the whole mind thing works for you now," he said.

Miranda looked at him expectantly.

"Well, I was thinking since you forgot how to do it since you lived on Earth, you closed off a part of your brain. I think we just have to crack into that head of yours," he chuckled and touched her head lightly. *Your beautiful head*, he continued.

Miranda blushed and looked away. Then her eyes snapped back to his face. Did he just say she was beautiful? Definitely not out loud.

His eyes grew wide, "So I am guessing now that we have closed your mind down we have also opened it up to hear others." He shifted uncomfortably, "I am sorry. That was unprofessional."

"It's alright Jackson," Miranda gave his hand a squeeze, "Thank you."

He gave her a shy smile and stood. "Well," he said, pulling her up along with him, "Shall we go learn some geography?"

Miranda laughed, "Sure."

# Twelve

★ ★ ★ ★

At the end of the day, Jackson walked Miranda to the front of the building. She stood between him and Alicia, unsure if Alex was going to pick her up on the roof where the faculty parked or if he would pick her up where the buses were. *Or if he is coming at all*, Miranda thought wearily. He did not contact her at all that day. Perhaps he wasn't coming.

"I can bring you home if he does not show up and your bus has left," Jackson said, "I just bought a new car." He smiled proudly.

Miranda smiled and nodded while Alicia swooned, "Oh that is very nice of you Jackson."

The three were interrupted by a fuss as a group of people beside them were looking up and pointing at a car headed towards them. It looked like Alex's race car but it did not have his number or fake name on the bottom. Either way, it was very noticeable. In the afternoon sun, it sparkled a metallic blue. Miranda rolled her eyes and swore under her breath, *if he is picking me up in his friggin race car, I am going to be so mad.*

Sure enough, Alex stepped out a minute later. The girls around started squealing and all seemed to move towards him.

"Hello everyone," Alex said politely to his fans.

Everyone wanted his attention, wanted to talk to him. He answered a few of their questions and signed their notebooks.

"Why are you here Alex?" some girl finally gushed out, "You are always appreciated but I am just curious."

"I am here to pick up a new member of our cast, Miranda," Alex smiled at the girl, nodding in Miranda's direction.

Miranda flushed. She didn't think he even noticed her in the back of the crowd and why was he officially announcing her as his co-star when she hadn't even been told yet.

Alicia squealed and turned to Miranda, "You did not tell me!" She hugged her tight, "Congratulations."

"Yes, congratulations," Jackson said, "You must be thrilled."

"I did not know, I swear," Miranda told Alicia and then she turned to Jackson, smiling in thanks.

The crowd had parted and Alex made his way over to her, smiling, signing notebooks and giving a few hugs on his way to her. Everyone's eyes were on either Alex or Miranda, who flushed deeper.

"Jackson," Alex nodded to his cousin.

"Alex," Jackson responded, equally as cool.

"Are you ready?" Alex asked Miranda.

"Yes," she snapped embarrassed, which only made Alex grin wider.

Alex stepped in front of Jackson and put his arm around Miranda's shoulders and turned to everyone, "Miranda will be starting on Northern Shores very soon," he said to everyone, "Make sure to keep watching." He winked.

Everyone nodded excitedly and started chattering amongst themselves. Alex pulled Miranda through the crowd and opened the passenger door for her. Miranda sent an apologetic look at Jackson and Alicia before she climbed in. She was so enraged.

Alex walked around the car, waved one last time to everyone and got in the driver's seat. He fired up the engine and they took off steadily.

Miranda didn't say a word with her arms folded across her chest, silently steaming until Alex chuckled and she lost it.

"Your race car?" she yelled, "You picked me up in your bloody race car? What was that all about? Why would you tell everyone I am your co-star when I don't even know yet! Aren't you giving away the plot? Evan will be furious!"

Alex laughed again and rolled his eyes, "Like you do not know already *and* this is my normal car and my race car. I do not need two."

Miranda glared daggers at him.

"Evan knew what I was going to do," Alex smirked.

"And I can't see him agreeing to it," Miranda grumbled.

"Well, it did take some convincing."

Miranda growled at him.

"Cheer up Maddie," Alex grinned, "I just made you popular."

"I do not want to be popular," she sighed, "I just want to learn and fit in."

Alex shrugged. "What were you doing with Jackson anyways?" he asked a minute later.

"He is my private trainer," Miranda snapped, still looking out the window.

Alex turned to face her ignoring the road, "He is?"

"Yes, why?"

"No reason," Alex said quietly. Miranda looked at him and he looked lost in thought. The rest of the ride to the studio was silent. Miranda fumed and Alex chewed on his lip. He parked on the top of the studio and they both got out.

Miranda walked ahead of him wanting to get away but she turned on him halfway to the elevator, "Why do you insist on embarrassing me?"

"I find it hilarious," Alex stopped walking and smirked.

"Well stop," Miranda snapped.

"If it bothers you so much, of course I will," Alex said, his smile fading.

"I..." Miranda paused. She didn't expect him to say that so she started walking away again, confused.

When they got to the elevator, Alex pushed one and they went all the way to the bottom. When the doors opened, Evan was there with a smile on his face along with Patricia, Sandy and another woman who was introduced as Melissa.

"So, as you know, you have the part," Evan smiled and rolled his eyes. The little party dissipated after offering their congratulations and Miranda followed Evan to his office to sign the contract. It was all digital and Miranda signed his computer screen with a wide smile. Now that it was official, she relaxed.

"As congratulations, we got you something," he said, reaching into his pocket and extracting six tickets.

He handed them to Miranda who read them silently. They read 'UHL' on the top and 'Mind Erasers vs. Razor Blades'. The tickets were for tonight.

"It is a hockey game," Evan said, cluing her in.

Miranda smiled, "Are you serious? You guys have hockey?" She jumped excitedly and hugged her brother.

"Yes that is one thing we stole from Earth. Ours is just a little different."

"Oh? How is that?" Miranda asked.

"We can also use our minds to control the puck into the goal."

"That's interesting," Miranda smiled, "I guess that would make it a lot faster."

"Yes, it sure is. My team is not playing but it will be great! I am so glad you like hockey!" Evan smiled, and turned to Alex who had been quiet, "Now Alex can give you a tour around the building. I have a bit of work to get finished before I leave today and I would not want to miss the game."

Alex scowled and Evan glared at him.

Miranda rolled her eyes at Alex and turned to her brother, smiling, "You are all keeping me so busy."

"We usually keep busy," Evan laughed as he walked with them back to the elevator, "and we want to make sure you like it here."

Miranda's smile faded a bit, "I do like it here Evan, don't worry."

Evan's smile widened, "Good. I will see you tonight and really… you did really well with your audition. I am so proud of you." He hugged her goodbye as the elevator door opened.

Miranda returned the hug, "Thanks Evan. See ya later!" The door closed and it was just the two of them again.

She followed Alex around as he showed her the room where they taped most of the indoor scenes and a few of the other studios in the building and finally, he showed her the dressing rooms where Miranda met one of her co-stars.

"I am Britany," she smiled, "I play Jeff's soon to be ex-fiancée Janet."

Miranda shook her hand politely, "Nice to meet you."

"You can have him," she laughed and playfully punched Alex in the arm.

Miranda smiled, "Not that I want him."

Britany and Miranda laughed and Alex just shot them dirty looks.

"Time to go," Alex said, slightly annoyed that it was two against one. He pulled Miranda down the hall and back into the elevator.

They took it to the parking garage and got in Alex's car.

"So, are you coming to the game tonight?" Miranda asked him as he pulled into traffic.

"Do you want me to?" he asked, turning to look at her.

"I really don't care but I assume you are coming? There are six tickets."

"You assume correctly considering I got them. Your brother asked me to get them yesterday. He thought it would be a great gift."

Miranda looked at him shocked, "You did?"

"Yes. While your dad can get concert tickets, I can get them for hockey games. I used to play when I was younger."

"When did you stop?"

"Two years ago just before I started on the show. I had to pick my career but I chose actor instead of hockey player."

"Well, I guess I should thank you then."

"Forget about it. I would have gone with your brothers anyways and just brought someone else."

Miranda felt like she was punched in the stomach. Of course he would just bring someone else. Like the girl he was dating.

"So how long have you had such a big ego? Do you like being idolized? 'Cause you would have if you had chosen actor or hockey player," she snapped.

He shot her a dirty look and ignored her.

"Just remember I beat you at hockey," Miranda smirked.

His jaw locked and he tightened his grip on the steering handles. The car punched forward as he accelerated. That didn't bother Miranda. At least she knew how to shut him up if he ever bothered her again. She giggled at this thought that she had found something to use against him. *Sweet payback*, she thought.

Alex sent her a glare.

*Oops*, she thought, *he can hear me*.

Alex tsked loudly and his lips set in a tight line. He didn't look at her for the rest of the trip. There must not be a speed limit the cars had to follow because Alex drove really fast. Miranda didn't mind though, it was fun!

In the elevator to their apartments Miranda finally broke the silence, "Why didn't you guys tell me you were going to be my co-star anyways?"

"Trust me, I am *not* happy with this arrangement either."

Miranda frowned, "Then why didn't you ask my brother not to cast me?"

"Will you speak properly... did not, ok? *Did...not*. Start practicing now because I will not have you messing up every day during the taping," Alex snapped, "And like I had a say in that."

Miranda looked at him, shocked. Leave it to him to ruin everything. "I said everything right in my audition did *I* not?" she snapped, "So you fought against me being on the show? What did I ever do to deserve that?" The elevator door opened to their floor and Miranda stepped out of it quickly, then spun around to block him in. "You know what? I do *not* even care what you think so leave me alone."

"That is probably why Evan suggested I go backstage with you at the concert," Alex grumbled after her and she stopped on the spot but didn't turn around, "We had an argument earlier that day about you. I expressed my opinion and he did not take it too well."

"Welcome to the show Miranda," she replied sarcastically, then she turned to face him again, "Why do you have to ruin everything? You were probably wishing I would fail miserably!"

Alex grumbled an incoherent response as he stepped out of the elevator before it closed on him.

"What?" Miranda snapped.

"Nothing," Alex said coolly.

Miranda left him there and went to her room furious. He embarrassed her often and he doesn't want to be her co-star. What did she do to make him hate her this much? She punched her pillow and lay down, tired from her long school day.


Greta knocked on her door, waking her. Miranda took a quick look at the time on her phone before sleepily answering, "Come in".

The door slid open and Greta was there in a hockey jersey, "Sorry to wake you but we should be leaving in a half hour."

Miranda smiled sleepily, stretched and sat up, "That's ok. I guess I was tired after school."

Greta smiled and handed her the jersey in her hand, "Here we have an extra one."

"That's awesome, thank you!" Miranda took it as she stood, holding it out in front of her. The jersey was white with red and gold stripes and details. It had a logo of a tornado coming out of a head. It had 'Mind Erasers' overtop. Greta sported another jersey. Hers was green and white with a skate cutting into the ice. It said 'Razor Blades' on the top.

"So, which team is better?" Miranda asked, as she opened her closet and tapped the screen to life. She chose a pair of dark red skinny jeans which matched the colour in the jersey and a pair of black running shoes that she had gotten the other day. They looked good with her skinny jeans since they were sleek and fitted to her feet.

Greta sighed, "Well, the Mind Erasers are doing very well this year and the Razor Blades are just behind them but that team is better, for now. It is Griffin's favourite team. He has two jerseys. Evan's favourite team is the Star Shooters. They are not doing too well this year," she grinned.

Miranda smiled back and Greta left her to change. Miranda quickly stopped in the bathroom to wash her face and then had it re-done in minutes.

Everyone was waiting in the living room. Alex sported a Razor Blade's jersey and his worn baseball cap. She eyed him wearily.

"Your girlfriend not coming?" Miranda asked. She hadn't meant for it to sound so snappish, but that's how it came out.

"She does not like hockey," Alex said, turning away from her and opening the door.

Miranda almost forgot to breathe. She didn't expect that he would answer like that, actually referring to a girlfriend. She followed them all once again out to the bus. Greta walked beside her talking excitedly but Miranda was lost in thought. That's probably who Alex is with when he isn't at the East apartment.

They made it to the arena ten minutes before the game started and found their seats quickly. The arena looked much the same as on Earth without all the rafters. The ceiling was smooth and decorated with banners. Miranda was seated as far from Alex as she could get, which was the way she liked best. Her father was on her right and Greta to her left, then Griffin, Evan and Alex.

Greta nudged her and Miranda looked over.

"What is wrong? You have been so quiet?"

"Nothing," Miranda lied.

"Lying is not easy around here," Greta smiled and then her voice dropped to a whisper, "It is not serious with Alex and Sidney. She likes him because he is on television and I know he cannot stand girls like that."

"I really don't care," Miranda said, not even convinced herself.

"Cheer up," Greta whispered back, then pointed and squealed, "Look, it is starting."

Miranda sat back and watched as the puck was dropped. It was faster paced then on Earth. She watched as the puck zinged around the ice, usually by stick but sometimes by mind. She got really into the game. It was so amazing and brought back so many memories. There was not a lot of violence, a few good hits here and there but no full out fighting.


"Are you blind? Offside!" Miranda and Alex both shouted at the same time, rising from their seats.

Everyone just gawked at them.

"Amazing how much alike they are and they do not even get along," Evan whispered to Griffin and Greta smiled. They all received dirty looks from both Alex and Miranda as they both sank back into their seats.

"By the way, you are wearing the wrong jersey if that call made you mad," Griffin said aloud.

Alex chuckled, "Maybe she likes another team. The Razor Blades are so much better."

"Are not!" Griffin replied stubbornly, "Only down by one and it is only near the end of the first. This is their year."

"Or maybe I think both these teams suck and I will find my own team," Miranda smirked, "How many teams are in the league?"

"There are 16 teams in each of the four divisions, north, south, east and west, and they play all year long. At the end of the year, the best teams play in the playoffs and the finals for the Earth Cup," Evan said, "See we dedicated it to Earth for giving us the idea."

"Last year, a team in the North won though after teams from the West held the cup since the league started about fifty years ago," Alex added, "And the year before that, the Razor Blades won it. They are in the West." He smiled.

"And the five years before that, the Star Shooters won it. Also, in the west," Evan said, jumping in with his favourite.

Griffin groaned, "Ok, so the Mind Erasers have not won in a while..."

"Try never," Alex cut in.

Griffin sent Alex a look, "But they always get so close!"

Miranda laughed, "I will find my team."

At the end of the first period, Greta volunteered her and Miranda to go get the snacks. They returned piled with treats and drinks for everyone.

When they came back the seats were rearranged. Evan was seated in Miranda's spot and Griffin beside him. Greta took the seat beside Griffin, of course, so Miranda was left at the end beside Alex.

She passed Alex a drink and then whispered to him, "What's going on?"

Alex shrugged and smiled, "I won this time." Miranda looked over at Griffin and Evan who looked a little miserable.

"Are you picking fights again?" Miranda said aloud.

"What? I do not pick fights," he said, then added, "Pancake." He started laughing and Greta giggled. Miranda was worried they had fought about her again. She sat back and took a sip.

"It was all about hockey, do not worry," Greta smiled, receiving a glare from Griffin, "You boys and your teams."

Mr. East chuckled and shrugged.

"Well you are a Razor Blades fan," Griffin said and chuckled, "You should sit on that side."

"What team do you like dad?" Miranda asked down the row.

He smiled, "I try not to let anyone know that. My team has also never won the Earth cup."

After the game was finished, they headed back to the bus. Alex's team had won by one goal and he wasted no time in rubbing it in.

"Thank you for getting the tickets," Miranda said to Alex as they waited, "That was so much fun!" He hadn't fought or embarrassed her in over an hour, so she hoped he actually meant what he said earlier.

"You are welcome," he smiled for what seemed like the first time at her.

"Thank you all," Miranda turned to everyone, "I really do like it here."

A look of relief passed over Griffin's face and Evan smiled and pulled his sister in for a hug. Mr. East looked happiest of them all.

When they got home, it was 29 hour but Miranda could not sleep. She had already taken that long nap. When she could no longer hear her family moving around, she left her room and headed for the Games Room. She figured if she played for a bit, it might make her sleepy. Back on Earth she might have played a game on her phone before falling asleep but she didn't have any on her notebook and she didn't know if she could even get games for it. Even if she did, she had no idea what they normally played here. She also thought she could read but all the books here were so full of information about the planet, it would be hard to get sleepy.

Nathan, Jane and Dave were there surrounding a pinball machine.

"Hi Miranda!" Nathan said, smiling wide when he saw her.

Miranda smiled shyly and returned his greeting.

She watched Jane play pinball, chattering about school, though the three of them had already finished. Dave and Nathan worked together at the bottle recycling building and Jane was shadowing a chef.

"Would you like to go for a walk?" Nathan asked after a while.

"Sure!" Miranda smiled, "Is there anywhere to walk around here?" A walk would definitely make her sleepy.

"Yes, there are paths between every building."

They went through the pool room and stepped out into the warm night. He led her to the path which was just short grass. Miranda asked if the grass ever grew and Nathan shook his head. It had been genetically altered not to grow more than an inch.

Miranda excitedly pointed out the flowers she had learned while hiking with her dad and brother. They were all so beautiful. He asked her about Earth and how she felt about this new place.

"I love it here. It is so different, though. I never seemed like I belonged on Earth, here I do," Miranda replied.

"Hmm…" Nathan mumbled, "It's nice to be different though."

"I suppose," Miranda smiled, "I noticed you use slang. Why is that?"

"I don't think it's necessary to sound so arrogant. I like different," Nathan said after some thought, "So, why did your brothers decide to get you from Earth?"

Miranda frowned, "They didn't know about me until my mother died. Not even my dad knew."

"That's so sad," Nathan said, putting an arm around her, "Why would your mother hide you."

"I think she believed I would not be allowed to stay here since I was a third child," Miranda's eyes welled with tears. She wished she had met her mother at least once and talked to her. She had no idea what she had been like.

"And the councillor said it was alright that you were here now?"

"Yes though he seemed so secretive. I was told to tell only people who are close."

Nathan smiled and gave her a squeeze, "I am glad you consider me close."

Miranda didn't realize she had spilled the beans. Oh well, he seemed like a great guy and it's not like he didn't know her situation anyways. He knew she had two brothers already.

"The river is just over there. Would you like to see?"

Miranda stopped to listen. She heard the sound of rushing water and nodded enthusiastically.

"Come on, I'll race you," he laughed and gave her a head start.

Miranda had always been a fairly fast runner with her long legs but, of course, everyone here had long legs and Nathan kept pace with her easily.

They reached a bit of a clearing and Miranda giggled as she dropped onto the grass beside the water.

She looked into the stream. It was so crystal clear. They talked more about Earth and her growing up. He sat beside her, so close. Miranda thought he was very attractive. He had a bad boy look to him, although no one on this planet was bad. Their talk turned to school again and Miranda told him about her tutor, Jackson.

"Jackson West is your tutor?" Nathan asked, incredulously.

"Yes, he seems like a nice guy."

Nathan scratched his chin, "Yes, he is. I had him in my class and he was always so studious. I remember he did want to be a teacher so that's great he's achieved it."

A branch snapped behind them and both turned at the sound.

"What are you doing here Miranda?" Alex snapped, marching up to them. He took Miranda's arm and pulled her ungracefully to her feet and away from Nathan.

"Ow! Alex!" Miranda cried, trying to pull her arm from his grasp.

Nathan stood and fixed Alex with a cold stare.

"You stay away from her," Alex growled, stepping between Miranda and Nathan.

"She's an adult. She can decide who she wants to hang out with," Nathan said calmly.

"Yes I can! Just what do you think you are doing Alex! You are hurting me," Miranda said, sending Alex a glare. She tried again to wrench her arm back but Alex was relentless.

"Not with him. He is with a different woman every night," Alex said through gritted teeth, turning to Miranda.

"You should talk Alex," Nathan smiled triumphantly, crossing his arms across his chest.

Alex snorted and sent him a glare.

"Well, I am going to bed," Nathan rolled his eyes. He looked around Alex and smiled at Miranda, "Perhaps we could go out sometime."

"That would be great!" Miranda replied at the same time as Alex growled, "That will never happen."

Nathan turned and went down the path without a look back. Alex didn't let her go till he was well out of sight.

"What the hell Alex?" Miranda screamed at him, rubbing her arm.

His eyes flashed, "What were you doing out here with him?"

"I couldn't sleep so I went down to the game room," Miranda started to say, "and then... wait, what do you care?" She was so confused. Why was he so angry with her?

"Do you remember what I said about people having sex for pleasure? Well Nathan does. You should stay away from him," Alex said, furiously.

"Well I sure wasn't planning on sleeping with him, Alex. He invited me for a walk and that's all," Miranda explained.

"Come on," he seethed, "I am taking you home. Do they even know you are here?"

"I can find my own way back," Miranda snapped, taking a step back. She put a hand on her arm and her eyes welled with tears. It really did hurt. She looked down and away so that he wouldn't see her face to know he had hurt her.

He stepped in close and tilted her chin up so that he was looking in her eyes. His eyes had softened. "I did not mean to hurt you," Alex whispered.

"I don't know what I did," Miranda said quietly, "What did I do to make you hate me so much? Whatever I did, I'm sorry. I just don't understand." She stared into his eyes and held his gaze.

Alex looked lost for a second as he looked down at her, but he dropped his hand and took a step back, looking away. "It is not like that. I do not hate you," Alex said, "You do not understand the kind of person Nathan is. Your brothers would not approve."

"I don't care what you or my brothers say about him. I am old enough to make my own decisions," Miranda tried to reason.

Alex rolled his eyes, "Fine. You can find out the hard way then. Go ahead and date him." He folded his arms across his chest and motioned with his head for her to walk ahead.

Miranda had nothing to do but start walking, scratching her head. He said nothing to her at all. Up the elevator, he waited till she went into her apartment and then went to his own.

* * *

Two men met at a coffee shop early the next morning. One was much older than the other.

"You asked to see me?" the older man asked as he sat down, "Your mother and father speak highly of you." He was very tall, nearly nine feet tall, and his hair was still jet black despite his age. His eyes were pools of black and his face looked as hard as marble.

"I have big news," the younger replied, picking up his napkin nervously. He played with it in his hands, tugging it tight.

They paused as the waitress took their drink orders.

"Go on," the older man urged.

"It is bad, sir. The chosen one exists."

The older man's mouth dropped and he banged an angry fist on the table. A few heads turned their way but the older man smiled to them. One by one, the heads returned to their own tables.

"How has this happened?" he whispered angrily, "We have been doing so well in keeping track of the third children."

"Councilman Hope allowed it. He knows of the legend, I know that for a fact."

"We must rid the planet of councilman Hope," the old man whispered, "I want you to stay close to the third child until we decide what to do about her."

"I will try. She already has feelings for me," the young man said with a smirk, not looking at the older man, "Her guardian is nearby."

The older man groaned, "You must make sure they never get together."

"I will do what I can," the younger said as the waitress placed their coffees in front of them.

"Do this and you will be ready to join," he replied, a fondness in his voice.

"Thank you, sir," the younger said.

"You may call me chief."

* * *

Miranda's eyes snapped open and she almost screamed aloud. She had dreamt that she was going to die. Falling forever and no one was there to save her. No one showed up this time. She wanted to cry. What happened to the one who always saved her?

No one was home when she left her bedroom even though she was awake before her alarm went off. She felt a little alone and still so confused as to what happened last night. Alex totally overreacted. He had no tact. If he had simply told her nicely that Nathan was a womanizer, she might have listened but since he didn't and Nathan was a perfect gentleman, *unlike* Alex, she figured she might as well give Nathan a shot. Besides, it seemed Alex was in denial. She saw how many girls fell over themselves for him.

She got ready and met Alicia on top of the building. At least she could talk to Alicia about it.

"What do you think about Nathan?" she said when she had finished telling her about the previous night, "Is he like Alex says?"

Alicia shrugged, "I do not know. I see him with a different girl all the time as well. Just be careful."

"Ya, that's what I figured, not to get too attached. Oh well."

"You never know though," Alicia smiled encouragingly, "He might really like you and not expect anything from you."

Miranda gave her a half smile. She didn't know how she felt about dating someone who had been with a lot of woman.

Alicia turned to her with a sad smile, "It sure sounds like Alex might have feelings for you too."

Miranda snorted, "Oh I do not believe *that* for a second."

Alicia pursed her lips, deep in thought. "I do. I do not mind though. He is not mine. I just want a boy like him."

"You deserve someone better than him," Miranda encouraged.


When the bus showed up, everyone smiled at Miranda as she walked down the aisle to an open seat. Could it be possible that the news that she got picked up by Alex and was going to be a star on Northern Shores got around?

When she got to the school it was confirmed. A few people introduced themselves to her when she walked in, asked her questions about the show and asked when she would be starting.

She politely answered what she could without giving away why her character was being introduced. Alicia smiled widely beside her, basking in the attention.

When an alarm sounded to signify class, Miranda had barely walked a few steps into the school. People slowly dispersed and Miranda still had to go all the way to the top floor.

When she got there, Jackson was already in the room.

"Sorry Jackson," Miranda said, breathlessly. She frowned. It was all Alex's fault. She didn't want the popularity.

"That is fine," Jackson said, "I guess I will have to deal with the fact that I am training a future celebrity."

Miranda coloured slightly, "Believe me. I did not want the popularity. Damn Alex!"

Jackson chuckled, "Well, that is my cousin for you. He has not changed much."

Miranda rolled her eyes, "So, what's up for today?"

"Today, I thought we would start on history." He pointed to a single book he had on the table in front of her.

She picked it up and read the front cover, *Forgotten Utopian Legends*.

"That is one history book we will use but there are several others. We can switch back and forth. After lunch, we can head down to the gym."

Miranda nodded enthusiastically and opened the book.

# Thirteen

★　★　★　★

Miranda's first week of school flew by and before she knew it, it was Friday night. Luckily for her, school was only scheduled Monday to Friday with two days off. She had learned so much that week about Utopian history, politics and philosophy that she didn't think her brain could take much more. Every day they went down to the gym to get some exercise for at least an hour. She learned that Amanuins was a handball kind of game. She wasn't very good at it, especially since it required moving the ball with the mind as well and she had just learned how to close her mind and read others.

She made plans to go shopping on Saturday with Alicia and her friends.

"Are we going to the track tomorrow night?" Miranda asked at dinner.

"No, there is no race tomorrow. It only happens every three weeks with one week off in between," Mr. East explained, "However, I was hoping you would let me throw you a party? To meet the family?"

Miranda smiled and she nodded enthusiastically, "That is a great idea! I would love to meet everyone."

"You may invite your friends if you like for them to come out after," her dad encouraged.

"Sure!" Miranda smiled and finished her meal. "So, what is going on tonight?"

Greta chuckled, "Are you getting restless with us already?"

Miranda grinned and winked, "Well, you all haven't kept me entertained the past few nights. Have you given up already?" She looked at each of them.

"Oh sorry Miranda," Griffin said, apologetically, "We have just been so busy catching up with work."

Miranda rolled her eyes, "Of course it's fine. I don't expect to be entertained all the time," she turned and spoke to her father, "Though would you mind, dad, if I went to the dance club tonight? I was thinking maybe I could see if anyone is in the game room."

Her brothers both made a face and Miranda raised her eyebrows in surprise.

"Well why not? I *am* an adult, you know."

"Of course you are," Greta smiled, "Do not worry about them. They are just going to be the typical over-protective big brother types." She put an arm around Griffin and patted his back.

"Well, as long as you are with friends it should be ok," Mr. East shrugged.

Evan made a face, "Maybe one of us should come with you?"

Miranda scowled, "No, that's not necessary. You are all busy. I will not be drinking anyways since I don't have any money. I just want to see what it's like. And I don't even know if they will be in the game room."

It was Griffin's turn to roll his eyes, "Oh, they will be. They head to the bar almost every night."

Mr. East pulled out his wallet and placed his card in front of Miranda. He gave her a stern look which didn't last long and smiled,

"I know you will not drink a lot but I would hope you could have a little fun."

Miranda took the card in her hand and flashed her dad the biggest grin, "Thanks dad!" She got up and gave him a quick hug.

She talked to her family for hours about her first week at school and when the sun went down, she headed to change.

She put on the black jean skirt that belonged to Helen and the same sparkly red tank top Evan had brought her for the concert. Compared to what she had seen other people wear, specifically Jane, the skirt was long so she felt a little more comfortable.

"I will see you all later!" Miranda said cheerfully as she chose a pair of high heeled black sandals. She wasn't used to high heels but these were so comfortable.

"Be careful," Mr. East said as he went to see his daughter out.

"Of course I will dad," Miranda assured him.


When the elevator doors opened to pick her up, Alex stepped out. He looked a little ruffled and was wiping his lips with the back of his hand.

He stopped short when he saw her standing there, "Where are you going?"

"None of your business," she snapped. She hadn't seen him since that night he had pretty much gone crazy angry at her. She looked down at her now faded bruise on her arm from where he had grabbed her.

Alex's jaw tightened as he seemed to hold back a retort as Miranda shot her hand out to hold the elevator before it closed.

"Are you going to move?" she asked, her anger starting to rise. She was excited for her night out and he was ruining it already.

"Are you going out with Nathan?"

Miranda rolled her eyes, "Even if I do you will be the last person I ask permission from. You definitely aren't the boss of me and you definitely can't tell me who to date looking like you do know. What are you doing making out with a girl you don't even like? I think you have a bit of lipstick here." Miranda made an exaggerated motion of her whole face.

"Who said I did not like her?" Alex snapped but he took another swipe at his mouth with his hand.

"Greta… my brothers. She is in love with the *famous* Alex."

Alex looked hurt, he stepped out of the way, "Have fun," he said quietly.

Miranda almost did a double take at the change of tone. She didn't want to hurt his feelings. She softened her gaze and stepped into the elevator, holding the door open, "Um… we are having a party tomorrow. I am allowed to have people over. Would you like to come?"

"I will see you tomorrow," he said, noncommittal and turned his back on her, heading towards the East apartment.

Miranda found a larger group down in the game room. Nathan, Rebecca, Pete, Dave and Greg were there along with Julie, Ivan and Kristin, who introduced themselves. Miranda looked around at their clothes, happy with what she chose. Rebecca and Kristin both wore skirts shorter than hers and Julie had on a tight strapless dress that looked more like a tube top then a dress.

"Are you all heading to the bar?" Miranda asked, hopefully.

Nathan put an arm around her waist, "Yes," he replied, excited, "Arc you coming too?"

"I hope you do not mind," Miranda asked everyone.

"Not at all," Rebecca exclaimed, squeezing her arms with both hands in excitement, "I am so glad you are coming. It will be so much fun, just wait!"

They piled into two vehicles. Nathan and Julie were going to be the drivers for the night.

They parked on the top of a small building with a neon blue sign that said 'Club 217'. They took the elevator one floor down. It was a three-level club, open in the centre to the first floor. There was a large dance floor in the centre. Miranda leaned on the railing and watched the blue and purple lights as they floated in the air lighting up the dancers on the floor for a second before moving on. She had never been to a club before. This was so exciting!

"We will go dance in a bit," Rebecca said excitedly, pulling on Miranda's arm, "Shall we get a drink?"

Miranda nodded and followed everyone to the bar. There were a lot of people there already.

She sat with everyone in a booth for some time talking and drinking, just listening to the music. It was really good. Most songs had an incredible beat to it. Miranda liked Rebecca most. She reminded her of Helen with her long blonde hair and heart shape face. Unlike Helen, her eyes were a fierce green and she was a lot taller, of course.

Eventually Rebecca pulled her on her feet to dance and Miranda stumbled a little. She felt like she was floating, it was a cool sensation. She had only three drinks so far, but it was the most she had drank since she moved here.

She bought one more before they headed out onto the floor. Miranda glanced around nervously watching everyone dance. She was worried they would break out into some dance she wouldn't know like they did in movies but nothing like that happened. They danced like they did on Earth.

After a few songs a slower song came on and most people paired off. Miranda had never really danced with a boy. In high school, she always turned them down when they asked because she wasn't interested in anyone then. She was about to leave the dance floor when someone tapped her on the shoulder.

She spun slowly, afraid that she would have to deny someone again but it was Alex.

"What are you doing here?" she asked, shocked and peeked around to see if anyone noticed.

"Dance with me," he ignored her question and took her hand, leading her to the centre of the dance floor apart from where her friends were. They were too busy to notice her anyways. Rebecca had been asked to dance with a guy who had been watching her for awhile.

She looked around again, this time to make sure everyone was still dancing like they did on Earth before she uncomfortably put her hands on Alex's shoulders and he slipped his around her waist, pulling her close to him.

She looked up into his face, confused. He was wearing his worn baseball hat pulled low which shadowed most of his face and Miranda finally realized he did that to disguise himself. Alex sent her a small smile and nodded.

"So, I wanted to apologize," he said, finally.

"Oh?" she eyed him suspiciously, "You followed me here to tell me that?"

"Do you accept?"

"Do you even know what you are apologizing for?" she asked, an eyebrow raised, "Well let's see. You've been mean to me ever since I moved here, you don't want me to be in the show, you embarrass me every chance you get and you think you can tell me who I can hang out with. Plus you bruised my arm." She pointedly looked down at her faded bruise.

Alex's lips tightened into a hard line, "Well, I am apologizing for you thinking that I am mean to you, for hurting your arm and for you thinking that I do not want you in the show."

"Then I accept but since you cannot apologize for everything, I think we are done here," she said and released his shoulders.

"Wait," Alex said and clasped her waist tighter. He moved in closer so she could take in his scent. She was drawn to him and her arms did not just find his shoulders, they wrapped around his neck. She sighed at herself for not being able to resist him.

"I saw the script for when you start," he said.

Miranda's eyes widened in excitement, "Really?"

"We have to dance," Alex said quietly so near to her ear. It sent a shiver down her spine. "Just like this."

Miranda felt her face heat up and her face fell, "Oh." She knew their characters were going to be together on the show but she didn't think it would be the first episode. What if they had to do more?

"Yes, they are going to be with each other from your very first episode," Alex answered her unasked question.

"Is that what this is about?" she asked, "You want to practice?"

"Why else would I be here?" Alex rolled his eyes.

Of course it is. She wondered if he felt drawn to her the way she felt to him. Probably not.

"So, we…" Miranda couldn't finish the question. She had never kissed a boy. Well, sort of, but not like she probably would have to in the show. The first episode too! She swore under her breathe. She knew eventually she would have to kiss Alex since they were going to be a couple, but did it have to be the first day! She thought she still had months to prepare.

"I do not want to be your first kiss Miranda," Alex said, stirring her from her thoughts.

"Why?" She narrowed her eyes at him.

"Do you really want me to be? It does not feel right. You have never been kissed before and well, I have, obviously. I just do not think it matters to me but it might to you if I am your first."

"Trust me. I knew what I was getting into. There will probably be a lot more I have to do. I *am* playing a twenty year old," Miranda fidgeted nervously. The song ended and another slow one started. Some couples broke apart but Alex didn't let her go. Miranda caught Nathan on the side looking at her. She knew he was trying to get her attention but she acted as if she didn't see him.

"Yes, twenty is a mature age here. People here start getting married around this age," Alex said. He didn't want to ruin her first kiss for her since kissing meant nothing to him, it wasn't special. Between his fans, the actresses and the girlfriends he had, it sometimes felt like he had kissed every girl in the city.

Miranda didn't understand why he cared about this but she could finally read his mind. Was it that terrible a thought to kiss her? What was wrong with her? Maybe if she had been left on Earth longer she would have had a chance. She did have a date.

Alex snorted loud enough for her to hear over the music.

"Not all Earthlings are bad, you know," Miranda retorted. She thought of her family and friends on Earth. What did Alex know about them? He didn't know them at all! He was terrible for feeling that way about all Earthlings, Miranda had the best of friends and now she had no one.

"It is not hard to make friends here. WE are all polite," Alex said.

"I beg to differ. You have been a jerk since I met you. At least now I understand the know-it-all snobby attitude. You think you are so hot with all your adoring fans. If only they knew you were such a mean person," Miranda said bitterly.

"Do you think I actually like that?" Alex snapped, his anger rising. She could feel his fists clench behind her back.

"You seemed to that night with all those girls around in the game room and at my school," Miranda made a face, then put on an innocent smile and batted her eyelashes at Alex looking up at him, "Oh Alex, you are so sexy! Can I have your autograph?" she said mockingly.

"Stop it," Alex said, finally letting her go.

Miranda panicked for a second. She didn't want to start anything now that he had finally apologized and was being at least halfway decent to her.

"Should I quit?" she asked him quietly, her eyes filling with tears. She looked at the ground.

He made a face and put his arms back around her, "No, this is a dream come true for you I bet." They had stopped moving in a circle and were just standing in the middle of the dance floor, arms around each other.

"Of course it is but how are we going to get through the first taping if you won't kiss me," Miranda said, looking away mumbling the last part. *Maybe this IS a bad idea. He hates me*, she thought.

Alex sighed, "It is not that Miranda, you have it wrong. I just do not want to ruin something special. Just try to get a boyfriend and kiss him before we have to do the scene?"

Miranda laughed at the thought. Getting a boyfriend was never an easy thing for her. She couldn't just snap her fingers and have boys crawling all over her like some girls could. She was sure

Nathan would kiss her but she wasn't sure she wanted him as her first though.

"Yes, please do not choose Nathan," Alex whispered. He seemed to realize they had stopped moving and started to spin slowly again.

Miranda rolled her eyes, "Alex, you can't tell me who to see."

"Well, I can try," Alex replied with a shrug.

The song ended and the music picked back up again.

"Thank you for the dance," Miranda said when Alex let her go. She stepped in close and kissed his cheek, then turned and left him, meeting up with Nathan at the stairs to the sunken dance floor. He looked sulky.

"Who was that?" Nathan asked.

"Not sure," Miranda lied, keeping a blank mind, "Some guy named Mike."

"I wasn't sure if you wanted me to rescue you but you didn't see me I guess?"

"Oh no, sorry Nathan," Miranda smiled apologetically, placing her hand on his arm, "It was alright. I wasn't really interested in him."

"That's fine," he replied, smiling back at her. He wrapped an arm around her waist and pulled her away from the dance floor, "Shall we get another drink?"

She nodded.

Later that night, Nathan managed to get a dance with her. She didn't feel as graceful as she did with Alex. She also looked down, knowing Nathan wanted to kiss her. She wasn't sure about him. Alex put these doubts in her head.

"Hey," he said, tipping her chin up, "I am not going to force you into anything. I respect any decisions you make."

Miranda smiled shyly, "Thanks Nathan." She wanted to ask him how many women he had been with but she didn't think she had the guts to or that she wanted to hear the answer.

A few songs later, everyone was ready to head home. Miranda and Rebecca sang happily in the back seat to the music on the radio. It was a Trees song so Miranda knew it.

Miranda felt giddy and light headed. She ended up having about six drinks and was definitely feeling a little wobbly. Once they got home, Miranda invited everyone to the East apartment the next night for her party.

Evan and Alex were watching television when she walked in.

"Hi," she whispered, smiling as she took her shoes off and flexed her toes. Her shoes were so comfortable. Her feet should hurt after all the dancing, especially in heels, but they didn't.

"Come here Miranda," Evan said, patting a spot beside him on the couch. "So Alex told you about the script?" he asked when she sat.

Miranda quickly glanced at Alex before turning to her brother, "Yes. It is fine Evan."

"Well, you did know that you two would be together before you signed the contract," Evan said, shrugging, "I just wanted you to know what was planned for you the first day."

Suddenly a thought occurred to Miranda. "Did you send him out to the bar?" she asked, flushed. She stood up, a little angry, "Did you send him out to check on me?"

Evan looked surprised and looked at Alex, "No, I did not. You went out to the bar? I thought you met her downstairs and told her."

Alex shrugged and stood, "Well, I will see you tomorrow at the party." He left, quickly.

Evan watched him go, shaking his head.

"You really didn't send him?" Miranda asked.

"No."

Miranda sat down again. She talked a bit about the bar with Evan until he yawned and she sent him off to bed. Miranda was still winding down, so she watched a bit of television before she turned in.

*Miranda was back at the club dancing. When the song changed to a slower song, she looked around for her saviour. Surely he would be here to dance with her. She weaved between the couples until she felt a tap on her shoulder. She was smiling as she turned around but her smile faded fast.*

*Behind her was an extremely tall, broad man dressed all in black with a black funny looking character drawn on his forehead. She barely had time to move before his hands were around her neck. She tried to pry his hands off her to no avail. Why was no one paying attention to them? she thought frantically.*

*She was losing consciousness. She dropped to her knees and the room darkened around her.*

Miranda woke up wide-eyed, choking. Her eyes were filled with tears. It felt like she had been gasping for breath even though she had been sleeping. She looked around her room, scared, but no one was there. Her clock read ten in the morning so everyone must have left for work. She had two hours until she was to meet Alicia for the bus to go shopping. Her father had left her a message on her phone that she could use his card for shopping today. She smiled as she looked down at her phone. He was such a great dad. She thought about her dad on Earth and frowned a little. She missed them so much in her moments alone here when she was able to stop and think about them. A few tears escaped before she wiped her face and decided to get ready.

# Fourteen

★　★　★　★

Miranda bought a new outfit for the party that night. It was a casual sundress that really flattered her eyes according to Tina, one of Alicia's best friends.

Miranda had a lot of fun with the girls, even though they spent a good part of the time asking her about her new character. She knew Evan would have her head if she let it out so she was very careful to put up her mind block, happy she had managed to perfect it. She also didn't need all the girls freaking out knowing that she was going to be with Alex.

"So I am having a party tonight," Miranda said once they were all seated for lunch, "First the family is coming to celebrate my return from studying Earth but then my father said everyone is welcome!" She sent Alicia a wink and Alicia smiled.

The four other girls agreed to come. Miranda worried a little that she was inviting too many people but her dad did say to invite her friends.

"Is Alex going to be there?" Tina asked, smiling in Alicia's direction.

Miranda tried hard not to roll her eyes, "I think so. I asked him last night and he *is* my neighbour."

Tina smiled wide but Alicia frowned at her and sighed, "I think I just might give up on him. He is not interested in me."

All the girls gave her a pitying look.

"Well, why do you like him?" Miranda asked.

Alicia looked thoughtful for a minute, "Well, he has always been very nice to me even though he is older. He was always doing something amazing or fun with your family or his own. He loved his sister and you can tell a lot about a person by the way he treats his family. He is really funny and intelligent," she smiled widely.

"Do not forget incredibly gorgeous," Tina added.

"And there is that," Alicia agreed, "When I asked him out on a date he took me to this great place and there were cameras all around. We ended up in the paper the next day and I have never been in the paper before! He acted all happy and he kissed me goodnight when we got back to the apartment but then he said he just wanted to be friends. I thought everything had been going well." Alicia frowned.

"Alex seems to be that way with everyone," Miranda told her, "He *is* an actor. I do not know what his problem is. He cannot see a perfectly great girl right in front of him."

"Thanks Miranda," Alicia said, giving her a small smile, "But I really think it is time for me to move on."

"I am so glad you said that!" Tina's smile brightened, "Lance was asking about you yesterday and I think he likes you! Right Taylor?"

Taylor smiled and nodded.

Alicia's eyes sparkled and she forgot all about Alex, "Really? What did he say?"

Taylor piped up, "He asked if you had a date for the senior dance."

Alicia squealed.

"He is so cute!" Tina giggled.

The girls spent the rest of the day talking about the cute boys in school and who they wanted to take to senior dance, which Miranda found out was the final celebration of the school year in December. It was still a couple months away and it was unlikely Miranda would go since it was just for the age 15 students. Miranda didn't know who any of the boys were so she mostly just smiled a lot. She was happy to have some friends to hang out with.

Miranda decided to message Jackson on the way home to see if he could make it to the party that night, which he had to politely refuse since he was away visiting family.

When she walked into the apartment, she found her father in the kitchen preparing some food for the evening and returned his card.

"Thank you so much dad," she smiled.

"You are welcome!" he replied, pulling a plate of biscuits from the oven.

"I only bought this dress," she assured him. She touched the teal material of the dress at her shoulder, so silky and soft. It was shorter in the front and longer in the back and probably a little too dressy for the small party but she liked it.

"Oh, it is very pretty," her dad said, sending her a smile. Then he turned back to his food preparation.

"Um, I hope you don't mind," she said, chewing on her lip, "But I think I may have invited too many people."

His eyes snapped back to her, "Oh?"

She smiled sheepishly, "I think about 12 people?"

Her dad chuckled, "Not to worry. I have had more in the house. When you have Evan and Alex on the same floor, you end up with some pretty big parties." He gave her a reassuring kiss on the forehead.

"Oh," Miranda snorted.

"I believe your grandparents will be here shortly."

Miranda smiled excitedly, "Would you like some help?"

"I think I am ok but you can watch! Tell me about your night. Did you have fun?"

Miranda told him about the bar and how much fun she had with her new friends today as she leaned on the counter and watched him expertly make food with the drops of liquid.

"Hello?" a woman's voice came from the front foyer.

"Hello!" her dad called, smiling.

Miranda's hands began to sweat as she followed her dad through the living room. An older couple were at the door and the man closed the door behind him. Both had darker hair and bright blue eyes like she did. The woman smiled warmly, a wise twinkle in her eyes as she took in Miranda.

"This is your grandmother and grandfather," her dad explained. He didn't have to say any more. Miranda knew it was her mother's parents.

"It is so good to meet you Miranda," her grandfather said taking her hand.

Her grandmother's bright eyes were shiny as she wrapped her arms around her, "Oh my darling granddaughter! I thought I would never meet you!"

Miranda's dad did a double take. "You knew?" he asked, shocked.

Her grandma bit her lip and she nodded. Even her husband looked at her, his mouth open in surprise.

"Sometimes you can only rely on your mother," she admitted quietly. She turned to Miranda, "I am so sorry you never met her."

Miranda didn't know what to say. She tried to smile at her grandma but inside she felt a little betrayed. Why didn't her grandmother fight to keep her here?

The door opened again to relieve the bit of tension that had built and Evan walked in with Alice and Ray and their two children, Mia and Jewel. They were talking about Evan's show.

"Oh Miranda!" Alice said excitedly when she saw her and gave her a hug, "Look at you! You look just like us!"

Miranda smiled wider and her uncle gave her a kiss on the cheek, "Congratulations on the show. Evan told us you got a part."

"Thank you," Miranda said.

Her dad greeted his sister with a smile and bent low to hug his nieces who were 12 and 10. They moved into the living room and about 15 minutes later, her Aunt Sally and Uncle Fred showed up with their children, Leah and Michael who were 16 and 13. Finally her father's dad showed and Griffin and Greta returned.

"Sorry we are late," Griffin said as he entered with Greta. He smiled secretively and waved a small bottle in his right hand at his father who took it to the kitchen.

Miranda's cousin Mia brought her real life game station which she showed Miranda how to play. There were several pairs of black sunglasses that when put on would put you right in the game. Mia explained that it tapped into your brain and you did not have to move physically. It was a lot of fun. Miranda played sports in the game against all her cousins. When it wasn't her turn, she talked with her family. She learned that her dad's mother had passed away just after she had her father's sister. She had been in a shopping centre that had been attacked by the bad people.

Alex showed up in time for the cake, which was what had been in the bottle Griffin brought home. It was a huge cake. Miranda had a piece and it was so delicious and moist. It tasted like vanilla and oranges.

Miranda's friends started to show just as her family started to leave. She planned it perfectly. She hadn't wanted to ignore her family or her friends if they were all there together.

When Mr. East announced he was going to bed, Alex suggested they move over to his place, which everyone agreed. Miranda hadn't wanted to surrender her party to Alex's house, but her father was going to sleep and she didn't want to keep him awake.

Miranda followed the party into the foreign apartment. She had never been in it before, of course. He didn't like her enough to invite her in.

It had the same setup as the East's apartment but different coloured walls and flooring. The furniture in the living room was a dark brown with some neutral accents. Miranda gazed around curiously as she walked into the living room. There were no family pictures on the walls.

Alex rummaged around in the kitchen coming back with an armful of bottles, which everyone picked up. Miranda took a purple one and went to talk to Nathan.

Nathan held up his bottle and she clinked hers against it and took a long drink.

After a few drinks, Miranda was starting to feel a little buzzed. Everyone seemed to be starting to feel it as the conversation in the room went up an octave.

Alex had put some music on a while ago and Tina and Taylor were dancing in the center where the coffee table had been. Miranda was very comfortable on the couch, feeling pleasantly light-headed but when she recognized a Trees song she pulled Alicia, who she had been talking to, into the middle of what they made as the 'dance floor'. Rebecca joined them with her enthusiastic and exaggerated dance moves which made them erupt into giggles.

Griffin and Greta went to bed around one in the morning and Evan was ready at about two. Laughing, he gave Miranda the day off from hiking before he left.

"Take care of her," he whispered to Alex on the way out.

Once he was gone, Nathan stopped the music.

"Now that the older brother is gone, how about something more exciting," he announced, staring mostly at Miranda as he picked up an empty bottle off the coffee table.

Miranda didn't know what to think. Spin the bottle? Wasn't that an Earth thing? She took a look at Alicia who smiled and nodded. She took a long drink from her bottle. Well, hopefully the drink would make her brave. At least she was attracted to Nathan. She stared at his medium build thinking that he had always been so nice to her. He wasn't rude or mean to her like Alex was. He reminded her a bit of Scott. Everyone around excitedly agreed, except Alex.

"Come on, spin the bottle? How old are we?" Alex said, rolling his eyes.

"Ya," Miranda agreed. Spin the bottle was an elementary school thing. Even on Earth her friends had moved on to something more mature. Feeling well drunk, she decided to get a little naughty, "You guys ever hear of 'Seven Minutes in Heaven'?"

Nobody had, so Miranda had to explain. She had never played herself because she chickened out in high school. She was worried she would get stuck making out with someone she didn't like and didn't want that to be her first *real* kiss. "All the girls' names are put in a hat and the guys draw one. Then they have to go into a closet and you can do whatever you want in there for the seven minutes."

Greg laughed, "You have to be kidding? That is an Earth game? I am going to Earth!"

Everyone agreed to do it Miranda's way, except Alex. It took a lot of coaxing before he finally agreed. Miranda could hear in his head that his reason was that he had already kissed every girl in the room. She rolled her eyes and shook her head at him. He had kissed everyone except her, of course.

"Awesome," Pete said, smiling.

Alex sent a glare at Nathan. He knew what he was up to.

It was even, boys to girls though they didn't have paper so they decided to put all the women's notebooks in a bag Alex got out from the closet.

"Do you have a big closet?" Miranda asked.

"How about we use the spare room Alex?" Greg suggested.

Alex sighed and rolled his eyes, "Fine."

The first to go was Greg. He pulled out Jane's phone and off they went down the hall. Nathan set a timer on his phone to go off in seven minutes.

While they were gone the others turned the music down to see if they could hear anything. Miranda giggled with Alicia on the couch. It had been awhile since she had been to a party and she was having so much fun, even if she was a little impaired. She tried to remember how many she had but couldn't. It was definitely more than she had had at the bar. Alex seemed to have an endless supply, she thought as she looked at all the bottles around the room.

"Do you think I will get Alex?" Alicia whispered.

Miranda thought about it for a second, "You have a good shot!"

Alicia smiled determined, "I hope I get him. It will be one last time and then I will try to give up on him completely."

Miranda laughed, "You are really giving up?"

Alicia nodded and shrugged, "I think I should. We shall see."

When the seven minutes were up, Nathan went up to the door and knocked.

"It is my turn! Get out!" he yelled through it, excited.

They both emerged, lips swollen from kissing, hair and clothes dishevelled and everyone cheered except Alex. He was pouting in the chair.

Nathan bounded over to the hat and pulled out Miranda's phone.

"Woohoo!" he shouted, dancing on the spot. He was about to take Miranda's hand when Alex sprang up from the chair and stepped in between.

"Maybe this is not a good idea," Alex said, glaring at Nathan.

"No way," Nathan argued, "The game has started and you can't stop it."

"Yes, but…"

"Alex, we have already started," Miranda slurred, rising from the couch, pushing past Alex and taking Nathan's outstretched hand, "Don't be such a party pooper."

Nathan chuckled.

"Can I ask you something first?" Alex snapped. Not waiting for an answer he grabbed her other hand and pulled her away, into the dining room where they were out of sight from everyone. Miranda held up one finger to Nathan and mouthed the words 'one minute' as she was pulled away. Alex closed the doors so they were cut off from any prying eyes.

"What now?" she crossed her arms in front of her chest when he had stopped and turned to her.

"Miranda, you are drunk. You do not want to go in there with him," Alex explained calmly, "He is what you would call a big jerk. He always has a different girl with him every time I see him and he uses them for a night and breaks it off. I am shocked he has not had any children yet."

She flushed angrily, "Alex, you have no right to tell me what to do."

"Your brother told me to look after you and he feels the same about Nathan," Alex tried next.

"I don't need a babysitter Alex! I know what I'm doing. Besides isn't this what you told me to do? Find someone and kiss him so that you don't have to be my first!" Alex was right. She shouldn't kiss someone for the first time on film. She really didn't know what she was doing and it would probably look terrible. Nathan was hot, who cares if he was a player, it was just a kiss and she would have to learn sometime.

"That is not what I meant. I do not care about how inexperienced you are. I just wanted to make sure your first kiss was special and not while you are drunk playing some stupid game or in front of the cameras for all of Utopia to see."

"You agreed to this game!" She poked him in the shoulder to emphasize this.

"I was wrong. I am slightly intoxicated," Alex smiled and shrugged.

"You agreed because you knew you had kissed almost every girl in the room anyways. I know exactly what you thought. Everyone but me," Miranda snapped.

"So you have learned how to read minds," Alex said with a smile.

"How could you do that to Alicia when you know she likes you?" Miranda retorted, angry. Luckily the music had been turned back up and no one could hear them.

"She likes the *famous* Alex just like you said," Alex frowned and rolled his eyes.

"How do you even know that? She likes you because she thinks you are a *super* nice guy and that she thinks you are a great person because of how you have always treated her. I asked her today." Miranda snorted because she had never been treated nicely by him.

"Oh please. She would not even give me a second look if I was not on television."

"Well you certainly don't think as highly of yourself as I thought," Miranda said, "Are we done here?" She turned to leave.

Alex grabbed her shoulder, "No, we are not done. Not until I talk you out of this."

"Alex. I won't find anyone else and Nathan has been perfectly nice to me."

"Just not him," he said, "You will regret it."

"Fine," Miranda said, her eyes flashed with anger, and without thinking twice she moved in close to Alex and pressed her lips to his. A surge of electricity went through her body and she gripped his shoulders tightly.

Alex stiffened, not expecting that at all. He almost pushed her away but seemed to have lost control of his arms. Instead of pushing her away he pulled her closer to him as he spun and pressed her against the wall. Miranda's hands slid up his neck and she wound her fingers into his hair. Alex opened his mouth, deepening the kiss further. Miranda could feel his heart racing against her chest as time seemed to stand still. She had no idea how long they had been kissing when she realized what was happening.

She had to push him away since she was pressed right up against the wall. Her whole body shook at the intense feelings that had bloomed inside her and she had to take in deep breaths. She looked into Alex's bewildered eyes. "I'm sure that will be my only regret tomorrow," she whispered harshly and slipped out of his arms, leaving him dumbfounded.

Miranda went back into the living room, everyone still lounging around.

"You know if you wanted Alex I could have set it up so you would get him," Pete laughed.

Miranda laughed, "Of course not!" She smiled but inside she was still reeling from what just happened. She grabbed Nathan's arm leading him into the back room.

Once inside, Miranda closed the door and closed her mind.

"What was that all about?" Nathan asked her.

"Nothing too important. He was just worried about what my brother would say." Miranda said, sitting on the bed. She patted the spot beside her and Nathan quickly sat down.

"Why does he care?"

"My brother told him to keep an eye on me and he seemed to take it seriously," Miranda rolled her eyes.

"Oh," Nathan said, nervously, "Are you sure about this then? I don't want to make your brother angry."

Miranda rolled her eyes, "Not you too. I've only had brothers for like two weeks and I've done fine without them since."

"Sorry," Nathan said quickly and smiled.

"So, what do you want to do then?"

Nathan's smile widened, "I don't know. Let's talk I guess."

"Ok," Miranda said, lying back on the bed. She took in the room. It was pink and had a pink floral bedspread. It must have been Alex's sister's room. There was nothing else in the room, not even a single picture. She must live with Alex's parents, wherever they had moved. "Tell me more about yourself. You have heard a lot about me."

"Well, I was born and raised in this city and I did not do that well in school. I live on the third floor with my parents. We moved here when I was eleven." Nathan started, running a hand through his blond hair, "I would rather talk about you though. Tell me about your earliest memory,"

Miranda thought about it for a second. "Well, I remember being really young and with my mother at the mall. I lost her and I was so frightened. But some woman helped me find her." Miranda could picture that woman's face even in her drunken state. She could remember the brown curly hair like hers and bright blue eyes. It had been her mother! It must have been! She had actually spoken to her mother when she was very young. Miranda leaned back on the bed as her eyes adjusted to the dark. "I think I remember it because it was traumatic for a young girl. I think I was three or four?"

"I am so glad to have met you," Nathan said as he touched her cheek, "Can I at least kiss you once?"

Miranda smiled and nodded. Nathan leaned over her and pressed his lips to hers just as there was a bang on the door and Pete yelled, "Ok, get out! I've got Rebecca now!"

Nathan smiled as he held a hand out to help Miranda up and she straightened her dress. Feeling a little embarrassed about seeing Alex again, she followed Nathan out closely behind him.

Alex didn't even look at her when she reached the main room. He had Alicia's phone in his hand and she sat beside him on the couch like a lovesick puppy, trying to make him laugh at the joke she just told. She nudged him playfully and then giggled. He just looked at her and smiled.

"You guys suck," Greg yelled over the radio at Nathan and Miranda, "You did not do anything, did you?"

They both ignored him and grabbed another drink. Instead of sitting down, Nathan pulled Miranda close to dance with her.

Miranda didn't know what to think and she could feel Alex's eyes burning into the back of her head. She tried her best to ignore it. Nathan seemed to really like her and he was such a gentleman asking to kiss her. Miranda could count on one hand how many guys liked her over her years. If Nathan was a player, perhaps he didn't want to be anymore. Maybe they would be together for a long time.

When the seven minutes were up, Greg got up to get the two out because Alex made no move to go.

They were definitely the most dishevelled when they got back to the living room. Pete even had his shirt on backwards and they basked in the applause and cat calls. Rebecca curtseyed and waved to everyone, laughing.

Alicia pulled Alex off the couch, "Come on, it is our turn."

He followed her to the back room without even a look back at Miranda.

"I wonder what's wrong with him?" Nathan asked, pulling slightly away from Miranda.

"Well, I did yell at him for butting in," Miranda laughed at her lie, "I don't think he likes that."

Nathan laughed and pulled her close to him again.

Miranda giggled, "My head is fuzzy." She moved her head side to side. She felt happy and uncoordinated at the same time. She had no idea how she was standing right now.

"That's all it really affects," Nathan told her, "I heard Earth's alcohol could actually hurt your liver and stuff. Not here. It is probably not even the same kind of alcohol, we just call it that. I believe long ago it was made the same way as on Earth but now it is something else entirely. It just gives you a nice buzz that goes away, depending on how much you drink and how fast. I'd say, judging by how much you had. You'll feel normal in a couple hours."

"That's good to know."

Nathan tried to make conversation with her but Miranda was not really answering his questions. She was wondering about Alex behind that door with Alicia. If he wasn't doing anything in there, why didn't he come out? It was obvious that unlike her, he didn't care about kissing someone he didn't want to. Miranda dismissed the fact that she could be jealous. Why should she be when she had Nathan? "Let's go," she said to him.

"To where? My place?"

"Sure, for a bit. I am getting tired."

They stopped dancing and said goodbye to those remaining in the room while Alex was still in the spare room. Miranda knew it was better that way, not wanting to argue with him again for even thinking about leaving with Nathan. She couldn't believe she kissed Alex. It had seemed like a good idea at the time but now she almost wished she hadn't. Miranda wondered if Alex was just talking too like she had with Nathan. At least she had more respect for herself that she didn't go make out with every guy. With Alex trying to keep his popularity up, as Evan put it, he'd probably kissed dozens of girls he didn't care about. Miranda vowed never to do that. She didn't want that kind of popularity. It must have been the alcohol because she never would have had the guts to do any of the events that night sober. She was almost shocked as she realized the whole 'Seven Minutes in Heaven' game had been her idea.

Miranda followed Nathan into the elevator and to the third floor. It was dark in his apartment and she could only make out shadows as he pulled her through his apartment and into his room.

Nathan's room was about the size of hers, but a dark blue in colour as the lights flicked on automatically when he walked in. He had a picture of a female model over his window. She wasn't wearing much clothing and that made Miranda feel a little uncomfortable. Is that what he liked on his walls?

They sat on his bed, neither of them talking. Miranda found this a little awkward until he reached over and pulled her to him.

He kissed her slowly at first. When his kisses grew more demanding, she pulled away. She didn't even know if he wanted a girlfriend and she wasn't going to do anything with him until she found out.

"What's wrong?" he asked.

She looked at her hands clenched on her lap, "Nothing."

"Like I said, I will respect any decision you make," Nathan whispered, taking Miranda's chin in his hand a raising her eyes to meet his.

Miranda nodded, "I know. Thanks."

They talked for a bit more about Nathan and he continued to ask her about Earth. He was really interested in where she grew up, which was very different from Alex who hated everything to do with Earth.

"How about we get you home and we can go out tomorrow night?"

"Sure. I would like that," Miranda agreed, giving him a quick hug before he led her out to the elevator where he kissed her hand again. She said 'good night' and the doors closed.

When Miranda reached her floor she jumped a little when she saw Alex waiting outside his door. He looked like he had been pacing.

"Lock yourself out?" Miranda smirked.

"Where did you go?" he asked angrily, taking a menacing step towards her.

"None of your business," she said moving away from him.

"It is my business. I was supposed to keep an eye on you and you just left with *him*."

"I told you I don't need a babysitter."

They glared at each other for a few seconds until Miranda asked, "Where's Alicia?"

"She left with the others after we got out of the back room. She was a little upset that I told her I did not like her that way."

"Smooth one," Miranda snorted and turned once again, "I'm going to bed."

"And I will be telling your brothers what you did."

Miranda spun around, her eyes flashing, "Don't you dare. I'm an adult. I can do what I want."

Alex moved closer to her so that they were almost nose to nose, "After how many times I tell you how he is, you decide to go home with him. And drunk nonetheless" he hissed.

"What do you think happened? I am not an idiot," she whispered angrily.

"No, but you are a stupid little girl who cannot take a little alcohol."

"What do you know?" she said, raising her voice. She felt so uncomfortable now to be so close to him.

"I know that you kissed me while you were drunk then you went over to some other guys place doing who knows what! I really did not think you were that kind of girl, Miranda but after you kissed me the way you did, I am not sure."

"The way I kissed you? You are the one who... You know what? You don't know me at all," Miranda hissed.

"Apparently I do not."

"What are you, jealous?"

"Not a chance," Alex said, rolling his eyes.

"Then leave me alone. I will do what I want!" Miranda said through clenched teeth.

"You will not do what you want," he whispered threateningly, "Your brothers will not be too happy with you."

"Stay out of my business!" she screamed and pushed him. She felt a heated energy escape from her palms. She hadn't pushed him hard, just enough to get him out of her face but he stumbled backwards pretty far hitting the wall behind him and Miranda looked shocked at what she'd done. "I'm sorry," she said quickly. She took a step towards Alex but paused as Alex sent her a glare. He turned abruptly and went to his apartment, the door shutting behind him.

Miranda quietly slipped into her own apartment and went to bed.

# Fifteen

★ ★ ★ ★

Miranda was having a nightmare again, the same one she always had. She was about to die and was looking expectantly around for her saviour. This time, she didn't have time to continue on when she was shaken awake.

"Miranda!" someone said angrily.

"What?" Miranda asked sleepily, rubbing her eyes. Turning to her notebook, she saw that it was only eight twenty-five. When she turned to look at Griffin, she noticed he wasn't the only one in her room. Both Evan and Alex were there as well.

"Oh God, this is worse than a hangover," Miranda groaned, rolling away from them and throwing her blanket over her head. She'd never had one before, but she remembered Helen after her birthday party. She was so ill the next day.

"What does that mean?" Griffin asked.

"Well, a hangover is what you get on Earth when you drink too much. It's usually accompanied by nausea and a headache. Pretty much an overall crappy feeling and I figured I'd say it out loud 'cause you guys would hear it in my mind anyways," she snapped, rolling onto her side and propping herself up on her elbow, "Can we skip the big brother discussion till later? I'm tired."

"Miranda, we need to talk to you now," Evan said, looking at her with concern.

"I don't know what that idiot told you," Miranda said, motioning to Alex, who rolled his eyes, "but it certainly isn't what you think."

"Oh really? Because he tells us you slipped away while he was busy and went home with Nathan," Griffin snapped.

Miranda snorted. "Busy? Oh yes, Alex was *very* busy and only *ever* speaks the truth," Miranda said sarcastically.

Her brothers looked at her, shocked. "How dare he!" Griffin said, pounding a fist on her desk.

"Oh please! If you think I did anything more than kiss him, you've got the wrong girl! I'm not like that!" she screamed at them, getting up from her bed in her tiny little baby doll nightdress. She really didn't care what she was wearing, she was furious. "How would you know anyways? You don't know me at all. I did fine before I met all of you and I don't need your protection. I'm an adult!" Griffin had taken a step back and she had all the boys cornered. They stared at her, not saying a word. Miranda turned to Alex, "I told you to stay out of my business. What is your problem?"

"I warned you about him and you did not listen!" he said, frustrated, "I just told you so you would not get hurt. I figured if you would not listen to me, you would listen to your brothers."

"I wouldn't let anything happen that I didn't want to and I don't need brothers to tell me what I want or don't want. I've done well without them so far. I've never done any drugs and rarely have I done any underage drinking. I've never been pregnant because I've never even *had* sex or got close to it," Miranda snapped, listing the things on her fingers, "Hell, I've never even kissed someone till yesterday. Maybe you guys didn't know this or didn't want to know but I'm old enough to make my own decisions!" She turned back to Alex, "Besides, you obviously didn't tell them the whole story, just your twisted version of it."

Alex looked at her pleadingly and Miranda smiled triumphantly. He obviously never told them about the game but if he was going to rat her out, she could do the same.

Miranda told them about the game and where Alex really was when Miranda left.

"Great job Alex! I leave you to watch my sister one night and you go and kiss Alicia! What about..." Evan stopped, thinking before he continued, "Sidney!"

"We broke up yesterday morning," Alex said defensively, "And you both know me. I told Alicia that I did not want to do this with her and that I was sorry but I was still not interested. She really did not care about what I thought. She wanted to kiss me anyways just to tell everyone that she did, again. I read it in her thoughts. She was all over me before I knew it and I was drunk but I pushed her away. How was I supposed to know Miranda would leave in the short time I was in that room?"

Griffin sighed. Neither he nor Evan knew what to say. It was true, Miranda had not had them her whole life and was perfectly capable on her own but they were just worried about her dating the wrong person, someone like Nathan.

"And I even waited to make sure she got back. If she had taken much longer I would have went and got her," Alex continued when no one said anything.

Miranda tried to calm herself down. She didn't want to hurt her brothers' feelings. She was very happy they were in her life now. She sat down on the bed and ran a hand through her hair, taking a deep calming breath. Her brothers both took a seat on either side of her.

"You are right," Evan sighed putting a head on her shoulder, "We do not know you very well."

Griffin put a hand on her other shoulder, "I am not angry with you. I just do not like Nathan, I never have. I see what he does to girls and I am not a really good friend to him. I only see him once in awhile around the building."

"I am sorry too," Evan agreed, "I guess we should get to know you better before jumping to conclusions. We overreacted but we do want to warn you about Nathan. I do not like him either and I am glad Alex told us."

"Yes and I think Mr. Perfect and I should have a little conversation," Miranda said, eyeing Alex angrily. He wasn't looking at her but was staring at the bookshelf defiantly.

Her brother's got up and Evan whispered a good luck to Alex as he passed him and shut the door.

"You are such a jerk!" Miranda whispered when the door had closed.

"Save it Maddie, you are just as bad as I am," he whispered back, "We were both drunk. I just have a better sense of responsibility."

"Oh please, YOU have a better sense of responsibility. Ha! You did more with Alicia than I even thought about doing with Nathan!"

"Jealous?" he smirked.

"Oh, please. You are so full of yourself," Miranda snapped, her arms folding across her chest.

"Am I?" Alex questioned, his eyebrows raised. He knelt in front of her putting a hand on either side of her, so she had to look at him. "You think I have not heard every word you have *ever* thought about me."

Miranda blushed out of anger, mostly, "If you didn't notice, I just think you're hot. Your personality stinks so that takes all your hotness points away!"

"What am I? A game?"

Miranda snorted, "You said so yourself. Alicia wanted to kiss you so she could go tell all her friends that she kissed the *famous* Alex West."

Alex looked hurt.

"And I did it too, Alex," Miranda whispered harshly, "I just wish I wasn't embarrassed by it or else I would tell all my friends."

Alex stood and turned away, "You are such a mean person. I cannot believe you are related to your brothers. I wish we had left you on Earth."

Miranda's eyes filled with tears. He was the one who was cruel. "Why would you tell my brothers?"

"I told your brothers because they deserve to know and tell you their opinion of Nathan."

"I don't need their opinion. I can make my own decisions and I don't need you to protect me!" Miranda said, hotly. She wiped away an escaped tear from her cheek.

"Yes you do!" Alex said. He turned back to her. "You had no idea what you were getting into."

"You want to be my hero, don't you? What do you want to prove?" Miranda said, standing as well. The strap on her nightgown fell down her shoulder, revealing a lot more skin than necessary for this conversation.

Alex's breath caught in his throat as his eyes lowered to what she was wearing and something in the air seemed to seize them. Both of them remembered the kiss they shared and both looked poised to spring into each other's arms to do it again.

Alex absentmindedly put his hand to her face and wiped away another tear before he withdrew it quickly. "N-nothing," he stammered after the brief pause, taking a step away from her, "I was just watching out for you because your brother told me to."

"Find yourself another damsel in distress! I don't need you!"

"Fine!" he said throwing his hands in the air, and walked out, closing the door behind him.

Miranda sunk to her bed slowly after he left and let the tears flow. *Why did I kiss him? He is so mean.* He even admitted right there how much he hated her. He wished they had left her on Earth.

Miranda tried to fall back to sleep but her mind was racing. Of course, she had probably deserved it for saying those things to him but he took it too far.

Eventually she fell back to sleep and when she awoke at one, there was no one home so she decided to go lay out in the sunshine and study. Jackson had given her some reading homework.

Soon after, Alicia joined her. Miranda had sent her a message asking if she wanted to meet her outside to do homework together.

"Hi," Alicia greeted her, a little glumly.

"Hey, I'm sorry. I heard about what happened with Alex."

"I will be fine. I thought I would try one last time but I guess I will truly give up now. He is still a great guy."

"Ya," Miranda snorted, sarcastically.

"So, how did it go with Nathan?" Alicia took a seat on the lounge chair beside her, her notebook in hand.

"Fine, we just kissed. I am still not sure what to think."

"I am sure you will make the right decision," Alicia smiled.

Miranda laughed, "Perhaps I should just forget them all and go for Jackson."

"Oh, he is so cute! Maybe you should!" Alicia agreed with a smile as she laid back.

"I know he thinks I am pretty," Miranda blushed, "I heard him think it."

Alicia giggled, "That is a good start."

Miranda thought about him for a minute but then shook her head, "Or maybe I should just concentrate on school and the show and let come what may." She held up the history book Jackson had given her. "I should get studying."

Alicia cocked her head to read the title, "Forgotten Utopian Legends? I have never heard of that book."

Miranda looked at the book in her hand, "Really? It is not a school book?"

Alicia shook her head, "I never studied from it." She sat up again.

*Huh,* Miranda thought and passed the book to Alicia's outstretched hand. She flipped it open and gasped.

"This is a real book!" Alicia exclaimed, "Made from a tree!"

"How is that possible?" Miranda asked, leaning over to see the date. It was about 3 billion years old.

"They preserved the pages with new technology but yes, this is very old." Alicia pulled out her notebook and looked for the book title but couldn't find it, "Hmm. That is odd. You cannot buy this book. What is it about?"

"So far just ancient war heroes and battles," Miranda explained, "I have only read the first two legends."

"Interesting. I wonder if that book is his family heirloom. I cannot believe what good condition it is in." She flipped it over in her hands and then passed it back to Miranda.

"It must be important to him then. Guess I should get reading!" Miranda exclaimed.

"You want to go for a swim?" Alicia asked after an hour of studying. She didn't wait for an answer and stripped down to her bathing suit. Miranda agreed and they went inside to the pool. The water cooled her sun-warmed skin as Miranda dove in.

Nathan sent her a message that he had to cancel their date that night and reschedule for Tuesday, which Alicia and Miranda then analyzed. Miranda was worried he was seeing someone else but Alicia tried to reassure her. Was this how Miranda was going to feel whenever Nathan was away? It didn't make for a good relationship.

When Alicia left, Miranda did a few laps before she was startled by Alex at the end of the pool.

"Hey Alex," she said as she pulled herself up and out of the pool.

He gave her a questioning look, surprised she wasn't bitter with him, before he returned her greeting.

"I am sorry about this morning. Some of the things I said were out of line," she said, swallowing her pride. It seemed with Alex, she would have to give a little to get a change of attitude in him.

"I accept," Alex said, narrowing his eyes. He was not sure if she was genuine or not.

Miranda stood under the heater which dried her quickly and she put her dress overtop of her bathing suit.

"Come on," Alex said, with a sigh, "I will make you dinner." He took her hand and headed for the elevator, "I have the script to your first day in two weeks."

Miranda smiled, excitedly, "Send it now!"

Once they stepped in the elevator, Alex took out his notebook and Miranda's vibrated. She pulled it out, tapped the new document and read the first few lines.

"I thought we could maybe practice," Alex said, "After dinner?"

Miranda nodded absentmindedly as she read a little more. She followed Alex into his apartment while she read.

"I am sorry too," Alex said, turning to her, "I did not mean it when I said we should have left you on Earth. I felt awful for making you cry."

Miranda looked up to meet his eyes, "Do you mean that?"

Alex nodded. Miranda was so happy she threw her arms around him, "Thanks Alex."

While they ate, Alex flicked the television on and tuned in to a hockey game. A team called the Knights were playing the Whales and Miranda was pulled away from her reading.

"Oh, my favourite team at home was the Knights!" she told Alex, "They were not professional or anything but Helen and I went to a lot of their games." She tried to explain to Alex about the draft picks and the different leagues they had on Earth. Once she was finished her mind was on Helen. Hockey reminded Miranda of her, especially since it was something they had both liked. She wasn't going to see her best friend ever again. A few tears sprang to her eyes as she watched the game in silence until the threat of tears subsided.

"Well, I suppose we should get practising," Alex said, turning the volume down.

Miranda tried to smile.

"So, this first scene is where we meet. There is a ball for one of Gould's birthdays. It will be a huge deal and very formal. Everything will be elegant. Do you want to stand?"

Miranda stood up and Alex flicked his wrist and the coffee table moved over slightly so they had more room. Miranda stared at the coffee table and concentrated hard on it. She flicked her wrist as Alex had done but the table didn't move. She flicked her wrist again and again but it still didn't move so she got angry and gave it a little push with her foot.

"Stupid table," she muttered, a little frustrated. She would definitely have to ask Jackson if they could work on moving things with her head. She looked at Alex who looked like he was trying so hard not to laugh, "Don't you dare laugh," Miranda said, pointing her finger threateningly, but smiling.

Alex forced his face into a frown, "Of course."

"Do we ever go over the script as a cast? I know on Earth they have like run-throughs and stuff like that," she said, changing the subject.

"No, our brains are more advanced. We remember things easily."

Miranda thought back to Earth. She did have an easy time remembering her lines for all the plays she was in which was probably why she always had so much time to perfect her body movements.

They ran through their lines quickly during that scene. Jeff was going to ask Cara to dance and they would be getting to know each other as they danced.

They practiced the lines just standing there first and then Alex suggested they dance as well. He took Miranda's hand and put his other arm at her waist, swaying her gently side to side, spinning in a slow circle.

Miranda flushed a little at the closeness remembering the kiss last night which sent chills down her spine. They ran over the lines as they slowly turned in a small circle.

*Hmm*, Miranda thought, *I wonder if Alex knows any good moves*.

Alex spun her and caught her in a low dip.

"Oh, I got moves," he teased, smiling down at her.

Miranda's face flushed deeper red as he pulled her back up and spun her again. Miranda let out a laugh as she flowed with Alex's every move.

"You really have not danced before?" he asked, when he once again pulled her in towards him.

"Yes, I have," she said. *Just the other night at the bar of course,* she added in her mind.

He stopped dancing but still held her with one arm around the waist, his right hand held hers "Liar."

"Shut up!" Miranda said, her anger rising. So she hadn't big deal.

"I was not going to make fun of you, I was just making conversation."

"Well, keep your conversation out of my business. Look at me! I was taller than all the boys on Earth. Who would dance with me?"

"Please do not get angry. Really, I was just going to compliment you. I think we could spice up the scene a bit. You know we *are* supposed to enjoy one another," he said, letting her go and sitting on the chair.

She followed suit and sat on the couch, "Ok, what did you have in mind?"

"Well, exactly what we did with the conversation in between and you have to laugh, just like you did. It was perfect."

Alex stood up again, "Come on, work with me," he said, holding out a hand to help her up. Alex choreographed the whole scene and timed the lines perfectly. Miranda watched Alex carefully. He was very good at what he did and she could tell he really enjoyed it.

They went over that scene a few times, exactly as Alex planned, then the next two scenes, which would take place on the boardwalk and by the water.

"Well that was perfect too! Shall we move to the next scene?" Miranda asked, as they sat down once again. She hated to admit it but she actually was enjoying herself and Alex had some great ideas.

Alex fidgeted. He looked nervous.

"What happens in the next scene?" Miranda asked. She knew something must be up with the way he was acting.

"We kiss," Alex said, looking away.

Miranda blushed again, thinking about last night. "Let's skip that scene and move to the next one," she suggested and Alex readily agreed.

There were only a few more scenes Miranda was in though. There was the next scene where they kissed, another where she sees him and his fiancée and only has a short monologue as she watches them walk away. That scene takes place the following day after the dance and the final scene was the one from her audition, but extended.

They went over the audition scene with the few extra lines that had been added, but Miranda knew it by heart so they moved on to the kissing scene.

They ran through it quickly standing side by side, which on camera would be filmed outdoors beside Cara's car. Miranda stopped when she read the words, *Jeff kisses Cara*, and laughed nervously.

"Can I kiss you Miranda?" Alex asked.

Miranda did a double take at Alex's face. *Was he kidding?* She nodded, thinking he was joking and to Miranda's surprise, Alex pulled her close to him and kissed her. It was short but Miranda could feel it all the way to her toes. She forgot everything, including her next line.

"Well, I figured since we have kissed already, it would not be your first time anymore," Alex snapped, "Now that we have gotten the first one out of the way, we may as well get it perfect."

"I'm sorry, I wasn't expecting that," Miranda mumbled, "Just give me a second."

"Are you going to do that when we film?" Alex asked, raising an eyebrow.

"No, I just…never mind," Miranda said, looking at the floor, "Let's try this again."

They went over all the scenes a few times. Alex kissed her every time and each time seemed to get longer and longer.

Alex had just kissed her again when someone cleared their throat from the foyer.

Miranda broke away, her face flushing.

Griffin was there, staring daggers at Alex, "Oh, there you are Miranda," he muttered through clenched teeth.

"S-sorry Griffin, I…uh… should have messaged to say where I was," Miranda stuttered, "W-we were just going over the script."

Griffin raised an eyebrow, "Oh?"

"You knew what Evan had written," Alex said, glaring back at Griffin.

"Right," Griffin said, his face still set.

"Well, I think we have had enough practice for one night," Miranda smirked and decided this was her cue to go, "Later Alex." She left her brother there.

Greta was sitting on the couch when she got to her apartment.

"Hi," she smiled and went to sit with her.

"You look happy," Greta replied, looking at her up and down.

"I got the script for my first day of filming," she said, excitedly, "Alex and I were just practicing."

"Oh?"

"Yes. And he was actually nice to me," Miranda replied. Now that she got to think about it, she actually had a good time.

"See? I told you he was a nice guy," Greta smiled and squeezed her leg.

Miranda shrugged as Griffin walked in.  She sent him a small smile, trying to assess his mood. She wondered what he said to Alex after he had seen them kissing.

"Oh!" Greta gasped.

"It was nothing Greta," Miranda rolled her eyes, "It was in the scene."

"Oh," Greta smiled and turned to her boyfriend, "Griffin, relax."

Griffin made a face, "I know." He sat in the chair, pouting.

Miranda stifled a fake yawn, "Wow, I'm tired. I think I'll go to bed. Long day of school tomorrow!" She left the room. Her brother was so over-protective. It was just Alex!

* * *

Miranda awoke with a start and took in a long breath. These dreams were really starting to worry her. Why was she dying every night?

It was still early so Miranda took out her history book. She read through the table of contents looking for something interesting. The *Legend of East* caught her eye. She turned to page 166.  As if the first time didn't process, she had to read it again.

*The Legend of East*

*Long ago, as Utopia was created, an evil resided deep in its core. This evil would never let the good planet find peace. Evil will always possess those who are weak of mind.*

*This account is taken from the dawn of the millennium in the year two billion six hundred, sixty six million, at the first awakening of the evil inside.*

*Possessed by evil, a man enslaved thousands, murdering them by the most atrocious means. At every murder, the oceans churned violently alerting the one true being who could stop it, the third child of East. For long ago, the power of good bestowed upon the cursed planet a lineage. Every third child of East would be able to harness the power of good to overcome the evil core.*

*When the man was defeated, evil was enraged and placed a new curse. This curse plagued the East family and every third child fell ill and died before the age of two. This continued for centuries but evil would not prevail.*

*Good saved a child from its untimely death and placed it in the care of the West. When it looked like all hope was lost, the planet shaking with every violent death by a group of men and women possessed by evil, Good returned and explained to the East and West the mighty powers they would now possess. Good granted protection over the first child of West so that evil could never again curse the East family. A new destiny was founded.*

*Only the powers of East and West combined could purge the planet from the evil core. Evil hid. Evil is patient and awaits the day to possess those weak of mind again.*

*When East and West face,*
*Join hands, exchange words,*
*White light will shine,*
*The evil is purged.*

*What are these words?*
*I cannot tell.*
*For only true hearts,*
*Can perform this spell.*

*You will know*
*When the time is here.*

*That evil is gone,*
*There's nothing to fear.*

*Find the ones you love*
*Dance and sing.*
*Your planet is saved,*
*And fear nothing.*

*What would happen,*
*Should East and West fall?*
*The chief of evil*
*Will help darkness prevail.*

*He will kill the chosen ones,*
*And good will mourn.*
*No new saviour*
*Can be born.*

Below the poem, the top portion of what looked like a ying yang character and the translation below it read 'Evil is in all good things'.

Miranda shook as she read the final words again. The tears spilled down her cheeks. This was a connection. She'd seen that character before in her dreams. *But how?* How did her mind know this character and produce it in her dreams? Was she this saviour? She was definitely the third child of East! Is this why her mother hid her?

As if on cue, the ground beneath her bed started to rumble and her stomach dropped. *What was she supposed to do?*

Her door slid open and she hastily shoved the book under her pillow. It was her dad. He had a frightened look on his face. The rest of her family were right behind him.

They all gathered in her room, waiting. No one spoke as the ground continued to shake.

"Why isn't it stopping?" Miranda cried, clutching at her bed.

Greta put her arms around Miranda, "It is close by," she whispered to her. The shaking caused the books on Miranda's shelf and her Earth pictures to fall over and onto the ground.

Evan suddenly looked even more worried, "I have to check on Alex."

Their dad nodded and motioned for him to go.

Evan struggled a bit on the un-sturdy ground but managed to make it out of the room.

Miranda clung to Greta, burying her face in her shoulder. Finally after what seemed like five minutes, the rumbling stopped. Miranda extracted herself from Greta's arms and got up quickly. She wanted to make sure her brother and Alex were ok.

They were walking in the door as the family reached the foyer. Miranda gave them both a quick hug.

She turned to her family. *Did they know?* "Why does this happen?" she asked. It seemed like a safe question. She shut her mind down.

"No one knows," Mr. East shook his head sadly.

"Isn't there something that someone can do?" she asked, looking to everyone. They all shook their heads. Maybe no one did know. Someone must though. She looked at Alex and he glanced her way. Is he a first child? She had no idea. The thought made her nauseous. Was that why she felt drawn to him?

It dawned on her though that it was Jackson's book. If Alex had no idea then it must be Jackson. She felt a strong attraction to him too. It could be him. She shook her head clear it again as she sat with her family.

"No one knows why and no one knows what to do," Greta said sadly, "How it could happen in this place is just awful."

Mr. East pulled out his phone to check on the family as Evan turned on the television. The attack was being investigated at an apartment very close to theirs.

"So, when it's like that, it means its close-by?" Miranda asked. Tears filled her eyes. What could she do to stop it?

"There is nothing you can do," Mr. East said, trying to reassure his daughter.

They all sat quietly, watching the news story. The footage on the screen showed a whole building in ruin. There were no confirmations yet if anyone had been in it. Miranda's heart sank. Of course people were in it. It was still the early morning when most were asleep.

Finally Mr. East stood, "I should get ready. Can we all travel together?"

"Yes dad. Alex and I can drop Miranda off at school before we go to the studio," Evan said. He stood up as well, pulling out his phone, "I will call and tell Melissa we will be an hour late."

"I can go to school early if you want," Miranda said quietly. She really needed to talk to Jackson. Just as thought this, her phone buzzed in her pocket, not once, but three times. There were messages from her friends group. Alicia was making sure everyone was ok. There were also messages from Nathan and Jackson. She told the latter two that she was fine and then sent a message to Alicia telling her she would be getting a ride to school.

"No, it is alright Miranda," Evan said, forcing a smile, "We can be late."

Miranda tried to smile back and went to her room. It seemed like she had a lot to talk to Jackson about today. She pulled the book out from under her pillow and tucked it into her purse. She sat in the chair by the window, thinking. What was she going to do? How should she approach the subject with Jackson?

There was a tap on the door which startled Miranda out of her thinking.

Miranda had to clear her throat before she could speak, "Come in."

Evan opened the door, "Are you ok?"

"Yes, I was just getting ready for school."

Evan looked down at her in her pyjamas and sitting in the chair, "Getting ready?"

Miranda forced a laugh, "I… uh… was just thinking I guess."

"Scary way to wake up?" Evan asked as he crossed his arms and leaned against the door frame.

Miranda nodded.

"We will be ok," Evan tried to smile, "Try not to worry."

She nodded again.

"The bathroom is free now but if you are already ready then I guess we can go," he smirked.

Miranda rolled her eyes, "You know what? I think I do need the bathroom." She stuck her tongue out at him and he chuckled.

The car ride to school was quiet. Alex dropped her off at the top of the building this time. They watched until the elevator picked her up and the doors closed.

She took the elevator to the bottom, hoping to catch Alicia before class. The mood at school was sobering. Everyone looked a little anxious. She found Alicia at her locker and they talked a bit about the morning before they separated for class. Alicia did not know who the victim or victims were either.

Miranda took a deep breath as the elevators opened to the sixth floor. She still had no idea what she was going to say to Jackson. Or if she should even bring it up. What if he had no idea either? Then maybe he wasn't *the* one?

She saw Jackson in the room even before she opened the door. He also looked anxious.

When she opened the door, she couldn't help herself. She started to cry. Sob uncontrollably, actually.

Jackson had his arms around her in seconds. He quietly rubbed her back as she let it all out.

"I'm so sorry Jackson," Miranda said, embarrassed, when she finally calmed enough to speak.

"Tell me what is wrong," he said, soothingly.

She pulled away and opened her purse. She handed him the book.

He mouthed the word 'oh' and leaned back on the desk, holding the book out in front of him and whispered, "You read ahead."

Miranda nodded, the tears glistening in her eyes.

"I did not want you to find out this way," Jackson said, sadly. He frowned and looked at the ground.

"You shouldn't have given me that book then," Miranda tried to smile, but it faltered. "So it's true? Us?"

Jackson nodded, "My mother told me last year and I believe your mother knew as well."

Miranda's eyes widened, "My mother knew? What about the rest of my family?"

Jackson shook her head, "No. I do not believe they know of the legend. Not even my family. My father and brother do not know of it either."

Miranda just stared at him, stared at this man who was supposed to be some sort of protector or soulmate to her. Could she love him? What if she didn't?

Jackson's looked up into her eyes, "This was definitely not the way I wanted this to happen. I was hoping we could go on a date and maybe take it from there. I was hoping you would give me a chance before you knew about the legend so that you would not feel forced."

"Don't you feel forced?" Miranda asked, searching his eyes.

"At first yes, but now, no," Jackson smiled, shyly, "Just spending one week with you was enough. I think you are everything I could ask for."

She blushed.

"I am sorry I could not make it to your party this weekend," Jackson smiled and took her hand, "I was very disappointed when you asked me and I was already out of town."

Miranda didn't know what to say. Today had already been very overwhelming and it was still the morning.

Jackson sighed. He was at a loss as well.

After a minute of thinking and silence, Miranda looked at him in the eyes, "Can I try something?"

Jackson nodded.

Miranda stepped in close to him and tilted her head up. She made it very clear what she was about to do and Jackson caught on and met her halfway. When their lips met, Miranda felt a familiar tingle run through her. It was nothing desperate or uncontrollable like she felt with Alex and it didn't feel wrong like it felt with Nathan.

Miranda pulled back, a smile on her flushed face. Jackson was also flustered.

"That was nice," Miranda said.

Jackson chuckled and turned to grab his notebook off the desk, "I think we deserve a day off. Will you spend the day with me?"

Miranda smiled wider, "Sure."

# Sixteen

★　★　★　★

Miranda put the legend to the back of her mind as she sat in Jackson's car. She wanted to try and forget about it, just for the day. Jackson was so far very smart, handsome and treated her amazingly.

Miranda looked down as they left the city limits and flew above the wall. There was not a lot to see aside from the trees.

"Have you not left the city?" Jackson asked, smiling. He gave her knee a squeeze.

"Not yet!" Miranda said excitedly, not turning to him, staring out the window, "Where are we going?"

He smirked, "It is a surprise!"

They drove for an hour asking simple questions, typical of a first date. Jackson grew up in City 217. He had always wanted to be a teacher and did very well in school. He had a brother who was one year younger named James. He lived at the opposite end of the city as the East's apartment. His mother had a clothing store and his father was a building manager.

Miranda could see the ocean before they had arrived. The blue-green expanse which stretched as far as she could see was breathtaking. She had learned from Jackson that Utopia was a planet about the size of Earth but with only two large continents. There were a few islands just off of the continents which were used as vacation spots.

They parked on a long plain of grass in front of the beach and together they walked to the shore.

"Oh Jackson! It's so beautiful," she smiled up at him and he returned her smile.

"Have you ever been windsurfing?" he asked.

She shook her head.

"Come with me," he said as he took her hand and they headed down the beach, "We will have to buy a change of clothes but that is ok."

"Jackson, please don't spend too much on me."

But Jackson was in a great mood and wouldn't hear it.

Miranda had so much fun learning to windsurf. They were out on the water for hours. Jackson was already a professional. Miranda leaned into his tall body as it held her firmly in place. She could get used to this.

When her arms couldn't take it anymore, she sat in front of him on a blanket he had in his car on the beach and he massaged her shoulders. Once in a while he would brush his lips on her shoulder. She smiled every time he did.

"Are you hungry?" he whispered in her ear and then looked at the time on his notebook, "Oh, it is almost dinner time. You must be starved!" He stood and pulled her up with him.

"You have already done enough Jack," she hugged him and rested her head on his shoulder. It was amazing how comfortable she felt with him already. "We can head back and eat at home."

"No," he smiled as he shook his head, "I want to have dinner with you as well."

"Alright," she returned his smile and rolled her eyes dramatically, "If you must."

He chuckled and pulled her off the beach and to the tiny restaurant nearby which had lobster. Miranda was amazed when the tiny dab of liquid turned into an already de-shelled lobster drenched in butter and a mixture of liquid into a garden salad. She had never tried to make anything like that yet.

They ate and chatted happily. She felt like she had known Jackson forever and was comfortable telling him all about her secrets and her worst fears. She told him about her nightmares.

Jackson frowned, "I do not have nightmares. I am so sorry. Maybe they will stop now that you know?"

"I hope so," Miranda said sadly, "They are so frightening sometimes."

He touched her arm softly.

"Anyways," she smiled, and waved her other hand, "Let's forget about that. Thank you so much for this amazing day!"

"Did you really enjoy yourself?" he asked, hopeful.

"Of course," Miranda smiled, "I definitely do not feel forced."

Jackson looked overjoyed and leaned to give her a quick kiss.

"You two make a cute couple," the waitress said, appearing at their table to refill their water glasses. Jackson smiled and put a hand on top of Miranda's and gave it a squeeze.

Miranda was having such a great time that she completely forgot about her phone and her family. She had left her phone in Jackson's car the whole day. When they were on their way home after dinner, she checked her phone. She had 12 missed calls and messages from everyone in her family as well as Alex.

"Oh no!" her smile faded as she could sense the panic in the messages.

"What is it?" Jackson asked, his smile fading as he glanced her way.

"I missed 12 calls and I have so many messages!" Miranda's eyes glistened with tears. She hadn't meant to worry her family especially after that morning.

She tapped her father's name and after seconds, his face appeared.

Miranda didn't have time to say a word before he cut in, "Oh Miranda! I am so glad you are ok!"

"I'm so sorry dad," Miranda said as a tear slipped down her face.

"What is wrong? Where are you?" he asked anxiously.

Miranda wiped her face, "I am absolutely fine. I am just upset at myself for worrying all of you. Can we talk when I get home? I will be there soon."

Mr. East's face softened, "Of course Miranda. Do not be sad. I am just so glad you are ok."

"I will be home in 25 minutes," Miranda assured him before they disconnected. She turned to Jackson, "I am so awful. How could I not think of them?"

"I am so sorry that I did not think of it either," Jackson frowned, "I was just having so much fun."

Miranda touched his arm, "Me too. Thank you so much."


Jackson dropped her off on the top of her building. She gave him a kiss on the cheek and thanked him again.

"I will see you tomorrow," Jackson smiled.

Miranda shut the door and watched the car as he drove away. When she turned towards the elevator, someone stepped out of the shadow and Miranda let out a small squeal.

"Do you have any idea how worried your family has been?" Alex snapped.

Miranda put a hand on her heart and sighed, "You scared the crap outta me Alex!"

He faced off against her, "You have no idea what you put your family through. You scared them."

Miranda's face flushed, "I know, Alex. And I feel horrible about it but I don't need a lecture from you right now. I want to go see my family."

"Who were you with?" Alex said and pressed the button to call the elevator.

"Jackson."

He made a face, "All day? Evan and I went to pick you up from school and Alicia said she had not seen you since the morning."

"We went to study the ocean," Miranda lied.

Alex snorted, "Do not lie to me."

"You know what?" Miranda snapped, "It is none of your business!"

Alex's eyes flashed with anger, "Yes, it is my business. He is my cousin and your family is my family. How dare you worry them the way you did after the attack this morning?"

"I know!" Miranda yelled as the door opened, "I feel awful. Just leave me alone!"

They arrived on their floor and Alex stomped over to the East's apartment. Miranda had barely a second to take a breath before she had to face her family.

Her father was so relieved to see her that he didn't even need an explanation. He hugged her tight and asked that she please keep him informed when she was not going to come home when he thought she would be. Evan and Griffin were a different story.

When their father went to his bedroom to read for the evening, both turned on her while Greta tried to keep the peace. Alex seemed to steam in silence.

"Where were you?" Griffin snapped, as soon as their father's door had closed.

"Griffin, I am so sorry for worrying you all," Miranda pleaded, "I never meant to do that."

"Where were you?" he asked again, ignoring her plea.

"She went to *study* the ocean with Jackson," Alex answered for her.

"Jackson? Your trainer?" Evan asked incredulously, looking from Alex to Miranda.

"Yes," Miranda said, looking down.

"I am calling the school tomorrow to have him released from that job," Griffin seethed.

"No!" Miranda said, raising her voice, "I made a mistake. It has nothing to do with him."

"Why were you with him?" Evan asked.

"He wanted to show me the ocean. He thought I might enjoy it and he taught me how to windsurf."

"I did not think that was part of the curriculum," Griffin said, his eyes narrowed.

"Do not be like that," Greta cut in as she rubbed Griffin's arm, "I am sure he is a very nice boy from what Alex has said before."

"That does not matter, Greta," Evan said, "The point is he is supposed to train her, not date her."

"He is training me," Miranda snapped, "I was sad after this morning and he thought he would cheer me up. Besides, even if we were going to date, he can still be my trainer. Both him and I know that my education is the most important." She was trying not to get angry at her over-protective brothers since it was her fault she had been late but they were being ridiculous.

"Miranda, you are not really making things positive for you," Griffin said, "First you go to Nathan's apartment and then I see you and Alex together," he said, shooting Alex an angry glare, "And now you spent the day with your trainer?"

Alex's face burned and Greta gasped, "Griffin!" Evan seemed to side with Griffin, though he wasn't worried about Alex. It *was* in the script. Miranda's mouth dropped open and her eyes flashed, "How dare you Griffin!" She rose from the chair and moved towards him, a finger raised. She planted herself right in front of him, "Don't you ever insinuate something like that about me again!" she threatened.

Griffin was about to say something but Miranda didn't let him continue, "Don't you dare! I am 16 years old and I will see whomever I please! I am not some slutty little tramp who sleeps around and even if I was, I am old enough to make that choice."

"She is absolutely right Griffin," Greta agreed, "You know your sister. Why are you so worried about her?"

Griffin gave Greta a hard look and rubbed his face with his hand. His expression changed to one of pain, "We were so worried Miranda. After the attack this morning, how could you let us worry like that? When our mother did not come home after an attack we found out she had been killed." His eyes glistened.

Miranda's hand fell to her side and her expression softened. She bent down and hugged her brother, "Griffin, I am fine. I was home with you today when the ground shook," she whispered softly.

He pulled her into a bear hug which took her breathe away, "I know. It had just happened so close by and the bad people could still have been near."

"But I am here and I am so sorry I worried you all. Jackson feels awful too. He honestly was just trying to cheer me up after this morning," Miranda said as she pulled away.

Evan made a face and looked at Alex who was quiet. Alex shook his head to himself and got up, "I am going home. Sleep well everyone."

"Good night Alex," Greta replied and waited till he left, "Are we done here now? Your sister is sorry and she is fine." She looked between the two brothers.

Griffin finally nodded.

"Ok good!" Greta smiled, "Now I am going to have some girl time with Miranda." She stood and held her hand out to Miranda, smiling.

Miranda returned her smile and took her hand. They went off to Miranda's room so she could tell her all about her day.

"So he bought you dinner after?" Greta smiled as she lay across Miranda's bed.

Miranda blushed and gave a small smile, "Yes. He was so nice to me all day. I think I really like him."

"No more Nathan?" Greta laughed.

Miranda thought about it for a second. What would she say to Nathan? They were supposed to have a date tomorrow.

Greta was listening, "Well, unlike what your brothers think, you do not have to see just one person. It is not like you officially are with one. You can give them both a shot and see what happens."

"I guess."

Greta smiled and then put a finger to her lips and whispered, "I was dating two boys in the beginning. But your brother won my heart. You are still young Miranda. You do not have to fall for someone right away. You just got here. Enjoy yourself."

Miranda nodded and put her feet up on the bed, stretching on the chair, "How come you two aren't married yet?"

Greta frowned, "I think your brother was going to ask but then your mother passed."

Miranda sat up straight, "Oh I'm so sorry."

Greta gave her a half smile, "It is ok. I am hoping he will work up the nerve again."

"So how do you know he was going to?"

"I found the ring," she smiled sheepishly, "It was hidden in his old jacket that I decided I wanted to wear one day."

"Oh! A ring is a sign of marriage here too? Was it pretty?"

"Yes, it is a very old tradition. A ring represents something that cannot be broken," Greta sighed happily, "And it was gorgeous!" She described the intricate band decorated with gleaming red stones.

"Sounds lovely! I hope he asks soon! I would love to see a Utopian wedding," Miranda winked.

"Not just see it but you would be in the wedding party!"

Miranda squealed with joy and hugged Greta.


*Miranda was back out in the ocean windsurfing when the wind picked up. She could no longer hold onto the sail and went tumbling into the water. When she resurfaced, she was far from shore and the board was drifting away from her.*

*She swam towards it in a panic. As she neared the board, something grabbed her foot and pulled her under.*

*Miranda kicked her feet trying to get whatever it was to let go. She couldn't see anything in the blackness around her only a fading light above as she got pulled deeper and deeper. She struggled against it, trying to break for the surface. She needed to breathe and felt an ache grow in her chest. When she could almost hold it no longer, she looked around for someone to save her, but he didn't show. She couldn't hold it no more and drew in a deep breath of water.*


Miranda woke up choking, gasping for a breath. She sighed as she turned to her clock which read that is was only just after three in the morning. She rolled over and started thinking about Jackson and Nathan. There was no point in dating Nathan now that she knew she was meant to be with Jackson. She didn't want to hurt his feelings though. Perhaps she could think of something tomorrow when she wasn't half asleep.

Miranda was exhausted when the alarm on her phone went off. She sleepily dragged herself out of bed and into the bathroom, hoping a shower would wake her up.

An hour later, she met Alicia at the top of the building to wait for the bus.

"Oh I am so glad you are here!" Alicia cried when she saw her, "I was worried when Evan and Alex came into the school looking for you."

"I'm sorry I worried you too," Miranda frowned, "I was with Jackson. We were having an outdoor lesson." She flashed Alicia a sheepish grin.

"Oh?" Alicia looked confused, and then it dawned on her, "Oh!"

Miranda full out smiled.

Alicia squealed, "How was it? What did you both do?"

Miranda told her about her day as they boarded the bus and sat. Alicia was so excited for her.

"So you kissed him?" she giggled.

Miranda blushed and nodded. She had gotten that over with right away.

Alicia laughed, hearing her thought and went on to compare Jackson to Alex, "Well sure they both have the West looks and charm but Jackson does seem to be more mature and level-headed even though he is younger."

Just as they exited the bus, laughing, the ground started to tremble though not as bad as it had the other day. The two girls stopped laughing immediately and backed against the bus. Alicia took her hand and squeezed it till it hurt but Miranda could hardly feel it. All the happy chatter around them had stopped in an instant. Everyone looked tense and gathered closer together.

It only lasted a minute and as soon as it was done, it seemed everyone pulled out their notebooks to call their loved ones. Shaky voices could be heard from around the school. Alicia had already whipped out her own to call home.

Miranda's buzzed in her pocket. She had three calls incoming in at the same time so she tapped all three. Her dad, Evan and Griffin and Greta all showed on her screen.

"Everyone ok?" their dad said. Everyone nodded.

"Alex is here too," Evan assured them, "We were in the middle of filming."

"Ok, be careful today," Mr. East said, "And please come home tonight Miranda."

"I will dad," she said, frowning, "See you later."

They disconnected and Miranda's phone buzzed again. It was Jackson sending her a message. She replied that she was downstairs and would be up in a minute.

"I am going up to class," Miranda said, disheartened.

Alicia, still on the phone, gave her a quick nod.


Miranda made her way through the tense crowd and up the elevator. Jackson was pacing behind the desk and when he saw her, he took two strides and engulfed her in a hug.

"Why us?" Miranda asked sadly, "Why now?"

Jackson pulled away to look at her face, "That book you were reading, no one on the good side knew about it till recently. We think that the evil know that we have discovered the legend and are doing this to make us reveal ourselves."

"Forgotten, I guess?" she tried to smile. That *was* the title of the book, "Who do you mean by we?"

"Our mothers were part of a group of individuals formed by the councilman who was killed yesterday. They were brought in because of their names and their traced lineages. They knew they would bear the children who would be saviours."

"Councilman?"

"Councilman Hope was killed in the attack yesterday."

Miranda gasped and shook her head, hoping it wasn't true, "He knew," her voice was shaky, "He knew of me. That was why he told me my presence should be kept a secret. That must mean that they know too. They killed him because of me." Miranda's stomach clenched. This was all her fault.

Jackson's eyes widened in alarm, "So then it *is* possible that they know. I was hoping they did not."

"This was why I was hidden?" Miranda's eye filled with tears, "Not because I was a third child but because I was being protected till I was old enough to come back and fight this?"

Jackson hesitated for a minute and nodded. He led her to the long desk and they both took a seat. Then he spoke in a voice barely audible, "A lot of killings have happened to many members of the East and West families over thousands of years. That is why your grandmother is no longer with you. They try to make it look random and take out other innocent people but the group our mother's belonged to discovered the pattern."

"That is all? No one else?"

"Well no, I should not say that. They attack those who get in their way… those who are really good people… at random. But if you look back through the past generations, there are missing Easts and Wests everywhere. Alex's sister two years ago and your mother only months ago."

"Alex's sister?" Miranda asked, shocked, "She's dead?"

"Oh, you did not know?" Jackson flushed, "His parents moved just after that. They could not bear to be in the same apartment. It seems Alex's quest for accompaniment started after that."

"You mean all the dating?"

"I suppose you could call it dating."

"You mean sex?"

Jackson coloured and shrugged, "So I hear."

Miranda shook her head, "He told me he was a virgin."

He snorted, "Well, he could be but I doubt it. Rumour has it, he is not."

Miranda flushed in anger, *What a liar!* How could he lie straight to her face?

"So, anyways, I was thinking that maybe it might be a good idea to start training for a fight," Jackson said, fidgeting, "We could train in the morning and work on your education in the afternoon."

"I suppose," Miranda said, hesitantly. What could she do? Could she do this? Of course she could! She had to protect her family and friends. It was her calling in life. "Do you know how?"

"I have spoken to my mother," Jackson said, a little shyly, "She thinks we might have special powers that when combined are able to defeat the bad ones. The only trouble is since no one has survived an attack, we do not know how they fight."

"Well, the ground moves," Miranda said, thoughtfully. Jackson nodded. "It must be some kind of mind thing. There are no guns or weapons. What do the bodies look like?"

"Usually crushed or cuts but the cuts look like they were burned."

"So maybe they throw things with their minds?"

Jackson shrugged, "That is possible but no one can move anything too large. Small things are easy but anything big like a person, not a chance."

Miranda's eyes widened, "Not a person?" Didn't she move Alex before when she was angry?

"You did?" Jackson asked, awed.

"Well, I pushed him at the same time but he really hit the wall hard. Seems I even shocked him though," Miranda said, thinking about the moment.

"That is it then," Jackson said, "You are stronger because you are the third child and I am just here to protect you. I do not have powers like that."

"You don't?"

"No. I cannot move much. Just small things like plates and notebooks… forks… things like that."

"Well, maybe we should both be training," Miranda laughed.

"Oh do not worry. I will be working just as hard as you," Jackson assured her, "I have been building myself physically since I found out. My mother wanted to wait until I was sixteen." Jackson blushed, "I was the slim, studious type but since I found out, I have been going to the gym every day."

Miranda nudged him playfully, "Well, you look pretty good."

Jackson kissed her temple, "I am glad you like because this is all for you."

Miranda blushed and stood, "So, let's get to it! I have not moved anything since Alex so I need lots of practice."

Jackson then became the drill sergeant as he normally did when he taught. He took out his notebook and put it on the other side of the desk.

She was unsuccessful for over an hour and getting frustrated. He told her to concentrate hard and try to pull the notebook toward her with her mind. Clear the way.

"You can do this Miranda," Jackson coaxed, "You know you can." He repeated the same lines over and over.

"I can't," Miranda rolled her eyes in frustration. She had tried everything, even beckoning the notebook like a dog, which Jackson had snickered at. He rarely laughed when he was training her.

"How did you move Alex?" he asked.

"I was angry."

"Well then get angry!"

Miranda closed her eyes for a minute. This was all the bad people's fault. They killed her mother, the councilman, Alex's sister. They could be after her family next. Well not on her watch!

She opened her eyes and focused on the notebook. She gestured with her hand to 'come' and it did. It slid across the whole desk and into her hand at lightning speed. She dropped it because it had stung, "Ouch!"

Jackson laughed, delighted, "That was amazing!"

She turned to Jackson saw the book on the table and pushed with her hand. The book went flying into the wall. She looked at the desk next and did the same. The desk was picked up and thrown across the room into the metal wall.

"Oops," Miranda said, shocked that she had sent the desk so far.

"Woah!" Jackson was amazed.

"Your turn!" Miranda smiled brightly.

Jackson put his hands up in surrender, "Please do not push me across the room!"

Miranda laughed, "Of course not! Show me what you can do."

Jackson took a deep breath and pulled the notebook toward him with his mind but it didn't travel as fast as when Miranda had done it. He pushed the book across the table, again, not as fast. He turned to the desk they had put back in place but it did not move. Not even an inch.

"Concentrate Jackson," Miranda coaxed, taking on his role, "You have to strengthen your mind as well."

They finished up the morning with Jackson practicing but he could not move the desk more than an inch. He sat down, sweating.

"Wow, that felt like a workout," he laughed, wiping his forehead on his sleeve.

"Well, you are improving," Miranda smiled, "You moved the desk a bit. So all it takes is a little practice to strengthen your mind too."

Jackson nodded in agreement. "Are you going to have lunch with your friends or can I take you out?"

"You don't need to do that," Miranda started to say, "You don't have to spend..."

"But I want to," Jackson cut in. He stood up and took her hand, pulling her off the desk. He flashed the famous West smile and Miranda couldn't resist.

"Ok but you don't have to do this every day."

Jackson smirked, "We shall see."

She followed him out to his car and they went out to lunch. Jackson sat on her side of the booth so that they could cuddle up to each other.

"This is why I want to take you out for lunch," Jackson explained, then gave her a light kiss, "I cannot do this in school."

"You are right, Mr. West," Miranda joked, giving him a playful nudge.

Jackson chuckled and they spent the rest of lunch wrapped in each others' arms. That afternoon, they turned to her education. A lot of it was history. Utopia had a very long record of history and it is learned every year of school. Miranda was fifteen years behind.

There was a knock on the door about ten minutes before school was finished for the day. Miranda and Jackson, who were sitting side by side looking through an old book, both looked to the door. Alex was standing there and Jackson motioned for him to enter.

Alex opened the door but didn't come in, "Can I talk to you for a minute Jack?"

Miranda narrowed her eyes at Alex but Jackson got up and headed out the door. She was tempted to go listen at the door but thought better of it. She tried to continue reading but couldn't. *What was he doing here?*

She sat impatiently wondering what they could be talking about until the bell rang. Should she get the bus or did Alex come to pick her up?

Miranda put her notebook in her purse and went out into the corridor. She saw Jackson and Alex in a heated conversation at the end of the hall and thought about going to intervene but instead just crossed her arms and leaned on the doorframe, tapping her foot impatiently.

They exchanged more words, totally ignoring Miranda and also the other students who were heading to the buses. A group of girls looked longingly at Alex but seeing he was in a conversation, they slowly walked away, hoping he would finish up and notice them. Miranda rolled her eyes and tsked loudly, though with the noise in the hallway, no one had heard.

After a few more tense minutes, she was fed up. She marched over there to figure out what they were talking about so heatedly.

"Is someone going to take me home?" she snapped, "I missed my bus waiting for you both to stop arguing."

Both of them turned to her with fake smiles and she rolled her eyes.

"I will," Jackson said, taking a step towards her.

"Do not be silly," Alex said, coolly "I was sent to pick her up. I live in the same building."

Miranda looked between the two. She seriously should have just left them both and got on the bus. She looked down at her phone. It was possible that the bus was still there and she was about to turn when Alex stopped her.

"Miranda, just come home with me," Alex said.

"Why should I Alex?" Miranda said, angry, "Why did you come here?"

"To let Jackson know that if he is going to have you out all day, he better make sure to clear it with your family first," Alex said, sending Jackson a warning look.

"And I said I totally understand that Alex," Jackson snapped back, "And…"

Miranda cut in, "And it is none of your business, Alex. The time got away from both of us. What makes you think I would go with you now when you think you own everyone?"

"He is my *younger* cousin," Alex said, "I am allowed to be a role model to him and tell him when he is crossing the line."

Jackson snorted. "You know what? You are right cousin," he said sarcastically and then turned to Miranda, "I know you have to get home anyways. Just go ahead with Alex."

Alex smiled triumphantly, even though he knew Jackson was being sarcastic. Miranda crossed her arms and pouted. Then she thought of something and smiled. She stepped in close to Jackson, kissed him quickly, "See you tomorrow?"

Jackson smiled, "Yes, tomorrow."

Miranda turned to Alex, smiling brightly. "Ok, let's go."

Alex's smile had faded. He turned on his heel and headed towards the elevator. Miranda winked at Jackson and followed Alex. Jackson's chuckle followed them down the hallway.

Once they were in his car, Alex shot up into the sky accelerating quickly. Miranda held the seat tight.

"What's wrong Alex?" Miranda smiled sweetly.

"Nothing," Alex replied, chewing his lip.

"Why shouldn't I date him?" Miranda said. She knew what he was thinking.

"He is not your type," Alex replied.

Miranda gave him a funny look, "How would you know my type?"

"Jackson is a good student, intelligent. He is not much of an athlete."

"So are you saying I am not good enough for him?"

Alex shrugged.

"Are you jealous?"

Alex snorted, "Why would I be?"

"I'm just trying to understand."

"He is just not right for you," Alex said flatly.

The rest of the trip was quiet until Miranda's phone buzzed. She saw it was Nathan calling.

"Hi," she said, smiling into the phone.

"Hi beautiful," Nathan responded.

Alex looked at Miranda's phone in her hand and at her with a look of disgust.

"I was wondering if we were still ok for the date tonight?" Nathan asked.

Miranda's smile faded, "I am sorry Nathan. My father wanted me home tonight."

His face fell, "Can we reschedule?"

"No!" Alex snapped and he grabbed for Miranda's phone, "She is never going out with you." He hung up on him.

Miranda's mouth dropped open and she snatched her phone back, "Don't ever touch *my* phone again!"

"Your brothers said you were not to date him."

"They do not know him and neither do you. He is perfectly nice."

"Yes, he is nice to you," Alex glared, "Of course he is. He will take his time, have sex with you and then find someone else."

"Well at least he tries. I bet the girls just fall all over you. It must make it so easy to not have to try at all."

Alex shot her a glare, "I am NOT like him."

"Whatever you say," Miranda said sarcastically.

They reached the apartment and Miranda was out the door the second it was parked. If only the elevator had shown up sooner, she would have tried to get away from him.

She called Nathan back to reschedule for the next week when she had reached the privacy of her bedroom. Miranda was too nice. After Alex had hung up on him, she had felt terrible. It was a harmless date anyways. It didn't have to mean anything and Nathan was nice. She enjoyed his company even if it was going to be just as friends.

# Seventeen

✯ ✯ ✯ ✯

That week there was an attack a day. Miranda was driven to school every day and picked up by Evan and Alex, though the latter did not take one step into her school after his talk with Jackson.

Miranda and Jackson worked hard at training, using the gym for a couple hours in the morning, pushing themselves till their minds and bodies hurt. He still could not move larger objects more than an inch but Miranda could move anything put in front of her. Jackson was amazed at what she could do.

They had lunch together every day off of school property. In the afternoon, Jackson still insisted that she had to learn, so they went through a lot more history.

Jackson had wanted her to meet his family, especially his mother, but Mr. East had everyone on lock-down since the attacks were increasing. So they planned to spend Saturday together if Mr. East allowed it.

On Friday night, Miranda cornered her father alone. "Dad? Can I please go out with Jackson tomorrow? We are just going to his apartment and his parents are going to be there."

Her father hesitated, worried for her safety.

"He is going to pick me up, bring me home and I promise we will not go anywhere."

Mr. East's face softened, "Of course Miranda. You must be so tired of staying here with just us."

"No dad!" Miranda assured him, "I just really want to spend the day with him."

Mr. East shifted uncomfortably, "Do you like him? He seems like a nice boy."

"No talks, dad," Miranda giggled, "I am a good girl."

He chuckled and gave her a hug, "I know you are. I just did not think you would be interested in him. I met him a few times when he was younger."

Miranda smiled, confused. Were they really that different?

When Evan got home, he was smiling but Alex looked miserable as he followed him in.

"I have all your scripts for the whole week," Evan announced to Miranda, "You will start on the show Thursday but just as a background character and Friday we will actually start with your scenes. We normally air the episode four days later but we are getting ahead on some scenes so you will air on television a week later!"

Miranda squealed and hugged her brother tight, "Let's celebrate!"

"Yes!" Evan agreed and held up a finger, "But first, we must send you your scripts." He pulled out his notebook and pushed a few buttons. Miranda's phone buzzed and she pulled it out. There were six documents, one for every day but Sunday.

Evan went to the kitchen and brought back some curved bottles to celebrate. Miranda took the purple one.

"So that means Miranda will be on television Thursday in the background and Friday for the debut?" her father asked.

"Well, her official debut will be the Friday," Evan replied, "She will be in the credits on Friday but not Thursday."

"We should all take the day off to watch it together," Mr. East said, squeezing Miranda's arm. She flashed him a smile.

Greta and Griffin walked in the door and Miranda told them the news.

Greta gave her a hug, "Congratulations!"

"Yes, that is wonderful Miranda," Griffin agreed.

They all talked excitedly, everyone but Alex. He sat miserably, tossing back a few drinks.

"Will you be back in time to go to the track tomorrow?" Mr. East asked after they all sat down to have dinner.

"I think so. If not, maybe we can meet you there?" Miranda said.

Griffin paused with his fork halfway to his mouth, "Where are you going tomorrow?"

"I am spending the day with Jackson," Miranda said, staring down her brother, daring him to say something.

He made a face but didn't say anything.

Alex stood up, "I am sorry Mr. East but I am not feeling well. If you excuse me, I am going to lie down."

"Of course Alex," Mr. East said, sincerely, "I really hope you feel better."

Evan watched him go, a suspicious look on his face.

"What's wrong with him?" Miranda asked.

Evan shrugged.

Miranda stood up. She had a pretty good idea, "Excuse me a minute."

She hurried to catch Alex before he went into his apartment.

"Wait up just a second," Miranda said, a little snippish.

Alex opened his door and motioned for her to follow. She went to sit on the couch and he brought back a couple more drinks from his fridge.

"So, you have been miserable since you got home. What's wrong?" Miranda got right to it.

Alex sighed, "Your brother has some interesting ideas with the scripts."

Miranda rolled her eyes, "I knew it. You still have a problem with me being on the show."

Alex took a long drink. He pulled out his notebook, tapped the screen a few times, scrolled and passed it to Miranda, "See for yourself."

Miranda took his phone and read, her mouth dropping open. Their characters were going to have sex.

"What script is this?"

"The sixth," Alex replied.

She passed Alex back his phone and shrugged, "Well, that is going to be awkward but I am sure you are a professional by now."

Alex glared at her, "You know I am not."

Miranda shrugged, "Well, you obviously have done a scene like this before? You are engaged on the show."

Alex shifted uncomfortably, "No I have not. We were saving it for marriage."

Miranda looked deep in thought for a minute, "Well you have seen me in a bathing suit. It will not be much different and it is not real."

"Oh I think it will be very different, Maddie," Alex sighed.

"So what do you want to do, practice?" Miranda said, raising an eyebrow.

Alex choked on the drink he just took, "Are you serious?"

Miranda thought about it a second. They were going to have to anyways and it didn't mean anything since they were practicing.

Jackson was just going to have to deal with it. She would have to kiss Alex on the show anyways. Perhaps that was something she would have to discuss with him tomorrow.

Finally, she nodded but Alex shook his head, "No, I do not think we should."

"Suit yourself," Miranda sat back. Alex turned the television on to a hockey game while Miranda messaged her father telling him that she was taking care of Alex and would be home later.

"Would you like another?" Alex asked, motioning to her empty bottle.

"Sure."

He got them a couple more each and they sat back in silence to watch the game. Miranda loved the Utopian hockey. She did very well against Jackson in gym even though it was on the floor and not on a rink. She hadn't actually skated in awhile, though she wasn't too bad. As she watched the game more closely, she noticed there were females on the teams. They were just as good as the men.

When she had finished taking a drink, she glanced at Alex and saw he was staring at her.

"Yes?" she said, giving him a puzzled look.

"You look different," he said, looking her up and down.

"I have been working out every day, I guess," Miranda replied looking down at her arms. They seemed to have toned up a little bit and she had definitely lost weight since she arrived on Utopia. It must be the food.

Alex shrugged, "I guess so." He still looked puzzled, "I am still trying to figure you out."

"There is not much to think about," Miranda looked down at the empty bottle in her hands, "I am pretty simple."

"Hmm… I do not believe that," Alex replied. He got up and got two more bottles each from the kitchen.

Miranda started giggling when she had finished the next bottle. Alex… puzzled? That was a new Alex. She stared at her fingers and they seemed to dance in front of her. *Oh gosh, I am a little tipsy!*

Alex chuckled, "Yes, me as well."

They both laughed.

"So really, Alex, what puzzles you?" she said, through her laughs.

"Well maybe the fact that you want to practice?" Alex said and stopped laughing, "It makes me wonder if you want to use me too."

Miranda stopped laughing, "Of course not, Alex. Unfortunately for me, I know the real you." She gave him a playful shove.

Alex shrugged, "No, Maddie. You have the wrong impression of me and a highly biased viewpoint."

"So you are not an arrogant, but super hot, and completely sex-driven ego-maniac?" Miranda laughed.

"Super hot and maybe a bit of an ego," Alex smiled.

Miranda rolled her eyes dramatically, "A lot of an ego."

"Fine," Alex smiled his charming smile that made girls swoon. Miranda's eyes flicked down to his lips and turned away, a slight flush rising in her cheeks. Stupid West charm. At least she wasn't the only one it affected.

"Ok. Maybe we should practice," Alex said, looking down at the bottle in his hands. He took another long drink.

"Well, geez Alex!" Miranda laughed, "Is it that bad of a thought that you have to get drunk first."

"Not really. But it helps," Alex laughed as he tipped the bottle back again.

Miranda giggled and did the same.

"So here?" Alex asked, watching her as she polished off her last bottle.

"Where is the scene?"

"In Cara's bedroom."

"What? Not Jeff's? Is he afraid of his *fiancée* walking in?"

"Well apparently they break it off that day, earlier in the episode."

Miranda stood and held a hand out to Alex, "Well, obviously my bedroom is a no-no. I'm sure Griffin would *love* that. Let's use yours."

Alex took her hand and she tried to pull him up. They stumbled a little, under the influence of the alcohol, laughing.

"Get your notebook!" Miranda laughed and he scooped it up as she led the way down the hall. She stopped in the middle of the hall "Which one is yours?"

Alex kept hold of her hand and led her through the last door, which was the master bedroom. It was a lot bigger than her dad's.

"Did you take a wall down?" Miranda asked, looking around. It was elegantly done in dark red with rustic looking furniture. He had a large king size bed in the centre of the far wall. She stopped short, wondering how many girls he had entertained in that bed. He had a picture of snow-capped red mountains over his window and she went over to look at it.

"Yes. I am the only one here so I thought I could have more space," he said and joined her by the picture, "No women have been in this bed, Miranda. I told you that."

Miranda looked into his eyes. There was no sign of a lie. "This is a beautiful picture. Where is it?"

"My parents live further north and you can see this mountain in the distance."

"Have you ever been skiing?" Miranda asked.

"Skiing?" Alex questioned and shook his head.

"I guess there is no skiing in Utopia?"

He shook his head again.

"We have snow-capped mountains like this on Earth," she said, motioning to the picture, "I went skiing with my Earth parents a few years ago."

"How do you ski?" he asked.

"Well, you get these things called skis. They are flat and long and you put them on your feet. They you just kind of swish from side to side downhill," she laughed. It was hard to describe skiing feeling like she did now.

Alex chuckled.

"So, what are the lines?" Miranda asked.

They both looked at the notebook. There is a short scene before the bedroom where Jeff comes to her house and they talk about how he had broken up with Janet. He then asks her to be his girlfriend and they start to kiss. Jeff picks her up and they go to the bedroom. From there, there are no words.

"Ok," Alex smiled, "I will go outside and knock. You let me in."

Miranda giggled, "Maybe. We shall see"

Alex winked at her and left the room, shutting the door behind him. In the few moments before he knocked, Miranda noticed a family portrait on the wall. *That must be his sister*, she thought, scanning her pretty face. She looked younger than him and had the same light brown hair and bright blue-green eyes. She was so beautiful.

Miranda's attention turned back to the knock on the door. She smiled and went to the door. Her smile faded when she opened the door.

"Hi Jeff," she said glumly, "What do you want?"

"I did it, Cara," Alex said, moving around her and into the room before she could invite him in, "I broke it off with Janet."

Miranda looked hopeful, "Really?"

"Yes," Alex nodded and smiled. He took her hands, "I want to be with you."

Miranda's eyes sparkled and she flashed him a smile, "I want to be with you too."

"Exclusively," Alex said, staring deep into her eyes, "I want you all to myself."

Miranda nodded and threw her arms around him, "And you, all mine?"

Alex nodded as well and leaned in to kiss her. It was no short kiss. Miranda felt her whole body heat as her hormones took over. Thankfully it was Alex who pulled away.

"I want you M-," he whispered, sending chills down her spine, and then shook his head slightly, "Cara."

"Ok," she agreed and Alex lifted her into his arms. "So now we go to the bedroom," Alex laughed and took a few steps then spun her around and put her on her feet. She swayed a bit. Spinning and alcohol didn't mix. She gripped his arms as he steadied her even though he looked a little unsteady.

"And so now comes the real practice," Miranda said, "And don't you dare try to actually get into my pants." She laughed nervously.

"I would not think of it," Alex chuckled, raising his hands in surrender, then he pulled her close to him and she forgot what she was going to say. He kissed her desperately, hardly giving her any time to think about what she was doing. She dropped his notebook that was in her hands, but neither noticed the small thump it made when it hit the ground. They stumbled slightly over each other as they made their way to the bed, continually kissing.

They pulled apart for a second and Miranda took a deep breath. She had almost lost control of herself. "This is where I pull your shirt off," Miranda said, light-heartedly, pretending to do just that.

Alex laughed and kissed her again. The heat returned, filling her every pore. This time she pulled apart long enough to pull Alex's shirt off for real this time wanting a view of his amazing body. Alex didn't seem to mind and leaned her onto the bed. Miranda ran her hands over his body, feeling every muscle under his warm skin. Alex grabbed her around the waist and slid her up slowly towards the pillows.

Suddenly a shrill ringing came from the floor and Miranda gasped, coming to her senses. Sometime in there she had lost her shirt as well and Miranda had her hands on the waist of his pants. Alex looked shocked as well and sat up quickly.

The phone was still buzzing but they just stared at each other breathing heavy. As Miranda found her thoughts she was worried that what everyone said was true. If they were only practicing why could she feel him digging into her thigh?

Alex got off of her quick, "What are we doing?" he whispered.

"Do you feel the same way I do when...?" Miranda asked but stopped herself.

"Reckless?" Alex offered.

"Why?"

Alex looked away. He couldn't give her an answer.

"We cannot do this anymore," Miranda said getting up quickly, looking around for her shirt. She tried to cover herself as best she could.

"Why?"

Miranda backed away from Alex as he rose off the bed. He handed her shirt to her, which was tightly gripped in his hand.

She snatched it from him, "Just leave me alone."

"I am sorry. I understand if you do not want to practice for the filming," Alex said, confused. He took another step towards her and she backed away farther.

"No, I don't want to," she said, shakily. How could she do this to Jackson? She was an awful person.

"Are you ok? I am sorry. I did not mean to make you feel uncomfortable, but it is like you said... uncontrolling."

Miranda turned away to slip her shirt over her head. She didn't understand why this was happening to her. "Yes, I'm ok."

"Why are you afraid of me?"

"I'm not afraid," Miranda lied, forcing herself to look at him again.

Alex could see right through her and got angry, "What are you thinking?"

"Nothing."

"Do you think I want to do this? I do not want to, I have to! This is all for the show!"

Miranda's eyes filled with tears. Of course it had been all for the show, but why did she feel like she betrayed Jackson. She was so confused. They were supposed to be practicing, but if he was practicing... she didn't know what to think. He was a guy. Sometimes their parts are uncontrollable. "I should go," Miranda said finally and turned away from him.

He didn't follow her. Greta and Griffin were in the living room when she walked in. She sort of hid her face, said hello and went to her bedroom.

Greta saw Miranda's tears and followed her.

"What is wrong?" she asked, closing the door behind them.

Miranda sat down on her bed and put her face in her hands, "I can't do this anymore. I can't be on the show."

"Why? What did Alex say?" Greta asked as she took a seat beside her on the bed.

"It's not him, it's me. There are so many things I have to do and I'm not sure I can handle it. We have to film a scene where Alex and I are in bed together."

Greta's eyebrows rose, "Really? That is going to be tough, but you can do it. It is just acting."

"I don't know, Alex was my first kiss and now…"

"You really like him, right?"

Miranda knew she couldn't lie. She looked down at her hands, "I think so but what about Jackson? I like him too. And Alex is always telling me, it is for the show."

"Look, I know Alex. He is like another brother to yours. He takes his job seriously and he enjoys being good at what he does. But he does not like to kiss onscreen. He said it makes him uncomfortable."

"He's said that before?"

"Yes. He has had to kiss many other co-stars. I do not think he has ever liked it."

"I just wish he liked me."

Greta smiled, "Do not worry about that and do not quit over this Miranda. This is wonderful. You are an actress! A beautiful, intelligent actress on one of the most watched daytime drama series on this planet. And like I said, if you think you can, date both. Date all three of them! Just when one wants to be exclusive, tell the others that you cannot be with them anymore."

Miranda frowned, "I wish it were that easy. And anyways, Alex hates me."

"He does not hate you, trust me."

"It sure doesn't seem that way. We fight all the time. Just like now," Miranda looked at her hands on her lap, "Well he has been nicer recently."

"Can I tell you something honestly?" Greta sighed, "I do not want you to get angry at your brothers and I just found out tonight."

Miranda looked to Greta who smiled apologetically.

"What?" Miranda asked suspiciously.

"I heard it in Griffin's mind. I think him and Evan talked to Alex about being nicer to you so you would not want to date Nathan, or even Jackson for that matter."

"WHAT?" Miranda screamed and she was up and out of her room in seconds. She banged on Evan's door, "Evan! Get into the living room now!" and she continued down the hall.

Griffin turned the television off seeing the livid look on Miranda's face and then saw the apologetic look on Greta's face and knew he was in for it.

Evan appeared in the living room and took in the scene. He almost turned to walk away when Miranda spotted him. "SIT!" she barked.

Mr. East had heard the commotion and peeked his head in.

"Uh...what is going on?" he asked, a half-smile playing at his lips.

Miranda forced a huge fake smile, "Just talking to my brothers, dad."

"Well, go easy on them," he laughed, "I see you got your mother's temper as well." Then he disappeared down the hall and they heard his door close.

"How dare you two ask Alex to be nicer to me so I won't date anyone!" she shouted.

Evan shot a glare at Greta, who shook her head, "You two were wrong and you know it. She would have found out eventually hearing it in someone's mind like I did."

Suddenly the culprit poked his head in the front door.

"I heard shouting," he said.

"You sit too!" Miranda shouted.

"Woah, your mother's temper, huh?" Alex joked, taking a seat.

"Trust me, now is not the time," Evan warned.

"Told you she would find out," Alex said and then turned to Miranda, "It was their idea, Maddie. Do not blame me."

"How could you guys do this to me?" Miranda raged, angry tears filling her eyes.

"We did not mean to hurt you Miranda," Griffin said first, "But that is how much we are opposed to Nathan. Jackson is ok, but still. He is not your type."

"Why does everyone keep saying that?" Miranda fumed.

"Well, he is studious and more of a homely person," Evan said, "From what I remember of him at least."

"Well, I like geeks," Miranda snapped, "But maybe you did not notice he has been coming out of his shell."

"They are just being over-protective," Greta said, trying to make light of the situation.

Miranda turned on Greta, "And they felt that this was a good way to deal with it, by asking Alex to treat me better and pretend to like me?" The tears spilled down her cheeks. Now she almost wished she hadn't called this meeting. What was she thinking exposing her true feelings for Alex?

"Alex is the only one we know who could possibly have changed your mind about Nathan. We thought about some of the other guys but you do not know them much," Evan said, he almost looked sorry though, now realizing what a terrible idea it had been to play with their sister's emotions.

"And when I saw you kissing Alex, I knew we had gone too far," Griffin said, "That is what I stayed behind to talk to him about. I thought he took it too far." Griffin sent Alex a glare.

"You make me sick!" Miranda said, "All of you, except you Greta. Thank you for telling me the truth but I don't know how you stand Griffin."

Greta frowned, "Miranda, please do not get so mad at them. They have never had a little sister and to get one at such an old, mature age must be hell for them."

"Alex had a sister," Miranda snapped but then she almost felt sorry for saying it. Alex's mouth dropped open in shock and he frowned.

"This is your own problem," he said quietly to the brothers on the couch, then turned to Miranda as he stood, "Miranda, I really did owe it to you to be nicer and the only reason I agreed was because I knew I should be. I did not know you at all and everything I have ever said to you has been the truth. I just bit back some of the rude remarks and let some compliments out." He turned abruptly and left.

"You two stay right there," Miranda snapped and then followed Alex. She reached him just as he was at his door.

She caught his shoulder and forced him to look at her.

"Oh Alex, I am so sorry," Miranda said quietly. She threw her arms around him.

"You have every right to be mad," Alex mumbled.

"I know, I am very angry," she said calmly, "but I had no right to-to-"

"Just forget it," Alex said, releasing her. He looked away, "I forgive you. Just go easy on your brothers. Their intentions were good though poorly executed."

Miranda looked away, "I wish you all would let me learn myself. I would not do anything I did not want to."

"So, you do not get reckless with anyone else?" Alex gave a small smile.

Miranda punched his arm lightly, "No. There is something wrong with me and you."

"Yes there is," Alex agreed, chuckling.

"I am still mad at you," Miranda frowned.

"I know. So no more practising?" Alex joked.

Miranda shook her head.

"Good because you smell like Earth sometimes." He wrinkled his nose, then slipped inside his apartment and shut the door quickly before she could retort.

She groaned then turned back to her own apartment.

Her brothers were still right where she left them, not saying a word. Apparently, her mother had taught them well.

"Ok," she said from the door to the living room, "I am going to go out with anyone I want to, no matter what you guys say or do and neither of you will meddle in my life again."

"Oh Miranda," Griffin said, "Just not Nathan! He..."

Miranda shot him a glare and he stopped what he was saying.

"Meddle in my life one more time and you may as well bring me back to Earth. I was fine by myself where I was."

"Miranda, no," Evan shook his head, "We want you here."

*It would be safer for her on Earth*, Griffin said in his mind and Evan shot him a look. *What about the dreams?* Griffin continued and Evan shook his head slightly.

Miranda didn't miss the exchange, "What is that have to do with anything? How do you know about my nightmares?"

"We hear you screaming sometimes," Evan said, sadly, "Griffin is worried our family is a target for the evil ones."

"And we are!" Griffin cut in.

"No, we cannot be," Evan said, his tone resolved.

Miranda looked between them, concentrating hard on them not hearing her thoughts. Did they know or didn't they? Jackson seemed to think they didn't.

Greta looked as confused as Miranda but she turned to her and said, "Why not have a nice, hot shower and relax. It is all right, you will see." She got up and put an arm around Miranda's shoulders and gave her a squeeze. Together they went down the hall towards Miranda's room.


"Is it really the most watched daytime drama on the planet?" Miranda asked after a minute.

"It sure is!" Greta smiled, "And you get to be a part of that!"

Miranda smiled, "Wow. Evan must be so proud of it."

Greta laughed and took a seat on her bed, "Yes but you would not know it. He is not very conceited, you know? Not very many people are on this planet."

"I've noticed. Everyone is so nice," Miranda agreed, "When I met the Trees. They were so cool and so nice, not conceited at all that they make great music. They sat and talked to me like I had been their friend for years."

"You met the Trees?" Greta said, stunned.

Miranda told her all about it. Griffin had forgotten to tell her that Miranda and Alex had gone backstage.

"That sounds amazing!" Greta smiled, "I wish I was not at my grandparents!"

"Yes, me too," Miranda smiled, "Then it would have been you instead of Alex!"

# Eighteen

★  ★  ★  ★

Miranda woke up with a scream. She was going to die again and no one was there to save her.

Evan ran into her room. He was half dressed. His pants were on but he had his shirt in his hands. "Are you alright? I heard you scream!"

"Yes, I am ok," Miranda said, taking deep breaths.

"What is wrong? What happens?" he asked as he pulled his shirt on.

"Just dreams, Evan," Miranda tried to smile, "I don't want to talk about it." She looked at her notebook. It was only the 7:05. She rolled her eyes and lay back, "I am going back to sleep. Ugh!"

Evan chuckled as he left to finish getting ready for work.

She couldn't sleep, though. Now that she was awake and she wasn't drunk, she could reflect on her night. She couldn't believe her brothers were really that opposed to Nathan. But why? And why did everyone think Jackson wasn't her type? She found nothing wrong with him and she was so attracted to him. Even if he was studious, he was a cute! And he had the muscles she liked.

Miranda wished she could talk to Helen. She was so much better at handling boy situations. Thinking about Helen, she thought about her Earth parents, her cat and her eyes filled with tears.

Miranda got out of bed to find her Earth phone. She tried to turn it on, but the battery had finally died and the tears started to fall. She had been here just over three weeks but she felt so much at home, which made her feel awful. She wanted to feel like she belonged more on Earth with her Earth parents but here it was so easy.

And then there was the daunting task of saving the planet. She didn't feel like much of a superhero. Sure she could lift heavier things with her mind than the average Utopian but it did not feel like much. If only she had super physical strength or could fly. Maybe she should get some tights. She chuckled, wondering how Jackson would feel about that.

Speaking of Jackson, her eyes turned to her notebook. It was almost 8:25. She might as well get up and get ready.

Once ready, she messaged Jackson to see if he was awake.

He called her back right away, his face smiling brightly.

"Hi!" Miranda smiled.

"I have been waiting for you to message," Jackson smiled.

"I didn't want to message you too early," Miranda winked.

"That is fine. I have been awake since 7."

"Oh? Me too!"

He laughed, "When can I come pick you up?"

"I am ready now," Miranda replied.

"Now sounds good. I will see you soon!"

They disconnected. Miranda smiled down at her phone. He seemed so happy to be hanging out with her that day. It felt nice to have someone who wanted to be near her unlike Alex, who was only nice to her *after* her brothers asked him to be. And that was only a lie because they didn't want her to date.

No one was home so she went up to wait for him on the roof. She sat on the ledge of the building and looked up at the sky. For once, it looked like a big rainstorm was coming in. She could see some dark, threatening clouds in the distance. Miranda smiled when she saw his car pull up in front of her.

They were talking about lessons when Miranda looked outside the window and gasped.

"Jackson stop!" she cried, "The ground is shaking! Really bad!"

Other cars nearby seemed to have noticed, already beginning their descent and Jackson pushed a button and the car descended vertically with them. As soon as it hit ground, it shook violently. Jackson clasped her hand tightly, regretting landing the car. It was not safe. The bad people were very close by.

Miranda took in her surroundings as she held the dashboard with her other hand, trying to figure out where they were in the city. Then she realized they were close to the studio!

Miranda jumped out of the car and Jackson yelled after her. She tried to walk unsteadily towards what she thought was the source. Jackson was right behind her, trying to catch up.

"No Miranda, stop!" he cried, "We are not ready!"

"It's near the studio!" Miranda yelled back, not stopping, "I have to go!"

People were fleeing from the area. Miranda and Jackson were the only ones headed in the opposite direction.

He finally caught up to her and threw his arms around her, pulling her back. Miranda screamed for him to let go and tried to slip from his grasp.

"Miranda! There is nothing we can do!" he yelled above the sounds of people running and screaming.

Miranda dropped to the ground, placed her palms down on the grass. She was so scared for her brother. What if it was the studio being attacked? "Stop!" she cried.

Unexpectedly, a force left her palms that almost knocked her on her back and the rumbling subsided. There were two glowing spots on the ground where her hands had been, which faded quickly.

Jackson dropped to the ground awestruck and put his palm on the faded spot, "Wow." He took her hand and felt her palm.

Miranda felt drained as she hunched over, her eyes closed.

"Are you ok?" he asked, his face full of concern. He put an arm around her and helped her to a sitting position.

"Just tired," Miranda slurred. Her phone started to ring and she fumbled with her purse and pulled it out.

Evan's face was on the screen and she came around a bit, happy to see his face.

"Oh Evan, you are ok!" her eyes filled with tears.

"Miranda, where are you? Are *you* alright?" Evan said, seeing her face.

"I am with Jackson. I was trying to get to you but..." Miranda tried to hold her head up but it was becoming difficult, "I just need to lie down a minute."

"Miranda!" Evan yelled as he watched her eyes close. Jackson caught her head before she hit the ground.

Jackson took the phone, "She is ok. She just fainted. She was trying to get to you."

"Where are you?" Evan said, his eyes wide.

"I assure you, I can take care of her," Jackson said calmly, "I will take her to my mother. We are not far from my car."

Alex took the phone from Evan, "Jackson! Tell us where you are!" he snapped.

Jackson rolled his eyes, "My dear *older* cousin. Trust me, I can handle this."

Alex glared at the phone and then his face lit up as he recognized the building behind him, "Stay there and we will come to you."

Jackson looked angrily over his shoulder at the building which gave them away and then turned back to the phone but they had disconnected.

Miranda couldn't see or hear anything but felt a drop of water hit her face. She felt lost in blackness. She thought she heard voices far away and tried to reach out to them.

"You both did not have to come," Jackson said. He sounded the closest but as if he were under water. Someone tucked a hair behind her ear.

"What happened?" Evan asked. He sounded stressed.

"We were driving to my apartment and saw the ground was shaking so we landed like everyone else but then Miranda jumped out. I caught up to her just as the ground stopped shaking and then she fainted. It must have been too much for her. She was so afraid for you, Evan. You were all she thought about."

A hand touched her cheek gently. The voices were so much clearer, right beside her now. She felt another drop of water hit her face.

"She is getting wet," Alex said, "We should get her out of the rain."

"Alex, can you take her home?" Evan asked, "We can continue filming your parts tomorrow."

"With all respect, Evan, Miranda is safe with me," Jackson cut in, "We were going to my apartment."

"Jackson," Alex snapped, "I am taking her home."

"No Alex," Jackson said, finally raising his voice, "Her and I have plans and I can take care of her. It was not necessary for you both to come."

"I want my sister at home," Evan cut in, "My father will want her there as well."

"You must listen to us Jackson," Alex said, raising his voice, "We are older and know better."

"No Alex," Jackson snapped back, "I am old enough now that I do not need to listen to you like when we were younger."

Alex sent Jackson a glare.

Miranda finally felt released from her blackness and she groaned. "Stop... arguing," she said weakly. All three turned to her.

Jackson touched her cheek, "Are you alright?"

Miranda tried to sit up but Alex pinned her back, "Take it slow Miranda. You may be dizzy."

Miranda lay back on Jackson's lap. She still felt weak, *what had happened?*

"Miranda, what were you thinking?" Evan scolded.

Miranda groaned again and closed her eyes, "Saving your ass."

Evan chuckled a bit and shook his head, "Please do not ever try that again. There is nothing you can do."

"Where was the attack?" she asked, opening her eyes again.

"The building beside the studio," Evan replied and looked at Alex, "So, will you take her home?"

"Evan," Miranda said. She sat up, slowly, "I am fine. Jackson and I are going to his place and we are going to be ok."

Evan looked torn. He looked at Alex again.

"Your brother would prefer you to go with me," Alex said, staring her down.

"I would not prefer that," Miranda snapped and looked at Jackson, "Help me up."

Jackson bit his lip and helped her to her feet, "If your brother wants you to go home, perhaps you should." He frowned. He had wanted her to meet his family and they were so excited to meet her.

Miranda gave him a wary look. She felt her strength returning and stretched her arms out. "I am fine. Is dad, Griffin and Greta ok?"

"Yes, they are fine. I did not tell dad the whole story though. I really did not want him to worry."

A commotion interrupted them. An excitement rang throughout the crowd that was in the streets.

Evan looked over, "What is going on?"

The man in front of them turned, "It looks like some were caught!"

The woman beside him smiled, "I knew those holding cells would be beneficial someday." The man smiled and nodded.

Evan looked anxious to find out what was going on. He looked torn as he glanced to the crowd and Miranda.

"Evan, I am fine with Jackson. Please just let me go," Miranda pleaded. She really did not want to spend any more time with Alex after last night and she had so much to talk to Jackson about.

"You will be safer with me Miranda," Alex said.

Jackson's lips formed a hard line.

Miranda tried to smile and stepped between them, "Let's not start, ok? I am going to go with Jackson and I will be just as safe with him."

Evan looked defeated, "Ok. Go with Jackson but do not leave his apartment for any reason and we will pick you up to go to the race tonight."

"Ok," Miranda smiled as she got her way. Jackson sent a small smile of triumph to Alex who made a face. Miranda didn't miss the exchange and she didn't like it. What was with those two?

Her and Jackson left the crowd and walked back to the car in silence. Miranda messaged her dad and her friends letting them know she was ok. All of them had checked in already and were accounted for.

Once they were seated and in the air, Jackson turned to her, "You stopped that," Jackson smiled, "You stopped the whole planet from moving."

Miranda thought for a second. "It may have been a coincidence."

"I do not believe that. Some people were caught," Jackson glanced her way, "*You* stopped the attack."

Miranda didn't think it was that easy. Was that all that she had to do? *Not likely*, she sighed.

Jackson touched her leg, "Well, it was a start and later I bet we will find out how they attack since some were caught."

Miranda shot him a smile. If he was so positive about it, then she should be as well.

Jackson's mother was waiting anxiously at the door when they arrived and threw her arms around him when he entered, "Oh Jack, I am so glad you are both ok!" She turned to Miranda, who barely had a moment to see her face before she was engulfed in her dark brown hair. His mother squeezed her tight.

"I am Marcy," she said as she pulled back, "My goodness you look like your mother. Your mother was so beautiful as well."

Miranda smiled hesitantly, "It is very nice to meet you."

"I am so sorry this was all brought down upon you. Your mother's plan was to wait until you were twenty. She thought you would be able to handle it better."

Miranda frowned. She wasn't going to be twenty for just over three years! How could her mother have wanted to wait that long?

"I wish I had known sooner." Miranda thought about her Earth parents and how much she missed them and her friends. Even if she had gotten three more years with them, it would still be hard to leave.

"It was a group decision. We all agreed."

Miranda's jaw tightened, "I should have been involved. You were all sitting and planning mine and Jackson's life. It doesn't seem fair."

Marcy took her hand, her eyes pleading, "Oh please do not be angry with us Miranda. We just wanted you to be safe. Councilman Hope checked back in the records and the last third child was killed very young."

Miranda sighed. Whether they made a bad decision or not, she was still the chosen one and she was still going to have to save Utopia. She just couldn't believe how much everything could have been different. Jackson took her hand and gave it a squeeze.

"I was angry for a long time too," Jackson admitted, "I wanted you brought to Utopia right away but I needed the time to strengthen myself and prepare to protect you."

Miranda sent him a small smile.

Marcy seemed to sigh, "It is so amazing to see you both together finally! Your father and brother went out to see what happened today. I hear some people were caught!" She turned to Miranda, "My husband and other son do not know. We all promised to tell as few people as possible."

Miranda sent Jackson a look as they followed his mother into the living room. She wasn't sure if they should tell her what happened today. Jackson gave his head a quick shake, wanting to keep everything between them for now.

Marcy told her about Councilman Hope, who had founded the group and how he had recruited Jackson and Miranda's mothers by tracing the lineages many years ago.

"I was so upset to know that my first child would be some protector and your mother... oh, she was upset for weeks. Especially when she found out she was having twins and the third child was coming sooner."

Miranda did a double take, "I'm sorry, twins?"

Marcy's eyes widened, "Oh no, I am so sorry. I guess you would not know."

"What happened to my twin? How am I the third?"

Marcy shifted uncomfortably and cleared her throat. Her big green eyes filled with tears, "I did not want you to find out this way."

Miranda rolled her eyes, "I wish everyone would stop keeping things from me." She looked at Jackson, who ran a hand nervously through his hair.

"Evan is your twin brother," Marcy admitted quietly.

"That is impossible! Evan is older than me."

"No, he is not," Marcy muttered, mad at herself for not thinking, "You are older than you think. The years are longer on Earth."

Miranda went quiet. Of course she was right! The years *were* longer! "How old am I?" she snapped, suddenly, "I am eighteen like Evan? Was I born here then? How could my father not know?"

"You were born here. They doctor who was taking care of your mother was a part of our group and she hid the twins from your father. Your mother gave birth to Evan first, so you are the third child."

Miranda's mouth dropped open. She could hardly believe this news. She looked at Jackson, "I want to go home." Her eyes filled with tears. She was eighteen? Way older than what she thought. Now she was older than Jackson and way older than she should be to go to school. She felt so stupid and so dumb for not realizing this sooner.

Jackson shot his mother a look and then turned back to Miranda, "I know this is a lot to take in. I really would like to spend the day with you but if you want to go home, I can take you there."

Miranda's mind raced. Should she tell Evan and her family this news? What harm could it do or would it raise more questions? She stood up to go. There was so much she had to think of. She paused. There were also a lot of things to discuss with Jackson too. Jackson stood and put an arm around her. "Come with me. We can talk privately in my bedroom and then if you need to, I will take you home."

Marcy stood as well, "I am truly sorry Miranda. I can tell you now that there are no more secrets." She frowned, hoping Miranda would forgive her.

Miranda tried to send her a reassuring smile, "I do not blame you and I am glad you let the news slip out."

Marcy smiled weakly back.

"Did you know too?" Miranda asked once they were in his room.

"Yes. I just did not know how to tell you," Jackson admitted, sitting on the bed, looking glum.

Miranda made a face. She was so angry. It was becoming overwhelming. And the strength it took for her to stop that attack. Was she always going to faint?

"It may have just been that time," Jackson said, interrupting her thoughts, "You know. It was your first time so it took all your strength."

Miranda nodded, taking a seat beside him on the bed.

"So, you wanted to talk?"

Of course she did but did her thing with Alex even matter now? There seemed more important things to discuss.

"What about Alex?" Jackson asked, quickly, his eyes widened.

"What is wrong with the two of you?"

"I am not sure exactly. It just seems we have grown apart and I just do not like the way he has been acting, thinking he is older so he knows better when we both know that I did better in school."

"You both really have to stop arguing."

"I am not trying to. He just keeps doing it again and again. Just like when he showed up at school."

"What were you talking about anyways? Me?"

Jackson rolled his eyes, "Do not worry about it."

Miranda pressed her lips into a line, "Well, you are going to have to deal with him." She might as well tell him.

"Tell me what?" he asked, nervously.

"Well, you know that Alex and I are going to be on the show together..."

"Yes?" Jackson answered when she didn't go on.

Miranda looked around his room. It looked a lot like Griffin's with an astronomy theme. He had a hologram of the stars on the ceiling. It was actually very pretty.

"Well, you know that we are going to be *together* together," Miranda continued.

"Well yes, I know that too."

"Alex and I are going to have to kiss. A lot it seems. I wanted you to know that."

Jackson made a face, "Oh." His face fell, "I guess I never really realized that."

"And, well, I wanted you to know that I have kissed him before in rehearsal."

Jackson's eyes locked with hers, "You have?"

Miranda nodded, "I wanted you to know. I feel guilty every time I kiss him."

Jackson looked in thought. "Well, I am going to have to deal with that I guess. It will be your job," he said eventually. He fidgeted and turned away from her.

Miranda nodded and they sat in silence.

"So, do you still want to leave?" Jackson asked. His shoulders were sagged.

"Not now Jack," Miranda said quietly, "I wanted to spend the day with you." She would have a lot of time later tonight or tomorrow to think about what to tell her family. They would have to know the truth about how old she really was. She couldn't pretend to be on the verge of seventeen when she was actually almost nineteen!

He gave her a half smile, "Well, I really wanted to spend the day with you. Shall we go down to the gym until my father gets home with the news?"

Miranda agreed.

They returned to Jackson's apartment after a long and trying workout and a swim to cool off. Both seemed to push themselves harder after that day. Jackson's father and brother were home.

Jackson introduced her as his girlfriend and she shook hands with them both.

"So what happened today?" Jackson asked his father. They were all seated in the living room after a bit of small talk about how they met and a few questions about her upbringing. Miranda used the story that she had been studying with her mother.

"Well, it looks like three people are being held in the cells. They are trying to say they were possessed. It appears they can harness some sort of energy and they use that to attack. The survivors reported a lot of red flashes," he explained, "Red beams of light that burn."

"There were survivors?" Miranda gasped.

His father smiled, "Yes. It is amazing. The survivors claimed this white light overtook the red and the bad people were thrown against the walls."

Miranda and Jackson shared a look, thinking the same thing. It *was* her that stopped it. Could it be that was all she had to do?

They spent the rest of the afternoon with his family. Jackson's brother was a lot like him, very studious and he wanted to explore space. Miranda saw pictures of the two of them and they had looked a lot alike until Jackson had put on some muscle and weight this past year. Miranda felt a little uneducated compared to his family. They were all very smart. She tried not to talk a lot about herself. She didn't want to say something wrong and then they would realize her lie. Of course, his mother already knew and she helped a bit by asking a different question or jumping in.

Miranda got a message at 27 hour that Alex would be picking her up since everyone was a little behind schedule and would be meeting there. She groaned aloud.

"What is it?" Jackson asked.

"Alex is picking me up shortly," Miranda said, rolling her eyes to Jackson only.

Jackson made a face.

"Alex, my nephew?" his dad asked.

"Yes, he is my neighbour. My father is a bit behind schedule so Alex will be picking me up." Miranda forced a smile.

"I have not seen him in some time," he replied, "How is he?"

"Pretty much the same," Jackson said before Miranda answered, "I have seen him a few times the past few weeks."

His father chuckled. Apparently Alex's ego was famous.

"I guess I should wait for him on the roof," Miranda said as she rose from her seat, "Thank you very much for dinner. It was lovely to meet you all."

Jackson moved to follow, "I will walk you out."

On the roof, they argued about their training schedule. They sat beside each other on the ledge. Miranda had her arms crossed and stared up at the sky. The rain had stopped long ago but there were still gray clouds in the sky.

"I really think we should just concentrate on fighting and strengthening our minds," Miranda argued.

"You still need your education," Jackson retorted, "I do want to train you like I am paid to do."

"They know though," Miranda replied, "What if we are targeted next? Or our families? Will they know that I am the reason they were stopped in their attack today?"

"I do not know Miranda, perhaps? We also are not completely sure that they actually do know about you."

"I think Councilman Hope was attacked because of me," Miranda said, sadly. She put her head down and uncrossed her arms. It was all her fault somehow. Someone must have found out about her and knew he was involved.

"But no one should know that you are here," Jackson said, "That you even exist. You are doing well with your story."

"There *are* some though. Friends from the building and I am sure people from the space centre know since my dad brought me there and introduced me. The bad people could be anywhere and could be anyone. Training for battle comes first. I have a bad feeling that we are not far from a showdown. I am still having bad dreams and they are getting worse."

Jackson looked a little frightened.

"We will be fine Jackson," Miranda put an hand on his shoulder and looked him in the eye.

He forced a smile, "I am supposed to assure you Miranda. I want you to know that I will protect you with all I have." He closed the distance between them and kissed her.

The rev of an engine startled her. Alex had pulled up beside them. He reached over and pushed the door open, his expression unreadable, "Are you finished?"

Miranda nodded and gave Jackson's hand a squeeze, "I will see you Monday."

Jackson smiled and nodded.

The ride to the track was silent. She was surprised Alex did not have much to say. His eyes glanced her way.

"Did you know that Evan is my twin?" Miranda blurted out.

Alex's whole head turned to her, "What?"

"I found out today. It was simple to calculate. My birthday is wrong. The year on Earth is longer so I was always following that."

"That is impossible Miranda. How would your father not know?"

"I have no idea but think about it. Evan is almost nineteen and I am almost seventeen. Is his birthday near the beginning of November? Because that is what I calculated mine to be. Jackson helped."

"Yes, it is," Alex said, deep in thought, "November 2$^{nd}$."

Miranda held her breath. It was true. She was eighteen years old. Her nineteenth birthday was just over a month away.

Alex shook his head, "Are you going to tell your family tonight?"

"I don't know," Miranda looked down, "It will raise so many questions that my mother is not here answer. Obviously she knew."

Alex was quiet.

"My father would have said something if he knew, right?" she continued.

Alex looked thoughtful and it was a few minutes before he answered, "Do not tell them yet. We will think about it first."

Miranda nodded, "I want to change my identification."

Alex checked the time, "We have a bit of time if you want to go now."

"Really?" Miranda smiled, "Thanks Alex."

They stopped in at city hall. It did not take a lot of convincing to the lady at the desk. Miranda had dealt with the same woman last time who knew of her situation and that she had been on Earth.

"I am glad you could have the correct day," the lady smiled handing her back a replacement card.

Miranda returned the smile and thanked her, and then they got back in the car and headed to the track.


Her brothers and Greta were there already. Griffin and Greta hugged her when they saw her.

"I was so worried all day," Griffin admitted, "I wish you had let Alex take you home."

"Oh Griffin," Greta said, rubbing his back, "She was fine."

"I know," he grumbled.

"Well, I am going to get my car ready," Alex said. He seemed subdued, not his normal self.

"Have a good race Alex," Miranda turned to him. She wondered if it was her fault he was upset. Maybe about last night?

He gave her a forced smile and turned away.

When he was gone, both her brothers started to chastise her about her day. They both felt she should have gone home with Alex. And what was she thinking running towards the fighting?

They didn't drop it until her father showed up since he had no idea she had been anywhere near the attack.

# Nineteen

★  ★  ★  ★

Alex was in the very first accident that race, which was set up differently from the last race. They must have changed it every week. His car, badly banged up, sank slowly to the ground and he got out. The family watched as he stomped frustrated to the awaiting vehicle and his car was towed.

"He seems... distracted," Miranda commented quietly to Greta, who was lying beside her.

"I think it was about last night," Greta whispered back, "He does not mention his sister often and the anniversary of her death is coming up next month. He did the same thing last year."

"I feel awful for mentioning that," Miranda frowned.

"Do not worry," Greta said, giving her shoulder a squeeze, "He will be ok."

The rest of the race was uneventful. They all found Alex in drivers' area after the race. He was alone and moody but his car had already been fixed and looked brand new.

Miranda yawned.

"Oh, I was going to ask if you had wanted to go to Ernie's but if you are tired, we can go home," Mr. East said.

"I am still not feeling well," Alex cut in, "You all go and I will take her home."

"Sure Alex," Mr. East said understandingly.

Alex was quiet on the drive home. Miranda touched his leg and he almost jumped a mile.

"Sorry Alex," Miranda said, "And I am sorry about last night. Is there anything I can do to cheer you up?"

"No," Alex said, grumpily. He didn't look her way.

"Are you really not feeling well?" she asked.

"I will be fine," he sent her a forced smile.

Miranda sighed and sat back. She liked the egotistical and argumentative Alex better.

When they exited the elevator to their apartment, Miranda stopped short. She felt something sinister and dark coming from her apartment. She took an automatic step back and bumped into Alex, who looked at her as if she had lost it, glanced at the door to the East apartment and back at her.

"Can I come over for a bit?" Miranda asked, trying not to sound alarmed.

"Sure?" Alex questioned. He led the way into his apartment.

"I will be right back," Miranda said, "I need to use your washroom." She didn't wait for his answer.

In the bathroom, she called Jackson.

"Hi," he said excitedly, seeing her face. His face fell at her expression.

"Jackson, I think there is someone in my apartment. I am at Alex's. I'm afraid to go home. What if they do not go away?"

Jackson's mouth fell open, "How do you know?"

"I can feel it," Miranda said, looking foreboding.

"Want me to come there?"

"No!" Miranda almost shouted, and then lowered her voice, "I just wanted to let you know. Training is the most important. They know."

"Ok," Jackson agreed, "Tomorrow? Can we workout together?"

Miranda nodded, "I will see you in the morning." She disconnected.

"Alpha," Miranda said quietly, hoping Alex wouldn't be alerted to his system being used.

A computer screen appeared and waited expectantly.

"Can you lock the front door please?"

"Yes, Miranda," she complied.

Miranda was a little shocked Alex's system knew her name, but then again, it probably knew the whole building.

Alex was on the couch watching television when she returned. She still felt a sinister presence when she passed the front door and it made her shiver. She shut her mind down hoping Alex had no idea what was going on.

He forced another smile at her as she sat.

"Would you like a drink?" Alex asked, smirking.

"Non-alcoholic please," Miranda forced a giggle, hoping it didn't sound forced. She felt on edge, just waiting for someone to burst through the front door. Alex got her a glass of water and brought back a bottle for himself. She could tell he was a little edgy too.

They sat in silence, watching a show Miranda didn't know the name of. They didn't laugh at the funny parts like they were meant to. Miranda heard the elevator about an hour after they arrived home and when it closed again, she felt the sinister aura leaving. She relaxed a bit. At least she wouldn't have to worry about when her family got home. What was someone dark doing in her home if not waiting for her to arrive? She almost wanted to go check but she was afraid. Miranda peeked at Alex who was staring stonily at the television. He did not drink more than two and the second bottle was still half full.

"I think... I think I should go home," Miranda said finally. She faked a yawn.

"Stay with me please," Alex pleaded, turning to her. He put a hand on her arm, "Just until your family gets home. I do not want to be alone."

Miranda frowned, "Oh Alex, what is wrong? Will you tell me?"

He scratched at the bottle in his hand with his thumb, "My younger sister. The anniversary of her death is coming up. I am just having a hard couple days."

"Ok, I will stay with you," Miranda gave him an encouraging smile.

"It was my fault she died," Alex's eyes filled with tears that threatened to spill, "I was supposed to be watching her when she was attacked. It should have been me."

"Oh no Alex," Miranda said, taking his hand, "Of course it is not your fault."

"My parents cannot even bear to be near me anymore. All I have is your family."

"That cannot be true Alex." She was shocked he could even think that his family didn't care about him.

"They took her death very hard."

"Of course they did. But that does not mean they love you less."

He frowned and turned back to the television.

"I miss her so much, especially now. She was a lot like you."

Miranda bit her lip, "Stubborn, I guess?" She tried to smile.

He smirked, "To the extreme."

"She was beautiful," Miranda commented, remembering her picture.

Alex nodded. "Just like you," he said, staring at the television.

Miranda sat back, her cheeks went pink. She didn't know what to say to that.

It wasn't till an hour later that there was a knock at the door.

"Alex," Evan called through the door, "The door is locked. Is Miranda in there with you?"

Alex looked at her finally, puzzled, "Why is the door locked?"

Miranda shrugged.

"Alpha, unlock the door please," Alex said.

The door opened and Evan entered the living room after taking off his shoes. He took in the room. Alex and Miranda were on opposite ends of the couch so there was nothing fishy about the situation. "Why was the door locked?" Evan asked.

Alex shrugged, "I am not sure."

Miranda didn't say anything and they seemed not to suspect her.

"Is everyone home?" Miranda asked.

"Yes, I think we are all going to bed," Evan said and then looked to Alex, "Everything ok? Can I take the spare bed tonight?"

Alex nodded.

Miranda got up to go. She had almost forgotten about the presence she had felt and had thought mostly about Alex for the last hour. She hesitated at the entryway to her apartment. She had been afraid but she had also wanted to protect Alex. She had never seen him vulnerable.

Everything looked normal as she peeked around the apartment and neither her father or Griffin and Greta mentioned anything wrong or missing. She stopped outside her room and shakily reached to slide the door open. She could hear her father moving about in his bedroom.

Miranda squeezed her eyes closed as the door slid open. She peeked through her lashes, gasped and stepped in her room, shutting the door behind her. Her pictures from Earth were torn apart and scattered, and the books were pulled down off the shelves and thrown across the room. She dropped to her knees in the middle of the room and gathered her torn pictures together, somewhat hysterically. She found a piece of Helen's face and her vision blurred with tears.

Now she knew for sure that they knew she was here but she didn't understand why they hadn't waited for her to get home. Maybe they could not feel her presence they way she felt theirs.

She picked up the torn pictures and put them in the suitcase in her closet, the tears streaming down her face at the lost memories she had of Earth and then she started to replace the books. She looked to see if anything was missing and the only thing she thought of was a picture she had of herself that she liked. It was of a trip she had taken to the Caribbean with her Earth parents. She had liked the way her eyes had sparkled in the evening sun.

"Well, everyone will know what I look like," Miranda thought glumly, putting the last book back on her shelf. She sent Jackson a message to tell him what happened. Her phone buzzed a minute later.

She saw his face on the screen.

"Miranda, are you alright?" he said, frantic, before she could say hello.

"Yes," Miranda said, "I just finished cleaning up."

"You must be so scared," Jackson said, his eyes wide. He looked frightened himself.

"Well, yes," Miranda replied, trying to sound calm, "but I guess I really do not have a choice. I am going to have to fight."

"Yes but I thought we would have lots of time."

Miranda made a face, "We could have had a lifetime of growing up and knowing this was coming but some people thought that we were too young."

Jackson took a deep calming breath, "I am sorry Miranda. I must not sound like much help. I am supposed to be the protector and I feel so helpless. I have no idea what I am doing."

"I don't know either," Miranda said, trying to sound positive, "We are going to learn together, Jack."

Jackson sighed and nodded, "You are right," Jackson said, sounding stronger, "I am not young anymore. This is what I am supposed to do."

Miranda tried to smile, "That's the spirit. Anyways, I just wanted you to know what happened."

"Hey listen," Jackson said before they disconnected, "I do not want you to go anywhere by yourself. Whether you need a ride or anything, call me."

"I will Jackson," Miranda said, "And you be careful too. I need you."

Jackson smiled, "See you tomorrow."


Miranda slept badly. She thrashed all night trying to escape death and no one could find her. Her protector was near, she could hear someone calling for her but he never reached her.

She decided to leave her bedroom at six in the morning. She checked the door and it was still locked. She had locked both hers and Alex's through Alpha after everyone had gone to bed and ordered that the door could only be opened by someone in her family or Alex. It was all she could do apart from telling everyone what was going on and she didn't want anyone involved. It was best they didn't know. Griffin, Greta and her father travelled together and so did Evan and Alex so she hoped they would be ok.

Miranda sat on the couch and turned the television on with the volume on low. She took the blanket from her bedroom and curled up on the couch. She couldn't stop thinking about saving Utopia and what they were supposed to do. She pulled out her notebook and read through the passage in the book that she had copied out, hoping that it would give her a hint of what to do.

Exchange words? What words could those be? It is possible she was supposed to even love Jackson. *Only true hearts*. Miranda thought about that. Sure, she liked him a lot but she had never loved anyone besides her family and friends. What did it feel like to be in love? She barely knew Jackson.

Her thoughts were interrupted by a thump at the front door followed by a small groan.

"Alpha, can you please unlock the door," she heard Evan's voice.

He appeared at the door rubbing his head, "What is going on with the locks? Alex's door was locked as well."

Miranda shrugged, "I am not sure Evan."

"You did not sleep?" Evan asked.

"Not well," Miranda replied, turning her attention back to the television.

"Alex neither. He was on the couch this morning. I had to wake him up, he looked distressed," Evan said, taking a seat by her feet.

"Is he ok Evan?" Miranda asked.

"He has a lot on his mind," Evan replied and turned the volume up, "All these attacks lately and his sister's anniversary coming up."

"Are you worried too?" Miranda asked, "How often *do* the attacks happen?

Evan frowned, "A lot more recently. We are all concerned. I was hoping I could talk to you a bit about it."

Miranda looked at him, expectantly.

"We do not think you should be going anywhere by yourself without anyone from the family or Alex. So no riding the bus and no going out with your friends until the attacks stop."

Miranda scowled, "And what do you think that will help Evan? You think one of you will stop them?"

"It would really ease our minds if you were with the family," Evan tried to explain.

"Alex isn't part of the family," Miranda rolled her eyes, "Evan, if this is about me dating Jackson, you guys are going to have to forget about it. Jackson and I are going to be together. And Jackson has agreed with you all. He will be picking me up and we will travel together."

Evan gave a frustrated sigh, "Miranda, you and him should not be dating."

Miranda sent him a glare as a door opened at the end of the hall. Mr. East appeared ten seconds later.

"Good morning kids," he said, smiling. His smile didn't reach his eyes.

"Morning dad," Miranda tried to smile back. She knew he was worried about them.

"I was thinking we should skip the hike today and just stay home," he said, taking a chair, "With all the attacks close by. I feel more comfortable with everyone home and sticking together."

"Can Jackson come here?" Miranda asked and then she shot Evan a glare daring him to say anything, "We were going to do some extra studying today."

"Sure Miranda," he said, "As long as you stay in the building."

"Of course dad," Miranda nodded. She got up and put her blanket away then slowly got ready before messaging Jackson. He messaged that he would be there within the hour.

When she was finished, she said 'good morning' to Griffin and Greta, who were in the living room and joined Evan and Alex in the dining room for breakfast.

"Have you both been through the scripts?" Evan asked.

Alex nodded but Miranda blushed. With her training schedule, she had only practiced with Alex that one time and that was mainly for the first day of filming. With everything going on, she had forgotten that this was the week she would start filming.

"Seriously Miranda," Evan chastised, "You should forget training and practice today. Alex does not have anything to do and he will be here all day."

Miranda made a face, "Ok but Jackson is coming over. I will practice with him and he can play Jeff."

"That is fine," Alex said icily, "I was not going to stay here anyways." Alex cast a look at Evan, "I know your father is worried but I am meeting Amanda."

Evan dropped his fork and it clanged loudly, "Amanda from work?"

"Yes," Alex said.

Evan's jaw clenched and he stood up. He put the excess food back in the oven and pushed 'U', poured it back into the bottle and then stomped away.

"Who is Amanda?" Miranda asked after her brother had left.

"She works on another show that they film at the studio," Alex said.

"Do you like her?" Miranda asked.

Alex shrugged, "At least she is famous herself though, so I know she does not just want attention by dating me."

A chill went through Miranda. They finished eating in silence.

"Well, I best be getting ready," Alex said taking his plate to the kitchen, "See you tonight Maddie!" He smirked and then turned to say goodbye to the rest of the family.

Miranda shook her head. He seemed back to normal.


When Jackson arrived, they headed straight downstairs to the gym. For an hour they worked on the weights, until Miranda said they had to try some more mind strengthening. She started lifting heavy weights with her mind. Jackson kept adding more and more and she picked each one up with ease. He watched her in admiration.

It wore her out but after awhile of sweating, it started to get easier. They decided to switch but Jackson could not lift anything at all.

"Maybe I am not supposed to," Jackson said, wiping his brow, "Maybe I am supposed to just be your bodyguard."

"I am not sure Jackson." Miranda looked thoughtful and then it dawned on her. *Joining hands!* "Come here Jack, I want to try something."

She took his hand and looked into his eyes. With all her might she tried to ease some of her power into him.

"Now try," she said, sounding strained.

Jackson looked at the weights and concentrated hard on moving them. But still, nothing happened.

Miranda lct out a frustrated sound and sent weights across the room where they left a dent in the metal wall.

Miranda's mouth dropped open, "Oops."

Jackson shook his head at her, smiling "Well, I think we are done for today. We should probably tell your building inspector."

Miranda whipped out her phone and sent a message to Alicia who replied that she would tell her dad. She typed back to make sure to let him know that she was very sorry but she had accidentally knocked the weights over and into the wall. She did not want to say how it had actually happened and Alicia did not ask anything else. Alicia told her not to worry, it was an easy fix.

They spent the rest of the day talking about the missing picture, the intruder and actually getting some school work completed. Miranda completely forgot about the scripts. Jackson stayed for dinner, talking politely to Miranda's father about his work at the space centre. Griffin and Greta were missing so Miranda talked to Evan since she wasn't interested in the conversation.

"Where are Griffin and Greta?" she asked.

"Gone out to dinner," Evan replied.

"I thought we were restricted to home?" Miranda asked, a little irritated.

"Well, they had plans that Griffin was not willing to break, again" Evan smirked.

Miranda smiled, "Is he proposing?"

Evan raised an eyebrow, "How did you know?"

Miranda shrugged, "I have my ways."

Evan chuckled, "Well, yes. He was taking her to where they had their first date and he is proposing."

Miranda motioned with her head to her dad, "Does he know?"

"I think he might have an idea," Evan smiled.

"Well, I am glad Griffin finally worked up the nerve."

Evan chuckled again.

After dinner, Jackson and Mr. East moved to the living room. Mr. East wanted to hear more about Jackson's brother, thinking he might be able to help him out with a job to shadow once he finished school.

Miranda was amused. Jackson was so excited to talk to her father. Evan decided to go to the pool so Miranda went into the living room. She flicked on the television and tuned them out.

"Well, I should be going," Jackson said finally, touching Miranda's arm.

She was snapped out of her daze, "Sure. I will walk you out."

Mr. East said 'goodbye' and hoped he would see Jackson again soon.

Miranda walked Jackson to the parking garage. He quickly kissed her goodbye and was gone. That's all he ever did was kiss her. He never tried anything else.

She sulked back to the elevator actually craving a make-out session. *Stupid hormones,* she thought as she waited, *Why didn't Jackson feel that way?* When it stopped to pick her up, there were two people in it making out. They barely noticed her there. All she could see was the back of the woman's head, long, blonde and silky and a man's hands on her backside.

She made an angry 'huff' and they broke apart. The woman gave her a sheepish smile. Alex seemed shocked to see her standing there.

"Sorry," the woman's voice rang, breathlessly, "Oh I have to get off here." She grabbed the door before it closed. "See you tomorrow Alex. I really had a great time." She winked and blew him a kiss.

The door closed on the uncomfortable silence and the air seized until it was released again when the doors open.

"Your shirt is done up wrong," Miranda said, icily. *Virgin my ass,* she added in her mind. What was she thinking when she kissed him. Oh right, she was drinking. Both times!

"Think whatever you want," Alex snapped back.

"I will!"

"Did you practice today?"

Miranda flushed.

"I thought not. You may as well quit now before you embarrass your brother on Friday."

"No! I am not going to quit so get used to it!"

Alex rolled his eyes.

"Ugh!" Miranda stomped to her door. She spun to face him as it slid open. "I wish I could slam these doors because I would on your stupid face!"

Mr. East chuckled as the door closed. "What was that about?"

"Alex," Miranda grumbled.

"Oh?" Mr. East asked, amused.

"He doesn't want me to mess up on Friday," Miranda continued, "I am going to practice."

Mr. East nodded and Miranda went to her room to practice for the rest of the night.

# Twenty

✦  ✦  ✦  ✦

Monday and Tuesday went by slowly. Miranda complied with her father and Evan and Alex were dropping her off and picking her up from school though she didn't speak to the latter. Jackson was happy that she was not alone so he never pushed to drive her himself. They trained hard in the gym all day. There were no attacks but Miranda worried that they were plotting the best way to attack. Jackson was more hopeful.

Miranda barely saw Griffin and Greta since he had finally proposed and they had been doing a lot of couple activities and acting so in love. It had made Miranda jealous. Her father wasn't allowing her to go out after school which was the only place she could see Jackson and he didn't feel comfortable acting as a couple there. She had asked him to come over last night but he had to refuse since his brother needed help with homework.

When she was picked up from school on Wednesday afternoon, Evan let her know that she would need to leave school at 15 hour to be at the studio the next day.

"I cannot move the shoot to a later time," Evan explained, "I have one of the other actors who need to leave."

Miranda nodded. She was so nervous for tomorrow even though she didn't have to say anything, "That should be fine."

Evan turned from the front seat and smiled, "You will do just fine. You were amazing in your audition."

"I am going to try really hard for you, Evan," Miranda said, trying to smile.

"Did you go over the scripts?" Evan asked.

"Yes but it is hard to do on my own," Miranda said looking down at her hands, "I really hope I have grasped everything correctly."

"Are you going out with Amanda again?" Evan asked, turning to Alex.

Alex smiled, "No, we have the night off from each other."

Evan frowned, "Well, you can practice with her."

"No," they both answered in unison.

Evan sighed, "The best way to practice would be together. I will not have you both messing up on the day of filming."

"I will not be the one messing up," Alex said, glancing in the rearview mirror.

Miranda glared at him.

"Do you actually like Amanda?" Evan asked Alex.

Alex shrugged.

"Ok, shall we practice?" Alex asked Miranda back at the East apartment.

"No," Miranda replied bitterly.

"Come on, Miranda," Alex said, "You do not want your brother to be upset, do you?"

"Fine," Miranda reluctantly agreed, "But we will stay here."

Alex shrugged.

Miranda flicked her wrist and the coffee table slid across the floor and into the metal wall with a loud thud.

Alex did a double take, "Remind me never to make you angry."

Miranda glared at him and he put his hands up, "Ok. Remind me never to make you *very* angry."

Miranda had an urge to send him flying across the room too but she refrained. She closed her eyes and took a few deep breaths to calm herself. She was on so much edge and she felt a lot of frustration. This whole show thing was nothing compared to what she was going through. How could she even be worried about it when there were evil ones out there?

They went over the script for Friday again but they both seemed a little icy towards each other. They didn't do the dancing part and basically faced each other with their arms folded.

"That was awful," Evan commented irritably from the foyer where he had been spying, "I thought you wanted to get the feel for the scenes Miranda. You certainly cannot do that by *not* trying."

Miranda sighed, "We have already done the first day of filming and its fine. Shall we just move to the second day?"

Alex made a face, "Sure."

Miranda turned to Evan, "Don't you have somewhere else to meddle?"

Evan rolled his eyes and went to his room to do some editing for the scripts in a few weeks. He hoped he didn't make the wrong choice as to where his show was headed by splitting Jeff and Janet but he really liked the thought of the new character to spice things up. He knew Miranda was right for the job so he did not regret that decision.

"So, the next script," Alex said, turning to her, "I know my lines, what about you?" He didn't remove his notebook at all having memorized all his lines for the next week.

Miranda, however, needed a starting point. She pushed a few buttons on her notebook and the script opened. Alex sighed, angrily and Miranda shot him a glare. She had highlighted all of the scenes she was in so she moved to those sections. So the second day of filming, Jeff and Cara are out on another date. Jeff seems to constantly be looking over his shoulder for people who could recognize him. They end the night at Cara's apartment and argue about how he hadn't broken up with his fiancée.

They went through the scenes delivering the lines in the same icy tone. It was nothing like how it should have been. At least in the scene where they argued, it was perfect because Miranda was already mad or frustrated. She couldn't decide which.


"That was also awful," Alex commented and sat on the chair, "How can we fix this?"

Miranda sat on the couch and put her head in her hands, "I don't know." She sighed, "I just have so much going on."

Alex snorted, "Like what? School?"

Miranda eyed him warily over her hands as tears filled her eyes, "You have no idea Alex."

Alex moved from the chair and sat beside her on the couch. He put a tentative arm around her, "What is it? You can talk to me." He tried to read her mind and for the first time, he couldn't. She had always been an open book to him, or at least he thought. "Is it Jackson?"

Miranda shook her head. She wanted to tell him everything.

"Well, if not Jackson then what?"

Miranda shook her head again, "Just drop it. I can't do this right now. I'm really tired." Miranda got up and went to her room. She laid face-down on the bed and let a few tears fall. Her new life was not simple and if it hadn't have been her destiny, she would have her brothers return her to Earth. She had only one person she could talk to about everything and she had only known him about a month. Actually, she only knew everyone on this planet about a month, including her own family. She was having a hard time only seeing Jackson at school, where he acted as her drill sergeant. When were they going to have time to fall in love?

Miranda fell asleep and did not dream at all. When she finally did awaken, she was surprised. It was probably because she had so many restless nights, that she was too tired to dream.

She looked at her clock and it was just after 3. Her stomach growled since she had missed dinner so she crept quietly from her room, careful not to wake anyone. She tried to do as much as she could with the lights off and it wasn't until she had made a bowl of oatmeal and sat at the dining room table before she asked Alpha turn the lights on at a dim setting.

She sighed. Her mind continued on the endless worry about her family, about Jackson, about herself and about how she was supposed to defeat the bad people when she had no clue what to do. She had almost finished her oatmeal when a she heard a low moaning which made her pause with the spoon halfway to her mouth. She kept perfectly still. *Were there ghosts? Was there someone in their apartment?* She didn't feel any sinister presence.

The moaning continued and it sounded like it was coming from the living room. Miranda asked Alpha to turn the lights back off and she waited a minute until her eyes adjusted before moving. She peeked around the kitchen archway and into the living room.

Miranda sighed with relief. Someone was on the couch. She moved quietly and sat near Alex's waist on the edge of the couch. He moaned again and lashed out but Miranda was quick enough to catch his arm before it hit her.

"Alex," she whispered softly, taking his hand and laying it on her lap. His body stilled but he continued to moan quietly.

"Alex," she tried again, gently shaking his shoulder.

His eyes opened slowly and he blinked several times.

"Are you ok?" she whispered.

He nodded and sat up, "Did I wake you?"

She shook her head, "You can go lay in my bed. I can't sleep anymore."

"Ok," he agreed. He kissed her temple, clumsily, as he got up. "Thank you."

Miranda's eyes closed at the kiss. He still had the same effect on her no matter how mad she was at him. "Goodnight," she whispered.

Once he was gone, she felt the spot on her head where his lips had touched. It still tingled. She smiled a little bit as she put her head down on the pillow he had just vacated. She drew in the smell of his scent and she sighed, falling asleep again.

"Miranda," Greta whispered, touching her cheek softly.

Miranda's eyes opened and she took in her surroundings. She almost forgot how she managed to get to the couch until she remembered that Alex was in her bedroom.

"Hi sleepy," Greta smiled, though her eyes were full of concern, "Are you not well? You slept a lot! We did not want to disturb you for dinner last night."

"Guess she had a night time snack," Griffin's voice came from the dining room. He sent her dirty bowl through the washer.

Miranda sat up, "I'm alright. What time is it?"

"It is just seven," Greta replied, "Would you like some breakfast?"

Miranda nodded.

"Are you excited for your first film day?" Greta smiled wider as she led Miranda to the dining room.

"Yes. A little nervous but tomorrow will be worse. I am glad I finally got a good night sleep."

"Oh good. I am very excited for next week to see you on television."

Griffin placed three plates of bacon and eggs down on the table. Miranda smiled, "Me too."

"I feel like we have not had a lot of time to talk. Would you like to go shopping tonight?" Greta asked.

"Sure. That would be fun!"

"Sorry to wake you but I figure you got a lot of sleep," Griffin said before putting a large mouthful of eggs in his mouth.

"No, that is fine. Thanks!"

Miranda finished her breakfast quickly, told Greta she looked forward to their shopping trip, and then went down the hall, pausing just outside her bedroom door. She thought about knocking and felt silly. It was her room but what if he was naked. *Why would he be though?* She couldn't even remember what he had been wearing last night.

She wished the door would just open a crack instead of all the way so she could at least peek in.

Miranda was still deciding what to do when Evan stepped out of his room. He gave her a questioning look.

"I sent Alex to my room when I woke up in the middle of the night," Miranda explained. "I spent the rest of the night on the couch," she added quickly when he raised an eyebrow.

"Just go wake him and tell him it is time to get ready for work," Evan whispered back and then headed towards the kitchen.

Miranda sighed and opened the door. Alex was still asleep on his back, his head pointing away from the door. When she sat on the edge of her bed, she noticed he had a peaceful look on his face and felt bad disturbing his sleep. She watched him for a minute. He wasn't wearing a shirt. She almost felt compelled to run her hands down his stomach.

"Alex," she said, giving him a little shake.

His eyes snapped open and he sat up quick, knocking her arm away, "What happened? What am I doing in here?"

"We switched last night. I was awake at 3 and you were on the couch having a bad dream so I told you to go lay down in my bed."

"Oh, right."

Miranda fidgeted uncomfortably, "Evan said to wake you to tell you it is time to get ready."

"Thanks," Alex said flatly. He pushed the covers off. He was wearing only shorts and Miranda looked away as he got up and left.

She got herself ready in her school uniform and then Evan and Alex drove her to school.

"Alex will pick you up at 15 hour," Evan reminded her.

"Yes," Miranda nodded nervously, "See you later." She walked slowly to the elevator and took it down one floor to meet Jackson.

"Hi!" he greeted her happily.

She smiled at his good mood. It was very uplifting since she had been in a terrible mood yesterday.

"I was thinking we should have a day off," Jackson continued.

Miranda smiled, "Really?"

He nodded enthusiastically, "Since you are leaving at 15 hour anyways I was thinking we could skip training today. We have been working so hard I think we deserve a break."

"I guess," Miranda said and she hopped up on the desk beside him, "What would you like to do?"

Jackson pulled out his notebook, "How about astronomy?"

Miranda's face fell, "Astronomy?"

Jackson frowned, "History?"

Miranda made a face. She thought he had meant a day off from everything. She got an idea and leaned in close to kiss him.

He allowed it for a few seconds before pulling away, "Miranda, we are at school."

"So?" she pouted. She pressed her lips again to his.

This time he allowed it longer before he pulled away, "Ok, seriously." He looked stern, "I cannot do this at school. I am being paid to train you."

Miranda sighed, her bad mood returned instantly, "Fine. Astronomy I guess."

Jackson smiled and opened a document on the desk notebook beside Miranda. She slid off the desk and into the chair in front of the document.

"I'll give you a minute to read that page and then we can talk about it," Jackson instructed.

Miranda sighed again and put her head down, pretending to read. She wanted someone to talk to so badly. Perhaps Greta? But she didn't want Greta to know about the legend and she could never understand her boy troubles since she didn't know Miranda and Jackson were supposed to be soulmates. She didn't know if Jackson would want to talk about how she's frightened and scared for her family and about how she wants to spend more time with him when she isn't even allowed out after dinner.

She didn't notice Jackson had come around the desk and put his arms around her.

"Ok Miranda," he said, nuzzling her neck, "What would you like to do?"

Miranda's eyes filled with tears and she turned to face him, "I am in such a bad mood Jackson. I just don't know."

"I do want to talk about it Mandy," Jackson said, "You can tell me anything."

Miranda half smiled at her nickname. She had told Jackson about it on Saturday.

"I'm just so afraid," Miranda said, a silent tear falling down her cheek, as she frowned again, "There was someone in my apartment. What if someone had been home? I cannot keep the doors locked all the time. My family is starting to get suspicious. I told Alpha not to let anyone else but my family and Alex unlock the doors but I am afraid she is going to tell them that I have instructed her to do that."

"Did you tell her not to?" he asked.

"Yes, but still."

"Then she will not. She will follow your instruction until you tell her otherwise."

"And I can't be there to protect them all the time. I am constantly worried that someone bad will hurt one of my family members to get to me."

"We still do not know if they know it is you," Jackson tried to assure her.

She gazed at him warily. Of course they knew. How could they not? "I still feel something dark is coming... soon," Miranda dreaded.

Jackson squeezed her shoulders, "And we will be here, ready for it. You are the strongest person I have ever met, in mind and body."

"What about my family? Will they be ok?" Miranda asked quietly.

"I know you will do anything to protect them," Jackson said, looking her squarely in the eye, "Of course they will."

"And you? Am I strong enough to protect you?"

Jackson kissed her quickly, "I am here to protect you."

Miranda still worried for him. Perhaps he still needed time to develop whatever powers he held. She was older. What if it didn't kick in until later?

"Can you ask to be picked up at my apartment?" Jackson asked, "We do not have to study today and it would be nice to have some alone time with you."

Miranda knew he was doing that for her but it still lightened her mood a bit, "I will message him when we get to your place."

Jackson nodded and together they went up to his car and headed for his apartment. When they arrived in the parking garage there, Miranda sent Evan a message asking to be picked up at Jackson's instead. Sure enough, a minute later, Evan called her.

"Do NOT leave the school grounds Miranda," Evan said before she could even speak.

"Well, hello to you too," Miranda snapped, "I am already here, Evan, so have Alex pick me up here at 15 hour." Evan was about to say something but Miranda hung up on him.

Jackson chuckled, "Shall I expect another altercation with my big cousin?"

Miranda sent him an apologetic glance as they waited for the elevator, "Sorry Jackson. I don't mean to get you in trouble with him. I just knew it would be easier to beg for forgiveness than ask for permission."

"An Earth philosophy?" Jackson chuckled again.

Miranda giggled, "I suppose."

The elevator picked them up and before the doors even closed, Jackson pulled her close and kissed her.

Miranda laughed breathlessly as they broke apart when the doors opened to Jackson's apartment floor.

"I guess I had better make it worth the fight," Jackson smiled and kissed her again quickly before pulling her out the elevator, through his apartment and into his room.

"Is there anything else you would like to talk about?" Jackson asked as they took a seat on his bed.

"Just that I know it's hard with me being on lockdown every night but I would like to see you more Jackson," Miranda smiled, but frowned as she continued, "The passage in the book speaks of two people in love fighting the evil. Maybe that is why your powers are not at the strongest they can be. Now I don't mean just tell me you love me. Obviously we haven't known each other long enough for that but we need time to develop that part of our relationship and not just training all the time."

Jackson nodded, "You are absolutely right."

"I am shopping with Greta tonight but come over tomorrow after I am done at the studio."

"Ok," he agreed, "I will gladly spend more time with you."

Miranda kissed him and he returned it, kissing her like he never had before. A warm tingle spread through her body and she slid her hands into his hair. She could feel the warmth of his hands through her uniform as they caressed her back. They paused long enough for Miranda to pull his shirt off. She ran her hands across his flat stomach and he groaned. Without breaking contact, he flipped them over so she was underneath him. He was running his hand up her leg when they heard her name.

They broke apart quickly. Jackson stood and grabbed his shirt and Miranda sat up so fast her head spun. Jackson had just slipped the shirt over his head when his bedroom door opened and Alex was there looking furious.

"Why is it that I was sent here to retrieve you when I should be on the set filming?" Alex snapped.

Miranda shrugged, "I didn't ask to get picked up now so I have no idea. Why *are* you here early?"

Alex turned to Jackson with a glare and watched as he finished pulling his shirt down over his torso.

"What did your family say about traveling only with a member of the family or me?" Alex continued, turning back to Miranda.

Miranda stood up, furious, "Jackson can take care of me as well. He wants the same as you all do and ..."

Alex cut her off, turning on Jackson, "You should know better. You are paid to train her during these hours."

Miranda stepped in between them before Jackson could respond, "If I want to skip school, I am old enough to decide that."

"Miranda, you lived on Earth! Obviously you have not reached the maturity level of a Utopian citizen," Alex snapped.

Miranda's face flushed angrily, "How dare you insinuate that I am still a child!"

"No Utopian adult would go against her family's wishes to go have sex with her instructor while she is supposed to be at school!"

Miranda's face burned, "We were not going to have sex!"

"Wow Alex," Jackson said, stepping up beside Miranda, "You crossed the line."

"No, you did Jack," Alex snapped, "I will have you released from your job."

Jackson took a menacing step towards Alex but Miranda took his arm, "Go ahead Alex, get him fired." Jackson looked at her quickly. Surely she did not mean that, "Do it! But do not think for one minute that I will stop seeing him."

Alex looked between them a few times as the seconds ticked by. "We will let your family decide," he said, finally, "Get your stuff. We are leaving."

"I will meet you on the roof," Miranda told him but he didn't move, waiting for her with his arms crossed.

She eyed him angrily and bent to pick up her purse where she had dropped it beside the bed. She turned to Jack and took his hand. *I'm sorry*, she said in her mind. He nodded and gave her a half smile.

"See you tomorrow," Jackson said aloud.

Alex snorted, "If you are lucky."

They both ignored him and Jackson gave her hand a squeeze before she turned to follow Alex.

They didn't speak up the elevator or on the walk to the car. Miranda crossed her arms over her chest. The time on the dashboard said 12:15. She was so early. Why couldn't Evan just have let her stay there? Why did he have to send Alex?

Alex slammed his door and pushed the ignition start. He jammed his foot on the gas and the car accelerated quickly up into the air and into traffic.

"You are unbelievable!" he snapped, "Why did you leave the school grounds while you are supposed to be learning?"

"Sometimes we all just need a break," Miranda replied, "I am overloaded. I just didn't want to do anything today and Jackson said since it was going to be a short day, we could just hang out."

Alex snorted, "You call that 'hanging out'?"

Miranda rolled her eyes, "Don't think you rescued me from a horrible mistake. I am not like you."

"Oh this again," Alex rolled his eyes, "Please tell me again what you think of me so I can act like I care."

Miranda just turned away from him. Alex sped up and they arrived at the studio in minutes.

"Come with me. I have never seen your brother so angry," Alex said, "Evan was always the calmer one."

Miranda followed him, reluctantly, sulking the whole way. She was so early and now she would just have to sit here and be nervous. Plus deal with whatever trouble she was in with Evan, not that she cared what her overprotective brother had to say.

Evan was in the studio on the set when Miranda and Alex walked in. He was explaining the atmosphere of the next scene and encouraging them to keep up the good work. He spotted Miranda and scowled. He strode over to Melissa, asked her to take over for a few minutes, and then marched up to Miranda and Alex.

"Save it, Evan," Miranda snapped, before he said anything, "What I do with my life is none of your business!"

"Dad did not want you to go anywhere without one of us," Evan retaliated, "Do you have any idea how much danger you put yourself in?"

"Of course I know, Evan. I know there have been a lot of attacks lately but I have to have a life too! I am sick and tired of staying at home every night while everyone else is able to go out," Miranda snapped back, "And Jackson can take care of me. He is my boyfriend."

"No, you cannot be with him," Evan said, assertively.

"Why not?" Miranda's eyes flashed angrily.

Evan glanced at Alex, "Because he is not right for you."

"There is nothing wrong with my cousin," Alex said quietly. Miranda did a double take at Alex. Was he really on her side? "That being said," Alex continued, "He is still your instructor and he is not up to the job of keeping you out of danger."

"What were you thinking leaving the school? I thought you were learning from him," Evan added.

"Well, *I* decided *I* wanted a day off. *I* was nervous for today and *I* am running through my lines for tomorrow in my head. *I* couldn't concentrate on school," Miranda lied, stressing it was all her idea and not Jackson's. She closed her mind and stared Evan down. Alex raised an eyebrow. He didn't believe her for a second but Evan finally sighed, frustrated.

"Fine, just do not let it happen again," Evan said, "Dad, Griffin and I do not want you going off with just anybody."

"Dad trusts me and he likes Jackson," Miranda said, "I am sure when I ask him tonight that dad will allow me to go with Jackson as well."

Evan's lips formed a hard line. He shot a glare at Alex but Alex ignored it. He turned back to Miranda, "You will go with Rachel to get ready." He turned around and motioned for Rachel to come over.

Rachel was not much taller than Miranda. She had flaming red hair tied back in a braid. Evan introduced them both. Rachel was the costume designer.


Miranda followed Rachel into the dressing room that she shared with Britany. Along the way, Rachel talked excitedly about Miranda's new role. Miranda was barely listening. She was too busy wondering why her brother didn't want her to be with Jackson.

Britany was in a chair, having her hair done when Miranda walked in.

"Well, here she is," Rachel announced, "Have a great day!" Rachel had been totally oblivious that Miranda wasn't paying attention.

"Hi!" Britany said excitedly, "You nervous?"

Miranda smiled weakly, "A little but I'll be worse tomorrow. I don't have to say anything today."

Britany smiled, "I would not worry about it. I heard you did wonderful in your audition."

"Thanks."

"Oh, that came for you this morning," Britany said, motioning to the flowers that sat by Miranda's area of the room.

"Oh, seriously?" Miranda asked shocked. She went over and took in the scent of the exotic flowers. It was from her dad, brothers, Alex and Greta wishing her good luck and congratulations.

She smiled to herself as she admired the flowers again.

"They are beautiful, are they not?" Britany said coming over to Miranda and admiring them as well. She was all ready for the taping and it was Miranda's turn.

"Yes, definitely," Miranda agreed as she sat down so that the hair stylist could do her hair.

"Well, I should get out there and get started. It will be awhile till the dance scene, but I am not in it. I have to go away on business," Britany winked, "That is where you steal my man."

Miranda smiled, apologetically.

"And like I said, you can have him," Britany giggled.

Miranda laughed, "Well, if it was not in the script, I would not want him."

"You are the first girl I have ever met that has said that!" Britany giggled, "Good luck today!"

Miranda talked politely with the stylist as she worked her magic. The stylist pulled Miranda's hair into a beautiful up-do and clasped it with a purple sparkly flower and did her makeup with light purple eye shadow.

When she was done, she told Miranda to put the dress on that was in the dressing bag so that she could make sure it was the right size.

Miranda was shocked at the beautiful dress they had chosen for her. It was a long, light purple strapless dress with an empire waist. There were tiny sparkles embedded into the silky fabric and it had long satin gloves matching the gown. The stylist said it looked beautiful on her, but it needed to be hemmed an inch, so she left Miranda there and took the dress to be fixed. Miranda was wearing a strapless white bathing suit so she went to the wardrobe and put on a dress. She needed the bathing suit for one of the later scenes even though she would not be doing that one today.

Miranda didn't know what to do. She was so nervous and so confused she couldn't sit down so she stood by the vase. She concentrated on the flowers to keep her mind off her problems. The flowers here were beautiful, looking nothing like the flowers of Earth. They were all so colourful, just like the ones she had seen on her hike with her dad and Evan.

When the dress returned, she put it on. It was perfect now. The stylist pointed her over to a pair of silver, sparkly high heels and she was worried she would trip when she danced with Alex tomorrow.

Evan showed up at her door about an hour after.

"Wow," he said when he entered her dressing room, "You look stunning."

Miranda blushed, "I feel beautiful," she said touching the fabric lightly, "This is a gorgeous dress!"

"Come. Let me show off my sister," Evan said and he took Miranda's arm and hooked it around his own, escorting her to the studio. Miranda was quiet.

"What is wrong?" Evan asked.

"Just a lot on my mind," Miranda replied a little preoccupied.

"Want to talk about it?" Evan asked, slowing their pace.

"Not really, Evan," and she smiled at him.

"I am sorry I got so angry," Evan said, "I guess I do not realize how over-protective I can be. It is hard since I have not had you in my life for so long."

"It's fine Evan," Miranda said, squeezing his arm, "I guess I just don't understand why you don't think I should be with Jackson."

Evan made a face, "I guess I just do not know him so well. I just assumed any sister of mine would be with Alex."

Miranda's mouth dropped open and she choked on a laugh, "He is already like a brother to you Evan. Why would you need to make it official?"

"I see the way you two are together. Do not think no one notices," Evan implied.

"If you mean that he is so mean to me and we are always fighting. Yes, I can see how that could be misjudged as love," Miranda laughed.

"He started as mean to you but now I can see he is just as protective of you as Griffin and I," Evan said, nudging her shoulder, "Plus, I know you care about him and think he is cute."

Miranda rolled her eyes, "Just stop Evan. Alex and I are far from compatible. He is like a brother to me, a brother who you don't like very much but are forced to love because he is family."

Evan snorted a laugh as they reached the studio. Everyone's eyes turned their way. She glanced around nervously but Evan pulled her into the middle and announced that she was the new cast member. Everyone applauded and Miranda blushed.

She could hear those around her saying "She looks beautiful" and "Wow, you can tell they are related" as she stood beside her brother. She looked to her brother, who smiled at the comments.

Alex entered the studio, after his stylist had him dress up in a dark grey suit for the dance scene, wondering what everyone was staring at until he noticed Miranda in the centre. He moved onto the set but stayed away from Miranda.

Evan was back up on his director's chair, barking out orders. Miranda was going to be standing by the line of drinks. Alex would get a drink and then take a second glance at Miranda, who would be looking at him.

They would smile at each other and Alex would walk away but stare at her from across the room. Miranda would continue on with her silent conversation with the extra, unaware of Alex's eyes on her.

They shot the scene quickly and a few others, Miranda doing exactly what she was supposed to do, and then Evan told everyone they could leave. They were done shooting for the day.

Evan came over to her and told her she did a good job.

Miranda looked down at her dress, "Hardly seemed worth getting all dressed up for."

"That is the business. We can only do so many scenes in one day. We will just have to make you look exactly the same tomorrow."

Miranda smiled, thinking about the next day when she would actually get to act.

She went to her dressing room and changed back into her normal clothes. She took the piece out of her hair, but left it pinned up.

When she left the dressing room, Alex was waiting for her.

"You can bring your flowers home," he said, "They would make your room smell great."

"Ok," she replied and went back into the dressing room to take the vase home. As a last minute decision, she grabbed the high heeled shoes as well. She wanted to practice dancing in them.

Alex led the way up to his car.

"I picked those flowers out," Alex said once they were in the air.

Miranda gave him a quizzical look.

"Your dad wanted to give Evan his card to get them this morning but Evan refused and bought them himself," Alex explained, "We stopped on the way to the studio this morning."

"Thank you. They are beautiful," Miranda smiled.

"Yes, I have good taste," Alex complimented himself.

Miranda laughed, "Well, maybe with flowers."

"What is that supposed to mean?" he snapped.

"Oh Alex, I was just teasing you," Miranda sighed.

Alex sent her a half smile.

"Why doesn't Evan or Griffin have a car?"

"Unnecessary. I have one and your father does as well. They are fine to get rides with me and your father or take the bus."

"Maybe I should get a car so I don't have to bother you for a ride all the time," Miranda sighed.

"I do not mind," Alex said.

Miranda looked at him, "You sure did this morning when you picked me up."

"That was different," Alex replied, sending her a look, "You were supposed to stay at school."

Miranda didn't respond. She didn't want to start again with Alex. In fact, she was hoping he would be staying at home when they got there so he could help her.

"What did you need?"

Miranda picked up her purse off the floor that held her shoes and opened it to show him.

"I am not wearing those," Alex joked.

Miranda giggled, "No, I have to. And I am going to fall flat on my face tomorrow. Can we please go over the dance scene again?"

Alex laughed and agreed.

Miranda moved the coffee table again with her mind once they reached the Easts apartment and had taken off their shoes.

"You are getting pretty good at that," Alex complimented.

Miranda smiled at him as she slipped on her heels and took a practice walk around the living room. They were very comfortable, just a lot higher than she was used to.

Alex tried not to laugh as he watched her walk around. She was not that bad at it. "Ok, come here," he said, holding a hand out to her and she tottered over to him with her arms out for balance.

He pulled out his notebook and picked a song, then tossed it on the couch as it started to play.

"Slow at first please," Miranda requested. They started first by just spinning in a slow circle.

"Try not to step down fully on your heel," Alex suggested, "Keep your weight on your toes."

"How do you know that?" Miranda asked, laughing.

Alex shrugged, "Ready for a spin?"

Miranda bit her lip, "Ok."

Alex tried it slowly. Miranda tripped a little over the heel and stumbled but Alex caught her. She giggled.

"Oh this is going to take awhile," she laughed.

They went back to the slow circle.

"Ok, how about we try a little more movement before the spin," Alex said. He quickened the pace, to a sort of waltz, taking bigger steps. Miranda flowed with him without tripping and smiled. Without asking her, he spun her around and she nailed it flawlessly so he moved to the full routine that he had choreographed. Not once did she stumble.

She threw her arms around Alex when they finished and thanked him for helping.

Alex shrugged, "I did not want you to hurt yourself tomorrow."

"Can we try one more time, please?"

He took her hand and again led her through the routine.


"That was great you two!" Greta smiled. She was in the foyer, just home from work.

Miranda and Alex, who were in their own world, jumped a little and both looked towards the front door.

Miranda smiled, "I had to try with the shoes on." She showed Greta her silver heels.

"Those are nice," Greta complimented, "And you looked very comfortable in them."

Miranda looked over to Alex, "Thanks for the help. I think I will be good tomorrow."

"Yes, you will be just fine," Alex smiled. He gave her shoulder a squeeze, "Ok, I am heading out with Amanda. See you tomorrow."

Greta rolled her eyes after he left, "I do not know why he keeps pretending to like Amanda. It is obvious he is crazy about you."

Miranda laughed, "You Utopians have a weird way of looking at things. Alex and I aren't happening. I'm with Jackson exclusively."

"Really?" Greta asked, her eyes sparkled, "You can tell me all about it at the shopping centre. Do you want to go now? We can have dinner there."

"Do you ever call it a mall?"

Greta cocked her head, "A mall?"

"We call shopping centres a mall on Earth."

"Oh!" Greta smiled, "Never heard it used here!"

When they got to the shopping centre, Miranda bought another pair of heels and kept them on as she walked around the shopping centre with Greta to get the practice. It really helped her height too. Greta bought them for her since Miranda had forgotten to ask to borrow her father's card. She would be able to use her own as soon as she got paid. Evan told her pay day is every Friday but she would not get her first pay until the next week.

Miranda told Greta all about Jackson. Greta was happy for her.

"I don't understand why you are the only one who is happy for me," Miranda sighed as she sat down at the restaurant they had chosen for dinner.

"Well I guess everyone was hoping you and Alex would get together," Greta commented, scrolling through the menu, "And so was I, of course, but I am happy if you are."

Miranda rolled her eyes, "That *is* what Evan said today. I just have no idea why anyone needs Alex to be any more of a family member than he already is."

Greta shrugged, "It would have been cute but you are absolutely right. Alex is already like a brother." She smiled, "I think I am going to try the stuffed chicken and rice. What are you having?"

"That sounds yummy," Miranda said, "I am going to try the fish and fried potato. We called them French fries on Earth, or chips. It was always fish and chips to me."

Greta laughed, "I do love it when you use Earth words Miranda. It is cute."

Miranda really enjoyed her time with Greta, until the ground trembled slightly. Greta's eyes went wide. She pulled out her phone and called Griffin right away, even as it still trembled.

Miranda closed her eyes and with her palms towards the floor, she wished with all her might that the attack would stop. Her hands shook but she held them in place. A quick flash of light lit up the underside of the table but no one in the restaurant noticed. They were all preoccupied with the Earthquake. Miranda felt weakened but it wasn't overpowering like it had been the first time. She pulled out her phone which vibrated in her pocket. It was Jackson.

"Hi Jack," she said, "Everything ok?"

"Yes, are you?"

"Yes, same thing happened as before," she said, hinting that she wasn't alone.

"Oh? That is great!" Jackson replied.

"I hope it worked," Miranda whispered. She didn't think Greta was listening anyways. She was talking to Griffin.

"I wonder if that is all you have to do. Just sit back away from the fight and send in your little light."

Miranda looked doubtful. She felt her phone vibrating again. "I have a call from my dad coming in. See you tomorrow." She clicked over to her dad, who was relieved to see her.

"I am shopping with Greta," she told him, "We are ok."

"We will head home now," Greta said, looking over at her while still on the phone.

"Be home soon dad," Miranda said and they hung up with each other.

"Look Miranda," Greta smiled. She showed her a message from Alex. He wanted to make sure they were both fine.

"As a friend and brother," Miranda told her, "And it was sent to you, not me."

When they got home, everyone was waiting for them in the living room. Griffin and Greta embraced.

"Now you see why we need you to stay with one of us," Evan said, hugging his sister.

"Greta was not on the list," Miranda shot back.

"Why would you say that?" Mr. East asked, looking between the two of them.

"Dad, I need to talk to you about Jackson," Miranda said. Everyone around them went quiet, "I think I should be allowed to go out with him. I am safe with him."

Evan and Griffin looked to their dad.

Mr. East shrugged, "If you think so, that is fine with me."

"No dad," Evan said.

"I do not agree either," Griffin added.

"But why?" Miranda asked them.

"He was supposed to be training her today and they left to go to his apartment. He is not acting like much of an instructor," Evan explained.

Mr. East turned to Miranda, "Is that true?"

"It was my idea dad," Miranda said, she shot a look at Evan, "Like I explained to Evan earlier, it was me that did not feel like studying today. I was too nervous for the show and I couldn't concentrate. Jackson is very professional. He knows the difference between how we act alone and at school."

Mr. East looked from Miranda to Griffin and Evan, "I do not see a problem with Jackson. He has a very level head on his shoulders," he said and then looked to the boys, "He is a very nice man and Miranda will be fine."

Miranda smiled. At least her father was on her side.

Mr. East turned to Miranda, "Just let me know where you are at all times."

"Ok, thank you dad," Miranda said. She gave him a quick hug then went to put her shoes away. She messaged Jackson to say her father was on their side and she would be able to go out with him. They made plans to go out for dinner tomorrow before coming back to Miranda's apartment.

# Twenty-One

★   ★   ★   ★

Miranda awoke with a start and took some deep breaths. She had been pushed from a cliff and fell for miles, until she awoke.

She got up from her bed, her legs shaking. Evan was in the kitchen.

"Morning," Miranda said.

Evan smiled, "Are you ready for today?"

"I am so excited!" Miranda returned his smile, forgetting all about her nightmare.

"Are you going to school?" Evan asked.

"Do I need to Evan?" Miranda asked, "I would really like to get to the studio."

"Dad will probably want you to go to school. Are you sure?"

"Dad will understand. I won't be able to concentrate today either. I am going to text Jackson and get a ride in with you and Alex."

She sent Jackson a message that she would be going straight to the studio today. He messaged her back wishing her luck.

Miranda went to her room and put on her jean skirt and a beige top with flowers in varying shades of pink. It really didn't matter what she wore since she would be changing into that gorgeous dress.

They reached the studio and Miranda headed to her dressing room

She sat patiently while the stylist did her hair and makeup in the same way it was the day before and then slipped on the dress. She didn't think it was possible, but today, she felt even more beautiful than yesterday. Her face fell a little. She felt bad for distracting herself with this TV show, when she should be preparing for a battle. What kind of battle would it end up being? She had no idea how many evil ones there were. According to the news, three more were in custody after she stopped the attack last night. She was sure that had made them angrier. What if they attacked her right here?

Miranda thanked her stylist and went out to the set. She was greeted by many of her cast members.

"You ready Miranda?" Evan said, coming over to her.

"Yep!" she replied, trying to sound excited. She followed Evan over to the set, where he was placing everyone. Alex strode over to where they were standing, wearing the same grey suit he had on the day before.

"Ok, you guys have been practicing, so, let me see it!" Evan said, sitting up on his director's chair.

Miranda worried a little about dancing in her high heels as Evan shouted "Action."

She was talking to the extra when someone touched her on the shoulder. She turned, smiling.

"Hi," Alex said.

"Hi," Miranda replied blushing.

"I was wondering if you would dance with me."

Miranda nodded, smiling and took Alex's hand as he led her to the dance floor.

"I am Jeff Williams," Alex said as he took the hand he was holding and the other found her waist.

"I am Cara Scott," Miranda said, breathlessly. Everyone behind the camera watched as Alex spun her around the room. Miranda couldn't help but smile. She never thought in a million years that she would be dancing with a very cute guy and performing in a television series. They moved around the dance floor with ease.

"I have never seen you here before. Are you new in town?"

"Yes. I just moved here yesterday."

"Job offer?"

Miranda looked down, "No. Just escaping the past."

Alex smiled, "Well, we always have to look towards the future, right?"

"Absolutely. Have you lived here your whole life?" Miranda let out a laugh as Alex dipped her.

"Yes. So I know all the good spots," he winked as he pulled her back up.

"Perhaps you could show me around sometime?"

The song ended and Alex nodded, "How about now?"

Miranda smiled and agreed. As they exited, two of the other cast members looked after them in shock.

"Cut!" Evan said, "How did you two make that look so great?"

Miranda smiled, "It was Alex's idea. We have been practising it that way."

"Well, it was really good. And great job from you all in the back turning to watch. Great improvisation. That was a great scene!" Evan smiled.

Miranda turned to Alex excitedly and threw her arms around him.

"Oh, that was so exciting," she said, bouncing on her feet.

"Yes, I did a great job," Alex laughed, releasing her finally.

She playfully punched him, "You are nothing without me."

Alex looked like he was thinking and Miranda slapped him again on the arm, "Don't say a word, *we* make a good team."

"Fine," Alex rolled his eyes but smiled in agreement.

They moved to another set to film the boardwalk scene. It occurred immediately after the dance. The screen behind Miranda, showed a starry night sky.


"This is the boardwalk," Alex, playing Jeff, explained, "There is always something going on every weekend here. Live shows, carnivals, it is a great city. I think you will like it here."

"It is beautiful out here," Miranda exclaimed. They strolled towards the edge of the pier. Miranda put her gloved arms up on the railing and looked out at the calm water, which of course, was a screen with surprisingly realistic waves on it. Alex stared at her. A few stray curls of Miranda's hair blew gently in the artificial wind and Alex brushed them gently behind her ear.

"How old are you?" Alex asked.

"Twenty, you?" Miranda replied, turning her gaze to him.

"Twenty-one. What do you do for a living?"

"I am a teacher for age six students" Miranda smiled, she looked to Alex for his response.

"I manage an office that takes care of banking transactions." Alex paused as they looked out into the water, "May I ask what you are escaping from?"

Miranda shook her head. Cara wasn't ready to disclose information to anybody, "Some other time, Jeff. How about a swim?"

"What?"

"A swim, you know, in the water," Miranda laughed.

"But… I am in a suit!" Alex said looking down at his clothes.

"Come on," Miranda laughed, "I am sure you have something on underneath! It will be fun."

"And what if I do not?" Alex asked with a playful smile.

Miranda smirked, "Well, that would be even better." She giggled and he joined.

Miranda walked excitedly down the pier pulling Alex along.

The next scene was down at the water's edge and they moved to an outdoor set. It was light out, but the editing crew would be able to make it night time.

Miranda took her dress off. She had her bathing suit on underneath, a plain white bikini.

"Do you always keep your bathing suit on underneath?" Alex asked, chuckling.

Miranda shook her head, "It just so happens that the top of this bikini fits perfect underneath my dress. I just wore the bottoms to match," she said, matter-of-factly.

Alex laughed and stripped down to his boxers and Miranda looked him up and down appreciatively.

"Nice Jeff," Miranda winked, "Do you work out?"

Alex laughed, "I try."

Miranda got in the water quickly, trying not to think that all of Utopia will be seeing her in a bathing suit. They had to cut the scene once again to get a close up of the two in the water where they joked and splashed around.

Miranda got a little nervous as the kiss approached. They had finished the water scenes, moved to another outdoor set where Jeff was walking Cara home. Before it happened, Miranda heard Alex sigh and say, *I do not want to do this again,* in his mind.

"Why not?" Miranda answered his question aloud.

"Cut" Evan said, "No line there Miranda, just kiss him."

Miranda looked at Evan, "I know that. He just... nevermind."

"Well, we will have a minute break and then we can take it from the kiss. You are doing great Miranda! It was only your first mistake today."

Miranda looked to Alex, "You don't want to?"

"Well no. You would not understand," Alex said.

"Try me," Miranda said.

Alex looked around, "It is just the camera. On film it is so public. I just do not like it."

"How are you going to feel next week?"

"When we have to..."

"Yeah," Miranda confirmed what he was about to say, when they have to film the sex scene.

"Well, I am supposed to be an actor, so I have to deal with it."

"You are a great actor Alex," Miranda assured him, "Let's do this!"

Alex chuckled, "All right."

Alex took her in his arms again and she smiled at him as her brother yelled "Action".

Alex didn't waste a second before he was kissing her and Miranda felt the same reckless feeling she always felt when kissing Alex. It spread throughout her.

"Woah, Cut!" Evan said and the two broke apart, "That is a little too much for the first kiss."

Alex closed his eyes and rubbed his face with his hand, "Sorry, Evan."

Miranda collected herself, "That was my fault. Got a little nervous."

Evan laughed, "Ok," he sighed, "Take it from the kiss again."

"Just breathe," Miranda coached herself before Evan said 'Action' again. Alex smiled at her. *Good advice*, he said in his head.

This time Miranda kept her hands at her side to try and control herself. Alex somehow had thought the same thing, so the kiss was very brief.

"Not enough now," Evan said.

Alex rubbed his face again and Miranda nodded.

"Let's get it right this time. You both ready?" Evan said.

Miranda took a few deep breaths again before Alex took her in his arms.

"Action."


Alex kissed her cheek and then she turned her face and captured his lips. She tried to keep control of herself but lost it again and before she knew what she was doing, her hands were tangled in his hair again.

"Cut!" Evan said, a little exasperated, "You two want a room?"

Miranda jumped back from Alex, "Sorry," she said and covered her face with her hands and her face burned with heat. She took a few steps back, shaking her head slowly, "Sorry, sorry, sorry."

"Ok, so when you guys first kissed, what was that like," Evan asked, "because from what I heard you both have practised before, but I need to capture the first time."

Miranda didn't mean to, but she snorted aloud thinking about the first kiss and how it was much, much worse than now.

"Ok, I really did not want to know that," Evan said aloud and glared at Alex "Last time I leave you two alone."

"Oh crap," Miranda rushed out, hyperventilating a little.

"Uh, can we get some water out here?" Alex laughed, "The suns are hot today." He held up a hand to shade his eyes. The editing team was going to have a harder time making it look like night with the sun shining off the cars.

Rachel rushed in with a glass of water for Miranda, who took a long sip and gave her the glass back empty.

"Would you like some more?" Rachel asked.

"No, thank you," Miranda said, taking deep breaths. She had just made a huge mistake and was afraid her brother would be angry. It was taking so long to film just one minute.

"It is ok, Miranda," Evan said, calmly, "Just take your time."

Miranda shot him a half smile, "Ok, I am ready."

"Are you sure?" Evan asked and Miranda nodded, "Are your hormones in check?" he added, joking.

"Evan!" Miranda said through clenched teeth, thoroughly embarrassed.

Miranda stepped up beside Alex again.

"Just pretend it is not me," he whispered under his breath, "Easy."

"Action!"

Alex caught her lips and Miranda pretended she was kissing Scott. She had never kissed him, so she tried to think about what it would have been like. Miranda pulled away, her thoughts still in check.

"Better," Evan said, "but I liked it better when you kissed her cheek first and then lingered just at her lips and then she kissed you. Kind of like the last time... but not so extreme in the end."

Miranda took another deep breath. Could she keep control of herself enough to do that?

She stood in front of Alex again as her brother called action. Once again, she just pretended it was Scott and executed it perfectly.

"Perfect," Evan smiled, "Moving on!"

They filmed other outdoor scenes while Miranda went inside to change into a pair of jeans and green tank top. She got back outside just before she was needed. It was the day after the party, and Miranda had to hide down an alley while she watched Alex and Britany.

"Jeff, Ocean and Katy saw you leaving the dance with another girl!" Britany exclaimed.

"Janet, I would never cheat on you. I love you," Alex lied, taking her in his arms.

"Why do I not believe you?" Britany said, leaning away from him.

"The girl needed a ride and she had drank too much. I was doing what anyone would do. Please believe me," Alex pleaded.

Britany looked into his eyes, "Promise?"

"I promise," Alex said and he kissed her, but it was nothing like their kiss.

They walked off the set and Miranda came out of the alley.

"He has a girlfriend," she said slowly to herself, "But, of course he does Cara. You cannot get your guys any other way." Miranda's eyes filled with tears, "How could he do this to me? I thought he was perfect."

"Cut! Miranda, you make that crying so believable!" Evan shouted from the director's chair.

The final scene was the fight scene from the audition, and when it was over, Evan came over to the two of them.

"You look great together. I am really happy with the results," he smiled.

"Good Evan, I'm glad," Miranda returned the smile.

Evan turned to Alex, "So are you ok with your new co-star?"

Alex shrugged and smiled, "I guess I cannot complain. It could be worse."

Miranda gave him a nudge and he smiled down at her.

Evan laughed, "I know that they would like to get some promotional shots of the two of you for the magazine. It will be published next Saturday after the air date, so get changed and then Alex can bring you back to the boardwalk set."

Alex and Miranda nodded and each went to their dressing rooms to change. Miranda was excited, she'd never modelled before and now she had a photo shoot. She thought of Mrs. Mahan on Earth who had always told her that she should model.

As the thoughts of saving the planet crept up on her, she pushed them away. For once in these past few days, she was just going to be happy to be here and in a show that millions of people watched.

Miranda's stylist fixed her hair and makeup, highlighting her eyes for the camera. Then she had Miranda change into a short-sleeved flowered shirt with a matching beige khaki skirt. She also had her put on an obnoxiously high pair of heels. Perhaps everyone felt she should be taller. She met Alex outside the door. He was wearing the same colours, beige and blue.

"Make sure I do not fall," she laughed, clutching at his arm.

"Oh Maddie," Alex chuckled, "If only you were not so tiny."

"Oh wonderful, you are here," the photographer said, excitedly, "My name is George Anderson from *Daytime Drama* magazine," he continued taking Miranda's hand.

He led her to the backdrop, on the boardwalk set which had changed from a starry night sky to daylight and placed the two of the beside each other on the pier.

"Ok, now just act natural," George explained.

Miranda looked at Alex confused and he laughed, "She has never done this before George."

George looked stunned, "She has never been photographed before? I do not believe it!" He turned to Miranda, "You are absolutely stunning!"

Miranda blushed and Alex shook his head.

George fussed around with his camera. "This will take a little longer then. I will guide you," George said and started telling her what to do, while he snapped pictures.

Miranda felt a little dazed as Alex put his arms around her in several ways, holding her close to his body. She could feel his every muscle and it made her forget every bad thing on her mind.

"Ok, now. Face each other," George told them, "Take her hands Alex, you know what to do."

Alex held her hands between them and moved his face inches towards hers. Miranda looked up at him. He was so close to her Miranda wanted so badly for him to kiss her and the camera kept clicking furiously.

"Now, kiss her Alex," George commanded and Alex closed the distance that Miranda had so badly wanted gone, "Miranda, move your arms up to his shoulders," he continued but her arms had moved there naturally. Miranda thought about her family, her friends, anything but what she was actually doing so she didn't lose herself. She thought of Jackson and felt horrible. Why did she want Alex to kiss her so badly? Maybe because he looked like Jack?

"Ok, now I just want to get a couple of just Miranda. The article will focus mainly on her arrival to the show," George said.

Alex waited nearby for her. George positioned her on the pier and then he switched the background to a beach scene. Miranda had been wondering what the pile of white sand had been for. He told her to go play in it and she laughed. She felt like a little kid in a sandbox.

"Miranda, that was lovely. If I had not known, I would have thought you had done this before. The both of you together make a great couple," George commented when they were finished and he showed them the pictures on a screen.

Miranda gasped, she did look beautiful. The best one was where she stood slightly in front of Alex both of them facing the camera and he had his arm around her waist and she leaned into him. One of her arms was pulling at his shirt and her head was slightly down and towards him. He was looking down at her and both of them were not smiling but it was a kind of passionate expression, the kind you find on the cover of romance novels. Miranda had never thought of herself as a passionate kind of person, so the feeling the photo gave off was a little strange for her. Did he really do that to her?

The photographer sent the best picture to a digital frame, one for each of them, in which they were both facing each other but smiling at the camera, and he also sent all the pictures to her phone so that she could keep them all.

She thanked him several times and then followed Alex to find Evan, who was in his office with Melissa.

"You both can go without me. I will take the bus home," Evan said when he saw them.

"I am going to message Jack to pick me up," Miranda said, "We are going to dinner."

"But..." Evan started to speak but Miranda cut in.

"Dad said I could go out with him so don't start with me, and should you really be taking the bus alone Evan?"

"I will wait for him," Alex said.

Miranda sent him an appreciative look, and then took out her phone and messaged Jack. She didn't even know if he was home.

"Miranda has the pictures on her phone if you want to see," Alex said as Miranda sent her message.

Evan came around the desk and snatched up her phone. Melissa looked at them over his shoulder.

"Wow," Melissa exclaimed, "These are amazing!"

Evan looked between the two of them, "Looks like we found you the perfect match Alex. You and Britany never photographed this well."

Alex shrugged.

Miranda's phone buzzed and it was a message from Jack. He would be there in a few minutes.

"Ok, I am going to get changed," Miranda said, turning to leave.

"That whole wardrobe in there is for you," Melissa told her, "You may use whatever you wear anytime. It should all be in your size."

Miranda smiled and looked down at herself. She supposed she couldn't look any better, so she decided to stay in the outfit she had on.

"Cool," she said, then turned to Evan, "I will see you at home tonight. I am going to wait on the roof for Jack."

She said goodbye and left. Evan made a face at Alex and motioned towards the door with his head. Alex followed her out the door, quietly tagging along.

"Do you guys really think something will happen to me out on the roof?" Miranda sighed as she pushed the button to call the elevator. If anything happened to her, she didn't want Alex to be there. She frowned.

Alex shrugged but remained quiet.

He followed her up to the rooftop and sat beside her on the

bench. He stretched his arms out so it appeared he had his arm around her. She leaned forward a little.

"You are quiet," Miranda commented, "What are you thinking about?"

"Us I guess," Alex said, chewing his lip.

Miranda's cheeks flushed, "What about us?"

"Just our relationship. It started out wrong and we still have our moments, but I am really happy you are here with your family."

"Well we all know whose fault that rocky start is," Miranda gave him a playful elbow in the ribs.

"Yes, well, I had to make sure you would not hurt your brothers, but you really showed me."

Miranda smiled at him, curiously. Is that what he really thought?

"If I asked you to play hockey, would you?"

"Of course! I love the game."

"And you do not mind when I drive fast?"

"No. It's exhilarating."

Alex sat up and rested his elbows on his knees. He looked deep in thought. Then he turned to face her and took her hand, "Do not go with Jackson," he begged, "Stay with me."

Miranda wrenched her hand away in shock, "Are you joking with me right now?" she demanded. "Did my brothers put you up to this?"

Alex shook his head and then put his hand on her cheek, stroking her face lightly. A car pulled up beside them on the bench and Miranda looked over. She could see Jackson through the window but couldn't read his expression.

"What? Are you done with Amanda and moving to your next target Alex?" Miranda pushed his hand away and stood, "I won't be next Alex. I'm sorry but I am with Jackson."

She took a step towards the car and turned back to look at Alex. He stared at her silently, begging her to stay. The window rolled down behind her.

"Is something wrong, Mandy?" Jackson called out.

Miranda turned back to Jackson and shook her head. He smiled at her and she took a few more steps towards the car. When she pulled the door open, she turned back to Alex, "I'm sorry Alex, but no." And she climbed into the car. She didn't look back at Alex. What was going on? Why did he say that to her now? It had to have been her brother's doing.

"What is going on Miranda?" Jackson frowned once they had put some distance between them and the studio.

"I have no idea Jack," Miranda shook her head again. She was still in shock and denial. It *had* to have been her brothers. There is no way Alex was acting on his own. After all, he was a great actor.

"You looked comfortable there with my cousin," Jackson said, suspiciously. Miranda fixed him with an angry gaze. "Well you really did," Jackson continued, "I am just telling you what I saw. I did not like it."

"Well, it wasn't my doing, that's for sure," Miranda touched his arm, "Please believe me. Alex didn't want me to go with you, but I said no. I am with you."

"I will fight him for you. He will not win," Jackson said, determined.

"That is not necessary," Miranda squeezed his arm again, "I am with you and there is nothing he can do to change that."

Jackson took one hand off the wheel and took her hand. He sent her a quick smile.

"I do not blame him, I guess," he said quietly, "You are pretty amazing."

Miranda laughed, "You are too."

They parked on the grass in front of a restaurant. Jackson told her they had the best steaks in the city and it was a popular hangout for actors and actresses. Miranda noticed that it had a long red carpet leading from the valet parking to the front doors. Just as they were headed to the side entrance a car pulled up and Britany stepped out. There were about five photographers who had parked themselves along the red carpet. They called out to Britany as she made her way to the door with a very handsome blond haired man on her arm. She smiled her sexy smile at the photographers and stopped to pose with her boyfriend while they took pictures. Finally she noticed Miranda standing by the doors.

"Miranda!" she called out and motioned for her to come to her. "This is someone you should all meet!" Britany exclaimed to the reporters. Miranda gave Jackson a look of horror before she pasted a smile on her face and pulled Jackson towards Britany.

"Miss Miranda East," Britany drawled, "is going to be a new member of show. Her debut episode is next Friday, exactly one week from today!" Miranda had just reached her.

The reporters went wide-eyed.

"A new character!" one of them shouted, "Who are you going to be?"

Britany put an arm around Miranda and they smiled as the reporters took some pictures.

"My name will be Cara Scott," Miranda smiled and winked, "I am new in town."

"Miranda will be adding some spice to the show to shake up some relationships and make some drama of her own," Britany said, smiling.

"Is this your boyfriend, Miss East?" a woman asked, "May we get some pictures of yourself and him?"

Jackson smiled, nodded at Miranda and stepped in, wrapping his arms around her. Britany took a step back and watched, happily.

"What's your name, sir?" the lady called, she had her notebook pulled out to take notes, "You look very familiar. And Miranda, you do as well. Are you related to any of the stars?"

"Evan East is my twin brother. He is the creator of the show," Miranda told them and they murmured their assent.

"Ah yes," the lady replied, "You look so much like your brother. I did not know he had a twin sister."

Miranda smiled, "We have always both been big into the entertainment industry, though this will be my first big acting position." Miranda turned to Jackson, "This is my boyfriend, Jackson West. He is Alex West's cousin."

"The family resemblance is definitely there," a man called out, "Can you please look this way for a second?" He took a picture.

"I know you cannot give anything away Miranda," a lady winked, "But who will be playing your love interest on the show?"

Miranda laughed, "That you will have to wait the week for. I am not sure I am even supposed to be talking to reporters right now."

Britany stepped in, "Definitely a surprise! Well, we should head inside! I am starved!"

Britany took Miranda's arm and led her up the carpet to the doors. The boys followed along behind.

"Oh Miranda, I am so glad I got to be the one to introduce you to the world!" Britany exclaimed, "Especially since you are stealing my man!" She laughed and then gave a little look over her shoulder and lowered her voice, "Oh my, does he ever look like Alex!"

Miranda laughed, "Yes, I guess."

Britany motioned to the man behind her and carried on with Miranda in a whisper, "That is Jonathan. He is so handsome! He works for the news channel in our office building. I have been dating him off and on since Alex broke my heart." She sighed, a little overdramatically.

Miranda gave her a quick look, "You dated Alex too?"

Britany snorted, "Who has not dated Alex? But like every girl, he broke up with me. Luckily I have not found *the one* myself. I see a few men here and there."

They reached the doors and stepped up to the podium.

"Will there be four of you this evening?" the host asked.

"Oh, I bet you want some alone time with your man," Britany said, letting go of Miranda's arm and taking Jonathan's. She turned to the host, "No, it will be two and two. Can we get a private booth in the back?"

"Why certainly, Miss Quartz," the host smiled and motioned for Britany and Jonathan to follow.

He returned a minute later to seat Miranda and Jackson.

"Who needs a private booth anyways?" Miranda laughed as the host walked away.

"I am sure by next week, he will know who Miss East is," Jackson winked, "Or maybe sooner, if you end up in the papers tomorrow."

Miranda's mouth dropped, "You think I will be in the paper tomorrow?"

"Well, that is who is out there. Two from the local paper and the other three are from the entertainment magazines," Jackson explained, "They need to get their articles and pictures from somewhere, so they have their employees stationed around the city, especially on Friday and Saturday nights."

"I don't think I should be flashing myself around the papers," Miranda frowned, "Perhaps I should go tell them not to print anything."

"Why not?"

"Because of who I am, Jack. If someone evil sees the paper, it will make them angry. I am responsible for putting some of them in the holding cells."

Jackson fidgeted, "It is no use now Miranda. They will definitely want to report on a new character on Northern Shores! I do not think you will stop them."

The waiter came over and Jackson ordered them a drink. He knew Miranda's favourite was the grape one.

"Have a look at the menu, Mandy," Jackson said, handing her the digital page, "Can we just forget about the whole saving the world thing and enjoy ourselves?"

Miranda took a second, but nodded, "Sure Jack. For tonight." For the whole day she had pushed the thoughts of the evil ones to the back of her mind. What if that was a mistake? She sighed and frowned as she scanned the menu.

# Twenty-Two

★ ★ ★ ★

When Miranda and Jackson arrived back at the East apartment that night, everyone was home, even Alex.

Greta jumped up, "Oh I heard you were amazing today!" she said excitedly. She turned to Jackson, "Hi Jackson."

"Have you two met?" Miranda asked.

"I do not believe so," Jackson said, smiling at Greta.

"This is Greta, my brother Griffin's fiancée," Miranda introduced.

Greta smiled at him.

"Hi Jackson," Mr. East called, "Come on in. Have a seat."

Miranda and Jackson went into the living room. Greta carried in two chairs from the dining room for them.

"Thank you Greta," Jackson smiled, taking a seat.

There was a hockey game on the television. Alex and Evan had their jerseys on since their teams were playing each other.

"Do you like hockey, Jackson?" Mr. East asked.

"Not really," Jackson replied.

Miranda looked at him in shock. She had no idea he didn't like it, but it really did not matter. They didn't need to have everything in common. Alex caught Miranda's bewildered look and smiled. She scowled at him.

"Actually, Miranda beats me every time we play in gym," Jackson laughed, "She is pretty talented at the sport."

Mr. East laughed and moved the conversation to something else. Griffin was polite too, talking to Jackson about his brother and about scientific stuff that Miranda had no interest in. She kept her eyes on the game, totally blocking out the conversation. Evan's eyes were glued to the television. His team was winning by one, so he was excited to watch. Alex's eyes kept wandering to her. She could see him out of the corner of her eye and did her best to ignore him.

"How about the races tomorrow?" Mr. East was asking Jackson, "You are welcome to join us."

Jackson took a peek at Miranda who turned and smiled encouragingly at him, and then turned back to Mr. East, "Of course I would be happy to join you."

Alex made a funny noise and stood, "I am going to watch the rest of this game at home."

Evan stood too, "I will come with you, there is too much talking."

Miranda made a face at her brother as he passed.

Jackson and Mr. East didn't notice their rude exit. They were too busy talking about some new constellation that was recently discovered. Griffin was pretty excited about it too. Miranda moved over to the couch to sit by Greta who was into the game.

Greta flashed her a knowing smile. "Get used to it," she whispered, "That is what you get when you date someone who is into the science thing. Not even hockey will keep their attention."

Miranda giggled, "Oh well. We can't have everything in common. It would be boring."

After the game was finished Greta convinced Griffin to go for a swim. Mr. East decided he wanted to go read in his room, so Miranda took Jackson into her room.

"I like your dad," Jackson smiled, "He is really nice. I am so happy he found someone my brother can shadow once he is finished school."

Miranda smiled, "That is pretty great."

"So you do not mind if I come to the races tomorrow?"

Miranda sat on her bed, tucking a leg underneath herself, "Of course not. It will be fun! Do you like the races?"

"Yes, though I have not been to them in years."

She motioned for him to have a seat beside her, "You know Alex races?"

He sat down as she indicated, "Oh does he?" He frowned, not wanting to talk about his cousin.

"Yeah, under some alias name," Miranda smirked, "He was hoping not to attract attention from his fans."

"Well, we really have not spoken much the past few years," Jackson admitted, "Not until you showed up in my life." He ran a hand down her back which sent a tingle down her spine. He looked like he was about to lean in to kiss her when his phone rang.

He groaned and pulled it out. "It is my mother," he said, and answered. Marcy reminded him that they were supposed to be leaving for her sister's house for the weekend.

"Oh mom, I forgot all about that trip. Can I just stay home this weekend? I made plans."

"Your Aunt Maggie will be so disappointed Jack. You know it is her birthday."

"It's fine Jack. I'll tell my dad you forgot about your trip," Miranda interrupted.

"Hi Miranda," Mrs. West called.

"Hi," Miranda called to her.

"I will be home soon," Jackson said and disconnected. He turned to Miranda, "I cannot believe I forgot that trip. Our plane is scheduled to leave in an hour."

"So late?"

"Not really," Jackson smiled, "Did I not teach you that our planes fly really fast?"

Miranda rolled her eyes, "I guess we haven't hit the aviation section yet." She stood, "I will walk you out."

They stood by Jackson's car for a few minutes in each other's arms until he said he should get going. He did not want to be late.

"Be safe while I am gone Miranda," Jackson said, "I do not want to worry about you rushing off into some attack."

"I will be fine, Jack," Miranda said, "You be careful yourself."

"Make sure you message me a lot," Jackson said, giving her one last kiss. She nodded and watched as he got into his car and left.

Miranda went back down to her apartment. It was going to feel like a long weekend without Jackson there to get her away from Alex. At least she had to work tomorrow and the races tomorrow night. Then maybe her dad would want to go hiking on Sunday. She would just make sure she kept busy.

It took Miranda a long time to fall asleep. Her mind wouldn't shut down. She kept worrying about being away from Jackson for too long. She hadn't wanted to worry him but she was frightened. What if they attacked while he was gone? Would she be strong enough without him? Of course she would. So far it didn't seem like he had any sort of powers, but maybe he wasn't supposed to? Miranda had no idea.

A loud knock on the door woke her from her disturbed sleep. She dreamt she was in a cage suspended over a boiling cauldron of water and every so often it would drop her closer. There were men and women surrounding her all in black with the mysterious character drawn over their eyes and they threatened and mocked her the whole time.

"Come in," Miranda said sleepily.

Evan was at the door. He had his notebook in his hand and stomped over to the bed, sitting down beside her. "What is this?" he snapped, "Just what did you think you were doing?"

Miranda rubbed her eyes and took his notebook. She stared down at the picture of the three of them from dinner last night, which graced the front page of the newspaper, *the front friggin page!* "I guess new characters are big news in Utopia," Miranda bit her lip. How could it make front page news? This was not good, at all.

"Do you think?" Evan yelled, as he stood up and threw his arms in the air. He started pacing back and forth, reading the article.

"Obviously I didn't give anything away Evan," Miranda said, "They asked, but I didn't say. And it was all Britany's fault. We just happened to arrive at the same time as her and she saw me and called me over. She made the announcement. Did you even read it?"

Evan started reading aloud, "Miranda East, twin sister of show creator Evan, will be playing the effervescent Cara Scott, a new arrival to *Northern Shores* debuting on Friday October 9th. She can be seen pictured above with co-star Britany Quartz and long time boyfriend Jackson West at Vacca Steakhouse." Evan sighed and looked over at her, "I guess we are going to go with the whole twin thing story?"

"Well, it's true Evan," Miranda said quietly.

"What? That we are twins?" Evan asked, "That is impossible."

Miranda bit her lip. She knew Evan deserved to know the truth. "I am going to be 19 on November 2nd."

Evan's mouth dropped open, "But that is my... I thought you were 16?"

"I am 16 on Earth. The year is longer," Miranda explained, "I figured it out with Jackson. He helped me calculate it."

Evan looked speechless, his mouth opened and closed like a fish. He sat down on the bed and took Miranda by the shoulders, "My twin sister," he repeated and shook his head. He gave her a quick hug, "Looks like I got all the height," he joked, then frowned, "Does anyone else know?"

"Alex does," Miranda said, "I told him a couple weeks ago when I found out, but he didn't know how to tell everyone so we decided to keep it quiet."

"I do not understand," Evan shook his head, "Was I born on Earth too or were you born here?"

"See this is the problem with it all," Miranda frowned, "There are so many unanswered questions."

Evan chewed his lip for a minute thinking. "Well, let me think about this for a bit. We will not tell anyone else yet."

"Ok," Miranda agreed.

"And about this," Evan said, holding up his notebook, "Thank you for not giving anything away. I am sorry I have not told you yet how to handle reporters."

"I would never give anything away Evan," Miranda assured him.

"Well, I suppose it is time for you to get up and get ready," Evan said looking at the clock, "We will leave in an hour."

When Evan left her room, she sent a message to Jackson telling him about the paper. Five minutes later she got a response, which told her she looked beautiful. She messaged back how worried she was about the evil ones seeing it, but he told her to try not to worry, the evil ones probably could not read. She laughed a little and got up to get ready.

Alex came over for breakfast but Miranda had no idea what to say to him anymore. She kept quiet and Alex never said a word to her either.

Evan tried to converse with the both of them but wasn't getting much back.

The ride to the studio was quiet until Evan finally broke the silence, "Ok, what is going on with the two of you? You have not said a word to each other."

"Nothing, Evan," Miranda said.

Evan turned to Alex, who shrugged.

"So are you mad at each other?" Evan asked.

"No," Alex said and Miranda shook her head.

"Upset?"

They both shook their heads.

He gave up and let the silence continue. When they got to the studio, they all went their separate ways. Miranda went down to her dressing room to get herself ready. Her makeup and hair were done quickly and she was told to put on any outfit she wanted. She knew she would be going out on a date with Jeff this episode, so she chose a flowered sundress that dipped low in the front and another pair of hot pink high heels which matched the dress.

The filming went smoothly. Miranda was so happy she did not have to kiss Alex that day. In fact, they had to argue, so that was a lot easier.

Miranda went up to her dressing room after filming and changed back into her own clothes. She couldn't wear the dress and heels to the races tonight.

Britany had already left, so Miranda was alone. She started to worry again about what could happen without Jackson there. She sat down on her chair and pulled out her phone to look at the pictures from this morning. She looked good, but Jackson looked a little awkward. Miranda's smile looked forced because she had been really nervous. She scrolled too far and came upon the pictures from the photo shoot with Alex. She looked through them all with a smile. They looked amazing.

Miranda scrolled back to the pictures of her and Jackson. She never looked at all the differences in them. Jackson's eyes were a little smaller and his hair was a slightly darker shade. She was looking between the two photos when Alex walked in looking for her.

"What are you doing?" Alex said, looking over her shoulder.

Miranda almost jumped a mile and turned to Alex, "Geez Alex, you scared me. I didn't hear you *knock*." She went to put her stuff back in her purse but Alex took her notebook out of her hands.

"Ah, I saw that this morning," Alex said, looking down at the picture. He swiped to the other picture. "Jackson is not quite as photogenic as you and me. We would make a better couple."

"Don't Alex," Miranda said, snatching her notebook back, "Have you no respect for Jackson? He is your cousin."

Alex paused. He looked deep in thought. It took him several minutes before he replied, "You are right, Miranda. I have not treated Jackson the way he deserves. I guess I am used to getting my way all the time."

"Can we just be friends?" Miranda asked, as she put a hand on his arm, "I don't want to ignore each other."

"Of course," Alex said, "I am sorry to you as well. I should not have said anything to make things awkward between us."

Miranda smiled and gave him a hug.

Evan entered and seeing them together he stopped, "So are we all talking now?"

Miranda and Alex broke apart. Miranda nodded.

"Ok, that is good," Evan said, "I have to stay late and work on the scripts with the team. If you both want to go home and have dinner then come back and pick me up before the race, I would appreciate it."

"Sure Evan," Miranda said and turned to Alex, "Are you ready to go?"

"Yes," he said and the three of them went to the elevator together.

"You did really great today Miranda," Evan said, smiling down at his sister, "I am so glad you got the part."

"Thanks Evan."

"I will see you both in a couple hours," Evan said when the elevator stopped on his floor, "I can send you a message when I am finished here."

Alex and Miranda took the elevator up to his car.

"Would you like to go out and eat?" Alex asked. "As friends," he added when she eyed him suspiciously.

"I don't have money till next week," Miranda replied, "We can just go home."

"I will pay," Alex said, as he opened her door for her, "Please? It would make me feel better if we could go out as friends."

Miranda bit her lip. *I suppose it wouldn't hurt*, she thought and tried to relax.

Alex smiled, "What do you feel like?"

Miranda thought about it a minute, "Do you guys have pasta here?"

His smile grew wider, "Yes, I know a great place."

Miranda looked down at Alex's outfit to make sure she looked ok for dinner. He was wearing long khaki shorts and a blue polo top and she wished she had left her dress on. She supposed her black shorts would have to do, but she felt a little underdressed with her plain blue tank top. She had her race shirt in her bag that she would put on later but that was also not an 'out to dinner' shirt.

"If you are worried about your clothes, we can stop at home and change," Alex smiled.

Miranda thought about it for a minute, "Ok. Can we please stop at home?"

Alex nodded and headed off to their apartment building.

"I will wait here in the car," Alex said, once they arrived.

Miranda scooted out of the car and went down to the apartment. Once in her room she called frantically for Alpha to get her a dinner outfit. Alpha's screen came down and made some suggestions, several dresses and skirts. Miranda scrolled through them again. She couldn't wear a skirt if they were going to the races after.

"No Alpha, I need shorts for the races after," Miranda explained, "Can we get a versatile outfit?"

Alpha came up with three suggestions and Miranda couldn't decide. She wasn't sure she liked any of them.

"Bring me all three out," Miranda said, "I will try them on."

And she did, as fast as she could. She settled on keeping her black shorts on but added a blue floral printed top and a dark blue short-sleeve cardigan. She looked at herself in the mirror. Her makeup and hair were good. She chose a pair of high heeled sandals and tucked her tennis shoes into a large purse. Then she took her wallet, racing shirt, notebook out of the smaller purse and transferred them over.

She had only taken about ten minutes and she laughed at herself when she was back in the elevator, not sure why she cared so much about what she looked like in front of Alex. But as a public figure, she wanted to keep up her appearance, just in case anyone recognized her from the paper that morning.

Alex was outside of his car stretching when she walked out. He smiled when he saw her and got back into his car and they headed off to dinner.

The restaurant was packed with people. It was a Saturday night after all.

"Hello Mr. West," the hostess greeted him with a smile, "Please follow me, your table is ready."

"I called ahead," Alex smiled to Miranda and took her hand, leading her through the restaurant. A few people glanced their way as they walked through towards the back. Of course everyone knew Alex from the show but Miranda heard her name once and that sent a murmur through the crowd.

"Oh, that is the girl on the front page!" someone said aloud.

Alex ignored the talk around them so she did the same although her cheeks did turn pink. She wasn't used to the attention. They were led towards a private booth at the back.

Alex ordered each of them a drink, also knowing Miranda liked the purple one the best before the hostess left.

The private booth was beyond a half wall and facing outwards towards the windows. It had a half wall on three of the four sides so once they were seated, they couldn't see around them.

"So these are the private booths," Miranda laughed as she peeked her head out into the aisle way, "Nice."

Alex handed her a menu, "Yes," he smiled, "I get special treatment. You will too."

"I didn't last night," Miranda laughed.

"You will," Alex said, scanning the menu. He already knew what he wanted and put the menu down.

"What are you having?" Miranda asked.

"The pasta with meatballs and their tomato sauce. It is the best in town," Alex smiled, "You?"

Miranda quickly scanned the list again, "The same."

When a waitress returned with their drinks, Alex ordered for the both of them. Miranda had ordered for herself last night. She supposed Alex would be a professional at chivalry with all the dates he's been on. Then she realized this was *not* a date.

A woman stopped by their booth, "Hello. I am from the City 217 Newspaper. Just wondering if I could get a picture and a statement?"

Miranda's mouth dropped.

"I know I am not allowed to in here but I was just having dinner myself in the next booth and I saw you both sit down."

"Yes," Alex said, "Just one quick statement."

"How do you feel about your new co-star Alex?" she asked, pulling out her notebook.

"Miranda is a very good friend both on the set and off. She is amazingly talented and an extraordinary, beautiful woman inside and out. I will be one of her biggest fans," Alex commented. He reached over and squeezed Miranda's hand.

The woman's eyebrow raised, "And Miranda?"

"Alex is one of my best friends. If he says that I am amazingly talented, it is only because I work with the best." Miranda smiled.

"Can you both move closer together?" she asked and turned her notebook to camera mode.

They had been sitting opposite each other but both moved towards the back bench so they were side by side. Alex put his arm around her waist and she rested a hand on his knee.

The woman took her picture and thanked them before she hurried out after her companion.

The waitress stopped by to check on them, "I am so sorry you were disturbed Mr. West, Miss East. Our owner apologizes and has asked me to bring you these complimentary." She took their empty glasses and replaced them with fresh ones.

"Not to worry," Alex replied, "It was harmless."

The waitress smiled and left them again.

"Thank you," Miranda said, turning to him.

"For?"

"For the compliments," Miranda said, "Gorgeous, talented." She laughed. "I would have thought you would say stubborn and a pain in the butt."

Alex laughed, "Well that too, but surely you do not want me telling that to a reporter."

The waitress returned with their food and placed it in front of them at their new spots side by side.

"Well, I guess not," Miranda said as she looked at her plate. It looked delicious and she was happy it was bigger noodles and not long spaghetti so she wouldn't make a mess of herself.

She tried a bite and swallowed, "Wow, this is delicious!" Miranda smiled at Alex.

Alex nodded, "Told you they are the best in town for their sauce," he smiled back, "I know all the good spots."

They ate in companionable silence, each finishing their drinks. Miranda ordered another and Alex got a glass of water.

"Drinking and driving a big no-no here as well?" Miranda asked.

"Of course," Alex replied, "Though there is no law, it is assumed." He picked up his water glass and drank deeply, then set it down and pointed to hers, "You however, can have as much as you like. We have a bit of time to waste." He checked the time on his notebook.

"Are you trying to get me drunk?" Miranda giggled.

Alex chuckled, "If you want me to. I am not forcing you."

Miranda took another sip of her drink as the waitress came by to clear their plates.

"Can I get either of you anything else," she asked.

"In a little bit," Alex said and she walked away.

"Is it ok that we sit here? Won't they need this table?"

"No, we should be ok," Alex smiled, "Remember who I am." Miranda rolled her eyes at him. "Can you tell me about Helen?"

Miranda did a double take. Was he serious? "Helen, my best friend?" Miranda asked, "Helen from Earth?"

"Yes," Alex smiled, "I know you miss her. I am just curious."

Miranda frowned. She did miss her best friend so much. "We met in grade school in Woodstock when we were five years old," Miranda told him, "By the time we got to high school we were like sisters. We pretty much spent every weekend together. She is pretty awesome, a great listener. She always gave me great advice and she was always more outgoing. She would talk to anyone and have them eating out of her palm. She was just an average height for a female on Earth, I was taller of course. She had beautiful long blond hair that I was so jealous of since hers fell in nice waves and I always had a big head of curls."

Alex chuckled, "What did you both do for fun?"

"Well, we were both on the cheerleading team. Evan didn't seem to know what that was though," Miranda giggled, "It is pretty much girls in short skirts parading around the sidelines of sporting events doing flips and stuff." Alex raised an eyebrow and smiled as Miranda continued, "I could do a few tricks, but I am pretty sure I was just on the team to throw people in the air. I was the tallest of course," Miranda sighed, but then smiled as she continued, "And of course we played ball hockey on the street and I was on the basketball and volleyball team. Helen played hockey too," Miranda smiled and then frowned, "I wonder how she is?" There was no way for her to contact her best friend to ask.

"Sorry Maddie," Alex said, squeezing her arm, "I did not mean to make you sad. I just wanted to know a bit more about you. We could go and visit her sometime. It *is* allowed."

Miranda sent him a smile, took a big drink and shrugged. Of course she wanted to see Helen, just so Helen would know that she would never abandon her best friend. She had no idea what her parents told Helen about her 'situation'. "What position did you play when you played hockey?" Miranda asked, reaching for a different topic.

"I was a goalie," Alex smiled.

"Really? And I beat you at that hockey game?"

"Yes, you actually did," Alex laughed.

"Were you any good?"

Alex shrugged, "I was asked to play on the Whales but I had just decided to take the job to play Jeff on Evan's show. I was balancing both hockey and acting up until then."

"Do you regret it?"

Alex shook his head, "No, I really enjoy doing the show. I mean, I probably would have liked playing hockey as well but I do not regret it."

"Is there anywhere to play for fun? Do you ever go?"

"I have some friends who rent the ice once in awhile but we have not done that for some time and every Sunday there are games. Depending on age and skill level, you can drop in and play."

"Can we go?" Miranda asked, excitedly, "Tomorrow?"

"You want to play? Or you want to watch me play?"

"Well I don't have skates, so maybe I'll just watch."

"You can borrow skates at the rink if you wanted."

Miranda made a face, "Ok so I am not a good skater. I can stick handle and I can score, I just cannot skate. Plus my Earth mom never wanted me to play hockey. She worried I would get hurt."

Alex chuckled as he reached over to tuck a loose hair behind Miranda's ear. Miranda flinched and drew back a little. She didn't realize she had been leaning towards him. Alex's smiled faded a bit, "Sorry," he said and also sat back, "I will ask Evan if he wants to play and you can watch us both. Maybe sometime we can go skating and you can show me how bad you are."

Miranda tried to smile and finished off her drink, "Evan plays too?" Miranda asked, playing with the empty glass in her hand. She was having a great time with Alex, but she was still suspicious of his actions.

"Yes. He plays on defence."

"What about ball hockey? Is there anywhere to do that?"

Alex scratched his chin, "I do not think so. Perhaps a side project of yours can be to start and run... ball hockey, you call it?"

"Oh, there is no ball hockey here?"

Alex shook his head.

"Well, it's the same as floor hockey you would have played in school but it is played with an orange ball instead of a puck."

The waitress stopped by and asked if they would like anything else. Miranda ordered another drink.

"A ball eh?" Alex asked, when she walked away, "Sounds like fun!"

"Yes, you would play on a concrete floor instead of on ice and you normally wouldn't wear all of the equipment like you do in ice hockey, except for the goalie," Miranda smiled looking off into space, thinking about playing in the parking lot in Woodstock. She turned to Alex, "Do you know where the washroom is?" then paused, "And don't you dare follow me this time!"

Alex chuckled, "It is to the right at the back there." He pointed the direction.

"Excuse me a second," Miranda said before she got up.

When she returned, the waitress was seated in her spot talking to Alex. They were both laughing. When the waitress spotted her, she got up quickly and apologized. Miranda shrugged and sat down, but on her side of the table, not at the back of the booth with Alex.

"Maybe you can call me sometime," the waitress said, and left. Alex tucked his notebook into his pocket. A fresh drink had been placed in front of Miranda and she picked it up and took a long drink.

"I wonder if Evan is ready yet," Miranda said.

"He should be soon."

An uncomfortable silence fell between them while Miranda gulped down the rest of her drink. She had to remember that they were just here as friends. Why should she be angry that he had gotten the waitress' number? Miranda's phone broke the silence. It was a message from Evan saying he was almost ready and that they could start heading over to the studio. She showed Alex the message.

"I will just go pay and we can go," Alex said and got up, heading towards the bar.

A few minutes later he returned.

"Thanks for dinner Alex," Miranda said, "I had a good time."

"Me too," Alex smiled. He offered her his hand, "Come with me, I will protect you from all the people out there."

Miranda laughed and took it. It was a harmless, friendly gesture. She only heard a few whispers as they walked back through the packed restaurant. It wasn't till they stepped out the door that the commotion started. Apparently the one news reporter let others know that they were inside, plus a crowd of women who were obviously fans of Alex's.

"Oh no," he whispered.

Everyone started talking at once and the women started cheering. "Alex, how do you feel about your new co-star?" "Alex, how do you feel about Miranda dating your cousin?" "Were you both on a date? Or are you just good friends?" "Miranda, how does Jackson feel about your relationship with his cousin?" "In the show are you both going to be together? What about Jeff and Janet?" "What is the next move for the show in adding a new character?" "May we get a picture?"

As the cameras went off, Miranda let go of Alex's hand. Something as harmless as that could definitely get misinterpreted. She looked at Alex who looked calm and was smiling at everyone. She rearranged her own look of shock to a smile.

"I am very sorry, but Miranda and I are headed out and we do not have much time," Alex smiled at everyone, "I can answer a few of your questions, but we really must go. As for how I feel about my co-star, yes, we are very good friends. Miranda is talented and beautiful. I have a lot of respect for my cousin and I am happy that they have each other. As for the direction of the show, I am obviously not obligated to comment on that. Thank you everyone for your continued support."

Alex took Miranda's hand again and they headed right for the crowd, which parted to let them through.

A few more questions were shouted out, but Alex ignored them. They made their way through and to Alex's car.

It wasn't till they were sitting that Miranda could feel her face burning. Alex rubbed his face and sighed, "Well, you survived," he chuckled. He pulled out his phone and sent Evan a quick message saying they were on their way.

"I can't believe they were waiting there for us," Miranda shook her head in disbelief.

"They must have been waiting awhile," he smiled a half smile, "Get used to it. It happens sometimes. Normally I would sign a few autographs or let some of the fans get pictures, but Evan is waiting." He started the car and slowly it rose into the air.

"Sign autographs?" Miranda asked, confused. There was no paper on Utopia.

"Sign the notebook with the stylus," Alex explained.

Miranda nodded. She *had* seen him do that before at the school.

Evan was waiting for them on top of the studio when they got back and hopped in the car. He had his race shirt on already. Alex smirked at his fake name on the shirt. "I really have to change that," he chuckled.

Miranda laughed, "I guessed it was you right away. I'm surprised no one else has put that together."

"Well, the camera crew know not to put my face on the screen. We have worked out an agreement. And the other racers know not to tell anyone or else the seating area will be packed with fans of the show instead of race fans," Alex explained, "It is busy enough. I am sure the race fans would not appreciate the screaming women."

"Ugh," Miranda sighed, and then told her brother about the people outside of the restaurant.

"You both went out to dinner?" Evan asked, smiling between the two of them. Miranda rolled her eyes. "You did not say anything about the show though, right?"

"Of course not, Evan," Miranda replied.

"Where did you go for dinner?" Evan asked, leaning forward from the back seats.

"Just to Joe's," Alex answered.

"And there were people from the newspaper there?" Evan asked incredulously.

"No, well, one was having dinner when we arrived," Alex said, "She must have called around when she saw us."

"I wonder if you will make the front page again tomorrow," Evan chuckled, turning to Miranda, "I suppose it is good for publicity. Everyone will be excited for your debut."

Dread passed over Miranda's face. The front page again! She may as well just wear a sign that says 'Come get me'. Alex gave her a confused look but Evan just sat back.

"What do you mean?" Alex asked. He threw a worried glance to Evan, and then back at Miranda.

Miranda threw up her mental block. It seemed to her that Alex was very attuned to the whole mind reading thing. He always caught on to what people were thinking very easily, especially with her so far.

Evan sat up again and leaned toward the front seat, "What?" he asked.

"Nothing," Alex replied, and changed the subject, "Do you want to play hockey tomorrow? Miranda wants to watch us play."

"Yes, I will play," Evan smiled, "At 27 hour?"

Alex nodded.

Alex won the race that night, so the whole family went to Ernie's to celebrate. When Miranda was finally alone, as she walked slowly to the washroom, she worried over the potential for her picture to be in the newspaper again and how she had spent no time on training today. At least tomorrow it was her family's plan to go for a hike, and then she could exercise her body. Perhaps she should go down to the gym tonight to throw the weights around with her mind.

As she stepped into the bathroom she caught the tail end of a conversation.

"...you heard wrong Alex. Stop worrying so much," Evan was saying. Evan and Alex turned to her as she entered. Evan smiled but Alex studied her carefully.

"What's up?" Miranda asked.

Evan shrugged and turned to wash his hands. Then they left, leaving her in privacy.

When Miranda got back out, she got another drink and realized she was starting to get a little tipsy. It made her forget her troubles and she was able to enjoy the time with her family.

Miranda drank too much that night. By the time they reached home she didn't feel like working out. She went straight to bed, promising herself she would work out in the morning before the hike.

# Twenty-Three

★ ★ ★ ★

Miranda awoke with a start. The ground had been shaking so hard in her dream that she was sure it was happening in real life. Miranda was out of bed in a second and in the hallway. There was no trace of her family. All the doors were closed.

"Dad!" she yelled frantically, knocking on his door, while trying to find the spot that would open it, "Daddy, please come out!" The tears started to stream down her face.

Griffin's door opened first, followed closely after by her father's. Miranda looked at the two of them and threw her arms around her father sobbing into his chest.

"What is wrong Miranda?" he asked, soothingly, rubbing her back as she cried. Greta's tired face peeked out from the door. Evan's door opened, he stepped into the hall and Alex appeared in the hallway from the living room as he slipped on his shirt.

Miranda couldn't speak and she had to take a minute to calm herself. Evan and Alex shared a look of concern. Greta stepped forward and started to rub her back. Miranda could feel everyone's eyes on her and knew they were all fine. She pulled away from her dad.

"I'm sorry," she whispered, "I... had a bad dream." She looked around and everyone was staring at her. She looked to the floor, "I'm sorry I woke you all."

Griffin squeezed his sister's shoulder, "Do not worry about waking us. Are you ok? Do you want to talk about it?"

Miranda squeezed her eyes shut and shook her head. Her face turned red with embarrassment. She wanted so badly to tell them all, but knew she couldn't. They all looked so concerned.

Alex stepped forward, "It is still early. Let me get you back to bed." He reached a hand out, which she took and he led her back to her bed and they sat down on the edge. "Lie down," he instructed. Evan, Griffin, Greta and Mr. East were at the doorway. Alex sent them back to bed saying he would take care of her. Mr. East smiled sleepily and nodded, then went back into his room. The others slowly dispersed.

Miranda laid down and Alex pulled the bedspread over her, tucking her in. "Tell me what happened," he said, cupping her face with his hand, stroking her cheek with his thumb.

Miranda turned her face into his hand. She touched his hand with her own, holding it there and she inhaled deeply, taking in his scent. It made her feel calmer. She glanced out the window and noticed it was still dark out. She turned back to him and studied his face. He looked so tired. "Lie down beside me," she said and he did but on top of the covers, facing her. After a minute, she spoke, "I had a dream there was an attack. The ground was shaking so badly I thought it was real. When no one ran to me like they have before, I just thought they were the ones who were attacked. I panicked."

"They are fine," Alex assured her and put an arm around her, "We all are."

"Now I just feel silly," she said and yawned.

"Do not worry about it," Alex said. He ran a hand down her arm. "Go back to sleep."

Miranda closed her eyes, enjoying the feel of him there beside her, but then felt guilty. Should she want Alex to be in her bed? She was sure Jackson wouldn't like it if he knew. When she opened her eyes again, Alex was still staring at her, longingly.

"Do you want me to go?" he whispered.

Miranda shook her head, "Is it wrong that I don't?"

"This is my fault," Alex sighed.

Miranda looked at him questioningly.

"I could have been with you from the start," Alex continued, "If I had not been such a jerk, this would be fine. You would be mine and there would be no questioning it."

Miranda's eyes welled with tears. She still would have to be with Jackson. She was meant to be with him. In that moment, Miranda was happy Alex had been a jerk. He was right. She was his from the first time she laid eyes on him. How would she break up with him when she found out the truth?

"What truth?" Alex asked.

"Nothing," Miranda said, "I can't talk about it."

"You can tell me anything," Alex insisted. He stared into her eyes, trying to read her mind.

Miranda shook her head. "I care about you a lot," Miranda said after a few moments and she touched his face. A tear escaped from her eye and fell onto her pillow. "If anything happens to me, I want you to know that."

"What do you mean?" Alex asked, quickly, "Nothing is going to happen to you."

She stroked his face. "I know, but just in case."

He put his hand on hers, "I would never let anyone or anything hurt you."

"I will never let anything hurt you either," Miranda returned, staring into his eyes. She leaned in and gave him one chaste kiss, pulling away before that familiar pull kicked in. She closed her eyes and cleared her mind. She couldn't tell him the truth. Not yet at least. There was nothing should could do. Jackson was her soulmate.

Eventually she fell back to sleep.


Light filled Miranda's room when she opened her eyes again. When her eyes focused she saw Alex sleeping next to her and sat up quickly. The arm that had been around her fell away.

Her phone had awoken her. It had been ringing. She got up quietly trying not to disturb Alex. She had a missed call from Jackson and two messages. The first was from Griffin saying they looked too peaceful to wake so they left for hiking without them. Miranda glanced back at Alex's sleeping form and rolled her eyes. They would like that, wouldn't they? The second was from Jackson, he wanted to talk about the front page. At first Miranda thought it was from the day before and then she remembered her and Alex were photographed yesterday.

Quickly, she opened up the newspaper on her phone and there she was again. *Really! Don't they have better things to report on?* she thought bitterly. This was the newspaper that had been in the restaurant so there was a picture of her and Alex in the booth and then another of them walking out hand in hand. It must have been before they realized a mass media was there waiting for them because they were just outside the door, midstride and they were smiling at each other. There was only a short article which made no insinuation that they were dating. Just that they were good friends and had complimented each other highly on acting skills. She sighed with relief.

Her phone started to ring again and she almost dropped it out of fright. She left her room to answer it, so she wouldn't wake Alex.

"Hey Jack," she said, answering the phone.

"Hi," he looked and sounded glum, "Did I wake you?"

"Actually yes," Miranda replied, "I'm sorry I didn't make it to the phone the first time but I was out late with my family last night."

"With your family? Or my cousin?" he asked, frowning.

"Both, Jackson," Miranda frowned too, "You know that he is also a part of my family."

"You had dinner with him," Jackson commented.

"Yes, we had to wait for Evan to finish at the studio, so we went out *as friends*," she stressed the word, "I talked to Alex yesterday. He is ok with me and you together and he said he wouldn't get in the way."

"He said that?" Jackson asked, surprised.

"Yes, I scolded him for not having any respect for you and he apologized. He is happy we have each other. Didn't you read the article or did you just insinuate?"

Jackson sighed, "I guess I was just jealous. You know I wanted to be home this weekend with you and to see you with my cousin... I guess it hurt."

"I'm with you Jack," Miranda said, "I *need* you."

Jackson put on a hesitant smile, "I need you too Mandy. I am so sorry to think the worst. I will be home today at 28 hour. Can I see you?"

Miranda knew that she had planned to watch Evan and Alex play hockey at 27 hour, "Can you meet me at the arena? I am going to watch Evan and Alex play hockey."

"I will be there," Jackson smiled.

Miranda smiled, excited to see him tonight, and they said goodbye.

Alex was standing quietly in the entrance to the living room, watching her.

"Good morning," she smiled, "How did you sleep? Want me to make breakfast?"

Alex raised an eyebrow and smiled, "Pancakes?"

Miranda laughed and got up off the couch, "Shut up." She went to the kitchen and got the pancake bottle, then correctly put enough liquid on a plate for the two of them and put it in the oven. She got out another plate, and by then the oven beeped. She put four on a plate for Alex, leaving two for herself.

"I slept really well, actually," Alex said, surprised. He took the plate Miranda offered and led the way to the dining room.

"Ya, me too," Miranda said, "I did not have any more dreams."

"Me either."

"You have bad dreams too?" Miranda asked taking a seat beside him.

Alex shrugged, "Sometimes."

Miranda could tell from his thoughts that he had bad dreams often.

"Where is everyone?" Alex asked.

"Apparently they left without us," Miranda snorted, "They thought we looked too peaceful to wake."

Alex rolled his eyes, "I am sure they loved that."

Miranda nodded.

Alex looked at the time on his notebook, "Well, they cannot have left long ago. Do you want to go catch up?"

"Sure!" Miranda was happy. She really wanted to get some exercise today. It had been too long.

They finished breakfast and Alex messaged Evan, asking where they were. Miranda and Alex both went their separate ways to change while waiting for a response.

Alex drove them out to the place Miranda hiked the first time. She saw her father's car parked in what she supposed was a parking lot. This time she had worn shoes from Utopia so she hoped her feet wouldn't be as sore.

"Evan said they are waiting for us at the bench about two kilometres in. They stopped to eat," Alex said.

Miranda stretched her legs a bit so they wouldn't cramp up. "Want to race?" she asked as she straightened up.

Alex eyed her suspiciously, "Really?"

"1... 2... 3... Go!" Miranda said quickly and took off.

Alex called her a cheat from behind her and broke into a run too.

"You are going to get tired," Alex said, catching up and keeping pace with her.

"Just you worry about yourself," Miranda said, and picked up the pace.

About a kilometre in, Miranda felt something before she saw it. A wave of dread passed over her and she felt evil nearby. She saw a beam of red heading straight for Alex. She reacted quickly by tackling him to the ground, but the red beam nicked her side, burning a hole through her plain, bright pink t-shirt and leaving a scratch on her skin. She yelped with pain and then they hit the ground, which started to shake violently. Luckily, they landed behind a bush which gave them some cover.

Alex looked shocked, "What the..." he started to say.

"Stay down," Miranda shouted at him, cutting him off and pushing him back down. She jumped up and took off after whoever had shot that light at them. She saw someone running away, and with her mind, she lifted him up and in her rage, threw him into the forest. The rumbling didn't subside, and Miranda knew that this person was just a distraction. They must be after her family. She dropped to the ground and wished for it to stop. *Please let my family be ok!* she thought hard. The white light escaped her palms and into the Earth. It drained away all her energy.

Alex looked at his blood-soaked hand which had been at Miranda's side. He rolled over quickly and got up to go after her. He saw her up ahead on the ground. She looked like she was glowing. Then he saw the white light draining from her body, out of her palms and into the ground.

The rumbling stopped and Miranda fell forward. Alex ran to her and kneeled beside her, but she was unconscious. He checked for a pulse which was slow but steady and gathered her into his arms, relieved. He took a panicked look around, hoping there was no one else.

Minutes later, a vehicle landed beside them and a medical team ran to them.

"Is she ok?" a paramedic shouted, pulling out her medical bag and running towards them.

"I think so," Alex replied, finding his voice, "She got hit by something, I did not see it, but she did. She saved me."

The woman saw the blood stain on Miranda's shirt and pulled it up. She sighed with relief, "It is very small and not deep at all. She will be fine." She wiped up the blood and applied a cream and then a square bandage. "Any other injuries, sir? Did she hit her head? Are *you* ok?"

"I am fine," Alex replied, "Our friends are farther up the trail. I have not heard from them."

"A medical team is taking care of them. They report that everyone is fine and the evil ones are unconscious. They will be put away," the second paramedic explained.

Miranda's eyes opened. She had heard everything. "There is another evil person just beyond those trees," she mumbled slowly and lifted her arm to point in the direction.

The two who were looking after her raced into the trees and found the body. They retrieved a stretcher and went to pick him up. By then Miranda was sitting up, supported by Alex. She shrank back against him when they got closer.

"He is dead," the woman said.

Miranda's eyes filled with tears, *I killed someone!* She put a hand over her mouth in shock.

Alex looked down at her with concern and regret on his face. He rubbed her back. Behind them, another medical vehicle pulled up and the East family jumped out and ran toward them, Mr. East was in the lead.

He dropped down beside his daughter and took her face in his hands, "Oh Miranda we were so worried. You did not answer your phone."

"Dad, are you all ok?" Miranda said, tears streaming down her face. She hugged him tight.

"We are just fine," he said, rubbing her back, "There were some evil people coming after us, but they did not even get close. They were all thrown back away from us by this glowing white wall of light. It was incredible!"

Miranda hiccoughed with relief and let him go. Alex's phone rang behind her.

"Hi Alex," Jackson said, "Is Miranda with you? She is not answering and I am so worried."

"Yes, she is here," Alex replied and passed Miranda his phone. A look of relief passed over Jackson when he saw her.

"I was so worried," Jackson said.

"My phone must be in Alex's car," Miranda told him, "We were all hiking and there was an attack here."

"Are you ok?" Jackson asked, and then corrected himself, "Is everyone ok?"

"I am fine and so is everyone else," Miranda said, "We will talk later. Come to my apartment when you get back."

Jackson nodded, "I will see you later." And they disconnected.


Mr. East took one of her arms and Alex took the other. They pulled her to her feet. Miranda swayed a little bit and Alex held her steady. The paramedic told her to wait a moment and retrieved something from her bag. She waved a bottle under Miranda's nose and Miranda perked up. She stood steadily on her feet.

"We can give you a ride to your cars," the second paramedic said. He went over to the vehicle and removed a bag from the backseat so they would have room to sit.

Mr. East put an arm around Miranda and ushered her to the vehicle. Once they were back, Miranda got her phone out of Alex's car and sent a message to her friends saying she was fine.

"I am sure the law enforcement would like to speak to you, but if you do not want to speak to the newspapers, you should leave now. We will send someone over later for a statement," the first paramedic said.

"I have had enough publicity the last two days," Miranda said, and looked at her father, "Can we go?"

Realization hit the second paramedic, "Right, you are the new cast member on *Northern Shores*," he said. He looked around at everyone, recognizing Evan and Alex. "Just give us your address and we will tell the law enforcement officers to meet you there."

Alex gave their address, and then turned to Evan. "Evan, come with me," he said, almost forcefully.

Mr. East drove home quickly, putting as much distance between the attack and them as possible. He kept looking in his rearview mirror expecting to be followed but only Alex followed. He rubbed his hand over his face several times, knowing how close he had come to losing everyone he loved today. Griffin and Greta were in the back seat. Griffin had his arm around his fiancée, holding her close. Silent tears streamed down Greta's face. She had never been more scared in her life. It was the menacing look on the evil people's faces and the weird character drawn over their eyes. She shuddered and Griffin drew her closer.

Alicia's dad, Bill, met them in the parking garage and escorted them down to their apartment.

"I heard what happened," he said to them in the elevator, "I came to get your statement."

Mr. East nodded and led the way into the living room, "I think I need something strong to drink," he half-smiled, "Anyone else?"

Everyone agreed and he went into the kitchen to get drinks.

"Where shall I start?" Bill asked, taking an offered drink, "I understand these were two separate attacks?" He had his notebook out to take notes.

Mr. East sat down next to Miranda on the couch and took a deep breath, "I suppose I can start. I was with Evan, Griffin and Greta at the Mountain Pass nature park. We were about two kilometres into the hike and we were waiting for Miranda and Alex to catch up. They slept in, so we decided to start without them. There is a bench there so we stopped to eat." Bill nodded, knowing the bench. He had walked that trail many times. "We were eating when the ground started to shake and we heard some shouts coming from the forest. Someone yelled 'let's go' and they emerged. There were about 10 of them, all dressed in black with that marking above their eyes. We were going to run for it, but we did not have to. This white light barrier stopped them and they were all thrown away from it.”

“And the marking above their eyes. Did it disappear like the others?” Bill asked.

“Yes,” Griffin answered when his dad said he was not sure, “I saw one of them unconscious. The marking was gone.”

“It makes it difficult to determine if they are possessed,” Bill sighed, “That is what everyone claims and we have no idea whether it is true or not. We do not know how long we will be able to hold everyone. We still have the others in the holding cells from the other attacks, but everyone claims to have been possessed.” He rubbed his face, worried.

“We cannot just let them go,” Miranda jumped in, “Even if they are possessed, it could happen again.”

“No, we do not intend to let them go easily,” Bill said, “Try not to worry. It is just getting difficult.” He turned to Miranda, “Now, can you tell me what happened where you were?”

“Alex and I were about a kilometre into the trail. We were jogging trying to catch up. I saw something coming for him, a beam of red light, and I pushed him out of the way. It hit my side, but just barely. I have a scratch.”

“Oh Miranda,” Greta gasped.

“I peeked out from behind the bushes in time to see the white light throw our attacker as well.” She put her face in her hands, “Apparently it killed him,” she added quietly. Alex could have died today. What if she hadn’t seen the red light coming at him? She looked at him and he was staring at her, his expression unreadable. She threw up her mental block as well. Now she knew they were after her family. What could she do to protect them all the time?

"If that is everything," Bill said, finishing his drink, "I will let you get back to your family time. Alicia wanted to see you Miranda, but I told her to just leave you alone for now."

Miranda turned back to Bill and nodded, "Please let her know I will call her later."

Bill shook her and Mr. East's hands. He said goodbye to the rest and left.

Silence ensued. No one spoke for a long time after Bill left. What does a family talk about after a day like today? Certainly not the weather, Miranda thought to herself.

After some time, Mr. East took his daughter's hand. She looked at him and there were tears swimming in his eyes, "Thank you Miranda," he said, "We could have lost someone very dear to us today if it had not have been for you. You put your own life at risk to save him." He gave her a hug. Greta took the vacant spot on the couch and hugged her too.

Evan looked at Alex. He was at a loss for words. He nodded to Alex and then asked Griffin if he could talk to him in his room. The three of them went to Evan's bedroom.

"I think I need to go lie down," Greta said, "I feel so drained."

"Me too," Miranda agreed, rising to her feet. She had been fighting sleep since the ride home.

Mr. East stood too. He kissed his daughter on the cheek and gave Greta a hug.

"I hope you both will set a date for your wedding soon," he told Greta, "You never know what tomorrow holds."

Tears filled Greta's eyes and she agreed.

Miranda lay in bed but couldn't sleep. She was stressed. She had no idea what she would do if anyone in her family had been hurt.

Her gut instinct had been to throw herself in front of Alex but she should have sent her own beam of light to meet it. Then maybe she would not have been cut. She would have to train herself to react faster. She rolled over onto her side. Today had drained her again. Was it because she hadn't worked out in a few days? Or maybe it was because she had been running with Alex and was already tired. She had no idea. She would have to ask Jackson what he thought later. Miranda was happy he would be over later. She didn't want another minute without him.

Miranda could tell her door opened but she pretended to be sleeping.

"I guess we will talk to her later," she heard Alex whisper to her brothers before the door closed again.

Were they going to scold her for saving Alex's life? She sighed. Of course they would be mad she threw herself in front of that beam of red, but they also didn't know that she was supposed to be the one able to stop it. Or did they? But they would have told her if they knew.

Miranda felt a hand touch her face and her eyes opened. Jackson was sitting beside her on the bed, looking down at her with concern.

"Oh Jack," she said and sat up to hug him tight, "I am so glad you are here."

"Your dad says you have been asleep all day," Jackson said, "I tried to call but when I got no answer I came straight here."

"That's fine, I missed you," Miranda said. Tears filled her eyes.

Jackson brushed her hair out of her face and kissed her forehead, "I have told my mother that I am not leaving you for a weekend ever again. She agreed. At least not until the trouble is gone."

Miranda nodded.

"You will be lucky if I let you out of my sight at all," Jackson said with a half smile. He took her face in his hands and ran his thumbs across her cheeks.

Miranda kissed him and it washed away everything from that day. All the fear she felt slipped away, now that he was here.

A knock at the door interrupted them. Miranda gave him a small smile and called for whoever it was to 'come in'.

It was Miranda's father. "Oh, I am happy to see you awake," he said, "Would you like something to eat?"

"No thank you," Miranda replied, "I will eat a little later."

"Did you want to take tomorrow off of school?" Mr. East asked.

Miranda looked at Jackson and shook her head, "I will be fine with Jackson, dad. He will pick me up and bring me home."

"Ok, but let Evan and Alex drop you off," Mr. East said, "Jackson can bring you to the studio after school so they do not have to leave."

Miranda agreed and Mr. East left her room, conveniently leaving the door open behind him.

Miranda got up, closed the door and turned to Jackson with a smile, "He left that open on purpose, I would say."

Jackson chuckled and held a hand out to her, "Tell me what happened today. I know you do not want to relive it, but I just want to know."

Miranda took his hand and sat beside him on the bed. She told him the story.

Jackson's mouth dropped open in shock, "You ran after him? What were you thinking Miranda?" He hugged her close, "Do not do anything like that again without me here."

She pulled away, "I had to Jack. They were attacking my family."

Jackson looked her in the eyes, "And that is why I am never leaving you again."

"That's fine with me," Miranda smiled and kissed him again. There was another knock on the door. Miranda pulled away and made a face. She got up and crossed over to open the door.

Evan was standing behind it, "Alex, Griffin and I have to talk to you. It is important."

"Can we talk tomorrow? I have company."

A sour look crossed his face, "I can see that, but..."

"Tomorrow Ev," Miranda cut in, "I haven't seen Jackson all weekend."

Evan was about to say something else, but Miranda hit the spot for the door to close. She went back to the bed, "Now where were we?" She smiled and leaned in to kiss him again when her phone rang. She pulled back again and stood up looking for her phone, "If that is my brother, I am gonna kick his butt, I swear." But it wasn't, it was Alicia.

"Hi," Miranda smiled, "I am so sorry I did not call, but I just woke up."

"Not a problem," Alicia replied, "I am just so glad to see you. I heard all about today and wow, Miranda. I cannot believe what happened."

"I know," Miranda frowned, "I am just so glad my family is fine."

"Yes, that is wonderful! Are you coming to school tomorrow?"

"Yes, I will be there, but Evan and Alex are driving me. Would you like a ride? I feel like I have not seen you in ages!"

"Yes, thank you! I feel the same!" Alicia replied, happy, "Tell me about your first days of filming! How did it go?"

"It was amazing!" Miranda replied, though with everything going on, the show was the last thing on her mind, "My brother said I did so well but I cannot wait till Friday to see the final product!"

"Oh me too!"

"I am sorry to say this because it has been so long since I talked to you, but I have Jackson over. Do you mind if we pick this up in the morning?"

Alicia flashed her a knowing smile and a wink, "Sure. I will see you in the morning."

Miranda hung up the phone. Jackson took it from her and shut it off, then he pulled her close, "No more distractions," he smiled and kissed her again.

Before he left for the night, Jackson helped Miranda practice her lines. Jackson was happy to play the part of Jeff, especially when it came to the kissing part, though it pained him to know that Alex would be kissing his girlfriend tomorrow. Miranda read his mind and assured him that he was a better kisser than his cousin. Not that it made Jackson feel any better since she must have kissed Alex to have something to compare it to.

By the time Jackson left, everyone was in bed. She didn't want to disturb anyone, but she was starving so she made herself some chicken and took it to her room. She sat awake for a long time since she had slept so much that day. To try and make herself sleepy, she lifted her bed up and down with her mind but after awhile got bored of that and decided to read a book.

When she finished the book, it was 5:17 and she sighed. Was there even a point to going to sleep now? She got up and decided to shower, carefully taking off her bandage. The cut was almost healed. She was shocked the ointment worked so fast.

Once she was dressed in her school uniform and ready for the day, she looked in the mirror, hoping the stylist at the studio could do something about the dark circles under her eyes. It was going to be a long day.

She went to the kitchen to fix herself something to eat, but even that didn't take very long and she was back in her room to wait it out until it was time to leave.


She was dozing in her chair when there was a knock on the door. She got up quickly and opened it. Her dad was there.

"Good morning," he said surprised, "I did not think you were awake yet but you are already dressed!"

Miranda half smiled, "I couldn't sleep last night, so I woke up really early and got ready."

"I just wanted to say, have a good day and be careful" he said and gave her a quick hug, "I do not know what I would do if something happened to you."

"I will be fine, dad," Miranda said, sadly, "You have a good day too. And be careful yourself."

Miranda followed him out and watched him as he put on his shoes. Griffin and Greta were waiting for him. As usual, they were travelling together.

As Griffin, Greta and her father were leaving, Alicia got off the elevator.

She brightened when she saw Miranda in the foyer.

"Hi!" she said and hugged her friend, "I know I talked to you last night but seeing that you are alright makes me so happy."

Miranda smiled a half-smile, "Yes, I am just fine. Are you hungry? Did you eat yet? Alex and Evan are just having breakfast and then I think we will be ready."

Alicia smiled and shook her head, "I did eat, but thank you."

Miranda led the way into the living room, "So tell me what is new with you!"

Alicia squealed a little bit, "Well, I went out with Lance on Friday! We had such a great time and he was such a nice guy. I think I really like him."

"Oh that is great," Miranda said, truly happy for her.

"I saw you had a couple dates this weekend," Alicia smiled, "I cannot believe you were on the front page twice!"

Miranda sighed, "Well, I had at date with Jackson. Alex and I just went to grab a bite to eat while we were waiting for Evan, completely just as friends."

Alicia lowered her voice, "Really? You can tell me, I do not mind if you like Alex too. I am over him."

"Yes, I am with Jackson exclusively."

"I guess it just did not look like it. You looked really happy with Alex and you looked great together."

"And I did not look happy with Jackson?" Miranda laughed.

Alicia giggled, "Well, your smile looked a little forced."

Miranda shrugged, "I guess it was noticeable. I think I was just nervous. It was my first big brush with the news."

Evan poked his head in the living room, "We will leave in five minutes."

"Ok Evan. We are going to give Alicia a ride too, ok?"

Evan nodded and continued down the hall.

Alex entered the living room and stopped when he saw them.

"Hi Alex," Alicia smiled, "I am glad to see you are fine."

He flashed her a smile, "Thanks."

"So tell me more about Lance," Miranda insisted, trying to ease the awkwardness.

Alicia smiled gratefully at Miranda, "We went to the new movie and then for a night time walk."

"And?"

"Well, you know," Alicia smiled wider, "He is a great kisser."

Miranda giggled, "Good. I am glad you are happy."

Evan returned to the foyer and said he was ready to go. Alex went to get some shoes on and the girls picked up their purses. Then they headed out to his car.

Alicia asked Miranda about certain actors and what she thought of them in real life, while Alex drove them to the school. Miranda told her everyone had been so nice to her but she still did not know everyone's name yet. Evan tried to help, describing them so it would jog Miranda's memory. "Oh him, right!" Miranda said as they reached the top of the school, "Yes, he was the first one to congratulate me. Really nice guy."

Evan stopped Miranda before she turned away, "Remember, we need to talk tonight."

Miranda frowned, "Ok."

"We will see you at the studio at 19 hour?"

Miranda nodded and waved goodbye to them.


Jackson was waiting for her in their training room. Before she could kiss him hello, he held up a finger. "Not in school," he chuckled.

She gave him a half smile and sat down in the first seat, "What shall we do today then, Mr. West?"

"How about we study history this morning and workout this afternoon?"

Miranda agreed.


She was only half listening to Jackson tell a story about the history of the planet, when a chill ran through her. She felt something dark and sinister nearby and she jumped out of her chair and ran to the window.

Jackson stood up from his seat on the desk in alarm, "What is it?"

There were about eight grown people dressed in all black entering the front door. Seconds later, the ground started to shake.

"No!" Miranda shouted and raced for the door. Jackson was close on her heels begging her to 'stop' and 'wait'.

Miranda wouldn't hear it. What if something happened to someone at the school? They were just students.

Jackson caught up to her before she reached the elevator and stopped her, "We do this together or not at all. Tell me what you saw or at least think it!" He was frightened. His brother was downstairs.

"They are coming!" She brought the image of the eight coming into the school into her mind.

"We will take the stairs to the first floor." Jackson led the way. They got to the first floor and stopped shocked. There were already bodies lying in the hallway.

"No," Jackson whispered in shock. He looked around at every young face, hoping he wouldn't find his brother.

Miranda tried not to look at who they were as she raced through the destruction. The bad people had already broken the invisible 'glass' of the atrium and were picking up the ground in large boulders and tossing it at anyone in their way. There were also streams of red light, which opened up bloody gashes on students who were trying to get away.

"Are you looking for me?" Miranda yelled as she slowed to a stop near the back of the pack.

The man closest to her turned and a wicked smile crossed his face. He yelled for the others' attention and more turned her way.

"Die Miranda!" the first man yelled and sent a stream of red light towards her.

Jackson had just arrived and he pushed Miranda out of the way. She rolled onto her side and got up quickly. The red nicked Jackson's arm and blood started to seep out.

"Jackson, are you alright?" Miranda asked. He didn't answer or flinch. He stepped between her and the bad people. She put a hand on his shoulder and made him look at her. "That is not how it works Jackson. I am stronger. You cannot stop them without me." She took Jackson's hand in hers.

The tallest man stepped forward laughing, his dark eyes, black as night, gleaming, "This pitiful being has nothing compared to your strength, chosen one. It appears you were right," he turned to another on his left, "She has no idea."

Miranda stared him down. She was confused but didn't want to let on. What didn't she know?

The woman on his left smiled wickedly and nodded, "Yes, chief. It is as I was told."

Miranda glanced at the speaker. Her features were familiar but Miranda couldn't place them. Her eyes locked again with the chief's.

"Well, I suppose we shall just dispose of your so-called *protector*," the chief mocked. He sent a large red bolt towards Jackson but Miranda threw her arms around Jackson and a white light engulfed them both in a bubble. The red stream of light redirected and killed one of the bad people who were tearing the building apart wall by wall. The building began to collapse.

"Oh she is strong," the chief chuckled, "But you are not strong enough without the powers of your protector."

Jackson pushed Miranda down at the same time as she lifted him and tossed him out of harm's way with her mind. From the floor she turned on the evil ones and threw her hands out on front of her. Bright streaks of white left her palms and the evil woman to the right and another one of the men fell dead. It gave her enough time to stand again.

"No!" the chief shouted. He turned to her enraged and attacked her.

She deflected again.

Those in the back began to turn and help their chief. Miranda was able to keep up and started to take them out one by one, while keeping a shield of white that glimmered like a thin mist in front of her. She was weakening though. It was taking all her strength to hold the barrier and attack at the same time. Miranda cast the glimmering mist towards Jackson, who had just gotten to his feet as someone launched a large boulder in his direction. The boulder seemed to bounce off the mist and rolled away without inflicting any damage.

"Jackson, run!" Miranda cried, "There is nothing you can do! You will get killed! Go!"

Miranda deflected another boulder coming her way, and fell to her knees, drained.

"Miranda!" Jackson yelled and ran to her. He made it just in time to save her from another streak of red which slashed his calf. He cried out in pain.

"No," Miranda said, quickly scrambling to her feet. She stepped in front of Jackson. Her strength returned as her fear and anger rose. She threw more streaks of white at them until there were only two bad people remaining. One hid behind a tree, scared and the chief took heaving breaths, enraged. He had a glowing red aura surrounding him.

"You cannot hide!" Miranda shouted. She uprooted the tree, and he was exposed. Miranda took him out next with a streak of white light to his chest and he flew backward into the metal wall.

She sank to her knees again. She took deep breaths, hoping not to faint. She couldn't now, not while the chief was still alive. Her mist of white faltered and broke when the next bolt of red hit it.

"Now you will die!" the chief yelled.

Miranda screamed as she watched the red beam rush towards her. She heard a low grunt and someone tackled her instead and they both fell backwards.

"Jackson!" Miranda screamed. His body was limp and she had to push him off before the chief attacked again. His head fell to the side, his eyes open. Miranda knew he was gone. "No!" she shouted and the glimmering mist erupted around her again, thicker this time. She stood and turned to the chief. Her eyes shone with a white light in the centre. She put her hands in front of her and cried, "Stop!"

The chief was lifted off of his feet, hit the wall of the atrium on the second floor and fell back to the first floor dead.

Miranda turned back to Jackson's lifeless form and kneeled beside him. She touched his face, knowing there was nothing she could do. She tried not to look down at the damage and took his face in her hands. It, at least, was unmarked.

She had no idea how long she sat there cradling his head, tears streaming down her face, and barely noticed as the school was flooded with parents and students looking frantically for each other. Everything moved in slow motion.

Alex was the first to find her. He had to put his hands on her shoulders and shake her slightly to get her attention.

"Miranda, are you hurt?" he asked frightened. She was covered in blood. He couldn't bear to look down at Jackson.

Miranda shook her head and sobbed.

He took her face in his hands and stroked her hair.

"I killed them all," Miranda whispered, tears still flowed down her cheeks as she closed her eyes.

"What?" Alex whispered, shocked.

"I did it," Miranda sighed just before her eyes rolled back and she fainted from exhaustion.

When Miranda awoke, she could feel a cold cloth on her forehead. She felt her strength returning and her eyes fluttered open. She was in a room she did not recognize. The one wall was dented and there were books scattered across the floor. The chairs and table had been overturned and even the couch she was on had a big rip in it. There was white padding sticking out just above her waist. Her family was around her, all looking down at her. Concern was written all over their faces.

Her father was the first to throw his arms around her, "Oh I am so glad you are awake!" He let a small sob escape, "When we heard the school had been attacked, we came right away," her dad explained.

"It was a madhouse," Griffin added, touching her leg, "with everyone looking for their family. I am so glad Alex found you."

"What happened, Miranda?" Greta asked, her eyes were red from crying, and she took a seat by Miranda on the couch. She threw her arms around her. "You were so close to the bad people!"

Miranda brought her hands up to her face. Someone had washed the blood off of her, but her uniform was still stained with his blood. She could tell, even though her clothes were burgundy. Her face scrunched, as she fought a wave of tears, "Jackson is dead?"

Mr. East looked uncomfortably at Griffin. Greta took her hand.

"I am so sorry Miranda," Greta said, "I know you liked him very much."

Miranda started to sob, "It's all my fault!"

"Oh no Miranda," Greta said, hugging her again, "It is not your fault. The bad people did it."

"No, it is!" Miranda sobbed hysterically, "It is all *my* fault."

Evan and Griffin shared a look of concern while Mr. East took her other hand and tried to calm her.

"No Miranda, it is not your fault," Mr. East said, soothingly, "The bad people kill everyone good and Jackson was a very good person."

Miranda couldn't calm herself. She sobbed loudly. Evan, who was by her head, knelt down and put a hand on her shoulder. He didn't know what to say, but he didn't want his twin sister to hurt.

Alicia entered the demolished teacher's lounge with her mother and father in tow. She was crying. Greta vacated the spot beside Miranda on the couch and Alicia sat down, throwing her arms around Miranda who hugged her back. Together they sobbed.

"Tina, my best friend, is gone," Alicia cried, "I heard about Jackson and I am so sorry but I am so glad you are alive."

Miranda hugged her tighter, "I am so glad to see you alive too. I am sorry about Tina. Is everyone else ok?" She felt Alicia nod.

Alicia eventually pulled back, her eyes red, "There was no one in the classrooms that collapsed. It could have been so much worse. I am so glad someone was fighting for us or the whole school may have been destroyed."

Miranda tears threatened to fall again and she nodded, "Yes and I hope that all the evil is now gone."

Alicia tried to smile, "Yes. I hope so too."

"Come Alicia," her father, Bill, said quietly, "I would really like to go home."

Alicia nodded. She hugged Miranda tightly one last time and stood to go.

"I am happy to see you are fine," Bill said to Miranda and touched her arm in farewell, "I know it is hard, but you have so many people who love you."

Alicia and her parents left, and Alex passed the family on his way in. He was carrying a cup that was steaming and took Alicia's vacated spot.

"I got this from the medical team," he said, "Be careful, it is hot but please drink it all. It will give you back your strength."

Miranda nodded and Alex helped her to a sitting position. He held the cup to her lips. Miranda took a sip which burned her tongue slightly. It was very light and tasted of lemons but as it slid down her throat, she could feel the burst of energy it released.

"The law enforcement officers will be here shortly," Alex said, tucking her hair back behind her ear with his free hand, "Do you feel up to talking to them today?"

She brushed her cheek against his hand. It always helped calm her. Miranda thought about it for a minute and nodded.

They sat in silence, Evan pacing back and forth, Griffin and Greta snuggled close on a nearby couch that they had righted. Its green upholstery was also ripped in several places. Mr. East was seated by Miranda's feet and Alex beside her, making sure she finished the drink until the officers showed up. They asked everyone to leave so they could talk to Miranda in private, since she had been found closest to the evil ones and alive.

"Can Alex stay?" Miranda asked, "Please?"

They nodded and Alex helped her sit up straight. He put an arm around her which kept her calm enough as she explained what had happened. She told them that she and Jackson were trying to get away and he stepped in front of one of the red streaks of light to save her. Then the white light appeared and they were all blasted off of their feet. They thanked her for the information before leaving. Only Mr. East came back into the lounge to tell her everyone wanted to go home. Alex helped Miranda stand and put an arm around her to help her walk. She still felt weak despite the drink, so she leaned on him heavily.

The paparazzi were outside. Miranda covered her face with her hands hoping they would just leave her alone.

They shouted so many questions asking about the events that took place. They had heard about Jackson and some offered their sympathies as she was ushered by. Miranda never looked up and they eventually went quiet.

# Twenty-Four

★ ★ ★ ★

Miranda just wanted to be left alone. As soon as she got home, she went straight to her bedroom claiming to be tired. She wanted to think about what had happened and what had gone wrong. Were the evil ones gone since their chief was killed? How many more were there if there were any left? Would she be able to do this without Jackson? That thought just tore her apart inside.

For hours, she sat pouring over the written passage in her notebook, though it didn't offer her much more except that evil had been defeated before. If it came back once, it could return again at any time.

When there was a knock on the door, she put her notebook under her pillow and her father opened the door after she said 'come in'.

His face fell when he saw that she was wide awake and crying, and he went to sit beside her on the bed, "I am so sorry sweetheart." She moved to give him room to sit, and he rubbed her back for a bit. "We have had far too many hard days these past few months. I know you may not see it now, but there must be some good on the horizon for us all."

Miranda nodded slowly.

"I was hoping you would come to the living room and spend time with us," he asked shyly, "We just want some family time."

"Of course, dad," Miranda replied. Her eyes filled with tears again and her thoughts would have to wait.

Greta was standing and waiting for Miranda when she rounded the corner to the living room. She hugged her tightly and pulled her to sit beside her on the couch. Griffin sat on her other side. Mr. East and Alex were in the chairs. Evan joined them a few minutes later.

"I am putting the show in reruns for two weeks. We will start filming again then. I was just on the phone with Melissa and Sandy. Sandy will be issuing a press release stating your debut will be moved to October 23$^{rd}$," he said. He looked to Miranda, "Is that alright?"

Miranda thought about it. *The show must go on, right?* She frowned at the thought. Everyone was staring and waiting for her to answer so she threw up her mental block. She felt like everything had been torn away from her. She was taken away from her family and friends on Earth to come here and find out she was destined to a path that was already laid out for her. And now, Jackson was gone too.

She looked up at Evan, her twin brother though only a few people knew it. *That* was something. She glanced around the room at everyone. She still had them and they were the most important people in her life now. She still had them.

After an endless internal battle, she nodded to Evan who sighed in relief.

"I want everyone to know," Evan said and the attention was shifted to him, "We found out Miranda is my twin sister."

Griffin looked at Miranda in shock, "What? How? I thought you were 16?"

Miranda shook her head, "The year is longer on Earth. I have been 18 this whole time."

"That is impossible," Mr. East said, shaking his head in disbelief, "How could your mother keep that from me? Evan was born here!"

"Were you there?" Miranda asked, finally realizing that her father must not have been at the hospital.

Mr. East bit his lip and shook his head, "Your mother called me after she had delivered and then she left for Earth the next day." His mouth dropped open, "I guess it is true."

"I calculated it," Miranda said, "It was pretty simple. I was a day or two off but when I went to the mayor's office, I verified Evan's birthday." It was actually Alex that had verified Evan's birthday, but she didn't want to give it away that he had known this whole time.

"No wonder you two are so much alike," Greta commented.

Evan tried to smile, "Though she did get mom's temper."

Miranda rolled her eyes, "And, like you said, you got all the height." She turned to her father, "What will happen with school?" She couldn't stay away from the subject for long.

"I think you have learned enough," Mr. East said, "You will be a wonderful actress."

Miranda was happy to hear she would never have to go to the school again. It would be so painful without Jack.

"The school will be repaired and the students have been given some time off as well," Griffin added.

Being surrounded by her family kept her mind off things and Miranda fell asleep on Greta's shoulder shortly after.

She put her arms around Alex's neck when he picked her up to bring her to her room. She opened her eyes once he laid her down and noticed his eyes were filled with tears.

"Alex, what is wrong?" she asked sleepily.

"Nothing," he replied, wiping at his eyes.

"I am sorry about your cousin," Miranda said. Her eyes filled with tears again. She couldn't believe she had any tears left.

"I am too," Alex said. He tucked a stray hair behind her ear and stroked her cheek, "You were so brave today."

"You know?"

"You told me when I found you. You told me you had done it."

Miranda looked down, "Oh."

"I do not understand though. I saw the light, Miranda, coming from you yesterday. When did this power come to you?"

Miranda shrugged. Obviously he did not know the whole truth and Miranda didn't want to tell him.

"I should have been there. I promised to protect you"

Miranda shook her head, vehemently, "You would have died too. I couldn't bear that."

A look of pain crossed his face and he looked away. He took a moment before he looked back down at her.

She closed her eyes and enjoyed the feeling of Alex's hand on her face. Before sleep overtook her again, she felt his lips brush hers.

"I am so glad you are alive," he whispered.

Her notebook woke her from her dreamless sleep. Miranda picked it up and saw Jackson's mother was calling. She took a deep breath and answered.

Marcy's red-rimmed eyes and tear stained face filled her screen, "Oh Miranda, I was not sure if I should call but now I am glad to see your face."

"I am so sorry," Miranda said. A tear escaped and slid down her face.

"I wanted you to know that you did wonderfully today. What happened was so painful but you must carry on," Marcy insisted as the tears flowed, "We all must carry on. You must keep the East lineage strong."

"But the West?"

"When the group spoke of this before, we talked about different outcomes and we assumed the lineage of the West would be passed on through my second son to the next generation just as we assume the East lineage would be passed on through your twin brother. That was easier to assume since you are twins. The passage said that only if East and West fail, there would be no other, but you have lived, so there must be some bright future."

"Do you think evil will return?"

"I do not know," Marcy shook her head, "If anything, you may have sent evil into hiding for generations."

"I hope."

Marcy's face scrunched as she fought another wave of tears, "We have set Jackson's funeral for Wednesday with all the others from the school. Please come. I know it will be hard but I want to see you again. And I want to give you the book. It is yours now to pass on to future generations."

Miranda nodded sadly, "Of course I will be there."


When she got off the phone, she went out to tell her family about the funeral. They were still gathered in the living room after eating dinner.

Mr. East got off the couch when he saw his daughter, "Can I make you something to eat?"

Miranda shook her head and he sat again, "I just spoke to Jackson's mother. His funeral is set for Wednesday." She looked around the room, "Where is Alex?"

Evan's jaw tightened, "He went... out."

"Oh," Miranda frowned, "Well, you can tell him." She went to the kitchen with the intent of making herself dinner but she wasn't hungry, so she went back to her room.

Miranda spent the next two days in her room. She had no nightmares and assumed it was because evil was gone, for now. She was torn up about losing Jackson, even though she had known him such a short time. He was her soulmate and now what? Would anyone ever take the place of her soulmate? She had never even had the chance to grow to love Jackson and she cried all night about her lost future with him.

The day the funeral arrived, Miranda dressed in the same black dress as she had worn to her mother's funeral. This time she added a pair of high heeled sandals. She looked at her reflection. It had changed over the time she had been here. She was thinner and more muscular from her recent workouts, but her face was the same aside from her red-rimmed eyes.

She sat on her bed, thinking and waiting. Jackson wanted her to be happy. She had dreamt of him last night and that is exactly what he had told her. He had said not to be sad for long, since their time together had been so short. She would love again. She had cried in her dream, saying that she never could and he put his arms around her and kissed her silent.

*"You did not love me," he stated simply and she tried to protest. "Yes, I did love you Jackson."*

*He gave her a half smile, "No and I do not blame you. We did what we could in the short time we had. I was not strong like you, but you will find someone who is and is deserving of you."*

*"I was not good enough for you Jack. And I blame myself. I ran towards the evil ones and got you killed."*

*"You did the right thing." He hugged her tight, "You were ready and you had people to save and you did it. Everyone has you to thank. I do not want you to blame yourself."*

*Miranda frowned and Jackson kissed her again.*

*"You saved so many," he continued, "They could have killed every senior school student in the city but you stopped them."*

When it was time, she met her family in the living room. They were also dressed in the same suits as before. Alex was not with them and Greta told her that he was going to the funeral with his parents and grandparents.

There were so many people at the funeral home when she got there. Jackson's was not the only one being held that day. All of the dead students were to be cremated on the same day.

The East family found Alex, his parents and his grandparents in the lobby. His grandmother rose from her chair as Miranda approached.

"Oh Miranda," she smiled, knowingly. The gleam in her eyes said it all. She knew everything. "You are a beautiful and brave girl."

Miranda's eyes filled with tears but Alex's grandmother held a finger up.

"Do not be sad. It is *written* that all will be well," she whispered so only Miranda could hear, "I cannot believe how well you did alone and without the powers of the West."

Miranda's eyes opened wide. She *did* know everything. Marcy must have shared with her mother-in-law. Alex's grandmother took her hands and gave them a gentle squeeze.

"Oh mother, leave the poor girl alone," Alex's father said with a half smile, as he approached the pair, "It is nice to meet you Miranda. Alex tells us you were right there and saw the white light."

Miranda nodded.

Mrs. West threw her arms around her. "Thank you so much for saving our son," she said, tears filling her eyes, "I am so glad you are ok."

"I am sorry about your nephew," Miranda whispered. Mrs. West gave her shoulder a squeeze, as the tears spilled down her cheeks.

Mr. East put an arm around Miranda. Together they all went down to the viewing room. There were so many people that they had to wait in a line. Alex's parents and Mr. East, Griffin and Evan spent the time catching up. Miranda, Alex and his grandmother were quiet.

They reached the viewing room. All 22 students and four teachers were each on their own table with the sheet pulled back. Their immediate families were nearby accepting condolences with dazed and sad expressions. Miranda, followed by her family made their way from family to family, offering condolences.

When they reached Jackson, Miranda could barely look. He looked so alive, like he was sleeping. There were no visible scars, not even the scratch he had received on his arm. Miranda touched his cold hand gently, her eyes filling with tears.

*I did love you Jackson and I will move on like you want me to,* she thought. She turned and was engulfed in a hug by Jackson's mother.

"Can I speak to you for a minute?" she asked. Miranda nodded and followed her a short distance away.

Marcy took the book out of her purse and handed it to Miranda who slipped it in her own.

"You did amazingly Miranda. Please do not ever forget that," she said, tears flowing down her cheeks.

Miranda tried to nod.

"Keep in touch, ok?" Marcy urged.

"Yes," she whispered in reply.

Alex's grandmother stepped over to them.

"What did you give her, dear?" she asked Marcy.

"Just a book," Marcy mumbled and waved her hand.

Miranda didn't stop her as Alex's grandmother reached into her purse for it. Her fingers traced the front cover, her lips pursed.

"Oh my goodness, no," she said, "No. This is not right." She looked speechless as she looked between Marcy and Miranda.

She tucked the book quickly back into Miranda's purse as Alex's father came up.

Alex's grandmother sent her another look as she was being led away, her expression unreadable. Miranda looked down at her hands, confused. His grandmother obviously knew a lot.

Miranda watched as they re-joined the family. Marcy followed them, taking her spot beside Jackson. The East family continued on, leaving Alex, his parents and grandmother to mourn with their family in private. Miranda had to leave. She excused herself, telling them she needed some air. She bypassed the rest of the dead but just as she reached the door, a light wind blew her hair. She turned her head to look in the direction of the source but found nothing.

She noticed Nathan amongst the crowd near the door, an odd look on his face. When he saw her looking his eyes narrowed but then he seemed to recognize her and nodded in her direction. Miranda gave him a small wave before leaving.

That night Miranda went to bed early, exhausted from crying all day. She dreamt of Alex's grandmother telling her she was wrong, of Marcy telling her to move on, of Jackson who warned her it was not over, and then of the familiar woman who tried to kill her. The woman looked so much like someone she knew, but she still couldn't figure out who it was. The wind picked up around her. Miranda couldn't see and then fingers closed around her neck.

She woke up in a cold sweat.

-End of Book One-